DARK HORSE

BY
B.J. DANIELS

MILLS &
BOON

First Published in Great Britain 2017
By Mills & Boon, an imprint of HarperCollins*Publishers*
1 London Bridge Street, London, SE1 9GF

© 2017 Barbara Heinlein

ISBN: 978-0-263-92906-5

46-0817

Our policy is to use papers that are natural, renewable and recyclable
products and made from wood grown in sustainable forests. The logging and
manufacturing processes conform to the legal environmental regulations of
the country of origin.

Printed and bound in Spain
by CPI, Barcelona

B.J. Daniels is a *New York Times* and *USA TODAY* bestselling author. She wrote her first book after a career as an award-winning newspaper journalist and author of thirty-seven published short stories. She lives in Montana with her husband, Parker, and three springer spaniels. When not writing, she quilts, boats and plays tennis. Contact her at www.bjdaniels.com, on Facebook or on Twitter, @bjdanielsauthor.

This Whitehorse, Montana book is for Sue Olsen,
who has brightened many a day for
me with her zest for life.
I just wish I had her energy.

Chapter One

Their footfalls echoed among the terrified screams and woeful sobbing as they moved down the long hallway. The nurse's aide, a young woman named Tess, stopped at a room in the criminally insane section of the hospital and, with trembling fingers, pulled out a key to unlock the door.

"I really shouldn't be doing this," Tess said, looking around nervously. As the door swung open, she quickly moved back. Nikki St. James felt a gust of air escape the room like an exhaled breath. The light within the interior was dim, but she could hear the sound of a chair creaking rhythmically.

"I'm going to have to lock the door behind you," Tess whispered.

"Not yet." It took a moment for Nikki's eyes to adjust to the dim light within the room. She fought back the chill that skittered over her skin like spider legs as her gaze finally lit on the occupant.

"This is the wrong one," Nikki said, and tried to step back into the hallway.

"That's her," the nurse's aide said, keeping her voice down. "That's Marianne McGraw."

Nikki stared at the white-haired, slack-faced woman

rocking back and forth, back and forth, her gaze blank as if blind. "That woman is too old. Her hair—"

"Her hair turned white overnight after...well, after what happened. She's been like this ever since." Tess shuddered and hugged herself as if she felt the same chill Nikki did.

"She hasn't spoken in all that time?"

"Not a word. Her husband comes every day to visit her. She never responds."

Nikki was surprised that Travers McGraw would come to visit his former wife at all, given what she was suspected of doing. Maybe, like Nikki, he came hoping for answers. "What about her children?"

"They visit occasionally, the oldest son more than the others, but she doesn't react as if she knows any of them. That's all she does, rock like that for hours on end."

Cull McGraw, the oldest son, Nikki thought. He'd been seven, a few years older than her, at the time of the kidnapping. His brothers Boone and Ledger were probably too young to remember the kidnapping, maybe even too young to really remember their mother.

"If you're going in, you'd best hurry," Tess said, still looking around nervously.

Nikki took a step into the room, hating the thought of the nurse's aide locking the door behind her. As her eyes adjusted more to the lack of light, she saw that the woman had something clutched against her chest. A chill snaked up her spine as she made out two small glassy-eyed faces looking out at her from under matted heads of blond hair.

"What's that she's holding?" she whispered hoarsely as she hurriedly turned to Tess before the woman could close and lock the door.

"Her babies."

"Her *babies*?"

"They're just old dolls. They need to be thrown in the trash. We tried to switch them with new ones, but she had a fit. When we bathe or change her, we have to take them away. She screams and tears at her hair until we give them back. It was the doctor's idea, giving her the dolls. Before that, she was...violent. She had to be sedated or you couldn't get near her. Like I said, you go in there at your own risk. She's...unpredictable and if provoked, dangerous since she's a lot stronger than she looks. If I were you, I'd make it quick."

Nikki reached for her notebook as the door closed behind her. The tumblers in the lock sounded like a cannon going off as Tess locked the door.

At your own risk. Comforting words, Nikki thought as she took a tentative step deeper into the padded room. She'd read everything she could find on the McGraw kidnapping case. There'd been a lot of media coverage at the time—and a lot of speculation. Every anniversary for years, the same information had been repeated along with the same plea for anything about the two missing twins, Oakley Travers McGraw and Jesse Rose McGraw.

But no one had ever come forward. The ransom money had never been recovered nor the babies found. There'd been nothing new to report at the one-year anniversary, then the five, ten, fifteen and twenty year.

Now with the twenty-fifth one coming up, few people other than those around Whitehorse, Montana, would probably even remember the kidnapping.

"There is nothing worse than old news," her grandfather had told her when she'd dropped by his office at the large newspaper where he was publisher. Wendell St. James had been sitting behind his huge desk, his head of thick gray hair as wild as his eyebrows, his wire-rimmed glasses perched precariously on his patrician nose. "You're wasting your time with this one."

Actually he thought she was wasting her time writing true crime books. He'd hoped that she would follow him into the newspaper business instead. It didn't matter that out of the nine books she'd written, she'd solved seven of the crimes.

"*Someone* knows what happened that night," she'd argued.

"Well, if they do, it's a pretty safe bet they aren't going to suddenly talk after twenty-five years."

"Maybe they're getting old and they can't live with what they've done," she'd said. "It wouldn't be the first time."

He'd snorted and settled his steely gaze on her. "I wasn't for the other stories you chased, but this one…" He shook his head. "Don't you think I know what you're up to? I suspect this is your mother's fault. She just couldn't keep her mouth shut, could she?"

"She didn't tell me about my father," she'd corrected her grandfather. "I discovered it on my own." For years, she'd believed she was the daughter of a stranger her mother had fallen for one night. A mistake. "All these years, the two of you have lied to me, letting me believe I was an accident, a one-night stand and that explained why I had my mother's maiden name."

"We protected you, you mean. And now you've got some lamebrained idea of clearing your father's name." Wendell swore under his breath. "My daughter has proven that she is the worst possible judge of men, given her track record. But I thought you were smarter than this."

"There was no real proof my father was involved," Nikki had argued stubbornly. Her biological father had been working at the Sundown Stallion Station the summer of the kidnapping. His name had been linked with Marianne McGraw's, the mother of the twins. "Mother doesn't believe he had an affair with Marianne, nor does she believe he had any part in the kidnapping."

"What do you expect your mother to say?" he'd demanded.

"She knew him better than you."

Her grandfather mugged a disbelieving face. "What else did she tell you about the kidnapping?"

Her mother had actually known little. While Nikki would have demanded answers, her mother said she was just happy to visit with her husband, since he was locked up until his trial.

"She didn't ask him anything about the kidnapping because your mother wouldn't have wanted to hear the truth."

She'd realized then that her grandfather's journalistic instincts had clearly skipped a generation. Nikki would have had to know everything about that night, even if it meant finding out that her husband was involved.

"A jury of twelve found him guilty of not only the affair—but the kidnapping," her grandfather had said.

"On circumstantial evidence."

"On the testimony of the nanny who said that Marianne McGraw wasn't just unstable, she feared she might hurt the twins. The nanny also testified that she saw Marianne with your father numerous times in the barn and they seemed...close."

She'd realized that her grandfather knew more about this case than he'd originally let on. "Yes, the nanny, the woman who is now the new wife of Travers McGraw. That alone is suspicious. I would think you'd encourage me to get the real story of what happened that night. And what does...*close* mean anyway?"

Her grandfather had put down his pen with an impatient sigh. "The case is dead cold after twenty-five years. Dozens of very good reporters, not to mention FBI agents and local law enforcement, did their best to solve it, so what in hell's name makes you think that you can find something that they missed?"

She'd shrugged. "I have my grandfather's stubborn arrogance and the genes of one of the suspects. Why not me?"

He'd wagged his gray head again. "Because you're too personally involved, which means that whatever story you get won't be worth printing."

She'd dug her heels in. "I became a true crime writer because I wanted to know more than what I read in the newspapers."

"Bite your tongue," her grandfather said, only half joking. He sobered then, looking worried. "What if you don't like what you find out about your father, or your mother, for that matter? I know my daughter."

"What does that mean?"

He gave another shake of his gray head. "Clearly your mind is made up and since I can't sanction this..." With an air of dismissal, he picked up his pen again. "If that's all..."

She started toward the door but before she could exit, he called after her, "Watch your back, Punky." It had been his nickname for her since she was a baby. "Remember what I told you about family secrets."

People will kill to keep them, she thought now as she looked at Marianne McGraw.

The woman's rocking didn't change as Nikki stepped deeper into the room. "Mrs. McGraw?" She glanced behind her. The nurse's aide stood just outside the door, glancing at her watch.

Nikki knew she didn't have much time. It hadn't been easy getting in here. It had cost her fifty bucks after she'd found the nurse's aide was quitting soon to get married. She would have paid a lot more since so few people had laid eyes on Marianne McGraw in years.

She reached in her large purse for the camera she'd brought. No reporter had gotten in to see Marianne McGraw. Nikki had seen a photograph of Marianne McGraw taken twenty-five years ago, before her infant fraternal twins, a boy and girl, had been kidnapped. She'd been a beauty at thirty-two, a gorgeous dark-haired woman with huge green eyes and a contagious smile.

That woman held no resemblance to the one in the rocking chair. Marianne was a shell of her former self, appearing closer to eighty than fifty-seven.

"Mrs. McGraw, I'm Nikki St. James. I'm a true crime writer. How are you doing today?"

Nikki was close enough now that she could see nothing but blankness in the woman's green-eyed stare. It was as if Marianne McGraw had gone blind—and deaf, as well. The face beneath the wild mane of white hair was haggard, pale, lifeless. The mouth hung open, the lips cracked and dry.

"I want to ask you about your babies," Nikki said.

Dark Horse

"Oakley and Jesse Rose?" Was it her imagination or did the woman clutch the dolls even harder to her thin chest?

"What happened the night they disappeared?" Did Nikki really expect an answer? She could hope, couldn't she? Mostly, she needed to hear the sound of her voice in this claustrophobic room. The rocking had a hypnotic effect, like being pulled down a rabbit hole.

"Everyone outside this room believes you had something to do with it. You and Nate Corwin." No response, no reaction to the name. "Was he your lover?"

She moved closer, catching the decaying scent that rose from the rocking chair as if the woman was already dead. "I don't believe it's true. But I think you might know who kidnapped your babies," she whispered.

The speculation at the time was that the kidnapping had been an inside job. Marianne had been suffering from postpartum depression. The nanny had said that Mrs. McGraw was having trouble bonding with the babies and that she'd been afraid to leave Marianne alone with them.

And, of course, there'd been Marianne's secret lover—the man who everyone believed had helped her kidnap her own children. He'd been implicated because of a shovel found in the stables with his bloody fingerprints on it—along with fresh soil—even though no fresh graves had been found.

"Was Nate Corwin involved, Marianne?" The court had decided that Marianne McGraw couldn't have acted alone. To get both babies out the second-story window, she would have needed an accomplice.

"Did my father help you?"

There was no sign that the woman even heard her,

let alone recognized her alleged lover's name. And if the woman *had* answered, Nikki knew she would have jumped out of her skin.

She checked to make sure Tess wasn't watching as she snapped a photo of the woman in the rocker. The flash lit the room for an instant and made a *snap* sound. As she started to take another, she thought she heard a low growling sound coming from the rocker.

She hurriedly took another photo, though hesitantly, as the growling sound seemed to grow louder. Her eye on the viewfinder, she was still focused on the woman in the rocker when Marianne McGraw seemed to rock forward as if lurching from her chair.

A shriek escaped her before she could pull down the camera. She had closed her eyes and thrown herself back, slamming into the wall. Pain raced up one shoulder. She stifled a scream as she waited for the feel of the woman's clawlike fingers on her throat.

But Marianne McGraw hadn't moved. It had only been a trick of the light. And yet, Nikki noticed something different about the woman.

Marianne was smiling.

Chapter Two

When a hand touched her shoulder, Nikki jumped, unable to hold back the cry of fright.

"We have to go," Tess said, tugging on her shoulder. "They'll be coming around with meds soon."

Nikki hadn't heard the nurse's aide enter the room. Her gaze had been on Marianne McGraw—until Tess touched her shoulder.

Now she let her gaze go back to the woman. The white-haired patient was hunched in her chair, rocking back and forth, back and forth. The only sound in the room was that of the creaking rocking chair and the pounding of Nikki's pulse in her ears.

Marianne's face was slack again, her mouth open, the smile gone. If it had ever been there.

Nikki tried to swallow the lump in her throat. She'd let her imagination get the best of her, thinking that the woman had risen up from that rocker for a moment.

But she hadn't imagined the growling sound any more than she would forget that smile of amusement. Marianne McGraw was still inside that shriveled-up old white-haired woman.

And if she was right, she thought, looking down at

the camera in her hand, there would be proof in the photos she'd taken.

Tess pulled on her arm. "You have to go. *Now*. And put that camera away!"

Nikki nodded and let Tess leave the room ahead of her. All her instincts told her to get out now. She'd read that psychopaths were surprisingly strong and with only Tess to pull the woman off her...

She studied the white-haired woman in the rocker, trying to decide if Marianne McGraw was the monster everyone believed her to be.

"Did you let Nate Corwin die for a crime he didn't commit?" Nikki whispered. "Is your real accomplice still out there, spending the $250,000 without you? Or are you innocent in all this? As innocent as I believe my father was?"

For just an instant she thought she saw something flicker in Marianne McGraw's green eyes. The chill that climbed up her backbone froze her to her core. "You *know* what happened that night, don't you," Nikki whispered at the woman. In frustration, she realized that if her father and this woman were behind the kidnaping, Marianne might be the *only* person alive who knew the truth.

"Come on!" Tess whispered from the hallway.

Nikki was still staring at the woman in the rocker. "I'm going to find out." She turned to leave. Behind her, she heard the chilling low growling sound emanating from Marianne McGraw. It wasn't until the door was closed and locked behind her that she let out the breath she'd been holding.

TESS MOTIONED FOR Nikki to follow her. The hallway was long and full of shadows this late at night. Their footfalls sounded too loud on the linoleum floor. The air was choked with the smell of disinfectants that didn't quite cover the...other smells.

Someone cried out in a nearby room, making Nikki start. Behind them there were moans broken occasionally by bloodcurdling screams. She almost ran the last few feet to the back door.

Tess turned off the alarm, pushed open the door and, checking to make sure she had her keys, stepped out into the night air with her. They both breathed in the Montana night. Stars glittered in the midnight blue of the big sky overhead. In the distance, she could make out the dark outline of the Little Rockies.

"I told you she wouldn't be any help to your story," Tess said after a moment.

Nikki could tell that the nurse's aide couldn't wait until her last day at this job. She could see how a place like that would wear on you. Though she'd spent little time inside, she still was having trouble shaking it off.

"I still appreciate you letting me see her." She knew the only reason she'd gotten in was because the nurse's aide was getting married, had already given her two weeks' notice and was planning to move to Missoula with her future husband. Nikki had read it in the local newspaper under Engagements. It was why she'd made a point of finding out when Tess worked her last late-night shifts.

Nearby an owl hooted. Tess hugged herself even though the night wasn't that cold. Nikki longed for any sound other than the creak of a rocking chair. She feared she would hear it in her sleep.

"I heard you tell her that you were going to find out

what happened that night," Tess said. "Everyone around here already knows what happened."

Did they? Nikki thought of Marianne McGraw. Her hair had turned white overnight and now she was almost a corpse. The only man who might know whether the rumors were true, Nikki's own father, was dead.

"What does everyone believe happened?" she asked.

"She was having an affair with her horse trainer, so of course that's who she got to help her get rid of the babies," Tess said as she dug in her pocket for a cigarette. "I'm trying to quit. Before the wedding. But some nights…"

Nikki watched her light up and take a long drag. "Wait, why get rid of the babies? She still had three other sons."

"I guess she figured they'd be fine with their father. But babies… Also they needed the money. Easier to kidnap a couple of babies than one of the younger boys who'd make a fuss."

"Still, they didn't have to kill them."

"The horse trainer probably didn't want to be saddled with two babies. Not very romantic running away together with the money—and two squalling babies."

That was the story the prosecution had told that had gotten her father sent to prison. But was it true? "I thought he swore he didn't do it."

She scoffed. "That's what they all say."

Nate Corwin, according to what Nikki had been able to find, had said right up to the end when they were driving him to prison that he didn't do it. Maybe, if the van hadn't overturned and he wasn't killed, then maybe he could have fought his conviction, found proof… Or maybe he'd lied right up until his last breath.

"But I thought it was never proven that he was even Marianne's lover, let alone that he helped her kidnap her own children?" Nikki asked.

The nurse's aide made a disbelieving sound. "Who else was there?"

"I'd heard the nanny might have been involved."

"*Patty?* Well, I wouldn't put it past her."

This caught Nikki's attention. "You know her?"

The nurse's aide pursed her lips as if she shouldn't be talking about this, but fortunately that didn't stop her. Anyway, she'd already broken worse rules today by sneaking Nikki into the hospital.

"She accompanies her husband most of the time. You can tell *Patty* doesn't like him visiting his ex-wife," Tess said. Nikki got the impression that Patricia McGraw also didn't like being called Patty.

"She won't even step into Marianne's room," the nurse's aide was saying between puffs. "Not that I blame her, but instead she stands in the hallway and watches them like a hawk. Imagine being jealous of that poor woman in that room."

"I also heard that Travers McGraw himself might have been involved," Nikki threw out.

Tess shook her head emphatically. "No way. Mr. Mc-Graw is the nicest, kindest man. He would never hurt a fly, let alone his own children." She lowered her voice conspiratorially even though they were alone at the back of the hospital and there was only open country behind them. "He hardly ever leaves the ranch except to come here to see his now ex-wife—that is until recently. I heard he's not feeling well."

Nikki had heard the same thing. Maybe that was

why he'd agreed to let her interview him and his family for the book.

When Nikki had first approached him, she had expected him to turn her down in a letter. The fact that she'd made a name for herself after solving the murders in so many of her books had helped, she was sure.

"You seem to have a talent for finding out the truth," Travers McGraw had said when he'd called her out of the blue. He'd been one of just three people she'd contacted about interviews and a book, but he'd been the one she wanted badly.

That was one reason she'd tried not to sound too eager when she'd talked to him. McGraw hadn't done any interviews other than the local press—not since a reporter had broken into his house and scared his family half to death.

"I work at finding the truth," she'd told him, surprised how nervous she was just to hear his voice.

"And you think you can find out the truth in our... case?"

"I want to." More than he could possibly know. "But I should warn you up front, I need access to everyone involved. It would require me basically moving in for a while. Are you sure you're agreeable to that?"

She'd held her breath. Long ago she'd found that making demands made her come off as more professional. It also shifted the power structure. She wasn't begging to do their story. She was doing them a favor.

The long silence on the other end of the line had made her close her eyes, tightening her hand around the phone. She had wanted this so badly. Probably too badly. Maybe she should have—

"When are you thinking of coming here?" Travers McGraw asked.

Her heart had been beating so hard she could barely speak. "I'm finishing up a project now."

"You do realize it's been twenty-five years?"

Not quite. She'd still had two weeks before the actual date that the two babies had been stolen out of the nursery and never seen again. She wanted to be in the house on anniversary night.

"I can be there in a week." She'd crossed her fingers even though she'd never been superstitious.

"I'll take care of everything. Will you be flying to Billings? I can have one of my sons—"

"That won't be necessary. I'll be driving." Though she was anxious to meet his sons. But the only other way, besides driving to Whitehorse, was to take the train that came right through town.

"I hope you can work your magic for us," McGraw said. "If there is anything I can do to help…"

"We'll talk when I get there. It would be best if no one knew I was coming. I'm sure in a small town like Whitehorse, word will get out soon enough."

"Yes, of course."

She'd left a few days before she'd told him she would be arriving. She'd wanted to see Marianne McGraw and get a feel for Whitehorse before she went out to the ranch. Once word got out about her, she would lose her anonymity.

Tess put out her cigarette in the dirt.

"If Travers McGraw is so devoted to the mother of his children, then why did he marry the nanny not long after his divorce?" Nikki asked, hoping to get more out of Tess before she went back inside.

"It was *nine* years after the kidnapping. I heard Patty showed up with a baby in her arms and a sob story. He's a nice man so I guess he was taken in by it." Tess definitely didn't like Patricia McGraw.

"A baby? *Was it his?*"

Again Tess shook her head stubbornly. "He adored his wife Marianne. He still does. Who knows whose baby Patty brought back with her."

"So what are the chances that nanny Patty had something to do with the kidnapping?"

Tess raised an eyebrow as she looked anxiously toward the back door of the hospital. "She got the husband, didn't she? Everyone says she married him for his money since there's a pretty big difference in their ages and she wouldn't have wanted Marianne's babies to raise. She has her hands full with her own child. Talk about a spoiled brat."

Nikki wondered what had brought the nanny back to the ranch after almost ten years. What if Patty Owens knew something about the kidnapping and Travers McGraw had married her to keep her quiet? But then why wait all those years?

"It certainly does make you wonder, huh," Tess said as she reached for the hospital keys. But she hesitated before she opened the door. "Something horrible had to have happened that night to turn her hair white. Something so horrible she can't speak."

"Something other than having her babies kidnapped?" Nikki asked.

Tess shuddered. "I try not to think about it. But if she was in love with the horse trainer..." She leaned toward Nikki and said conspiratorially, "What if she killed the babies before she dropped them out the window?"

Nikki felt a chill race through her. That was something she'd never considered. From what she'd read about the case, it was believed that someone—Marianne, according to the prosecutor—had given the babies cough syrup containing codeine so they would be quiet. Maybe she'd given them too much.

Her head ached. She'd thought of little else but this case since she'd stumbled across the old newspaper clippings in her mother's trunk and learned about her father, Nate Corwin—and the McGraw kidnapping.

At first she hadn't understood why her mother would have kept the stories. That was until she recognized the man in the photograph. The photo of him had been taken on the day Nate Corwin was convicted.

"I always wondered why if you loved my father, you didn't keep the Corwin name since you were legally married, right?" she'd asked her mother, and had seen horror cross her features.

"Why would you ask—" Her mother had never remarried but had gone back to her maiden name, St. James.

"You told me my father died."

"He *did* die."

"You just failed to mention he died on the way to prison for kidnapping and murder."

"He didn't do it. He swore he didn't do it," her mother had cried. She was convinced that her husband hadn't been involved with Marianne McGraw nor had anything to do with the kidnapping, let alone the double murder of two innocent babies.

But *someone* had. And if not her father, then someone had let him be convicted and die for a crime he hadn't committed.

Nikki was determined to get to the truth no matter what it took. She had just short of a week before the twenty-fifth anniversary of the kidnapping to get the real story. Travers desperately wanted her to do the book. It was the family she was worried about.

She'd been thinking about how to get close to at least one of the sons before she headed for Sundown Stallion Station and met the rest of the McGraws.

If there was one thing she believed it was that the people in that house had more information than they'd given the sheriff twenty-five years ago. They just might not realize the importance of what they'd seen or heard. Or they had their reasons for keeping it to themselves.

"So how did you get into writing crime books?" the nurse's aide asked as if putting off going back down that long hallway by herself.

"It's in my blood," Nikki said. "My grandfather was a Pulitzer Prize–winning newspaper reporter. From as far back as I can remember, I wanted to be just like him."

"He must be proud of you," Tess said almost wistfully.

Nikki nodded distractedly. Proving herself to her grandfather was another reason she would do whatever it took to get the real kidnapping story— or die trying.

Chapter Three

Cull McGraw put down the windows on his pickup as he drove into Whitehorse. It was one of the big sky days where the deep blue ran from horizon to horizon without a cloud. In the distance, snow still capped the top of the Little Rockies, and everywhere he looked he saw spring as the land began to turn green.

Days like this, Cull felt like he could breathe. Part of it was getting out of the house. He just felt lucky that he'd intercepted the newspaper before Frieda, the family cook, had delivered it on the way to the kitchen.

He didn't need a calendar to know what time of the year it was. He had seen the approaching anniversary of the kidnapping in the pained look in his father's eyes. He could feel it take over the main house as if draping it in a black funeral shroud.

Every year, he just rode it out. The day would pass. Nothing would happen. No one would come forward with information about the missing twins. Another year would pass. Another year of watching his father get his hopes up only to be crushed under the weight of disappointment.

What always made it worse was the age-progression photographs in the newspaper of what Oakley and Jesse

Rose would look like now and his father's plea for any information on them.

Ahead, he could see the outskirts of the small Western town. Cull sighed. He should have known there would be a big write-up in the paper, since this would be the twenty-fifth anniversary. He glanced over at the newspaper lying on the seat next to him. He'd read just enough to set him off. When would his father realize that the twins were gone and would never be coming back? Knowing Travers McGraw the way he did, Cull knew his father would hold out hope until his last dying breath.

But this year, the publisher of the paper had talked his younger brother Ledger into an interview. As he drove down the main drag, he spotted Ledger's pickup right where he knew it would be—in front of the Whitehorse Café.

JUST AS NIKKI had done for the past few days, she watched Ledger McGraw enter the Whitehorse Café. He had arrived at the same time each morning, pulled up out front in a Sundown Stallion Station pickup and adjusted his Stetson before climbing out.

Across the street in the park, Nikki observed him from behind the latest weekly newspaper as he hesitated just inside the café door. She saw him looking around, and after watching him for three mornings, she knew exactly what he was looking for. *Who* he was looking for.

He tipped his hat to the young redheaded waitress, just as he had the past three mornings, before he took a seat at a booth in her section. He had been three when the twins were kidnapped, which now made him about twenty-eight. There was an innocence about him and

an old-fashioned chivalrous politeness. She'd seen it in
the way he wiped his boots on the mat just outside the
café door. In the way he always removed his hat the moment he stepped in. In the way he waited to be offered
a seat as if he had all day.

She'd keyed in on Ledger when she'd realized that
no one else in the McGraw family had such a predict-
able routine. That wasn't the only reason she'd chosen
him. In the days she'd been in town watching him each
morning, she had seen his trusting nature and hoped he
would be the son she might get to help her.

Nikki didn't kid herself that this was going to be
easy. She'd heard from other journalists that the family hated reporters and all of them except Travers had
refused to talk about the kidnapping. She desperately
needed someone on that ranch who would be agreeable
to help her. Ledger might be the one.

Nikki wished she had more time before making her
move. But the clock was ticking. The twenty-fifth anniversary of the kidnapping was approaching rapidly. It still
gave her a chill when she looked at the photographs she'd
taken of Marianne McGraw. It hadn't been her imagination. The woman had risen up from her chair, eyes wild,
hands clenched around the "babies" in her arms.

If Nikki had had any doubt that the woman was still
in that shell of a body, she no longer did. Now she had
to find out if the rumors were true about Marianne and
Nate Corwin.

From across the street, she watched Ledger take a
seat in his usual booth. A moment later, the redhead put
a cup of coffee, a menu and the folded edition of what
Nikki assumed was the *Milk River Courier* on his table.

The local weekly had just come out this morning.

Ledger had been interviewed, which surprised her, since it was the first time she knew of that he'd spoken to the press, but it also made her even more convinced that Ledger was her way into the family.

Inside the café, she watched Ledger looking bashful as he picked up the menu, but he didn't look at it. Instead, he secretly watched the redheaded waitress as she walked away.

Nikki saw something in his expression that touched her heart. A vulnerability that made her turn away for a moment. There was a yearning that was all too evident to anyone watching.

But no one else *was* watching. Clearly this young man was besotted with this redhead. Today, though, Nikki noticed something she'd missed the days before.

As she watched the waitress return to the table to take his order, she saw *why* she'd missed it. Along with the obvious sexual tension between them, there was the glint of a gold band on the young woman's left-hand ring finger.

Her heart ached all the more for Ledger because this was clearly a case of unrequited love. Add to that an obvious shared history and Nikki knew she was witnessing heartbreak at its rawest. The redhead had moved on, but Ledger apparently hadn't.

High school sweethearts? But if so, what had torn them apart? she wondered, then quickly brushed her curiosity aside. Her grandfather had often warned her about getting emotionally involved with the people she wrote about.

She knew in this case, she had to be especially careful.

"Care, and you lose your objectivity," he'd said when, as a girl, she'd asked how he could write about the pain and suffering of people the way he did. "The best stories are about another person's pain. It's the nature of the business because people who've lost something make good human-interest stories. Everyone can relate because we have all lost something dear to us."

"What have *you* lost?" she'd asked her grandfather, since she'd never seen vulnerability in him ever.

"Nothing."

She'd always assumed that was true. Nothing stopped her grandfather from getting what he wanted. He'd go to any extreme to get a story and later to run the newspaper he bought, even if it meant risking his life or his business. But then again, that was one of the reasons Nikki suspected her grandmother had left him to marry another man. Not that her grandfather had seemed to notice. Or maybe he hid his pain well.

Ledger McGraw was in pain and it couldn't help but touch her heart. Nikki knew her grandfather would encourage her to use this new information to her advantage.

"Keep your eye on the goal," he'd always said. "The goal is getting the best story you possibly can. You aren't there to try to make things better or bond with these people."

That had sounded cold to her.

"It's all about emotional distance. Pretend you're a fly on the wall," he'd said. "A fly that sometimes has to buzz around and get things going if you hope to get anything worth writing about."

Nikki now felt anxious. She had to make her move today. Ledger would be finishing his breakfast soon. She couldn't put this off any longer. Just as she decided it was time, she saw Ledger grab the redhead's wrist as she started to step past his table.

Nikki saw those too shallowly buried emotions arc between them as the waitress reacted to whatever he was saying to her. The waitress jerked free of his hold and looked as if she might cry. But Nikki's gaze was on Ledger's face. His pain was so naked that she couldn't help feeling it at heart level.

Ledger McGraw was incredibly young, his protectiveness for this woman touching. *He's still a boy*, Nikki thought, and felt guilty for what she was about to do.

LEDGER IMMEDIATELY REGRETTED grabbing Abby's wrist. Without looking at her, he said, "He's hurt you again."

"Don't, Ledger."

As she jerked free of his hold, he raised his gaze to meet hers again. "Abby." The word came out a plea. "Any man who would hurt you—"

"Stay out of it, please," she whispered, tears in her eyes. *"Please."* Her lowered voice cracked with emotion. "You don't understand."

He shook his head. He understood only too well. "A man who hurts you doesn't love you."

Her throat worked as she hastily brushed at her tears. "You don't know anything about it," she snapped before rushing toward the kitchen and away from him. "He just grabbed my wrist too hard. It's nothing."

He swore under his breath, realizing he didn't know anything about it. He'd never understood what she saw in Wade Pierce. He especially didn't understand why Abby stayed with the man.

Ledger finished what he could eat of his breakfast. Digging out the cost of his meal and tip from his jeans' pocket, he dropped the money on the table, grabbed his hat and left.

Once outside, he stopped in the bright sunlight as he tried to control the emotions roiling inside him. It wasn't the first time he'd seen the bruises, even though Abby had done her best to hide them. The bastard was mistreating her—he was sure of it.

He wanted to kill Wade with his bare hands. It was all he could do not to drive over to the feedlot and call the man out. But he knew that the only thing that would accomplish was more pain for Abby.

When was she going to see Wade for what he really was—a bully and a blowhard and... With a curse, he realized that Abby might never come to her senses. She was convinced he couldn't live without her.

"Ledger?"

He turned at the sound of a woman's voice.

Marta, the other waitress and a friend of Abby's, held out the newspaper to him. "You forgot this," she said, sympathy in her expression.

That was the trouble with a small town. Everyone knew your business, including watching your heart break. He hadn't looked at the newspaper, wasn't sure he wanted to. He hadn't been thinking when the publisher had cornered him.

He took the paper from Marta and mumbled, "Thanks," before the door closed. Gripping the newsprint, he turned toward his ranch pickup. He felt light-headed with fury and frustration and that constant ache in his heart. Not to mention he was worried about what would happen when the rest of the family saw the story in the paper.

And yet, all he could think about was driving over to the feedlot and dragging Wade out and kicking his butt all the way from Whitehorse to the North Dakota border.

But even as he thought it, he knew he was to blame

for this. He'd let Abby get away. He'd practically propelled her into Wade's arms. He hadn't been ready for marriage. As much as he loved her, he'd wanted to wait until he had the money for a place of his own. He couldn't bring Abby into the house at Sundown Stallion Station. He could barely stand living on the ranch himself. He'd told himself he couldn't do that to her. Then Wade had come along, seeming to offer everything Ledger couldn't.

Head down, he was almost to his pickup when he heard someone call his name.

THE COWBOY WHO got out of the second Sundown Stallion Station pickup made Nikki catch her breath. She'd seen photos of Cull McGraw, usually candid paparazzi shots over the years, but none of them captured the raw power of the man in person.

From his broad shoulders to the long denim-clad legs now striding toward his brother, he looked like a man to be reckoned with. The one thing he had in common with all the photos she'd ever seen of him was the scowl.

"Ledger!" Cull looked like he wanted to tear up the pavement as he closed in on his brother. "Have you seen this?" he demanded, waving what appeared to be a newspaper clutched in his big fist.

Ledger stared at him as if confused, as if he was still thinking of the waitress back in the café. Clearly, he hadn't bothered to look at the newspaper he was now gripping in his own hand.

"Why in the hell did you talk to the press? Not to mention, why you didn't tell me that Dad had raised the reward. *Again!*" Cull slapped the paper against his muscular thigh. "Patricia is going to lose her mind over this. All hell is going to break loose."

"We probably shouldn't talk about this out here," she heard Ledger say. "Enough of our lives is open to public consumption, don't you think?"

Cull swore and looked toward the café. Two waitresses stood looking out the large plate-glass window along with several patrons.

"Fine. We'll take this up at home," Cull said through gritted teeth as he turned on his boot heel and headed back toward his pickup.

With an expression of resignation, Ledger turned toward the café window. The redheaded waitress was no longer at the window. He stood for a moment, looking as if he had the weight of the world on his shoulders before he headed for his truck and climbed behind the wheel. The engine revved and he roared past, sending up dust from Whitehorse's main street.

Nikki shifted her gaze to Cull, realizing her plan had just taken a turn she hadn't expected. She hesitated, no longer sure.

Cull had reached his truck, but hadn't gotten in. He was watching Ledger leave, still looking angry.

If Cull was this upset about the article in the newspaper and new reward, wait until he found out that she would be doing a book about the family and the kidnapping case.

She almost changed her mind about the truly dangerous part of her plan. Almost.

Jerking the door of his pickup open, Cull climbed in, angry with himself for coming here this morning to confront his brother. He should have waited, but he'd been so angry with his brother... He knew Ledger hadn't meant any harm.

Tossing the newspaper on the pickup seat, he reached for the key in the ignition. Like most people in Whitehorse, he'd left his keys in his rig while he'd confronted his brother. Had it been winter instead of a warm spring day, he would have left the truck running so it would be warm when he came back.

The newspaper fell open to the front-page story. A bold two-deck headline ran across the top of the page. Twenty-Five Years After Kidnapping: Where Are the McGraw Twins?

The damned anniversary of the kidnapping was something he dreaded, he thought with a shake of his head. Like clockwork, the paper did a story, longer ones on some years like this one. He hadn't seen anything but the first few quotes, one from his brother Ledger and the other from their father, when he'd grabbed up the paper and headed for his truck.

It was just like the publisher to talk to Ledger. His brother was too nice, too polite. If the publisher had approached *him*, the man would have gotten one hell of a quote. Instead, Ledger had said that the loss of the twins was "killing" his father after twenty-five years of torture.

How could their father still be convinced that Oakley and Jesse Rose were alive? Travers McGraw had this crazy fantasy that the twins had been sold to a couple who, not realizing the babies were stolen, had raised them as their own.

Cull and his brothers had tried to reason with him. "How could this couple not have heard about the kidnapping? It was in all the newspapers across the country—not to mention on the television news nationally."

His father had no answer, just that he knew the twins were alive and that they would be coming home one day soon.

He knew his father had to believe that. The alternative—that his wife and her alleged lover had kidnapped and killed the twins for money—was too horrible to contemplate.

Under the newspaper fold were the photographs of the babies that his father had provided. Both had the McGraw dark hair, the big blue eyes like their other siblings. Both looked angelic with their bow-shaped mouths and chubby cheeks. They looked like the kind of babies that a person would kill for.

When he'd seen that this year his father was doubling the reward for information, Cull had lost it.

With a curse, he could well imagine what his stepmother was going to say about this. Worse, a reward that size would bring every crank and con man out of the woodwork—just as it had over the years. What had his father been thinking? He was desperate, Cull realized, and the thought scared him.

His father had been sick and didn't seem to be getting any better. Was this a last-ditch effort to find the twins because he was dying? Cull felt rattled as the idea sunk in. Was their father keeping the truth from them?

Accompanying the story were also photos of Oakley and Jesse Rose digitally age-progressed to show what the twins could look like now. Cull shuddered. How could his father bear to look at these? It was heartbreaking to see what they would have looked like had they lived.

The rest of the story was just a rehash of the kidnapping that summer night twenty-five years ago. What wasn't in the story was that Travers McGraw had sold his most prized quarter horse to raise the ransom demand, and that even after horse trainer Nate Corwin's arrest, the $250,000 ransom had never been recovered.

Nor was there anything about what Travers and Marianne had lost. Not to mention the children left behind. Their mother was in a mental institution and their father had fallen into a debilitating grief and held on to a crazy hope that might be killing him.

Cull wadded up the newspaper and threw it onto the passenger-side floorboard. Had he really thought he could keep this from his family? It was only a matter of time before everyone back at the ranch saw this. His stepmother, Patricia, had long ago tired of this yearly search for the twins. This latest story would set her off royally.

The local weekly paper was only the beginning, he thought with a curse. With the twenty-fifth anniversary of the kidnapping mere days away, other papers would pick up the story and run it, including television news shows.

A part of him wanted to leave town until things died back down again. But as upset as he was with his father, he knew he couldn't run away. His father needed his sons, maybe now more than ever before. Because he might be sicker than they thought. Because once the story was out about the huge reward…

He backed out of his space, wanting to get home and put out as many fires as he could. He'd just thrown the pickup into first gear and gone only a few feet when a young woman stepped off the curb right in front of his truck.

Cull stomped on the brakes, but too late. He heard the truck make contact and saw her fall, disappearing from view before he could leap out, his heart in his throat, to find her sprawled on the pavement.

Chapter Four

Cull knelt beside the dark-haired woman on the pavement, terrified that he might have killed her. He heard people come running out of the café. Someone was calling 9-1-1 as he touched the young woman's shoulder. She didn't stir.

"Is she alive?" someone cried from in front of the café. "The 9-1-1 operator needs to know if she's breathing and how badly she's injured."

Cull took the young woman's slim wrist and felt for a pulse. But his own heart was pounding so hard, he couldn't tell if she had one. He leaned closer to put his cheek against her full lips and prayed.

With a relief that left him weak, he felt her warm breath against his skin. As he drew back, her eyes opened. They were big and a startling blue as bright as the Montana day. A collective sigh of relief moved through the crowd as the woman tried to sit up.

"Don't move," Cull ordered. "An ambulance is on the way."

She shook her head. "An ambulance?" She seemed to see the people around her. "What happened?"

"You stepped out into the street," he said. "I didn't see you until it was too late."

"Please let me up. I'm fine."

"But I hit you with my truck."

She sat up, insistent that she was fine. "Just help me to my feet." She glanced around on the ground next to her. "Where is my purse?"

Just then Sheriff McCall Crawford pushed her way through the crowd. "What happened?" she asked as she knelt beside the woman.

"She stepped into the street," Cull said. "I hit my brakes but—" He'd had so much on his mind. He hadn't even seen her until she'd stepped off the curb.

"I told you," the woman said. "You didn't *hit* me. You might have bumped into me and then… I must have fainted." She looked around her. "If you would just hand me my purse…"

The sheriff glanced around as well, spied her large shoulder bag and handed it to her. "Are you sure you're all right, Miss…?"

"St. James. Nikki St. James."

"Still I'd like the EMTs to have a look at you," the sheriff insisted.

"That really isn't necessary. I feel so silly. If I had been paying attention…"

"No," Cull said. "I was the one not paying attention."

The ambulance arrived and two EMTs jumped out. Cull stepped back to let them get to the woman. Nikki St. James. He frowned. He'd seen that name somewhere recently.

The sheriff pulled him aside. "I'm going to have to write up a report on this. I suggest you call your insurance agent."

"She said she was fine."

"It doesn't appear that you actually *hit* her," the sheriff said. "More than likely she just stepped off the curb and fainted when she realized she'd stepped in front of your truck. But as a precaution, let your insurance office know. They might want you to get her to sign something."

In front of his pickup, the EMTs were helping the woman to her feet. Cull heard her say she needed to go to her rental car. She was late for an appointment.

"I'm not sure you should be driving," one of the EMTs said.

"I can take you wherever you need to go," Cull said, stepping forward. "I agree. You shouldn't drive."

Tears welled in her eyes. "Actually, I would appreciate that," she said. "I'm not familiar with this area. As shaken as I am, I would probably get lost."

"Where are you headed?"

"A ranch outside of town. The Sundown Stallion Station—are you familiar with it?"

Cull stared at her, feeling all the blood drain from his face. He remembered now where he'd seen her name before. On a scratch pad on his father's desk.

Sheriff McCall Crawford watched Cull help the woman into the passenger side of his pickup. He looked more shaken than Nikki St. James did.

She tried to still the bad feeling that had settled in her stomach as she watched Cull slip behind the wheel. She'd seen his face when the woman had told him where she'd been headed—to his ranch.

McCall could no more help her suspicious nature than she could flap her arms and fly. She'd heard about scams involving people who appeared to have been hit by vehicles. It usually involved a payoff of some kind.

As she watched Cull start his truck and pull away, she couldn't help wondering who Nikki St. James was and, more to the point, what she was after. Did she really have an appointment at the ranch? Or was she a reporter trying to get a foot in the door?

Travers McGraw had been forced to get a locked gate for the ranch entrance because of the publicity about the kidnapping. With the twenty-fifth anniversary coming up next week, McCall worried that Cull had just been scammed.

She looked toward the café, suspecting someone in there had witnessed the accident. Wouldn't hurt to ask and still that tiny voice inside her that told her there was something wrong about this. Also she could use a cup of coffee.

As Cull drove past, she saw him glance at the woman in the passenger seat of his pickup. He looked worried. McCall thought he should be.

Nikki St. James was looking out the side window as they passed. She seemed to be interested in someone inside the café.

McCall turned to see redheaded waitress Abby Pierce standing in the window.

NIKKI TRIED TO RELAX, but she could feel Cull's gaze on her periodically as he drove. That had been more than risky back there. He could very well have killed her.

Her original plan was for Ledger. She'd seen how kindhearted he was. It was one thing to have Travers on her side, but she needed at least one family member she could count on. She'd hoped her stunt would make him more amenable to helping her once he knew who she was.

With Cull, she wasn't sure. At first, he'd been so scared that he would have done anything for her. But then she'd seen his shock when she'd told him where her appointment was.

As he drove south, she said, "Thank you for doing this. I hate to have you going out of your way for me."

"It's not out of my way. Your appointment is with Travers McGraw?"

"Yes."

His gaze was like a laser. "He's my father. I'm Cull McGraw, his oldest son."

She'd feigned surprise. "I knew Whitehorse was a small town, but…"

Nikki saw suspicion in his eyes as they met hers. He would have been a fool not to be suspicious and Cull was no fool. She could see that right away.

She recalled the change in him she'd seen after she'd mentioned her name—and where her appointment was. Had the sheriff said something to him to make him question the accident?

He'd said little since they'd left the small Western town behind them. This part of Montana was rolling prairie where thousands of bison had once ranged. In the distance she could make out the Little Rockies, the only mountains on the horizon.

Wild country, she thought, watching the cowboy out of the corner of her eye. It took a special breed to live in a place where the temperature could change in a heartbeat from fifty above to fifty below zero.

Nikki tried to relax but it was hard. There was an all-male aura about Cull that seemed to fill the pickup cab. She would have had to be in a coma not to be aware of the handsome cowboy, even with his scowling. Did he suspect that what happened back there had been a stunt? She should have stayed with her original plan and waited for Ledger.

Too late to worry about that now. With relief, she saw the sign for the turnoff ahead. Her pulse jumped when she saw the Sundown Stallion Station horse ranch come into view. It reminded her of every horse movie she'd ever seen as a girl. Miles of brilliant green grass fenced in by sparkling white-painted wooden fence that made the place look as if it should be in Kentucky—not the backwoods of Montana.

Cull McGraw hit the remote control on the massive white gate that she knew had been erected not long after the kidnapping to keep out the media and morbidly curious. People not so unlike herself.

The gate swung open without a sound, and after he drove the truck through, it closed behind them.

She was really doing this. Her grandfather had taught her that nothing was out of line to get a story. She would get this one. Her head ached and she was regretting her stunt back in town. It almost got her killed and it hadn't worked. Cull seemed even more distrusting of her.

Out of the corner of her eye, she saw him glance over at her. "How are you feeling?" he asked.

Nervous, scared, excited, terrified. "I have a little headache," she said. She'd hit the pavement harder than she'd planned.

He looked worried and guilty. She felt a sharp stab of her own guilt. But she quickly brushed it away. She had to know the truth about her father. Even as she thought it, a lump formed in her throat.

What if her grandfather was right and she couldn't handle the truth?

This case was definitely more than just a book for her; she could admit that now. She'd come here to prove that Nate Corwin had been innocent.

"Nate Corwin was a philanderer," her grandfather told her the day before she'd left for Whitehorse, Montana. "Of course, he was having an affair with Marianne McGraw. He loved women with money. It's why he married your mother."

"I don't believe that."

"Too bad you can't ask your mother, but she's off on some shopping spree in Paris, I hear. But then again, she'd just defend him like she always did," Wendell St. James had said. "Don't come crying to me when you find out the worst."

"I've never come crying to you," she'd pointed out.

"Smart girl," he'd said.

When she'd first confronted her mother about what she'd found out, Georgia had told her that her father had never liked Nate.

"It was because Nate was his own man," her mother had told her. "Daddy tried to hire him right after we got married. But your father flat out refused. 'I'm a horse trainer, not some flunky who sits behind a desk, especially a newspaper one.'" She'd chuckled. "You can imagine how that went over."

Nikki could. "So there is no truth in the newspaper accounts that he was cheating on you?"

Her mother had smiled. "Your father loved me and adored you. He couldn't wait to finish his work at the ranch and get back to us."

"Why would he leave us if that were true?" she'd asked.

"Because his true love was his work and horses. Yes,

he was away a lot because of his job, but he wouldn't have cheated," her mother had said simply.

Cheated? Or done much worse?

"I'll get you some aspirin when we reach the house," Cull said now as he drove along the tree-lined drive. "If you feel too ill, I'm sure you could get your appointment changed to another day."

She shook her head. "Aspirin would be greatly appreciated. I really can't put this off."

The sun flickered through the dark green of the leaves. Ahead, the big white two-story house loomed.

Nikki looked over at him, torn between apprehension and excitement. She was finally going to get into the McGraw house. "I'm a little anxious about my appointment."

"Yes, your appointment."

She didn't like the way he said it and decided to hit him with the worst of it and get it over with. "I'm nervous about meeting your father. I'd thought maybe he would have told you. I'm a true crime writer. I'm going to write a book on the kidnapping."

Cull swore as he brought the pickup to a dust-boiling stop in front of the house. He seemed at a loss for words as he stared at her and she stared right back as if unable to understand the problem. A muscle jumped in his jaw, his hands gripping the steering wheel so tightly she thought it might snap. Those blue eyes had turned to ice and peered out just as cold and hard.

Fortunately, they were both saved. The front door of the house opened; a woman appeared. Nikki knew at once that she was the notorious Patricia "Patty" Owens McGraw.

She'd been able to learn little about Patricia Owens,

the nanny, or Patty Owens McGraw, the second Mrs. McGraw, other than the fact that she was from a neighboring town and had gotten Ted to divorce Marianne so he could marry her sixteen years ago.

The only photo she'd seen of Patty the nanny had been a blurry black and white that had run in the newspaper at the time of the kidnapping. It showed a teenager with straight brown hair, thick glasses and a timid look in her pale eyes.

That's why Nikki was surprised to see the woman who came out to the edge of the porch. Patty was now winter-wheat blonde, sans the ugly eyeglasses, and any sign of timidity was long gone. She wore a large rock on her ring finger and several nice-sized diamonds on each earlobe—all catching the sunlight and glittering wildly. The dress she wore looked straight from some swank New York City boutique, as did her high heels and the rest of her tasteful adornments.

Patty had been nineteen the summer when she'd gone to work as a nanny at the ranch, which would make her about forty-four now. Her husband, Travers McGraw, was sixty.

Frowning, Patricia spun on one high heel and marched back into the house, leaving the front door standing open. She didn't look happy to see that Cull had a woman with him. Had Travers told his wife about Nikki?

She stared at the rambling, infamous house she'd only seen in grainy newspaper photographs—and always from a distance. Was she really going to pull this off? Her heart was a low thunder in her chest as she opened her door and stepped out of the pickup.

She tried to wrangle in her fears. The clock was ticking. She'd done this all before. Once she showed up, anyone with a secret started getting nervous. It usually didn't take long before the mystery began to unravel.

Nikki had only days to discover the truth before the anniversary, which was usually plenty of time to make progress on a book. But from the look on Patricia's face before she'd disappeared back inside the house, and Cull's cursing inside his pickup, it was going to be an uphill battle.

CULL KNEW HE'D acted impulsively. He should have listened to Sheriff Crawford. Instead he'd offered the woman a ride only to realize she was going to the same place he was—and for a reason he would never have imagined.

"True crime writer?" he repeated as he climbed out of the pickup after her. Had his father lost his mind?

He'd looked up to see his stepmother appear in the open doorway looking like she'd sucked on a lemon before she'd gone back inside in a snit. Did she already know about this? If not, when she found out, she would go ballistic. He felt the same way himself.

Cull wanted to storm into the house and demand to know what the hell his father had been thinking. Not that it would do any good, he thought, remembering the newspaper story.

He saw Nikki St. James rub her temple where she'd hit the pavement. Even if she'd stepped in front of his pickup on purpose, he grimaced at the thought that he could have killed her. He reminded himself that he'd promised her aspirin, while a part of him wished he'd almost hit the gas harder back in town.

Mostly, he was just anxious to see his father. The

only one more anxious, he noticed, was Nikki St. James. His father had no idea what he'd done.

Raised voices came from the house. Had Patricia seen the newspaper article and the increased reward her husband was offering? If so, she was already on the warpath. Even after twenty-five years, there was too much curiosity about their family. So much so that they seldom had guests out to the house. They'd isolated themselves from the world and now his father had invited the worst kind of reporter into their home.

What did his father even know about this Nikki St. James? Had he checked out her credentials? One thing was obvious, Cull thought as he walked with her toward the house. All Hades was about to be unleashed.

He hesitated at the porch steps, noticing something he hadn't before. Clearly this woman wasn't from around here, given the way she was dressed—in slacks, a white blouse, pale coral tank and high heels—and the faint accent he hadn't been able to place. It definitely wasn't Montanan.

"Hold up," Cull said to her backside as she continued up the steps.

She stopped midway but didn't turn until he joined her. She looked pale and for a moment he worried that she was more hurt that she'd let on. She touched her temple. He could see that it was red, a bruise forming, and his heart ached at the sight. No matter who she was or what she was doing here, he hadn't meant to hurt her. If only he'd been paying attention...

"Maybe you should sit down for a minute," he suggested.

"I'm fine. Really."

She didn't look fine and he felt guilty in spite of how

he felt about her being here. He actually felt sorry for her. She had no idea what she was getting into.

"Look, I'm not sure whose idea this was, but it was a bad one. What you're about to walk into... My family—"

He didn't get the chance to warn her further, let alone try to talk her out of this before it was too late. His stepsister, Kitten, stormed out of the house and across the wide porch to block their path. Kitten was sixteen and at the age that she thought everything was about her. He could see from the scowl on her face that she'd been arguing with her mother—as usual.

"My mother is impossible," the teen said around a wad of gum. She was dressed in a crop top and a very short skirt and strappy sandals, as if headed for town, a big expensive leather purse slung over one shoulder. "Can I borrow your truck?"

"No, Kitten," he said, and started to push past her.

"One of these days you'll regret being so mean to me," the girl said, then seemed to see Nikki. "Who's this?" she demanded, narrowing her eyes suspiciously as she took in the woman next to him. "You finally get a girlfriend, Cull?"

Chapter Five

Nikki guessed this teenager blocking their way must be Patty's child, the one she'd brought back with her to the ranch when the girl was just a baby. That would have been about sixteen years ago, making the young woman standing in front of her sixteen, if Nikki's math was correct.

The nanny, Patricia "Patty" Owens, had left the ranch after the kidnapping only to return nine years later with a baby. The father of the child had never been revealed. Was it possible this teen was Travers's?

"Back off, Kitten," Cull said as he and Nikki ascended the rest of the steps. "I'm not in the mood."

"Why is everyone in such a bad mood today?" the teen demanded, clearly taking it personally.

Nikki stepped through the front door, followed by Cull, then stopped, wanting to take it all in. But she wasn't given a chance.

"Cull? Is that Ms. St. James with you?" a deep male voice called from an open doorway off to her right. "Please have her come in."

"I'll get you those aspirin," Cull said as Nikki turned toward the open doorway.

Travers McGraw seemed preoccupied, one hand on

his forehead, his elbow resting on the large oak desk in front of him.

Nikki stopped in the open doorway, studying him for a moment. She'd seen dozens of photographs of Travers McGraw, most taken right after the kidnapping. He'd been a big, strong, handsome man, dark-haired with the same pale blue eyes as the two sons she'd seen.

The past twenty-five years had not been kind to him. While his hair hadn't turned as white as his ex-wife Marianne's, it was shot with gray and there were deep lines etched around his eyes. He seemed to have shrunk in size, his body thin, his shoulders stooped.

But as he looked up, his smile was welcoming.

"Mr. McGraw, I'm Nikki St. James," she said, stepping forward to extend her hand. "The crime writer."

He seemed to come alive as he got to his feet. Hope burned bright in his eyes with such intensity that the weight of it hit her hard. He was depending on her to solve the case.

"Please, call me Travers," he said as he shook her hand, clasping it with both of his. "I'm so glad you're here. I didn't hear you come in." He glanced toward the open doorway. "I thought you were going to call for directions to the ranch."

"Actually, I ran into your son Cull in town—" literally, she thought "—and he brought me out."

"Wonderful," Travers said a little distractedly. "All that matters is that you're here and you're going to find out what happened to the twins." He rubbed his temples as if he had a headache, too.

She hoped she didn't make it worse. She started to reiterate that she couldn't make any promises, but she didn't get the words out before Patty burst into the room.

"Tell me I'm misinformed," Patricia said, looking from Nikki to her husband, her blue eyes wild with anger. "Tell me you haven't brought this…this…woman into our home."

"Patricia." He sighed, looking defeated again. "This is not the place to—"

"*Not the place?* This has to stop. I thought we decided—"

"*You* decided," he said, looking a little less beat down. "I will never stop looking for them."

His words fanned the flames of the woman's fury, but seemed to leave her speechless for a moment.

"We need to talk," Patricia said to her husband between gritted teeth.

"I'm sure we will," he agreed as he sat back down behind his desk and motioned for Nikki to take a seat. "But right now I need you to leave and close the door behind you."

All color drained from the woman's face. Clearly appalled, she stormed out, slamming the door behind her.

"I apologize for my wife's behavior," he said after a moment. "I hope this doesn't change your mind."

Nikki shook her head. "Not at all." It wasn't the first time she'd run into a relative who didn't want anyone digging into the past. It wouldn't be the last.

She hadn't expected to get much out of Patty Owens McGraw anyway. But if the answers were on this ranch, she told herself she would find them even without the woman's help.

"You said that I would be allowed the run of the ranch," Nikki reminded him. "I hope you haven't changed your mind."

He shook his head. "If there is even the slightest

chance that you might find out the truth… Just let me know what you need from me. I should warn you. My wife isn't the only one who might be opposed to this."

"Your sons."

He nodded. "Also my lawyer and a close family friend who was in the house that night. They both are quite adamant that this is a mistake. I completely disagree with them, understand. But you might find getting information from them difficult, and I'm sorry about that."

"I've worked with families before that were…skeptical," she said.

He smiled at her understatement of the current situation and raked a hand through his graying hair, looking apologetic. "I had hoped that once you were here it might be easier. Please don't think I'm a coward for not telling my sons. They don't want me to be disappointed again and I really wasn't up to arguing before you got here. With so much time having passed and no new evidence…"

"I hate to get your hopes up as well, but I can promise you that I will do everything I can to find out the truth. I'd like to take a look around the house and the ranch," Nikki said, getting to her feet. "But first if someone can show me to my room. I'm afraid my car and luggage are still in town."

"Not a problem. I'll have someone pick it up for you," he said as he rose from behind his desk.

There was a tap at the door before it swung in. She turned to see Cull silhouetted in the doorway. He stepped forward, holding out a glass of water and two aspirin. She took them as she listened to Travers asking his son to see that Nikki's car was brought out to the ranch.

"But first if you wouldn't mind showing her to the guest room," the older man finished.

"I'll show her to her room," came a voice from the open doorway. It was the teenager who'd accosted her earlier on the porch steps. It was clear that Kitten had been close by, eavesdropping.

The insincere smile had an almost demented quality to it. Nikki wondered again about Patricia's daughter, the mystery child she'd brought back to the ranch years ago.

"Kitten, this is Nikki St. James," Travers said, introducing them. "She will be staying with us while she works on a book about the kidnapping."

The girl raised one brow. "Fascinating." She sounded like her mother, the word just snide enough.

"I want you to be nice to her," he said.

"Of course, Daddy," Kitten said, almost purring. "Later, can I borrow your car to go into town? I'm meeting some friends."

"You just got your license. I'm not sure that's a good idea. What did your mother say?"

"She said she didn't care if I went after dinner, but…" She mugged a face. "She's afraid I'm going to wreck her precious car."

"You can take mine," he said, sounding tired. "Just promise me that you'll be careful and come home whatever time your mother tells you."

The teen rushed to him and kissed his cheek. "Thank you, Daddy." As she turned, she mugged a face at Nikki.

Travers turned to Nikki. "Leave me your keys. Cull will see that everything is taken care of."

She thanked him as she handed them over, only to find Cull standing behind her. He scooped the keys up from the desk and pocketed them, then left without a word. She figured he'd been too surprised earlier to voice his displeasure, but his swearing had given her a clue as to how he felt about her being here.

"We can talk after dinner, Ms. St. James," Travers said as she and Kitten started out of the room.

"Nikki, please," she said, stopping in the doorway.

He smiled. "I can't tell you how glad I am that you're here, Nikki. Dinner is at six. It's informal."

She nodded and followed Kitten out the door. "Can you point out the wing where the twins' nursery was?" Nikki asked the girl.

Kitten smiled. "Of course."

They'd barely left the room before Patricia, who'd clearly been waiting only yards away, rushed into her husband's office, slamming the door behind her. Nikki could hear her raised voice as Kitten led her up the wide stairway.

CULL COULD HAVE handed off the job of retrieving Nikki St. James's car and luggage from town to a couple of the hired hands. After all, he was as unhappy about this turn of events as his stepmother. He was also anxious to talk to his father.

But right now Patricia was chewing Travers's ear, and the best place to be was far from the house until some of the dust settled.

Also, he wanted to know more about Nikki St. James before he confronted his father.

"I could use your help," he said when he found his

younger brother in the barn. "Can you drive me into town?"

"Can't Boone do it?" Ledger asked as he rubbed a hand down the long neck of the newest horse.

"He's gone to pick up that stallion Dad bought last week."

Ledger sighed. "Fine. What's going on in the house, or do I even have to guess?" he asked as they walked along the path next to the house.

Even from here, Cull could hear Patricia's voice raised in fury. He and his brother usually escaped to the horse barns when their father and Patricia were arguing. That's how he'd known where he would find Ledger, especially today after the newspaper article.

"We have a surprise guest."

Ledger blinked. *"Guest?"* He perked up so much that Cull realized for some unknown reason his brother had hoped it was Abby Pierce, the waitress at the Whitehorse Café and his brother's former love. For some reason, Ledger thought that Abby was going to come back to him.

"Dad has hired a crime writer to do a book on the kidnapping," he said before Ledger's unrealistic hopes could be raised further.

"What?"

"I'll tell you all about it on the way into town."

True to his word, he told his brother everything he knew, which wasn't that much.

"Dad has lost his mind," Ledger said when he'd finished.

"Seems that way. She's going to be staying at the house. That's why I need to pick up her car for her. According to what it says on the key, it's a blue compact with Billings plates. We should find it parked near the café where I found you this morning."

"Wait, how did she get to the ranch?"

"I drove her. It's a long story. But suffice it to say, we're apparently stuck with her for a while," Cull said.

"So what does she look like?" his brother asked, turning toward him as they reached town.

He hesitated a little too long.

Ledger laughed. "I've never seen you at a loss for words when it comes to describing a woman."

"It's not like that with this one. She's all right to look at, but I don't trust her."

"Well, once she realizes there is nothing new to write about, she'll leave."

"Let's hope so. I'm just worried about how much damage she'll do before that. Dad—"

"He looks bad, doesn't he?"

Cull nodded around the sudden lump in his throat as he pulled up behind the rental car parked on the main drag of Whitehorse. "I'm going to do what I have to to protect him. Starting by finding out everything I can about Nikki St. James."

NIKKI AND KITTEN were almost to the top of the stairs when Kitten turned abruptly. Swinging around, her large purse hit Nikki, throwing her off balance. Her gaze shot up to Kitten's.

The teen looked surprised for a moment, then a small smile curled her lips as Nikki teetered on her high heels. She grabbed wildly for the handrail. The tips of her fingers glossed over it, but she couldn't find purchase. She could feel herself going over backward.

At the last minute, Kitten grabbed her hand, the

two of them almost tumbling down the stairs as Nikki fought to get her feet back under her.

"That was a close call," the teen said in a mocking tone. "You really should be more careful. People in town say this house is cursed. Terrible things have happened here." She blinked wide blue eyes. "We should get you to your room. You don't look well."

With that she turned and started up the stairs. It was all Nikki could do not to grab the back of her shirt and fling her down the stairs. She was shaking from the near fall and still a little unsteady on her feet. It didn't help that the two aspirin Cull had given her hadn't started to work yet on her headache.

Nikki had faced opposition before. She'd also put herself in dangerous situations. It went with the territory. But as she stared after Kitten, she realized that she'd glimpsed something in the teen that frightened her more than the near accident.

She would have to watch her back in this house— just as her grandfather had warned her. Except it wasn't the kidnapper she apparently had to worry about. But it could be the spawn of one of the kidnappers, she thought, reminded of the look in Kitten's eyes moments ago.

While Nikki thought the purse incident had been an accident, the girl hadn't been that sorry it had happened.

Chapter Six

When McCall wanted information about Whitehorse, she went to her grandmother. Even though Pepper lived on Winchester Ranch miles from town, she had always known what was going on in the county sooner than most.

McCall hadn't doubted that she would remember the McGraw kidnapping.

"Remember it?" Pepper exclaimed after the two of them were seated in the living room. For most of her life, McCall had never laid eyes on Winchester Ranch—or her grandmother. Pepper had denied that McCall was her granddaughter until events had thrown them together. Now they had a mutual respect for each other that verged on love.

"I dug this out after you called," Pepper said, and handed her a file stuffed with newspaper and magazine articles.

"All this is about the kidnapping?"

Her grandmother nodded.

McCall glanced at a couple of articles, but this wasn't what she was looking for. She turned to her grandmother. "I need the dirt. The rumors. The things your old cook used to bring you."

Pepper laughed. "I'd almost forgotten about her." The woman had drugged her grandmother to keep her from demanding too much. McCall had never understood the relationship between the two women, since her grandmother knew what was going on and did nothing about it. Apparently Pepper had some affection for the woman to put up with it for so long.

"There were lots of rumors, if that's what you want. Marianne McGraw and the horse trainer, Nate Corwin. Travers McGraw and the nanny, Patricia Owens. Then there were disgruntled ranch hands looking to make a buck. There is the former ranch manager and close friend Blake Ryan. But I always suspected the lawyer. He was one sleazy bastard, that one."

"Jim Waters? But he's still the McGraw lawyer."

Pepper raised a brow. "That should tell you something."

"That he's trusted?"

"That Travers lives in a houseful of vipers and doesn't realize it," her grandmother said. "The man married Patricia Owens." She raised a brow as if that said everything.

"I suppose you heard—"

"About the true crime writer?" Pepper laughed at her granddaughter's surprise. "Also heard that Patty threw a fit."

"Nikki St. James is writing a book about the kidnapping," McCall said.

Her grandmother lifted another finely tuned eyebrow. "You don't trust her?"

"Something happened in town—"

"That little *accident* in front of the Whitehorse Café?"

McCall laughed. "You must have thought the same thing I did."

"The young woman staged it."

She nodded. "I'm just not sure what she thought it would get her. Cull McGraw was driving the pickup. He's the oldest. He was upset and gave her a ride out to the ranch. But when he found out who she was, I'm sure he was suspicious."

"Probably," Pepper agreed. "Those McGraw sons are smart as well as good-looking."

"I've heard there is no love lost between them and Patricia."

"What do you expect? No one in town can stand her," Pepper said. "The question you should be asking yourself is why Travers married her to begin with."

"He's a nice guy. She was young, had a baby, needed his help," the sheriff suggested.

"Or she had something on him," her grandmother suggested. "Guilt is a huge motivator—if not blackmail."

NIKKI PAUSED AT the top of the stairs for a moment to look back at the house. She felt she needed to catch her breath—and not just from her near fall. She still couldn't believe she was in this house—her father had once walked some of these halls. From what she'd gathered in her research, Nate Corwin had been a frequent guest.

But she wondered if it had been at Travers's request—or his wife's.

Pushing that thought away, she turned to look back down the stairs.

She'd wanted to see the inside of this house from the

moment she'd found the newspaper clippings and discovered how her father had really died.

Now she looked around at all the grandeur, not surprised how beautiful it was. She'd read that Travers McGraw had built the house for his first wife as an anniversary gift. The two had started out relatively poor, living in a small house some distance away. But when he'd begun siring prize-winning quarter horses, he'd had the house built for Marianne. By that time, she had already given him three sons—Cull, Boone and Ledger.

He'd spared no expense on the house and it had no doubt become the talk of the town as well as the county. Was that what had given the kidnapper the idea of taking her two youngest children?

After meeting him, Nikki had hated to get Travers McGraw's hopes up. He seemed a fragile man who'd been through too much. She wondered if another disappointment might kill him.

But she had hoped that there was something here to find—someone who had something to hide. She thought of Patricia. The former nanny had ended up with Travers, and if she played her cards right, she could end up with the ranch, since he didn't seem long for this world.

Except for the fact that Travers still had three grown sons. Did she plan to get rid of them, too? So why would she have kidnapped the twins all those years ago? What would have been her motive?

True, she'd implicated Marianne McGraw. But even if she wanted to be rid of both the wife and the babies, it seemed a little too desperate as a means to an end. Especially if that end was getting Travers McGraw.

Kidnappings usually were about money. But as far as Nikki knew, the ransom money had never been spent.

Because the kidnappers had accidentally killed the twins and had gotten too scared? She thought of the broken rung halfway down the ladder. Had the kidnapper fallen? Had he dropped one of the babies or both of them?

For all the research she'd done, Nikki had too many questions still. All her instincts, though, told her that the answers were here in this house. Someone in this house knew at least a piece of the truth. Once she had all those pieces...

"Are you coming?" Kitten demanded from down the hall.

Nikki sighed and turned to follow the teen. She couldn't help looking into each room they passed, feeling a tingle of excitement. The house was beautifully decorated. Had that been Marianne's doing? Or the new Mrs. McGraw?

Kitten had stopped at the end of the hall. Nikki knew the layout of the house. Downstairs was the large living room, Travers's office, the master bedroom and a huge farm kitchen and dining room.

Upstairs at the back part of the house were the bedrooms for the children and nanny. They were arranged down a long hallway that ran north to south, with the nanny's larger room and the playroom at the south end.

When Nikki joined Kitten, she turned north down a short hallway. Nikki recalled that the twins' nursery had been on the south wing—next to Patricia's. She glanced in that direction. The hallway was dark. A heavy silence seemed to hunker in its shadowy depths.

"This way," Kitten said, and walked to the end of the hall, where she opened a door into a room decorated in shades of blue. "This was Cull's room growing up." She smiled at Nikki's surprise.

She shot Kitten a look. "This is the room I'm staying in?" She'd distinctly heard Travers tell her the guest room.

The teen gave her an innocent smile. "You want to be in this wing, right? Otherwise, they're going to stick you away somewhere since no one stays on these wings anymore."

Nikki looked out the window and saw the addition to the house that had been added after the kidnapping so Travers would be closer to his remaining children. Past it, she saw what appeared to be a pool and pool house.

While what the girl said made sense, Nikki knew what Kitten was up to. The one person who would be most upset about her staying in his room would be Cull. But she decided she would play along and deal with Cull when the time came.

"It's a lovely room." She glanced around, chilled a little at the thought that he hadn't stayed in this room since the kidnapping. This entire wing had been left exactly as it had been. What had he heard that night? Or was it true that he, like the others, had slept right through the kidnapping?

She realized she was rubbing her bare arms as if to warm them. It wasn't cold in the room. On the contrary, the air felt heavy. It was being in Cull's childhood room, being in this house, being this close to the room where the twins had been taken from, she told herself.

"Creepy, huh," Kitten said, no doubt seeing her reaction. Kitten didn't miss much.

"Yes," Nikki agreed. Something horrible had happened in this house. A kidnapping that had probably led to the murder of two innocent babies. And Nate Corwin had been in this house. Possibly climbed the same stairs she had, maybe even walked down this very hallway. What if her grandfather was right? What if she found out that her father had been part of the kidnapping? Part of something even worse?

She thought of Marianne McGraw's snow-white hair and blank, empty eyes, and shuddered inwardly.

Kitten moved to the window and pulled back the drapes, blinding her for a moment. Past the teen, Nikki could see the barn and corrals where her father had worked. Beyond them was the bunkhouse where he'd lived. She'd seen the layout of the ranch from an aerial photo that had been shot after the kidnapping. Since then, some cabins had been added at the back of the property. Was that where Travers's sons lived?

Turning, she watched Kitten pick up a toy cowboy on a plastic horse from a shelf near the bed. "No one comes up here but Tilly to clean. So," she said as she put the horse back on the shelf and met Nikki's gaze, "you'll have it all to yourself. Good luck. Tilly swears she's seen ghosts up here and heard babies crying."

Kitten was trying to scare her *again*, not realizing that what scared her most would be the truth about that night.

"Thank you for showing me to the room, Kitten."

"It's Katherine. Only my family calls me Kitten."

"Duly noted." Her head throbbed. She couldn't wait for this young woman to leave. "I might lie down for a while before dinner."

"Yes, dinner," Kitten said, and smiled. "All the family and my father's attorney will be there. I can't wait for everyone to meet you."

AS HE RETURNED from town with Nikki's rental car, Cull heard Kitten's and her mother's raised voices. He quickly stepped into the office, hoping to find his father and avoid the latest upset.

The room was empty. A small fire burned in the fireplace and the latest edition of the *Milk River Courier* was spread on his father's desk. He stepped closer. One glance at the headline about the kidnapping and he let out a curse. Getting rid of the other newspaper before the cook brought it into the house hadn't done any good. Wadding up this newspaper, he angrily tossed it into the fire as his father came into the room.

Travers spotted the burning newspaper and gave Cull a sympathetic shake of his head. "I appreciate you trying to spare me, but I've already read it." He joined him in front of the fire and laid a hand on his shoulder. "Even if I hadn't, you can't burn every newspaper in town."

"I hate for you to have to go through this again," Cull said.

His father smiled wearily. "*I* was the one who contacted the newspaper, son. Anyway, it isn't something I can ever forget."

"We should talk about this woman—"

"Nikki St. James. Thank you for bringing her out to the ranch. You and Ledger, I understand, went in and brought back her car. Please see that her luggage is taken upstairs."

"I intend to take it up myself," Cull said. "But I have to ask you. Are you sure about this?" He'd gotten on his phone after Ledger had dropped him off and done some research on the woman. He'd hoped to find something that would dissuade his father from going through with this.

Unfortunately, what he found was a professional website, heartwarming reviews and a pretty astounding track record for unearthing new information on true crimes. He could see how his father might have been impressed that she wanted to do a book on the kidnapping.

Travers McGraw didn't answer right away. He lowered himself into his chair before meeting Cull's gaze. "It's been twenty-five years. Your stepmother is right about one thing—I can't keep doing this to myself or to all of you. This is it, Cull. If nothing comes of this book, then I'm done."

Cull let out a sigh of relief. "I know how much this means to you, but I'm glad to hear you feel that way. I'm worried it's going to kill you otherwise."

His father nodded. "So please, help this woman with anything she needs and ask your brothers to do the same. I'll appeal to Patty and Kitten, though I don't hold out much hope for their cooperation." His smile was sad. "I can't help but hope."

Cull wanted to change his father's mind, to argue that he didn't know anything about this woman and that bringing her into the house could lead to disastrous consequences.

He put a hand on his father's shoulder and quickly swallowed back the words, surprised how thin the shoulder felt, how weak his father looked. "I best get her luggage to her."

As he left his father's office, his stepmother came flying in, slamming the door behind her. Cull picked up Nikki St. James's designer suitcase and, taking the stairs three at a time, was at the top when he heard his stepsister call to him from the ground floor below.

"I put her in your old room," Kitten said. He stopped, nearly losing his balance as he turned to look back at her. She stood smiling that impish smile at him.

"Why would you put her in my old room?" he demanded through gritted teeth.

"Because that's the one that Tilly says is haunted the worst." She laughed and took off out the front door.

He almost forgot himself. That girl had needed a good tanning for years. Although he doubted it would do any good. She was just like her mother, spoiled and impossible, he thought as he heard the raised voices coming from the office. Maybe it wasn't his father's loss that was killing him. Maybe it was Patricia and her…daughter.

He often wondered why his father put up with the two of them. Travers had raised Kitten as his own. According to the scuttlebutt in town, she *was* his own. The story was that they'd been lovers all along and that—on top of the kidnapping of her babies—their affair pushed Marianne McGraw over the edge.

For the story to be true, then Patty and his father had renewed their relationship in secret. He and Ledger would have been in high school when Kitten was conceived.

Cull shook his head as he topped the stairs. He didn't have time to speculate on the past. Right now, he was headed for his childhood bedroom in the wing of the house that he hadn't entered in years.

After the kidnapping, he and his brother had been moved to other rooms, closer to his parents. That was

back before they took his mother away one day, never
to return.

As he walked down the hallway, he couldn't help
being furious with Nikki St. James for bringing up bad
memories already—and she hadn't even begun writing
the darned book.

Who knew what she might discover?

That thought turned his blood to slush. He'd buried
so many memories of that night and the days after. And
now she would be poking around, forcing him to relive
them. Worse, reminding him of the secret he'd sworn
he'd keep until his dying day.

NIKKI FRESHENED UP, waiting to make sure that Kitten
had left. Cull's childhood bedroom was all boy, from the
blue decor to the many male toys. He'd just turned seven
at the time of the kidnapping, so he must not have spent
much time in this beautifully decorated room before this
wing was abandoned. Which explained why the room
looked as if a little boy might return at any moment.

Hoping the coast was clear, she went to the door,
opened it and peered out into the hallway. It was empty.
Hearing nothing, she stepped out, easing the door closed
behind her, and started down the hall. All of the doors
to the rooms were closed.

Where the other hallway she and Kitten had come
down intersected, she stopped and peered around the
corner. Seeing no one, she headed for the south wing
of the sprawling house. This was where the nursery
was located, along with a playroom and nanny quar-
ters. This was where Patty Owens had lived before the
kidnapping.

The twins' bedroom room was at the end of the hall-way across from the nanny's room next to a back stairway.

As Nikki neared the end of the hall, she slowed and glanced over her shoulder. That same uneasy feeling she'd felt earlier in Cull's former room now washed over her. While immaculately clean and cared for, the wing still had an abandoned feel. No wonder the housekeeper, Tilly, thought she felt ghosts up here. That is, if Kitten hadn't just been trying to scare Nikki with the story.

Though it wasn't necessary, she found herself tip-toeing the rest of the way. The door to the twins' room was closed. She took hold of the doorknob and jerked her hand back as if she'd been burned. It wasn't until she touched it again that she realized it wasn't hot—it was ice-cold. The heat must be turned off in this wing.

She turned the knob.

Chapter Seven

As the door swung into the former nursery, Nikki was hit with a draft of freezing cold air. Movement. Her heart slammed against her ribs. It took a moment for her eyes to adjust to the dim light. A curtain billowed in the wind. It snapped, then fell silent for a moment before another gust raised it like a ghost coming through the window.

She let her heart rate drop back to normal before she stepped into the room. The wall by the window was painted in alternating blue-and-pink stripes. Someone had started a pastoral mural on the wall opposite the cribs. It had faded. This room, like Cull's, gave her a feeling of being transported back to another more innocent time.

Two cribs were positioned side by side on the opposite wall. She could see the horse patterns on the matching mattress sets. One with a blue background, the other pink. Nikki moved closer, stopping when she saw the tiny covers pulled back. Was that how the kidnapper had left them?

She thought she caught the scent of baby powder, a sick sweetness that turned her stomach. She fought her revulsion and moved to the window, careful not to touch anything. The room still felt like a crime scene.

At the window, she saw the faint dark residue where

fingerprints had been lifted off the windowsill and frame. Nikki wondered if the window had been left open by the housekeeper or if the kidnapper had left it like this.

The breeze stirred the cute pink-and-blue curtains and the white sheers under them. On closer inspection she saw that the fabric had faded pink-and-blue prints of tiny ducks. Something about that brought a lump to her throat.

As often as she'd thought of the twins since she'd found the newspaper clippings and discovered her father's involvement with the McGraws, this was the first time she'd felt the full weight of what had happened here.

The cold draft of air seemed to move through the room. She shivered as it curled around her neck. She couldn't imagine anything worse than losing a child—let alone two.

She rubbed her bare arms to chase away the chill as she considered the nursery. Whoever had prepared this room for the twins must have been excited for their arrival.

Had it been their mother, Marianne? Or had they paid someone to get it ready? Nanny Patty Owens had been here several weeks before the twins were born. Nikki couldn't imagine the woman she'd met downstairs taking such pains to prepare for another woman's infants. But maybe Patty had been as unthreatening as she'd appeared back then.

Nikki moved closer so she could look out the window to the ground below. The FBI had found boot prints in the soft earth where a ladder had been placed against the side of the house—just like in the Lindbergh case.

"What are you doing in here?"

Nikki jumped, startled by the low husky male voice directly behind her. She hadn't heard anyone come down the hall, let alone enter the room. She suspected the tall, broad shouldered, slim-hipped cowboy now standing only inches away had planned it that way as she met Cull's blue-eyed glare with one of her own.

"Your father gave me the run of the house, including this room," she said defiantly. He'd scared her and she could tell he was glad of it. She'd scared him earlier. Did he think that made them even?

He looked toward the open window. "There's nothing here to find."

"Thank you, but I'll be the judge of that."

His hair was long and dark, in stark contrast to the pale blue of his eyes. The resemblance between the McGraw men made her think of Kitten, with her long dark hair and intense blue eyes. She could have been a McGraw.

"Is the window always left open like that?" she asked, looking past him. She could see part of the horse barn where her father had worked as the window parted the curtains.

"Tilly closes it, but when my father comes up, especially this time of year, he opens it so it's as it was that night when the twins were found missing." His gaze, which had been on the window for a moment, moved to hers. There was a primal maleness to Cull that resonated in those eyes. It was as if he could see his effect on her. That, too, seemed to please him.

"You really have no idea what you've gotten yourself into," he said with a shake of his head.

"I've done other books that involved murders and—"

His laugh cut her off. "You feel it, don't you?" She

started to ask what he was talking about, but he didn't give her a chance. "This house, this…" He waved his arms, his gaze boring into hers. "Evil that an open window will never blow from this house."

"If you're going to tell me about the ghosts—"

"That Tilly has seen?" He smiled as he shook his head. "No, I'm talking about a place where something horrible has happened. The evil stays. Like a residue. Like a bad feeling. Like part of the furnishings. You can never get rid of it."

"So why do *you* stay here?"

"Because raising horses is in my blood. But I don't live in the house. I have a cabin on the ranch. You couldn't get me to spend a night on this wing or even under this roof. You don't believe in ghosts? You will."

She thought of how Travers McGraw looked ghost-like. He didn't appear to have fared much better than his former wife. He was thin to the point of gaunt, his face ashen, making her fear he hadn't been well. More than ever, she thought that was why he'd allowed her the opportunity to write the book on the kidnapping.

"What is wrong with your father?"

The abrupt change of subject caught Cull off guard for a moment. "What do you think? All this has taken a toll on him."

"Has he seen a doctor?"

"You seriously can't see what has caused his decline?"

"It has to be more than the kidnapping. He really doesn't look well."

Cull sighed. "I've been trying to get him to see a doctor. He's stubborn."

"Like his son."

He shot her a warning look. "Let's say you are as

good as your book publicist claims. What you uncover about the case could kill him."

"Is that what you're afraid of? Or is there a reason you don't want the truth to come out? Maybe some secret of your own?"

Something flickered in those deep blue eyes, but he quickly hid it. "I had just turned seven years old."

"Plenty old enough to remember that night. Maybe remember more than you've ever told anyone."

She thought she saw him flinch as if she'd hit too close to the truth. "I've found that often family members know more than they want to tell. They're covering for someone or they're worried what will happen if they tell."

Cull shook his head. "I'm just worried about my family and what you're about to do to it."

"You could help me."

He shook his head. "Have you not heard a word I've said?"

"Your father needs to know what happened that night. Can't you see that?"

Cull let out a low curse. "He already knows what happened."

"No, I don't think so. I don't believe your mother had anything to do with the kidnapping. Nor do I believe Nate Corwin did."

He looked surprised. "Then who?"

She cocked a brow at him. "That's what I'm going to find out. With your help."

"Sorry, but there isn't anything to find. You're wasting your time. Worse, you're giving my father false hope."

"What if hope is the only thing keeping him alive?"

"I almost feel sorry for you," Cull said. "You start

digging in the past and all you're going to do is stir up more trouble than even you can handle."

"That almost sounds like a threat."

He shrugged. "Just remember. I tried to warn you." He turned toward the door. Over his shoulder he said, "Dinner's ready."

"I'm going to find out the truth with or without your help," she called to his retreating backside.

He stopped in the doorway to look back at her. "Let me know when you have it solved because I've spent years trying to figure out what happened that night and I was actually in the house. I heard Patty's screams. I still hear them."

NIKKI STARED AT HIM. The man threw her off balance. She would have to be very careful around him, she thought just an instant before the sound of high heels could be heard making a noisy, angry tattoo in the hallway as they approached.

They both looked toward the doorway as Patty Mc-Graw appeared. Nikki heard Cull curse under his breath.

"What are the two of you doing in here?" Patricia demanded. She looked from her stepson to Nikki and back. "You brought her in here, Cull? What is wrong with you and the rest of this family?"

"She found her way on her own," he said, his hooded gaze taking in Nikki again. "I dropped her suitcase in my room where Kitten put her."

"You have no business in here," Patricia chided her as if Nikki were a child in a china cabinet. "If Travers caught you in here…"

"He gave me permission to—"

"He shouldn't have done that." Patricia motioned

frantically for Nikki to leave. "This room, this entire wing, is off-limits. I've had your things moved downstairs to the pool house."

"The pool house?" Cull said with an arch of one eyebrow.

Nikki shot him a puzzled look as she tried to understand why he seemed amused by this.

Cull shook his head in disapproval at his stepmother. "The pool house will allow her to have the run of the entire ranch while the rest of us are asleep in our beds."

"Well, what did you expect me to do with her?" Patricia demanded. "Your father wouldn't hear of putting her up in a motel in town or better yet sending her back where she came from."

Nikki wanted to remind them that she was still in the room. "I'm sorry, I didn't mean to cause any trouble."

"Oh, please," Patricia said, spinning on her heels. *"Everyone* knows what you're really about. You aren't the first one who's come here wanting to satisfy your morbid curiosity."

"I hope to help."

The woman's laugh could have shattered crystal. *"Help?"* She seemed to be choking on laughter. "You've thrown the entire house into turmoil. You call this helping?"

Nikki could feel Cull's keen gaze on her. She rubbed at the painful spot on her temple, still surprised she'd hit as hard as she had. She really was lucky she hadn't been hurt worse or killed.

"Cull will show you to the pool house after dinner." With that, Patricia made a rude sound and stormed away.

Her leaving the room, though, didn't cool the heated anger in it. Nikki could feel it coming off Cull in waves.

"This must give you great pleasure, this front-row

seat into our family drama," Cull said through clenched teeth.

"The kidnapping has been a lot of stress on your family for twenty-five years," she pointed out.

He smiled at that. "You think?" His intense blue gaze seemed to drill into her skull as he locked eyes with her. "You know all about us, though, don't you? I suspect you knew who I was when you stepped in front of my pickup. That you've known everything about this family for some time."

She lifted her chin a little higher. There was no reason to deny it. He'd seen through her stunt. She could have mentally kicked herself. Hadn't she known that Cull was the wrong person to cross?

"You know so much about us and yet we know so little about you," he was saying. "It makes me wonder why you chose our...tragedy for a book." When she didn't respond, he continued. "Well, seems you're going to be our guest for a while. Until you get what you need." His deep, soft voice reverberated through her. While Ledger had seemed impossibly young and innocent, Cull was anything but. This was a man not to be fooled with.

"But I have to wonder what a woman like you needs," he finished, his voice so low and so seductive that it felt like a deep, dark well drawing her in. "I have to wonder just how far you will go."

Nikki swallowed and asked, "Has anyone been staying in the pool house? I don't want to put them out of their lodgings."

Cull's smile filled her with dread. "The pool house has been empty since the night of the kidnapping. It's where an item from one of the twins' beds was found.

Apparently, the kidnapper and accomplice met there before at least one of them disappeared with the twins."

A chill rattled through her. Nikki hugged herself. That information hadn't been in *any* of the research she'd done on the case. It was the kind of thing that the FBI held back. What item had been found in the place where she would be staying? That meant that at least one of the kidnappers had been in that building that night. Her father? Marianne? Or someone in this house right now?

"You should be quite comfortable there since the place has its own set of ghosts," Cull assured her. "It's far enough away from the house that you won't be able to hear my father and stepmother arguing and yet no one will hear you should you run into trouble and need help. I'll try not to be too far away though. For your own sake. Wouldn't want you to have another...*accident*. How is your head by the way?"

She ignored the sarcasm laced with accusation. "The aspirin helped, thank you." Picking Cull had definitely been a mistake. Why had she thought he would be more helpful to her if he thought he'd almost killed her? From the look in his eye, he was wishing he hadn't braked.

"So you and your brothers live..."

"I would imagine you saw our cabins from the twins' window."

She had seen what looked like cabins set back in the trees some distance from the house. "You really are afraid of the ghosts," she only half joked.

His handsome face grew serious. "You think I'm joking? We'll see how you feel in a few days."

Chapter Eight

As Nikki and Cull descended the stairs, Ledger came out of his father's office.

"I don't believe you've met our houseguest," Cull said to his brother. "This is Ms. Nikki St. James, the famous true crime writer."

Ledger had clearly already heard about her, Nikki thought. He shook her hand warily.

"Patty has decided our guest would be more comfortable in the pool house," Cull said.

Ledger looked surprised, but added, "Whatever makes Patty happy."

"I need to make a quick call. Why don't you show Nikki to the dining room," Cull said.

"I'm glad we finally get to meet," she told the young man.

"You realize we're all shocked that our father would hire you."

"He didn't hire me. He's just giving me access to the ranch and the family so I can write about the kidnapping and hopefully uncover what really happened that night. I hope you'll help me."

Ledger let out a nervous laugh. "Me? I can't imagine how I could help. I was three."

"You might be surprised what you remember," she said, making him appear even more nervous. She quickly changed the subject. "I'm afraid I've upset your stepmother."

"Don't worry about it," he said as they walked toward the back of the house. "She's often upset over something."

"She caught me in the nursery."

He slowed so he studied her. "Oh. No one is allowed in that wing except the housekeeper, and even Tilly hates to go in there. The nursery is exactly as it was twenty-five years ago. My father insisted it be left that way. At first so that no evidence was lost. He was convinced that the FBI and local law enforcement would find the twins. Later it was left because he couldn't bear to change it."

"How awful for your family."

"Yes," he agreed as they reached the dining room. "Not to mention the glare of the media over the years. You can't believe the extremes some reporters will go to in an attempt to get a story."

She felt her face heat at his words.

"That's why I'm surprised my father opened the doors to you. Here we are," he said.

Stepping through the dining room doorway ahead of Ledger, she saw that Patricia and Travers were having a muted discussion in the far corner. At the center of the room was a huge cherrywood table and chairs that seemed to dwarf the large room. Kitten was already seated, and so were two men she didn't recognize.

Nikki felt a draft move across the back of her neck and shivered as it quilled the tiny hairs. She turned, expecting... Not sure what she expected to see. One of the ghosts?

THAT NIGHT AT DINNER, the sheriff told her husband about the woman who Cull McGraw had nearly run down. "I think it was staged. Too much of a coincidence that she steps in front of a McGraw pickup when she's on her way to the house anyway. But unfortunately, no one in the café saw anything."

"You have a very suspicious mind," Luke said, looking up from his meal. "What do you think she's after?"

"Supposedly, she's there to write a book about the McGraw kidnapping for the twenty-fifth anniversary."

"That sounds reasonable. I'm sure you checked her out."

McCall nodded. "She was born Nikki Ann Corwin."

"Corwin—why does that name ring a bell?"

"Because her father was Nate Corwin, the man who was convicted of the kidnapping," she said. "I can't help but wonder if Travers McGraw knows that."

"No wonder you're suspicious." He reached over onto Tracey's high chair to drop more finely chopped beef roast. She'd named her daughter after her father, Trace Winchester.

Tracey beat the high-chair tray with her spoon for a moment before laughing, then, ignoring the spoon, began eating the beef with the fingers of her free hand.

McCall smiled at her daughter. She never got tired of watching her, fascinated by the simple things the child did. She'd been so afraid of motherhood and hadn't admitted it until she was nine months pregnant.

Luke had talked her into taking a three-month leave while she decided if she wanted to be a stay-at-home mother or keep her job as sheriff.

"It's whatever you want," he'd told her. "I know you can do both. It's up to you."

McCall was glad she'd taken the time off. She loved being with her baby, but she also loved her job. She'd been afraid he was wrong and she really couldn't have both.

"I think I might drive out to the Sundown Stallion Station in the morning," she said as she straightened her daughter's bib and was rewarded with a huge toothy smile.

Being a game warden with the Fish, Wildlife and Parks Department, Luke was trained and served as an officer of the law. She didn't have to tell him why this year in particular, the McGraw kidnapping was on her mind.

"I have the day off tomorrow," he said. "Pepper's invited us out for lunch. Ruby's going, too."

McCall lifted a brow in surprise. "My mother and grandmother at lunch together? We need to get Tracey a bulletproof vest."

He chuckled as he rose to pull their daughter out of her high chair. "Probably a good idea."

The sheriff had to smile. That her mother and grandmother could be in the same room together and not kill each other was nothing short of amazing. For years Pepper Winchester hadn't acknowledged that McCall was even her granddaughter because of her dislike for Ruby.

Ruby had married Pepper's favorite son. Pepper had believed that Ruby had trapped Trace by getting pregnant and had wanted nothing to do with her—or the baby she had been carrying. Until a few years ago, McCall hadn't known anything about that side of her family, since her father had disappeared before she was born.

She'd never even laid eyes on her grandmother who'd

become a recluse after Trace's disappearance. Nor had she known why Pepper Winchester wanted nothing to do with her. Her mother, Ruby, certainly hadn't been a wealth of information.

Then McCall, who'd been working as a deputy back then, had stumbled onto an old shallow grave. In the grave was proof of her father's identity. Everyone had thought that he'd left town, run out on her and her mother. Finding his remains had brought more than his murder to light.

It had opened up a world to her that had always been a mystery. McCall would never forget the first time she'd seen the Winchester Ranch—let alone met her grandmother Pepper. It had changed all of their lives.

"Give my regards to Pepper tomorrow," she said now. "I'm sure she understands why I can't make lunch."

"Your grandmother loves that you're sheriff. You know she would have been disappointed if you had quit."

McCall did know that. She just hoped her grandmother didn't have an ulterior motive for inviting them to lunch. It wouldn't be the first time Pepper had something going on that she didn't want the law involved in.

As her husband began to get their daughter ready for bed, McCall felt a shiver. Just the thought of the kidnapping sent a spike of cold terror through her. She couldn't imagine losing her daughter. It was no wonder Marianne McGraw had lost her mind and was now locked away in the mental hospital.

McCall had been a child herself at the time of the kidnapping, but she'd heard stories about it and read both the newspaper accounts as well as the police file on it.

The FBI had been called in almost at once and taken

over the case, but from what she'd read about the investigation, there had been several suspects, including the babies' own mother, Marianne. But it had always seemed that the dalliance between the stable manager, Nate Corwin, and Marianne McGraw had been conjecture without any solid evidence.

The person who'd testified about the affair had been the nanny, Patricia Owens—now Travers McGraw's second wife.

It was speculated that Nate and Marianne had come up with the kidnapping of the twins for the ransom money. Nate Corwin was a mere horse trainer. Marianne had no money of her own. What they'd planned to do with the twins after they collected the ransom was unknown since neither had confessed. Marianne had gone into shock. Nate had denied his involvement right up until his death.

McCall knew what it was like to fall so deeply in love that you could lose all perspective. But she shuddered at the thought that a mother would jeopardize the lives of her babies for money and a man. Any man.

TRAVERS SAW NIKKI as she entered the dining room, and said something quietly to his wife before greeting her. "I don't believe you've met our attorney. Jim Waters, this is the woman I told you about," Travers said.

The attorney was fiftysomething with thinning brown hair and small brown eyes. He turned awkwardly, a deep frown burrowing between his brows, and held out his hand. His handshake was limp and slightly damp, and his eyes didn't meet hers.

"And this is Blake Ryan, our former ranch manager and a close friend."

Blake was about the same age as the other man, but unlike Waters, he was distinguished and cover-model handsome. His dark hair had grayed at the temples, bringing out the steel of his gray eyes. His handshake was strong and he met her gaze with both suspicion and wariness.

"Why don't you sit over here by me," Travers said to her after making the introductions. He didn't need to tell her that both men had some concerns about her being here.

She'd just sat down when she heard the sound of boot soles on the wood floor. She sensed rather than saw Cull enter the dining room because she kept her gaze averted. She didn't glance over at him as he took a chair next to his father, directly across from her.

Suddenly the room felt too small. She took a shallow breath and dared to look at him. His gaze was on her, those blue eyes drilling her to her chair.

Ledger had taken a seat down the table next to Kitten, who looked far too happy, all things considered, since she hadn't gotten to go into town yet.

Nikki tried to relax but the tension in the dining room was dense enough to smother her. Patricia had lowered herself into her chair at the end of the table with a sullen dignity, only to glare down the length of it at her husband.

Boone was the last brother to come in. She hadn't met him yet because he'd been out of town picking up a horse, she'd heard. He stopped in the doorway. He could have been Cull's twin. He had the same thick dark hair, the same intense blue eyes, the same broad shoulders, the same scowl.

"What's going on?" Boone asked as if feeling the tension in the air before his gaze lit on her.

Travers got to his feet. "Please sit down, son." He waited for Boone to take a chair before he said, "This is Nikki St. James. She's a true crime writer and will be investigating the kidnapping for a book. I want you all to cooperate with her."

"Like hell." Boone shoved back his chair and stood, towering over the table. "I'm sorry, Dad, but this was a huge mistake. I'm not having anything to do with this…book or—" he turned his gaze on Nikki "—or this woman." With that he stomped out.

"I apologize for my son," Travers said wearily.

"You don't have to do that," she said as she heard the front door slam and the sound of an engine rev after it. "I know how hard this is on your family." She glanced around the table. She could feel Cull's gaze on her. Like Boone, he didn't want her here.

Kitten was giving her that snotty look she'd apparently perfected. Her mother's steely blue gaze could have burned through sheet metal. Ledger was the only one who gave her a slight smile as if he felt sorry for her.

"I will try to make it as painless as I can, but I need all of your help if I have any chance of solving this," she finished.

"Solving it?" Patricia said with a snort, but quickly reverted her gaze to her plate as her husband gave her an impatient look.

"I'll speak to Boone," Travers said. "I should have told him about this. He doesn't do well with surprises." Though Boone had been only five when the twins were kidnapped, he might still have memories of that night.

"I should help Frieda." Patricia got up and went into

the kitchen. A few moments later, she returned with the cook, who was carrying a large tray full of small bowls of soup. Patricia put a bowl in front of Travers and another in front of Cull before she sat down. Frieda placed soup in front of Patricia, then worked her way around the table until she came to Nikki. For a moment, she looked confused. "I guess I left yours in the kitchen," the cook said.

"Let me," Kitten said, jumping up and hurrying after her.

The two returned moments later. Kitten, all smiles, put a bowl of soup in front of Nikki before sitting down again.

"Thank you, Kitten," Travers said, smiling at the teen, though looking surprised she would get up to help.

Cook placed two large plates of sandwiches in the center of the table and left.

Nikki picked up her spoon. Steam rose from the soup. She caught a scent she didn't recognize. Kitten leaned behind Waters to whisper, "Aren't you afraid it might be poisoned?"

Normally she had a good appetite. Even without Kitten taunting her, she wasn't that hungry. She started to dip her spoon into the soup, when Cull reached across the table and switched bowls with her. He gave his stepsister a challenging look. Kitten rolled her eyes and waited for him to take a bite.

"What is going on?" Patricia demanded.

"It seems Kitten thinks Nikki's soup may be poisoned," Cull said. The man had remarkably good hearing. Or he knew Kitten too well.

"What?" Patricia seemed beside herself.

Kitten gave her a shrug as if she had no idea what Cull was talking about.

"This is ridiculous," Patricia said, and started to get up. But before she could, Travers reached over and switched bowls with Cull.

"Kitten, I will speak with you later," he said. He picked up his spoon and took a sip of the soup.

"I didn't do anything," the teen whined, and glared over at her brother who hadn't touched his soup.

Travers started to take a second spoonful, when he suddenly dropped his spoon. It hit the edge of the bowl. The sound was startling in the silent room. Everyone looked in his direction as he clutched his chest, his eyes wide and terrified before he toppled to the floor.

Chapter Nine

Cull studied the toes of his boots. Anything to keep him from looking at Nikki St. James sitting a seat away from the family in the hospital waiting room.

If his fool stepsister had tried to poison the woman... He glanced at Kitten. She was sulking in the corner. On the way to the hospital, all of them piled in Patricia's Suburban, Kitten had continued to protest that she hadn't poisoned Nikki's soup, that she'd just been teasing and that maybe the cook had done it.

Finally, Cull had told her to keep quiet, at which point Patricia had gone off on all of them for mistreating Kitten. "She's as upset as the rest of you and she's just a child!"

Cull had concentrated on the road ahead, determined not to get into it with any of them. They'd followed the ambulance to the hospital and were told to wait.

Earlier Ledger had gotten everyone coffee. Cull had watched him ask Nikki if she wanted some. She'd volunteered to go with him to the machine. After hearing how it was that Cull had brought her to the ranch, Ledger had accused him of "literally running her down on Main Street."

Since then Ledger had been especially nice to the

crime writer in spite of Cull telling him that he didn't trust the woman. He could see what Nikki was up to and he planned to put an end to it once they were alone.

At the sound of footfalls, Cull looked up—as did the rest of them—and saw Boone storming in. *"What happened?"* he demanded. He had beer on his breath, which answered the question as to where he'd gone after he'd stomped out earlier.

"We don't know for sure—" Cull didn't get to finish.

"Someone poisoned Dad," Ledger said. "At least that's what we think happened."

"Poisoned him?"

"We don't know for sure," Cull said.

Patricia jumped to her feet. "This is all her fault," she accused, pointing a finger at Nikki. "It was her bowl of soup   "

Boone shot a look at Nikki.

"Hold on, everyone," Cull said, raising his hands as they all started talking at once. "Nikki was the intended *victim*. Perhaps, Patricia, you should be talking to your daughter. She was the one who brought the bowl of soup out of the kitchen."

Patricia sputtered as if unable to get the words out fast enough. *"Kitten?* Kitten wouldn't... How can you possibly think..."

"I was just teasing." Kitten burst into tears and ran from the waiting room.

"Now see what you've done?" Patricia demanded before she went after her daughter.

"Let's all just calm down," Cull said. "I called the sheriff when we got here. I'm sure McCall will be able to—" He stopped as he saw the doctor and the sheriff coming down the hall toward him. Heart in his throat, he waited, fearing what the news was going to be.

NIKKI WATCHED THE two come down the hall. She couldn't tell from their somber faces what they'd discovered. If Travers had been poisoned... Her stomach knotted at the thought. Was there someone in this family *that* determined to keep her from learning the truth? What if because of her, Travers McGraw lost his life? She couldn't bear the thought.

Boone started to speak, but the sheriff cut him off. "Your father wasn't poisoned."

Nikki felt a wave of relief wash over her. She'd been so afraid that Kitten had done something stupid in an attempt to get rid of her.

"He's had a heart attack," the doctor said. "He's in stable condition, but not out of the woods yet. Were any of you aware of your father's heart problems?"

The attorney, who'd been sitting at the edge of the group, spoke for the first time. "Travers knew he had a bad ticker?" Jim Waters asked.

The doctor nodded. "I've warned him how important it was for him to relieve stress and eat healthy and slow down. I had hoped he might have shared that information with his family."

Cull groaned. "It was just like him not to."

"I want to see him," Boone said.

"If anyone should get to see him, it should be me," Patricia said as she came down the hall.

The doctor held up his hands. "None of you are going to see him. Right now the last thing he needs is more... stress." As Patricia started to argue, the doctor said, "You will be able to see him possibly in the morning, but only one at a time. And I won't have *any* of you upsetting him."

They all fell silent for a moment before Cull said, "You heard him. Dad's in stable condition. Let's all go home."

Nikki's head ached. She couldn't wait to get back to the ranch and take a couple of aspirin.

"I'm not riding with *you*," Kitten announced to Cull. "I'm riding with Boone."

Patricia took her daughter's hand. "No one's leaving until you all apologize to my daughter."

Cull let out a curse. "An apology? Have you forgotten that no one would have thought that Dad had been poisoned if it wasn't for Kitten? Fortunately the doctor recognized his condition as a heart attack, otherwise they would have been pumping his stomach while he was dying of heart failure."

"All that matters is that Dad is going to be all right. But this constant bickering has to stop," Ledger said.

"Then get rid of *her*!" Patricia said, pointing again at Nikki. "Now with Travers in the hospital, the whole idea of a book on the kidnapping should be scrapped."

"Patricia's right," Boone said, speaking up. "You just heard what the doctor said. Dad doesn't need the stress of having someone digging up the past, and for no reason, since we all know who kidnapped the twins."

Cull shook his head. "This isn't the time or the place to discuss this, and if any one of you dare bring this up when you see Dad..." He saw from their faces that they got the message. "In the meantime, Nikki stays and does whatever it is she does. If Dad changes his mind, *he'll* send her packing—but not us and not before Dad is well enough to make that call. Boone, I'm going to take your pickup. You can ride in Patricia's Suburban since you've obviously been drinking. Nikki, you come with me. The rest of you can go with Patricia or walk, I don't care." He reached for Nikki. "Let's go."

CULL GRIPPED THE steering wheel so hard he was white-knuckled as they left the hospital.

"Thank you for sticking up for me back at the hospital," Nikki said once they were on the road headed toward the ranch.

"I didn't do it for you," Cull said through gritted teeth without looking at her. "I did it for my father."

Out of the corner of his eye, he saw her turn away to look out her side window. Open prairie ran for miles, broken only occasionally by farmland all the way to the Little Rockies. He loved this country. Where some people saw nothing, he saw the beauty of the wild grasses, the rolling landscape, the huge sky overhead that ran from horizon to horizon, living up to the name Big Sky Country.

The night was clear and cool. Stars glittered in a canopy of navy velvet. He rolled down his window as they left town behind. The smell of sage and dust and wild grasses filled his nostrils. He breathed it in and tried to calm down. This was home. The prairie soothed him in a way no other landscape ever had. He loved this part of Montana the way others loved the mountains and pine trees.

For a moment, he wondered what Nikki saw when she looked out there. Or did she yearn for towering mountains studded with pine trees? He'd found few women who appreciated his part of the state. It was one reason he'd never settled down.

"I feel responsible for what's happened," she said. "I'm so glad your father is going to be all right."

He glanced over at her, his expression softening when he saw the tears in her eyes. "It's not your fault. Dad hasn't been well. You heard what the doctor said. The anniversary of the kidnapping is just one more weight piled onto all the stress he's normally under."

"I'm sorry," she said. "I wish there was some way I could help. If my leaving would help…"

He slowed for the turn into the ranch. "You would give up that easily? I thought you were determined to find out the truth about the kidnapping?"

"I am, but I can't promise—"

Cull laughed. "*Now* you play coy?" He shook his head. "Sorry, I'm not buying it. I think you'd do anything to get this particular story and that makes me wonder about you."

"What you see is what you get," she said, then added quickly, "You know what I mean."

He smiled. "You would have eaten that soup, wouldn't you?"

"Yes. Why does that bother you?" she asked.

Cull scoffed. "Because it shows me the kind of woman you are. You don't back down."

"I'm going to take that as a compliment."

"Suit yourself." He could feel her gaze on him as he pulled up in front of the house and parked.

"You know what I think? I think the reason you and the others are frightened of my digging into the kidnapping is because you have something to hide. There's something you held back all those years ago. Maybe it's just a memory that has haunted you. A sound, something that was said, something that you saw but didn't understand at the time."

He wanted to tell her how crazy she was, but she'd gotten too close to the truth. But some secrets were best kept silent, since they wouldn't change the kidnapping. Nor would they change who'd been behind it. "That's what you're counting on to solve this? Good luck."

"I was hoping that all of you would want this solved as much as your father does," she said.

Cull turned off the engine and turned to face her. "You just don't get it. We've been living with this for twenty-five years. Do you have any idea how painful all this is for us to have to relive every year? Can't you now see that it's killing my father?"

"That's why he needs to know what really happened."

Cull shook his head as he took off his Stetson and raked a hand through his hair. A dark lock fell over his eyes before he shoved the hat back on. For a moment, he simply studied her, wanting to look deeper, clear to her soul. If she hadn't already sold it for a story.

"I swear this tops it all. A *true crime writer*? And I thought the psychic he hired was bad enough."

"The sooner I can get to work, the sooner I will be gone."

He cocked his head, narrowing his eyes. "Gone, but not forgotten."

She seemed to ignore that and met his gaze with a steely one of her own.

"Why? What does it matter to you? I'm sure there are other tragic stories for you to delve into out there. So what is it about our particular story?"

Nikki looked away, giving him the impression that

for some reason this time it was more than finding out the truth for a bestseller. Again he found himself wondering, *Who is this woman?*

All his instincts told him that she was hiding something but he couldn't for the life of him figure out what it was. She was already a *New York Times* bestselling author. From what he could tell, she didn't need the money or the attention. She'd already made a name for herself. Writing another book about some horrendous crime wasn't going to get her anything she didn't already have.

Or would it?

"I'm not sure what you're after," he said carefully. "But I saw the way you were with my brother. You're not using Ledger to get whatever it is you're really after. Right now because of another woman who took him for a ride, he doesn't know his ass from a teakettle. You stay away from him. He was too young to remember anything about the kidnapping. I won't have you using him."

"I'm not using your brother."

Cull scoffed. "And you just happened to be in Whitehorse today sitting across from the café where my brother has breakfast on the days his ex-girlfriend waitresses there."

He caught her moment of surprise before she carefully hid it. "That's right," he said with a bitter chuckle. "For whatever reason, you will do whatever you have to, use whoever you have to, tear this family apart to get what you want." He frowned as he studied her. "For a book? I don't think so. Just know that while you're digging into every dark corner of our lives, I'm going to be digging into yours. I can't wait to find out what your real story is, Nikki St. James."

With that he opened his door and climbed out. He heard her open her door and exit, as well. A set of headlights washed over him as Patricia pulled the Suburban up in the yard.

Cull was in no mood for any of them. He didn't bother going inside, but instead took the path beside the house and headed for the stables. He was breathing hard, sucking in the cold night air as he tried to cool his anger. Chill down the heat that filled him whenever he got around that woman. Nikki St. James rattled him more than he wanted to admit. No good could come of this for any of them. He had to find a way to get rid of her and soon.

NIKKI STOOD NEXT to the ranch pickup feeling as if she'd just gone three rounds in the ring. Cull suspected there was more to her story for being here. He hadn't found it. Not yet, but he suspected enough that he wouldn't stop until he discovered the truth about her.

She let out a humorless chuckle. He said she wouldn't stop at anything? He was just like her. She watched him take off and realized he'd left her not so she could deal with his family, but so he could escape all of them.

"He's not usually so…rude."

Nikki spun around to find Ledger standing right behind her. "You startled me."

"Sorry." Ledger glanced toward the rest of his family entering the house. Patricia was arguing with Kitten about something as they started up the porch steps. Nikki was reminded of earlier when the teen almost knocked her down the stairs.

Jim Waters and Blake Ryan both walked past without looking at her. Patricia stopped on the porch and called down, "I'll get cook to put sandwiches out. I don't know about the rest of you, but I'm starved." Her gaze lit on Nikki. She turned quickly and went into the house.

"I heard that Patricia moved you out of the wing upstairs and put your belongings in the pool house," Ledger said. "Why don't I go with you to make sure everything is ready for you?"

"Thank you. That would be nice," she said, happy to have some time alone with Ledger. She was reminded, though, of what Cull said about not using his brother. "But Cull might not approve. He's worried that I'll take advantage of you."

Ledger chuckled. "Cull's the oldest so he always thinks he has to protect us all. His heart is in the right place, though."

"Why do you think he feels he needs to protect you from me?" she asked innocently enough as they walked down a path that led around the house.

"He thinks I'm a fool."

"Because of the woman at the café," she said as they left the house behind and walked through a stand of aspens. "I was sitting across the street this morning. I couldn't help but notice."

His smile was sad. "Abby."

The darkness felt good. So did being around Ledger. There was a quiet confidence about him that was nice, especially after the intensity of his older brother. "You're in love with her."

"It's that obvious, huh?" He laughed. "I guess Cull's right. I'm pretty transparent. He thinks I should forget her." He shrugged. "Can't."

"You're worried about her."

"With good reason. Her husband is…" He waved his hand through the air as if he couldn't come up with a name that was appropriate in front of her.

"But she won't leave him."

"Nope," he said with a shake of his head. She could hear the frustration in his words. "She says he needs her. I don't get it."

Nikki said nothing. There was nothing she could say. Women often stayed with controlling men for their own reasons. Who knew what Abby's real reason was.

"What do you remember about the night of the kidnapping?"

He glanced over at her, clearly a little taken aback by the quick change of subject. But she also noticed that his guard had gone up.

"I told you, I was three."

"Oh, I thought you might be able to help, especially given your father's health. I want to find out the truth for him more than ever now."

He nodded, looking guilty. "I think I remember… little things. Waking up to hear Patty screaming. The sound of people running down the hallway toward the nursery. My father on the phone to the sheriff. But I've heard my brothers say the same thing over the years, so maybe they are actually their memories and not even mine. There is one memory that I think is mine because when I think about that night I see myself standing at the end of the hall until someone noticed me."

"Who noticed you?"

"Patty. She was our nanny then."

"Did she say anything?"

"I'm sure I asked her what was going on." He shrugged.

"I have a faint memory of her saying something about making pancakes in the morning. See, I really have nothing that could help."

Pancakes? That sounded like a very strange conversation, if that's what it had been.

Ledger stopped in front of a small building. Next to it was a large swimming pool. The breeze ruffled the surface of the water, making it lap at the edges. He looked back at the house. Golden light spilled from most of the windows as if all the lights had been turned on.

"What if you find out who kidnapped Oakley and Jesse Rose only to discover that they're dead?"

"I think not knowing is worse for your father. Maybe if the truth came out, it would let everyone heal."

He shook his head. "Dad lives with hope. If you take that away..."

In the silence that fell between them, she heard voices coming from the back porch. Two figures were silhouetted there against the lights coming from the house. One was clearly Patricia. The other was a man, but she couldn't be sure who.

She turned, trying to catch their words on the breeze. Behind her, she heard Ledger open the door to the pool house. A moment later, a bright light came on.

"There you go," Ledger said in a voice loud enough that it would carry to the back of the house. "If you need anything, just holler."

The voices silenced. She turned to look at Ledger, surprised to realize that he'd signaled Patricia and whoever she'd been in an intense conversation with that they weren't alone. When Nikki looked back, the two figures had bled into the shadows and were gone.

Cull was so sure that she had Ledger wrapped around

her little finger. That he would do anything she asked. That he would let her use him.

As Ledger met her gaze, she saw something in his eyes before they darted away that gave her a start. Ledger was just as protective of the McGraw secrets as his brother Cull.

They were definitely hiding something, but she couldn't be sure it had anything to do with the kidnapping. What had the boys seen or heard that night that they were afraid she was going to uncover? Was there a secret they'd been keeping all these years? But if true, *who* were they protecting?

Glancing toward the stables, she thought she saw a figure standing just inside out of the light. Cull? Over her shoulder, she said to Ledger, "I know there is something you're all keeping from me. What I don't understand is why."

There was no answer. When she looked back, she saw that he was headed for the house. He appeared to be in a hurry.

Seeing her suitcase waiting for her just inside, she pushed open the door to the pool house. The place was beautifully furnished. As it hadn't been used since the kidnapping, she had to assume that Marianne was the one who'd decorated not only the pool house but the main house, as well.

She would be quite comfortable here instead of Cull's former room on the haunted wing, she thought, even though this small building might have even more persistent ghosts. Why, though, did Patricia want her out of the house so badly?

Before she walked through the door, she glanced again toward the house.

Her pulse jumped, her heart taking off like the wild stallion Boone had brought home earlier. Someone was standing at a second-story window. Her chest constricted as she realized that the window was at the end of the south wing. Someone had been watching her and Ledger from the nursery.

A shock wave moved through her as she saw the figure was a woman dressed in all white. Even her hair appeared to be white. For just a heartbeat, she thought it was Marianne.

The breeze billowed the curtains. Nikki blinked and the figure was gone as if she'd only imagined it—unlike the chill that moved through her, turning her blood to ice.

Chapter Ten

Patricia called from the back porch saying cook had set out the sandwiches as Nikki started to close the pool house door. She felt her stomach growl. They'd missed lunch and now it was way past dinner.

"I can bring you a sandwich if you'd rather not go back to the house tonight."

She saw Cull come out of the darkness on the path from the barn. "I'm not that hun—" Her stomach growled again. By then, he'd reached her. He grinned, clearly having heard her stomach, and turned toward the house. "I'll be right back."

"Thank you, but I hate to have you go if you aren't hungry."

Cull stopped to look back at her. "If you want to eat by the pool, I'll bring back enough for both of us. Then we can talk."

She nodded, although she wasn't sure she liked the sound of that. Had Travers called and told him to send her packing? Or was Cull willing to help her with the book?

Nikki had yet to step inside the pool house, where she would be staying. She did so now, then picked up her suitcase and carried it into the bedroom.

It had been a long day. All she could think about

was climbing into the bed and sleeping. But even as she thought it, she wondered how much sleep she would be able to get. So much had happened today and her list of suspects just seemed to continue to grow.

Not to mention the fact that she was starving.

Hearing a tap at the open door a few minutes later, she looked up to find Cull standing there. He had a tray with sandwiches, glasses of milk and cake. Chocolate cake. Her stomach growled loudly.

"Let's get you fed," he said, motioning toward the pool rather than coming inside. She'd been surprised that the McGraws had a pool since it was so seasonal in Montana. She said as much as she joined him at the outdoor table.

"My mother loved to swim. Now Kitten enjoys it. I take a dip occasionally." He handed her a plate with several sandwich options.

"But no one uses the pool house?"

"My mother used to come down here and read when she needed a break from all of us," Cull said. "It was her…sanctuary." He seemed to remember that the kidnappers had possibly met here that night before the twins were whisked off, never to be seen again. His expression soured.

Nikki wanted to ask him questions about his mother but right now seemed the wrong time. She took a bite of one of the quartered sandwiches. Chicken salad. It tasted wonderful.

"How is your father?" she asked after she'd swallowed.

He didn't seem surprised that she would know he'd call the hospital after they got back. "Resting comfortably, the doctor said."

Nikki took another bite and noticed that Cull hadn't touched his yet. He was watching her.

"What?" she asked as she finished and picked up another.

"You. I'm used to women who don't eat carbs. Hell, don't eat anything, from what I can tell." For a moment, she wanted to defend her eating habits and her rounded though slim figure. He didn't give her a chance. "I like women who have curves."

Cull seemed to realize what he'd said. "I mean—" He laughed softly and picked up a sandwich. "I should just shut up and eat, huh."

They ate in a companionable silence for a while. He'd turned on the pool lights. The water shimmered invitingly.

"You're welcome to go in," he said, clearly having noticed the longing in her expression.

"I didn't bring a suit."

"I wouldn't let that stop you."

She laughed at that. "I've already caused a stir around here. I can well imagine what your stepmother would say."

"Yes, Patty." He shook his head. "Life is strange, isn't it?"

"Do you remember her when she was your nanny?"

He nodded thoughtfully. "Quiet, shy, mousy, I think is how the press described her. I've often wondered about the change in her." He eyed her closely. "I'm sure you do, too."

She met his gaze for a moment before she lowered hers and hesitated as she looked at the chocolate cake.

Cull picked up a piece and put it in front of her. "Enjoy—you deserve it after the day you've had."

"I could say the same to you."

He nodded and looked toward the pool. "I'm sorry I gave you such a hard time earlier."

"Speaking of earlier, I heard Patty talking to someone behind the house. It sounded rather heated."

"I think it was Blake. He's been with Dad from as far back as I can remember. They were probably arguing over Dad's health. Blake thinks Patty could be more…agreeable."

Nikki wondered if Cull really expected her to believe that's what they were arguing about. She hadn't been able to make out much of the argument but it hadn't been about Travers's health. And she suspected Cull knew that, since the barn was closer to the house—and the argument.

"I really doubt that was what they were arguing about and you know it," she said, calling him on it. "Why lie about it? What is it you're all trying so hard to keep from me?"

He looked up at her in surprise, his gaze suddenly calculating. "You don't miss much."

"It's my job," she said defensively.

"For the book."

There was that suspicion again. She felt her heart quicken—from his look, from his words. "I know it's hard. A stranger coming in who might uncover your most intimate secrets. It's hard for me, too. I often get emotionally involved with the family. I'm human. But I'm not here to hurt any of you. I just want—"

"The truth." He nodded as if he still had his doubts about her real reasons as he rose from his chair. "You look as if you are going to fall asleep right out here by the pool." He removed the other piece of chocolate cake from the tray and picked up the dirty dishes. "I'll take these up to the house. The cake…well, you might wake up in the middle of the night and need something."

It was such a sweet gesture, bringing down the sandwiches, eating with her out here by the pool, leaving the cake and taking the dirty dishes. She couldn't help but be touched. "Thank you."

"I'm sure I'll see you in the morning. Breakfast is at seven but if that is too early for you, Frieda will see that you get whatever you need." He seemed to hesitate for a moment as if there was more he wanted to say. But then he smiled almost sadly and said, "Good night, Nikki. Sleep well."

"So THAT'S WHAT'S going on," Patricia said the moment Cull pushed open the door to the kitchen and put down the tray. "Conspiring with the enemy."

He shook his head. It was late and he was too exhausted from the day he'd had to argue with her. "Let's not get into it." He started to turn away, but she grabbed his arm.

"Your father is lying in a hospital bed and it is all that woman's fault!"

He turned to face her. "*No, it's not.* If anyone is to blame, it's you. You harp and harp at him until I'm amazed he doesn't just tell you to shut the hell up."

Her eyes widened in shock. "How dare you—"

"Oh, I dare," he said, taking a step toward her. "I have been wanting to tell you how I feel for a very long time. My father took you in, married you and has helped raise your daughter and neither of you have ever said thank-you. You both just demand and demand. Nothing is ever enough."

She was shaking her head furiously. "You can't blame me for his heart attack. It's this stupid kidnapping. He just won't leave it alone."

Cull took a step back giving her an incredulous look. "*Stupid* kidnapping? Patty, his children were taken. For all he knows they're dead. Are you that self-centered that you can't understand that?"

She looked chastised for a moment, but quickly recovered. "Well, it's been twenty-five years. How long do you expect me to put up with this?"

"He is *never* going to forget. If you can't accept that, then there's the door. No one is forcing you and Kitten to stay here."

"You'd love to see that, wouldn't you?"

He said nothing, his earlier anger receding, leaving him feeling sorry for his harsh words, no matter how heartfelt. "Can't you just be happy?" He opened his arms to encompass not just the kitchen but the entire ranch. "Look where you live, look how you live. Can't you just embrace that?"

She sniffed and looked as if she might cry.

"And leave Nikki alone. Let her do what she came here to do."

"She's not going to find out anything more than the FBI and the sheriff did all those years ago." Something in her voice gave away her hope that that was the case. He'd often wondered if Patty had something to hide about the night of the kidnapping. If so, was she worried that Nikki would be able to uncover it? That could explain why she'd been so upset about the crime writer's appearance here.

"Only time will tell, I guess. I figure she'll be gone soon enough." He started to turn away again but this time it was her words that stopped him.

"Are you sure that's what you want?" There was accusation as well as mocking in her tone.

He stopped at the door, but didn't turn. "It's what we all want." And he was betting that each of them had their own reasons for wanting Nikki gone.

AFTER CULL LEFT, Nikki went inside the pool house, locking the doors before heading to the bedroom. She was so tired that she quickly brushed her teeth, stumbled into her pajamas and fell onto the bed.

She'd been so sure she wouldn't be able to sleep with everything that was going on. Everything including Cull. She thought of his intense blue eyes. He saw too much. But that meant he always had—even as a child. There was no doubt in her mind that he knew more about the kidnapping than he'd told anyone.

He was her last thought before she dropped into the deep, dark hole of sleep. That was why it took more than a few minutes for her to drag her way up and out of the dream.

She sat up in bed, rubbing her hands over her face as she tried to let go of what had started as a nice dream and had turned into a nightmare. Even as she thought it, she could feel the dream slipping away, leaving only that heavy, suffocating feeling of doom.

Nikki tried to hang on to the thread of her nightmare. Something to do with Cull and the horses in the barn and her father. She shook her head. Clearly not one of those dreams that made a lot of sense. She'd never even known her father. But he was in the dream. He was in the stables. And something horrible was happening.

That's when she woke up. She sat listening to the night sounds. An owl hooted in the distance. Closer she heard a horse whinny. Then another horse, then another.

She frowned as she got out of bed and padded barefoot into the living area of the pool house to look out toward the stables. A light was on. She caught movement. Someone was in the horse barn.

Remnants of her nightmare made her heart beat faster. Maybe it hadn't been a dream. Maybe she'd heard something...

She opened the door. The Montana night was clear,

the stars glittering overhead, only a slit of silver moon dangling over the barn. She made her way along the path, hugging herself against the slight chill in the air.

As she drew closer, she could hear the horses, restless in their stalls. A shadow moved along the edge of the horse barn. A moment later she heard raised voices. Male voices.

Her bare feet were beginning to ache from the cold of the stones along the path. She shivered, debating turning back. But curiosity won out. Her showing up at the ranch had caused a stir. If whoever was arguing in the barn this late at night had something to do with the kidnapping…

She moved to the edge of the barn door so she could hear better over the whinnying and stomping of the horses inside.

"You're making a terrible mistake. If you're wrong…" She didn't recognize the male voice and wondered if it could be the former ranch manager who'd apparently been arguing with Patricia earlier.

"I know what I'm doing. I'll do whatever I have to." Her heart slammed against her rib cage. This voice she recognized. *Cull.*

"You said you don't want anyone to get hurt. I don't see how that can be avoided under the circumstances. This crime writer—"

"Don't worry. I'll take care of her myself if this all goes south."

Nikki felt the air rush from her lungs. She stumbled back, her shoulder hitting the gate. The metal latch rattled.

"Did you hear that?" the unfamiliar male voice asked a second before Nikki heard someone moving in her direction.

She flattened herself against the side of the barn but

quickly realized she would be seen by whoever came out. Her only hope of getting away unseen was to go around the side of the building. But that meant climbing into the corral.

Nikki hurriedly climbed over the corral railing, dropping down to the soft hoof-turned earth. Her bare feet sunk into the dirt, slowing her escape. Just a few more yards and—

Suddenly out of the corner of her eye, she saw a horse come galloping out of the barn and into the corral. It headed right for her, ears back, hooves throwing up dirt clods as it barreled forward.

Nikki lunged for the corral fence as the huge horse bore down on her. Her hands brushed the railing and missed. Not that she would have been able to climb out before the horse reached her anyway.

Two strong, large hands grabbed her from around the waist and swung her up and over the railing. She felt the horse's breath at her neck. Before she knew what was happening, she slammed into a very solid male chest. Behind her, the horse stomped and snorted just feet away past the corral railing. She realized it must be the stallion that Boone had delivered to the ranch earlier.

The arms that had wrapped around her now set her down hard at the edge of the corral. *"What the hell do you think you're doing?"* Cull demanded as he held her at arm's length. "You could have been killed. What were you thinking getting into the corral?"

She couldn't speak and realized she was trembling all over from the close call. Worse, as she glanced toward the barn, she began trembling harder when she realized that someone had set that horse free in the corral. Cull? Then why save her?

"What are *you* doing out here?" she demanded.

"Checking the horses. I heard something."

She nodded. "So did I." She'd heard enough, that was for sure.

His gaze never left Nikki's face. He was studying her in the dim light from the barn as if he was trying to understand her. "You have no business in the corral. That's a wild horse in there."

She nodded and tried to swallow down the lump in her throat. Tears stung her eyes as she realized how close she'd come to being trampled. Worse, that she couldn't trust Cull.

He shook his head. She couldn't tell if he thought her silly and stupid. "Come on. I'll walk you back to the pool house."

She glanced toward the barn. The horses had settled back down. She saw no movement deep in the stalls. Whoever Cull had been talking to, he was gone. Which left the question of who had let the stallion out and why. Had he hoped to scare her? Or kill her?

She could smell Cull's very masculine scent intermingled with saddle leather and fresh air. If the purpose had been to scare her, then the stallion had done his job. She would have to be more careful, given what she'd overhead. Especially more careful when it came to Cull McGraw.

Chapter Eleven

Nikki drove into Whitehorse as the sun arced over the prairie. The day was beautiful, sunny and warm, the big sky blue and dotted with white fluffy clouds. She'd awoken before dawn with a suspicion that had felt like a douse of ice water.

She'd hurriedly done research on her phone before giving the sheriff a call and asking if she could come by and see her.

Sheriff McCall Crawford looked up from her desk as Nikki came in. She was a slim, pretty woman who Nikki had heard was a no-nonsense law officer. Mostly she'd heard that McCall could be trusted.

"Thanks for seeing me," she said, and closed the door behind her.

The sheriff raised a brow. "You sounded so cryptic on the phone." She motioned to a chair and Nikki sat down. "I was planning to drive out this morning to the ranch and see how you were doing."

"I'm sorry we met the way we did yesterday," Nikki said honestly. "Now I am hesitant to even voice my suspicions, but I hope you will take what I have to tell you seriously."

"Your suspicions after only one day at the Sundown Stallion Station? You really do work fast. I'm intrigued."

"Were you aware of Travers McGraw's health before his heart attack?"

"I'll admit I hadn't seen him in a good while," the sheriff said as she leaned back in her chair. "I was taken aback by his condition."

Nikki nodded. "His family seems to think the cause is his obsession with finding out what happened to the twins."

"But you don't think that's it?"

She shook her head. "I think he really *is* being poisoned." She pulled out her phone. "I've seen this once before. His symptoms are consistent with those of people who are being slowly exposed to small amounts of arsenic over time. Headaches, loss of weight, confusion, depression. In his case, finally cardiac arrest."

The sheriff looked skeptical. "I'm assuming you have no proof of this?"

"No, and I had the same reaction at first that you are. But then I remembered that his wife Marianne had the same symptoms."

"Twenty-five years ago?" The sheriff sat up, leaning her elbows on her desk, definitely interested now.

"But in the same house. The same house *and* the same people living there," she said. "If I'm right, that would seem like too much of a coincidence, don't you think?"

"Marianne's depression was blamed on postpartum. Her other symptoms on possibly an illicit love affair."

Nikki nodded.

"No one else is experiencing these symptoms at the house?" the sheriff asked slowly, studying her.

"No, so I doubt it's tainted water or any other factor in the house causing it other than the obvious. Someone is intentionally poisoning him."

The sheriff said, "He's in the hospital. If he was being poisoned, it probably wouldn't still be in his system, except possibly in a strand of hair from his head."

Nikki nodded. It was one way to find out if there was any basis for her suspicion.

"Speaking of suspicion," the sheriff said, "how are you since your accident in front of the Whitehorse Café?"

"Fortunately, I wasn't hurt other than a knock on my head."

"Fortunately," the sheriff said, smiling.

Nikki got to her feet. "I won't keep you, but I was hoping you might see if my suspicions are valid. Given Travers McGraw's condition, I didn't think it was something that could wait."

"I suppose you have a suspect to go along with your suspicions?"

"It's a short list," Nikki said. "But I'm sure you can guess who's on it. The person who has the most to profit if Mr. McGraw should die. The same person who had reason to want to get rid of Marianne McGraw twenty-five years ago."

CULL FELT THE full responsibility of keeping peace at home along with running the ranch, with his father in the hospital. Blake Ryan had handled that job for years. But a couple of years ago he had stepped down, and Cull, as oldest son, had moved into the position alongside his father.

Running the ranch, he could do. It was keeping peace

in the house that was the problem. Patricia had been on a rampage since yesterday. He'd heard her yelling at Frieda, their elderly family cook, this morning. He'd broken that up only to find that Nikki St. James had taken off before breakfast and no one knew where she'd gone.

Had she seen how useless this was and left? He could only hope, but even as he thought it, he knew better. Nikki wasn't a quitter. Wherever she'd gone, she'd be back.

As crazy as things had been, he hoped that his father's heart attack would be a wake-up call for him. Something had to change.

"How is he?" Cull asked the nurse when he reached his father's hospital floor after driving in from the ranch.

"He's doing well," she said. "You can see him. Just keep your visit short and don't upset him."

That meant not mentioning Nikki or the twins or Patty or Kitten or the ranch, Cull thought as he walked down the hall. He hesitated at his father's door. He'd watched the man get sicker and sicker and hadn't been able to do anything. Travers McGraw was stubborn; Cull knew that only too well. But maybe now he was ready to face things.

As he walked into the room, he saw that his father's eyes were closed and he was breathing steadily. He stood for a moment, simply relieved. He was glad to see his father's color was better. Stepping to the bed, he touched his hand.

His father's eyes opened and he smiled. "Hope I didn't give you a scare."

Cull chuckled. "Naw, we all just finished our meals before rushing you to the hospital," he joked.

"I'm fine," his father assured him. "The doctor said it was a minor heart attack and he's already lectured me, so you don't have to."

He nodded. Travers McGraw was anything but fine. He needed to make some changes in his life. If he didn't realize that now...

"Is Ms. St. James still at the house?"

Technically, she'd spent last night in the pool house, where Patricia had exiled her, and was gone before he'd gotten up. But he said, "She is," hoping his father would ask him to send her away.

"Good. I still want her to do the book, no matter how it turns out."

He wanted to argue with his father, but he bit his tongue. "Okay."

"I'd appreciate it if you would help her, do whatever she needs."

His father was asking too much, but he nodded, thinking of working closely with Ms. St. James. He had a sudden vision of her swimming half-naked in the pool on a moonlit night— Where had that come from? He smothered the thought, but it took a while for the heat in his belly to go away.

"Is Kitten all right? I hope I didn't scare her."

Cull chuckled at that. "Little scares Kitten."

"So you'll see to it that Ms. St. James gets everything she needs."

He'd love to see to her...needs. "I will."

"Good." His father seemed to relax. He closed his eyes and for a moment, Cull thought he'd dropped back to sleep.

"I can't tell you how much it means to me to have you for a son, Cull." His father opened his eyes again and reached for his hand. "I know I can depend on you and your brothers."

The nurse came in then and shooed Cull out. He promised to come back later and left the hospital.

On the way back to the ranch, he spent most of the time grumbling to himself. By the time he reached the front door of the house, he'd made up his mind.

He would do exactly what his father asked him to do. He'd help Nikki in every way possible. And once she realized there was nothing new to write, she would leave. His father would be disappointed, but he was going to be disappointed anyway.

As he parked in front of the house, he saw that Nikki wasn't back. He wondered where she'd gotten off to so early in the morning and if she'd tell him if he asked. He headed for the pool house only to cross paths with Kitten.

"She's not there," the teen said. "I heard her tell Frieda that she was going into town to do some research." Kitten made it sound like Nikki had lied. "I bet she's meeting a man." Her eyes glinted with mischief. "Which means you got dumped. Looks like you'll never get a girlfriend, even once you had to run over with your truck."

He had wondered how long it would take for that little tidbit to get around. Now he knew. "Kitten, there is a big, black spider on your shoulder."

The girl screamed and began running around swatting at her shoulders.

"Sorry, it wasn't a spider. It was that chip you have on your shoulder."

She mugged a face at him. "I'm going to tell Mother."

"Be my guest." He headed for the stables, wondering what kind of research Nikki was doing in town. Or if Kitten was right and Nikki had lied.

ALL THE WAY back to the ranch, Nikki told herself she'd done the right thing going to the sheriff. If nothing came of it or if she was dead wrong, then at least she'd shared her suspicions.

Now she had to get on with her work. As soon as she reached the ranch, she went looking for Patricia. As a true crime writer, she'd learned that where she found the truth was in the inconsistencies. Not just slight changes in a person's story, but new information that they hadn't remembered before. It always surprised her. Small tidbits were often drawn up from some well of memory to surprise both her and her interviewee.

While she also looked for changes in the stories, she found that those who had the most to hide had almost memorized their statements. They would provide an almost word-for-word account even as many as twenty-five years later.

After something horrible happened, of course people often changed. How much or how little was also often a clue. In Patricia's case, the change had been huge.

Nikki had read Travers's testimony as well as Patricia's from the sheriff's reports along with hundreds of newspaper articles. Travers had awakened to find his wife gone and had rushed out into the hallway on hearing Patty's screams. He raced down the hall to find the window near the twins' cribs wide-open, the cribs empty and a ladder leaning against the side of the house.

He saw no one, but had raced outside only to find

footprints in the soft dirt under the window. He'd immediately called the sheriff.

It wasn't until later that he saw Marianne. She'd apparently gone for a swim in the middle of the night because she was coming from the pool house.

Nikki had a pretty good idea that Patty's story would be the same one she had told dozens and dozens of times after the kidnapping. But still she needed to hear it herself.

As she entered the house, she heard voices coming from the kitchen. Patty's voice carried well and while Nikki couldn't make out her words, she could hear the tone. Patty was unhappy with someone.

She found her at the breakfast bar in front of a muffin. From the tension in the room, Patricia had been having a heated discussion with the cook, Frieda Holmes. Clearly Nikki had just interrupted it.

The cook turned her back to the stove, but not before Nikki had seen her blotched red face and her tears.

"I hope this is a good time," she said, knowing full well that it wasn't. What had the two been discussing that had them both so upset? "Mrs. McGraw, I need to ask you some questions."

"You can't be serious," Patricia said, shoving away her crumb-filled plate. "My husband is in the hospital possibly dying and you're intent on—"

"Doing what he asked me to do. I know you told the authorities what happened that night, but I need to hear it from you. The sooner I get everything I need, the sooner I will be gone."

Patricia sighed. "Not here," she said, glancing at the cook's back. Frieda didn't seem to hear. Or at least didn't react. "Let's go into Travers's office."

Nikki followed her, thinking about yesterday and the first time she'd seen Travers. She was glad to hear he was doing better and would be allowed to have visitors later today.

As if thinking the same thing Nikki was, Patricia said, "When I see my husband this afternoon, I'm going to convince him to put an end to this book of yours."

"You do realize I can write the book without his permission."

Patricia huffed as she sat down at her husband's desk. "Well, I have nothing to add."

Maybe. Maybe not. "I wanted to ask you about Marianne. You were living in the house. You would know if there were problems between her and her husband. If there was another man." She looked down at her notes and turned on her digital recorder. "In other interviews, you've said she'd been acting...strangely."

Clearly Patricia had expected to simply tell the same old story she'd been telling about that night. Her dislike of Marianne became quickly evident. "*Strangely* was putting it mildly. She would wander around the backyard as if lost. I thought for sure she'd lost her mind and as it turns out..."

"What about her relationship with her husband?" Nikki purposely avoided saying Travers's name.

Patricia rolled her eyes and seemed to relax a little. Gossip was clearly something she could get her teeth into. "I knew the minute I was hired that there was trouble in that marriage. I'd seen the signs. It wasn't my first rodeo. Marianne was miserable and not just because of this unexpected pregnancy. That's right, the twins were an accident." She nodded enthusiastically as she leaned closer. "From the start I could tell that she didn't want them."

"Was there another man?"

With a sigh, Patricia sat back. "You should have seen the way she was with that horse trainer. She made a fuss over him. It was so obvious."

"I'm sure her husband must have noticed."

Patricia shook her head in disgust. "He was blind to anything she did. Sure he noticed, but he thought she was just being nice to him since he was away from his wife and child and clearly lonely."

"Maybe that's all it was."

"Then why would the two of them cook up this kidnapping scheme?" Patricia demanded.

"Maybe they didn't. When the horse trainer was arrested, he didn't have the money. Neither did Marianne. So what happened to the ransom money?"

Patricia shrugged. "Maybe he hid it, waiting until the two of them could run away together."

"Strange, though, that it hasn't been found. I know the authorities searched the ranch for any sign of the money—and the twins."

"You mean searched for graves."

"But they found nothing."

"Have you taken a look at this country around the ranch? It's Missouri Breaks, miles and miles of nothing but gullies and cliffs and pines, millions of places to hide anything you want."

Nikki couldn't argue that. "Let's talk about that night."

Patricia proceeded to tell her story almost verbatim from her other accounts. Just as Nikki had assumed, she got the same old, same old.

Patricia claimed she'd been awakened by a noise and gotten up to check the twins. As she'd crossed the hall, she'd been surprised to feel the breeze coming in—convinced she'd left their window closed.

On entering the room, she'd gone to close it when she noticed that one of the cribs was empty. She'd quickly checked the other and panicked.

"I stepped to the window, saw the ladder and the footprints below and started screaming."

"Tell me where everyone else was at that point."

She frowned. "It's really a blur. Everyone came running down the hallway toward the nursery. Travers got there first and then the kids. Travers told me to take the children to my room and stay there to wait for the sheriff. That's about the time Marianne showed up, her hair wet. I didn't realize until later that she'd been for a swim—in the middle of the night." She rolled her eyes, making it clear she thought the woman had been crazy even back then.

"Let's not forget that Jesse Rose's blanket was found in the pool house after the kidnapping," Patricia said and raised an eyebrow.

Jesse Rose's blanket. So that's what the kidnapper had left behind? She tried not to give away her surprise in her expression. "And you had all three boys with you?"

The woman started to nod, but stopped. "No, Ledger was always the one lagging behind. I saw him down the hall and called to him."

"Had he come from his room?"

"No." She frowned, seeming surprised by her answer. "His bare feet were all muddy. I had to wash them in my tub in my room before I let him get into my bed.

But that was nothing unusual. Ledger often went out at night and wandered around. Like Marianne."

"Did he say anything to you that night about where he'd been or what he might have seen?"

"Seen?" She scoffed at the idea. "He was a child. Three years old. Cull was only seven and Boone, he was barely five. None of them said a word. I put them all into my bed. Like me, they were wide-eyed with terror and listening to what was going on outside my room."

AFTER TALKING TO PATTY, Nikki went looking for Ledger. But when she reached the barn, it was Cull who she found feeding the horses.

"Have you seen Ledger?" she asked.

"He's gone into town for breakfast," Cull said without looking at her.

Abby, she thought, and her heart went out to him.

"Well, since I have you..." she said.

He stopped what he was doing to give her his full attention. "So you think you have me, huh? You think you have the entire family now." He shook his head.

She ignored him. Patricia had proven Nikki's theory this morning. There'd been a slight change in her story, giving Nikki new information that Patricia hadn't remembered before. It was something small, something that even Nikki wasn't sure mattered.

"What part of 'it's not safe for you to be here' don't you get?" he demanded.

"I've been around horses before—just not unbroken stallions let out into a corral I happen to be in."

He ignored the accusation. "Not *here* in the stables. On this ranch. Didn't dinner last night teach you anything?"

"The soup *wasn't* poisoned," she said as she stepped closer to rub a horse's neck.

"The point is in this house it could have been," he said without looking at her. "You have no idea. The past twenty-five years…" He shook his head as if he couldn't go on. "Everyone is sick of hearing about the kidnapping let alone talking about it."

"Everyone but your father."

A muscle in his jaw jumped. "My father is the kind of man who just doesn't give up."

"What kind of man are you?"

He shifted those blue eyes to her, welding her to the spot. "The kind who knows a lost cause when he sees one."

"We've already had this argument. I'm not leaving and I'm guessing your father isn't giving up. He still wants me to do the book." She narrowed her eyes at him. "And unless I'm wrong, which I don't believe I am, he asked you to help me."

He chuckled as he shook his head again. "All you're doing is making things worse for everyone, including yourself."

"Don't you want to know the kind of woman I am?" When he said nothing, she continued. "I'm like your father. When I start something I finish it."

Cull seemed to consider that before he turned toward her, his lips quirking into a grin as his eyes blazed with challenge. "Is that right?"

Before she could react, he grabbed her and dragged her to him. His mouth dropped to hers in a demanding kiss as he pushed her back against the barn wall.

Fleetingly she wondered how far he would go. He

was angry, frustrated with what was happening to his family, scared. She knew those emotions only too well.

But she thought she also knew Cull McGraw. No matter what her grandfather said, she thought she was a pretty good judge of character. Cull wasn't the kind of man who would force a woman. He didn't have to. He was trying to scare her—just as he had with his talk of evil here on the ranch.

She did her best not to react to the kiss. It was a fine one even though she hadn't asked for it and his heart wasn't really in it. But she'd felt his fire, his passion fueled by the well of emotions surging through him.

The kiss made her want a real one from him, which was more dangerous for her than a wild stallion. The kiss ended as abruptly as it had started. Cull shoved off the barn wall and took two steps back. If anything, he looked more upset than he had before.

"You should be afraid of me," he said, his voice rough with emotion as he jerked off his straw cowboy hat and raked a hand through his thick dark hair. "I even scare myself."

"You don't scare me."

"Then you are more foolish than I thought. What happened here changed us all. If you can't feel the malice…" His gaze shifted toward the open barn door. She could see the house in the distance.

Nikki looked toward the nursery window. The curtain moved but it could have merely been the breeze stirring it.

When she looked at Cull again, all she saw was his backside headed out to pasture. She watched him go, aware of the lingering taste and scent of him, both more disturbing than she'd wanted to admit earlier.

Now she found herself alone in the barn where her father had worked all those years ago. An eerie quiet seemed to fall over it in Cull's absence.

She moved to the horse she'd petted earlier and again rubbed its neck, needing to feel the warmth. Cull was right. She could feel malice here, but unlike him, she didn't believe in dark spirits.

Instead, she believed that evil lived in the heart of man—and woman. She thought of Sheriff McCall Crawford and wondered if she'd do anything about her suspicions. Nikki was anxious to find out if she'd been right, if her instincts hadn't let her down.

Meanwhile, those instincts told her that someone in this house knew what had happened to the twins. She'd never felt it more strongly.

A breeze rustled the nearby pines, making the boughs groan softly. A hinge creaked somewhere deep in the barn. The hair quilled on the back of her neck, a gust of cold air rushing over her skin to raise goose bumps.

Suddenly she had the feeling she was no longer alone. She shuddered at what felt like breath on the back of her neck. As she rushed toward the barn door, she told herself she didn't believe in evil ghosts. Whatever she'd just felt in the barn was only her overactive imagination, nothing more.

And yet the feeling hung with her all the way to the pool house.

Chapter Twelve

Nikki closed the pool house door behind her, shaken by whatever that had been in the barn. She told herself it was a reaction to Cull. Every run-in with him left her off-kilter. He was angry and afraid—she could understand that. But kissing her? That had scared him more than it had her.

At least that's what she thought. He wanted her gone. Well, it couldn't be soon enough for Nikki, she thought, surprised she felt that way. She wasn't safe here from herself. She didn't scare easily, but Cull was right. There was something on the wind that turned her blood to ice.

Not that she could leave before she was done. Which reminded her that she needed to take advantage of whatever time she had here. She glanced through the window toward the house. Earlier she'd heard just enough of what Patricia had been saying to the cook this morning, to make her anxious to talk to Frieda.

At the main house, Nikki entered the kitchen to find Frieda Holmes sitting in a chair in the corner. The cook had a threaded needle in her hand and a quilt lay over her lap. Nikki had seen her elderly neighbor sew on a quilt binding enough times that she knew at once what the woman was doing.

"What a beautiful quilt," she said. "Did you sew it yourself?"

Frieda nodded almost shyly. She was a small, almost homely woman with dark hair shot with gray. She was in her early sixties, by Nikki's calculations, and had been the cook for years.That was back before they could afford a full-time nanny. Back before the twins.

Nikki moved closer. "I love the colors, and your quilting is amazing. My goodness, it's all done by hand." This surprised her, since her neighbor quilted with a sewing machine and only hand sewed the binding.

"It relaxes me," Frieda said proudly as she ran a hand over the tiny, closely spaced stitches.

At the sound of footfalls behind her, Nikki turned as Patricia came into the kitchen. "What's going on?" she demanded.

Frieda stuck her finger with the needle as she hurriedly tried to put the quilt away. She tucked the needle in the fabric and shoved the quilt into a bag next to the chair. She wiped the blood from her stuck finger on a corner of her apron and rushed to her feet.

"I was waiting on the pies in the oven," the cook said as if feeling guilty for getting off her feet for even a break.

"And I was just admiring Frieda's quilt," Nikki said.

Patricia dismissed that with a flip of her hand. "I've never understood why anyone would want to cut up perfectly good fabric and then sew it back together. It makes no sense."

"It makes beautiful quilts," Nikki said, seeing how Patricia's remark had hurt Frieda's feelings. "My neighbor quilts. Unfortunately, I've never taken the time to learn."

"Well, if you like quilts that much, you should drive out to Old Town and visit the Whitehorse Sewing Circle." Patricia turned to Frieda. "Don't you still meet in the community center down there? It's not that far from here. There are always a bunch of old ladies in the back working on a quilt. Isn't that right, Frieda?"

Frieda looked even more upset. Was it the crack about old ladies? Or something else? "I would love to do that," Nikki said. "Is there a certain day I could go?"

But it was her boss who answered for the cook. "Frieda goes on her day off, Wednesday. I'm sure she'd be happy to take you." There was something in Patricia's tone, an underlying menace, that made no sense to Nikki.

The timer on the oven went off and Frieda quickly picked up two hot pads and opened the oven without saying a word.

"I'm going into town to the hospital to see my husband," Patricia announced as she looked at Nikki. "You might not be here by Wednesday if Travers has decided to stop this ridiculous book." She waved a hand through the air, not giving Nikki a chance to remind the woman that she could do the book without Travers's permission, before she turned to Frieda.

"There are fresh vegetables from the garden that need to be washed and refrigerated right away," the woman said to the cook. "Please don't keep Frieda from her work," she said to Nikki. "I believe Cull has a horse saddled and waiting for you. He told me to tell you to have Frieda provide you with a picnic lunch. Apparently, he's taking you for a horseback ride." Her gaze took in what Nikki was wearing. "You might want to change."

With that she spun on her heel and stormed out in a cloud of expensive perfume.

Cull was taking her on a horseback ride? That was news to her. Frieda still seemed upset even with Patricia gone as she took out four beautiful apple pies from the oven. Nikki noticed that the woman's hands were shaking. Patricia had upset her and it was unclear to Nikki how exactly other than the woman's demanding and demeaning tone. So why was Frieda still working for her? Surely she could get a job elsewhere.

"I'll put together a picnic lunch for you while you change," the cook said, clearly wanting Nikki out of her kitchen.

"Thank you." She left to go change and when she returned, Frieda handed her an insulated bag heavy with food. As she thanked her again, Frieda busied herself washing the vegetables as per her boss's orders.

On the way to the barn, Nikki wondered if this horseback picnic ride was Cull's idea—or Patricia's. Either way, it would give her time alone with him away from a lot of the drama.

CULL WATCHED THROUGH the open doorway as Nikki made her way down to the barn. She'd changed from the slacks, blouse and high heels she'd been wearing earlier. Now she was in a pair of jeans, a T-shirt and tennis shoes. He should have realized she wouldn't own any cowboy boots.

Still, she looked good. She had a bag in one hand, no doubt their picnic lunch. He smiled to himself. The horseback ride had been Patricia's idea when she'd found him in the barn.

"Get her out of here for a while," the woman had

said, and he hadn't needed to ask whom she was referring to. "Take her for a horseback ride. Even better, leave her out there in the wilds. Or…" A look had
come over his stepmother. "Or cut her cinch so she has
an accident. Just joking," she added quickly at his mock
shocked expression.

Patricia had caught him at just the right time. He felt
antsy and knew exactly what he needed, and it was to
get on the back of a horse and ride out of here. "I'll take
her for a ride," he said, making Patricia smile.

As Nikki approached the barn, he said, "I should
have asked you if you rode."

"Or if I wanted to go on a picnic with you," she said
but was smiling. "I have ridden before. Once at a fair
when I was a child."

Great, he thought. Green. Just what he needed. "I
have a mild-mannered horse you'll like." He could see
that she was trying to think of a good reason to say no.
Who could blame her after earlier in the barn? That had
been stupid kissing her. What had he been thinking?

And then springing this horseback ride and picnic
on her. If he was her, he'd be suspicious.

"You should see the ranch," he said, determined that
she would go with him. "Consider it research. Also I
know you're dying to get me alone so you can…grill
me."

She was looking skeptically at the horse he'd saddled
for her. "I'm not sure about this." It had been too long
since she'd been on the back of a horse, but he didn't
like leaving her here alone with almost everyone gone.

"Where is that woman who will stop at nothing to
get what she wants?" he asked her.

She smiled and looked resigned.

"Hey, it's going to be fun. Trust me. You're in good hands with me."

Clearly, she wasn't so sure about that. But he'd promised his father he would help her. And wasn't that what he was doing? But how long before she realized there was nothing new to write about? How long before she realized that she'd wasted her time coming here?

Soon, he hoped. She didn't want to believe it, but she'd put herself in danger. She had a reputation for getting to the truth. What if there was someone on the ranch who had more to hide than he did?

He hadn't been trying to scare her. There was something evil in that house. He'd felt it too many times. But unlike Nikki, he couldn't leave here. His father needed him. So did his mother.

He thought of Marianne. He needed to go visit her and tell her about his father's heart attack. Not that she might hear him, let alone understand. But he felt he owed her that. She had the right to know. He often told her about things going on at the ranch.

She would rock, holding those horrible dolls, and he would tell her about the horses they'd bought and sold. His mother had always loved horses, loved to ride. It was something she had shared with her husband. Unlike Patricia, who didn't ride and complained that horses smelled. Kitten was just as bad. Which was fine with Cull. It meant that they never came down to the barns.

Cull shoved away any thoughts of Patricia as he led the horses out of the barn. Soon he and Nikki would be lost in the wilds of the Missouri Breaks. Just the thought stirred an unexpected desire. Nikki St. James was more dangerous than she realized.

Fortunately she wouldn't be with them long.

Chapter Thirteen

Nikki's mind was still racing with what had happened in the kitchen. The relationship between Frieda and Patricia perplexed her. Why wouldn't Patricia want her talking to Frieda? What was she worried the cook would tell her? And yet she'd suggested Frieda take her to her quilt group?

Just her showing up at a crime scene like this was often a catalyst that brought secrets to the surface. Nikki thought of the other books she'd researched and the times she'd uncovered so much that it had almost cost her her life. While that should have been a warning, she knew she had to get Frieda alone so she'd have a chance to talk to her without Patricia being around.

But right now she had something more troublesome to occupy her thoughts. Getting on a horse and riding off into the wilds with Cull. He took the picnic lunch, stuffed it into a saddlebag on his horse, then grabbed a straw cowboy hat hanging on the wall and dropped it on her head.

"You'll be glad you have it, trust me," he said as he cupped his hands to hoist her up into the saddle. She hadn't been completely truthful about her experience with horses. Her mother had been deathly afraid of them and had passed that fear on to her. Which was strange, since Nikki's father had trained horses.

Sitting high in the saddle, she watched Cull swing gracefully up onto his horse. He gave it a nudge with his boot heels and started out of the corral. For a moment, she thought her horse wasn't going to move. She gave it a nudge with the heels of her tennis shoes. Nothing. Cull looked back over his shoulder at her. Grinning, he let out a whistle and her horse began to follow him.

Nikki clung to the saddlehorn, feeling as if she might fall off the horse at any moment.

"You'll get use to the rhythm," Cull said, still grinning as her horse trotted up next to his. "Just relax."

"Easy for you to say. You've probably been riding since you were born."

"Not quite. I must have been close to a year old the first time."

They rode out of the corral, past the stand of trees behind the house and into the pasture. Ahead, the land opened into rolling prairie that stretched to the Little Rockies. She could see steep cliffs of rock shining in the sunshine and huge stands of pines.

"You're doing fine," Cull said, his voice gentle. She looked over at him and tried to relax. She had a stray thought. Cull was the kind of man a woman could fall hard for. She watched him run one of his big, sun-browned hands over his horse's neck, an affectionate caress. She imagined his hand touching her like that and had to look away.

"It's beautiful out here," she said. The afternoon light had an intensity that made the landscape glow. She sat up in the saddle a little straighter, feeling a little more confident. The horse hadn't taken off at a dead run, hadn't bucked, hadn't lain down and tried to roll over, hadn't ditched her the first chance it got.

All in all, she thought things were going pretty well—if she didn't think about the fact that soon she would be entirely alone with the man next to her. The same one she'd heard say he would "take care" of her.

CULL FELT AT home in the saddle. He felt the strain of the last twenty-four hours drain from him as they rode toward the Missouri Breaks. What he loved most about this country was the wild openness and the lack of people. He'd read that the population was only .03 persons per square mile out here. He didn't need anyone to tell him that there were more cattle than humans.

He glanced over at Nikki. She seemed comfortable in the saddle. He'd chosen a gentle horse for her, one of his favorites. His gaze shifted to the country ahead of them. It dropped toward the Missouri River in rolling prairie, becoming wilder with each mile as they skirted the Little Rockies.

They didn't talk as they rode, the sun lounging overhead in a brilliant blue sky filled with cumulous clouds. A faint breeze bent the deep grasses and kept the day cool.

"What an amazing day," Nikki said when they stopped near an outcropping of rocks in a stand of pine trees. There was plenty of shade, so Cull thought they could have some lunch here.

They hadn't talked on the ride. He had gotten the impression that like him Nikki was enjoying the peace and quiet, something sorely missing on the ranch. But he was smart enough to know it was temporary. He hadn't forgotten why she was here.

He watched her push back the straw cowboy hat and squint at him. Even though he knew what was coming, he didn't care. The warm afternoon sun glowed on her face. She really was stunning in a not-so-classical way.

Sure she was attractive, but he liked to think he wasn't the kind of man who could be taken in by looks alone. A part of him admired the hell out of her. The woman had fortitude—that was for sure. He thought of all the journalists who had tried to get stories over the years. Where they'd failed to get a foot in the door, Nikki St. James had the run of the house—and the ranch.

They ate, both seemingly lost in their own thoughts. He was curious about her childhood, but didn't want to break the peaceful quiet between them to ask.

As he was putting away the last of the picnic, she finally brought up the kidnapping. He'd been waiting, knowing she couldn't possibly not take advantage of the two of them being alone.

"I need to ask you about that night and even the days leading up to it," she said almost apologetically. "I'd rather do it out here than back at the house, if you don't mind."

To his surprise, he realized he didn't. His father had asked him to cooperate, so he would. He'd rather get it over with out here than back at the ranch anyway. He lay back against one of the smooth rocks and looked out toward the Breaks, dark with pine trees and deep gullies.

"You were seven," she continued. "I'm guessing the sheriff and FBI didn't question you at any length."

He shook his head. "Because I didn't know anything."

NIKKI HAD HOPED after the horseback ride that Cull would be more forthcoming. She wasn't going to let him put her off. She moved so she could look into his blue eyes, determined to find out what he was hiding.

"You've had years to think about that night. I think you know more than you've ever told anyone. I think you're protecting someone. Your mother?"

Cull looked away for a moment. "My mother had nothing to do with this."

"You know why the sheriff and the FBI believe it was an inside job and that your mother might have been involved," she said carefully. "A bottle of codeine cough syrup that had been prescribed to your mother was found in the twins' room. That's why they speculated that the twins had been drugged to keep them quiet during the kidnapping."

"It wasn't my mother," Cull said with more force than he'd obviously intended as he turned back to her.

Nikki heard something in his voice. Fear. "The cough syrup wasn't just her prescription. Her fingerprints were the only ones on the bottle, but," she said quickly before he could argue, "maybe the twins weren't drugged with the cough syrup. Maybe it was left there to frame your mother."

He stared at her for a long moment. "Why are you giving her the benefit of doubt?"

"Because I've often found that things aren't what they seem. If I'm good at anything, it's realizing that."

She saw him waver. "Still, there had to be someone inside the house who had access to the cough syrup and helped get the twins out of their cribs and to the window and the person on the ladder," he said.

"Patricia had access to the cough syrup. Maybe she'd given one of you older kids some. Do you remember having a cold or cough?"

He shook his head. "Are you saying Patty—"

"Not necessarily. That wing is isolated from the rest of the house and has an entrance and exit just down the stairs from the twins' room—anyone could have been let in. Someone inside the house could have taken the cough syrup before the kidnapping to frame her."

"Exactly. Which brings us back to the same spot. Someone in the house was in on it. Someone let the kidnapper in. Someone got hold of my mother's cough syrup."

"Which is why I need to know what you remember."

"I told you—"

"I know you're holding something back, Cull."

He sat up and for a moment she thought he might get up to leave. But instead, he settled again, then snapped, "You're a mind reader now?"

"No, I just know that often when people are afraid, it's because they know something that they fear will hurt someone they love. You and your mother were close, weren't you?" Cull still visited his mother. She knew that from her visit with Tess at the mental hospital. "Isn't it time that you told someone what you saw that night?"

He looked away. A muscle jumped along his strong jawline.

"What is it that you're so terrified I'm going to find out?" Nikki demanded.

Cull didn't move. "Why did you have to come here?"

She heard such anguish in his voice that it broke her heart, but she said nothing, waiting.

"I saw my mother."

Relief flooded her. "That night?"

He nodded as he returned his gaze to her. He looked

resigned and she wondered if a huge weight hadn't come off his shoulders. She knew only too well what secrets could do to a person.

"It was earlier that I saw her. She'd just come out of the twins' room," he said as if seeing it all again. "She looked right through me. It was as if she didn't see me until I spoke."

"Is it possible she was sleepwalking?"

He seemed surprised by the question. "She did walk in her sleep and had since she was a child, which according to the doctor implied a neurological problem that had gone undiagnosed. But to me, she seemed completely out of it. Now I wonder if she wasn't in shock."

"You think she'd already been to the nursery and found the twins missing?"

"I don't know." Cull shook his head before leaning back against the rocks where they were sitting. "I saw her walk down the hallway. I followed her, afraid she might hurt herself. I didn't think to check on the twins."

She heard the naked guilt strain his voice. "You were a child. It wasn't your place—"

As if he'd said all this to himself already and not believed it, he said, "If my mother was in on the kidnapping, then maybe the twins were already gone. Or maybe that's when she gave the twins the cough syrup. It wasn't much later that the twins were found missing. If I had told someone, they might have caught the kidnapper before he could get away with them."

Nikki considered that for a few moments, her heart aching at the guilt she saw in his face. "You said you followed your mother that night?"

"She must have heard me behind her, because she stopped and told me to go back to bed. That everything was going to be all right. She said she was going for a swim." His blue eyes shone with unshed tears. "Do you see why I have kept that to myself all these years? It only makes her look more guilty since we know the kidnapper was in the pool house that night after the twins were taken."

She knew that the FBI agents were convinced that Marianne had met her co-kidnapper in the pool house that night and that the swim had just been a ruse.

Nikki gave him a few moments before she asked, "What were you doing in the hallway that night?"

He frowned as if he'd never asked himself that question. "I was looking for Ledger. When I woke I looked into this room and saw that he wasn't in his bed. He had a habit of wandering around the ranch at night. I had gone looking for him."

"Did you go outside?"

He shook his head. "That's when I heard Patty screaming. She was standing outside the twins' room screaming that they were gone. My first thought was that my mother had taken them somewhere, which was terrifying enough given the way she was acting. The way she had been acting since their births."

"It was speculated that she was suffering from post-partum depression."

He nodded. "She kept saying she was fine but something was definitely wrong. She seemed confused a lot of the time and complained of not feeling well, but when my father took her to the doctor, he couldn't find anything wrong with her."

Nikki knew that he'd just described his father's recent condition. They'd all just assumed it was over the anniversary of the kidnapping just as they'd assumed Marianne's was postpartum depression.

"Did you see anyone else in the hallway that night?" Nikki asked.

"Everyone came out of their rooms after they heard Patty screaming and ran down to the nursery. I just remember Dad going past."

She stared at him. "But you didn't go." She saw it on his handsome face, the anguish, the fear, the regret.

He shook his head. "Somehow, I knew the twins were gone and something horrible had happened. I was terrified that my mother had done something to them."

"What about your brothers Ledger and Boone? When did you see them?"

Cull frowned again as if picturing it in his mind. "Boone came out of his room, but I don't remember seeing Ledger until later."

From what Patty had told her, there was a good chance that Ledger had been out roaming the ranch that night. Three was old enough to remember in some instances. Nikki herself could remember things that had happened at that age. Maybe Ledger remembered something. But hadn't been old enough to realize that what he'd seen at the time had been the kidnapper.

"ENJOY YOUR RIDE?" Patricia demanded when Cull came into the house, Nikki at his side. "Your father is being released from the hospital. Ledger and Boone have gone in to pick him up. I wanted to go, but you know how they can be."

The woman picked nervously at the suit jacket she was wearing. "I want everything to be perfect when he gets here." Her gaze shifted to Nikki. "I think it would be better if she wasn't here."

"Patricia—"

"I don't care what your father wants at this point. He could have died. All this is too upsetting for him. He needs his rest."

Cull shook his head. "I talked to the doctor this morning. Dad is doing well. In fact, his health has improved since he's been in the hospital or the doctor wouldn't be releasing him."

"I just don't want him upset," she said, holding her ground.

"Well, sending Nikki away would upset him, since he was very specific about that."

The woman let out a sigh. "Fine, but if she kills him, don't blame me." With that, she turned and stormed off toward the kitchen.

Cull cursed under his breath. "That woman is going to be the death of all of us."

Nikki watched her go, thinking again of the symptoms that both Marianne and Travers shared—although twenty-five years apart. The common denominator was that both had been living in this house at the time.

Well, she'd done what she could by going to the sheriff. Now it was in McCall Crawford's hands.

"I think I'm going to go rest for a while," she said, looking at the time.

Cull nodded as if he thought it was a good idea for her to be away when his father arrived back at the house.

The horseback ride had been wonderful, but she felt sunburned and tired. While glad Travers was being released, she worried about what he was coming home to, given her suspicions.

Surely, if she was right, no one would try to harm him now. Nikki had been afraid that Travers would change his mind about letting her stay here for the book. Fortunately he apparently hadn't. She couldn't help feeling bad for him. When she'd seen him collapse, it brought home just how serious this was. She didn't want to inflict any more pain on this family than it had already been through.

She'd seen Cull's pain earlier when he'd told her what he'd seen that night. Like what Patricia had remembered and told her, it was another piece of the intricate puzzle. There were still so many pieces missing, though. Worse, she hated what the final picture would reveal. Maybe her grandfather was right and she was too emotionally involved in this one.

She walked toward the pool house. The wind had come up. It whipped the branches of the cottonwood trees, lashing the new green leaves against the glass. Past the trees, she saw the horses running, their manes and tails blowing back as they cavorted in the deep green of the pasture. She thought about Cull and his brothers and their obvious love for the horses they raised. The reminder of Cull's hand gently stroking the mare's neck sent a shiver through her.

Nikki told herself that her reaction to Cull was normal. She hadn't met anyone like him and was now thrown together with him in a household where she had few to no allies. What worried her was that the man seemed able to see into her soul. That made him more than a little dangerous. Not to mention he already suspected that her motives for being here had to do with more than just the book. What was he going do when he found out that Nate Corwin was her father?

As she entered the pool house, she walked directly to her bedroom. She would have a shower before dinner, but right now, she just wanted to lie down for a while.

At a sound behind her, she turned to look back into the living room. Had someone been there? A movement near the door caught her eye. She stared as a single sheet of paper slid under the door and was caught by the wind from the window. The paper whirled up off the floor.

Hurriedly stepping to it, Nikki chased the sheet of paper down until she could catch it, then rushed to look out to see who had shoved it under her door.

She saw no one. Wind shook the nearby trees, sending dust and dirt into the air. She cupped a hand over her eyes as she looked in the direction of the house. The curtain moved on the second-floor window of the nursery and then fell silent.

With a shiver, she turned back inside, closing and locking the door behind her before she looked at what she held in her hand.

With a start she saw what appeared to be a page torn from a diary.

Chapter Fourteen

Nikki leaned against the pool house door, her heart pounding as she looked at the sheet of paper in her hand. It appeared to have been torn from a diary or journal, but there were no dates on the page. She began to read it as she walked over to the window, closed it and dropped into a chair.

I heard the screaming last night. Travers said it was just the wind, but I've never heard wind like that ever.

I got up and went up to check the children. I hate having them on a separate floor even knowing that the nanny is close by. But Travers insisted that we move to the lower floor master bedroom as soon as it was finished. He says I need my rest. I feel like all I do it rest. Sometimes I feel like I am going crazy.

In the nursery, the twins looked like sleeping angels. I call them the twins because their names seem too large for such small babies. They scare me they are so small, so fragile.

Just looking at them makes me cry. I feel such anguish, such guilt. When I found out I was pregnant with them, I was upset. I didn't want them. Still don't feel a connection to them. I want to love them, but they are so needy, so demanding. Even when I help Patty with them, I don't feel like I'm their mother. I can tell that she knows, that she's judging me and finding me wanting. I asked Travers to fire her and let me take care of them, but he refused. I'm sure Patty heard us arguing about it.

As I started to leave the twins' room, I saw the light in the stables. I thought about waking Travers, but I have awakened him too many times terrified only to be told there is nothing out in the darkness. Nothing that wants to hurt me, let alone destroy me. So why do I feel this way?

I know I shouldn't go out there alone, but I won't be able to sleep until I know that the horses are all right. That there is nothing out there to fear. Maybe it is only Nate working late. He is such a kind, caring man. I can talk to him. He seems to understand. He doesn't judge me. He lets me cry without looking at me as if I'm crazy. I'll go for a swim after I check the stables. That seems to help me sleep.

On the back, the text continued.

The light was on again tonight. I am trying to ignore it. Just as I am trying to sleep after my swim. But I'm restless. I know I should stay in the house and not go out there. But I need to see Nate. He is the only—

The words ended abruptly. Nikki turned the page over, forgetting that it was only one diary page. So where was the rest? Her heart was in her throat at the mention of her father. Was this how it had started? Marianne afraid at night and going out to the barn to talk to Nate. *He is such a kind, caring man.* Her father. What had this kind, caring man done to help Marianne McGraw?

She stared at the paper. Who had left this and why? Had they wanted her to believe that her father and Marianne had been lovers? Had the two of them made a plan to get rid of the twins—and have enough money to run away?

More to the point, why had she never heard that Marianne kept a diary? Who had known about it? Not the FBI or sheriff, or Nikki would have found the information during her research. The diary would also have been mentioned in the court transcripts—even if the judge had excluded it.

And where was the rest of it? Clearly someone on this ranch had the diary.

But why hadn't they turned it over to the FBI at the time of the kidnapping? Because it incriminated Marianne? Or incriminated the person who now had it in their possession?

They wanted her to believe Marianne and Nate had been lovers, had been the kidnappers. But in their attempt to convince her, they'd now made her aware of the diary.

Instead of convincing her, they'd only managed to make her more convinced her father was innocent on all counts.

So who had put it under her door?

NIKKI FOUND CULL in the pasture inspecting one of the horses' hooves.

"Your mother kept a diary?" Nikki demanded.

He looked up in surprise. "I beg your pardon?"

"Why is it that this is the first time I've heard that your mother kept a diary?"

Cull rose slowly to his feet, stretching out his long legs and then his back, before he said, "Because I didn't know she did—if she did."

Cull and his mother had been close, but it was clear he hadn't known. He looked as surprised as she'd been. "Well, someone knew she did," she said, waving the page she held in her hand.

He caught her wrist with warm strong fingers and slowly pried her fingers open to take the sheet from her.

"Is that your mother's handwriting?" she asked, half afraid he would say it wasn't and that someone was playing an elaborate joke on her.

"It looks like her handwriting." Stepping out of the horse's shadow, he held the page up to the waning sunlight. "Where did you get this?" he demanded after reading it.

"Someone slipped it under my door."

He looked angry as if he wanted to crush it in his big hand, but she snatched it from him before he could. "Whoever gave you that wants you to think my mother had an affair with the horse trainer."

"If true, then why not produce the entire diary?" She shook her head. "Whoever put this under my door wants me to believe that. But if this is the most incriminating part, it doesn't prove your mother had an affair." Nikki prayed she was right. If her father hadn't fallen in love with Marianne, then he had no motive for being involved in the kidnapping.

Cull pulled off his Stetson and raked his fingers

through his thick dark hair. "I can't imagine who would have known about the diary."

"And kept it from the FBI and sheriff all these years."

He nodded, frowning.

"You must have seen her with Nate," she said quietly, hating that she couldn't let the subject go.

"No more than I saw her with anyone else. Nate was a nice guy. He gave me a pocket knife and taught me how to whittle so I didn't cut myself."

"You don't think he was involved in the kidnapping."

Cull looked away for a moment before he shrugged. "How well do we really know another person?" His gaze locked with hers just long enough for her to wonder if he knew the truth about her.

HIS MOTHER HAD kept a diary. Cull hated to think what might be in the rest of it. Something even more incriminating in the rest? If so, then why did whoever had it wait so long to share even this much of it?

Nikki didn't think whatever was in there would be more incriminating. He hoped she was right. For years he'd believed in his mother's innocence. The last thing he wanted was to know that he'd been wrong.

But who in this house had it?

There were times he'd certainly wanted to be anyone but a McGraw. All the media attention had been horrible over the years, not to mention the suspicion that had fallen on every member of the household.

Nikki seemed surprised when he showed up at the pool house door, insisting that she come to dinner that night. "Wouldn't it be better if it was just family?"

"Probably, but Patricia invited my father's attorney

and friend Blake. I'm sure she thinks they can convince him what a mistake it is having you here."

"I would think everyone would be happy if I was gone, you included," she said.

He met her gaze. "Don't presume to know how I feel."

She looked at him as if surprised by that. "So you don't want to get rid of me?"

"Maybe I just want to see an end to this. My father promised that if nothing comes of your…book, then he will quit searching for the twins."

So that was it. "Is there a reason the attorney and former ranch manager wouldn't want the truth about the kidnapping to come out?" she asked, recalling what he said about Patricia using them at dinner tonight.

"They're both protective of my father—and Patty, for that matter. Blake knows my father will always take care of him because of the years he put in here. As for the family attorney, Jim Waters is pretty happy the way things are now with my father continuing to pay him to look into claims by those believing they either know something about the kidnapping or are one of the twins. If Jim didn't have a gambling problem, he'd be quite wealthy by now."

"So if I find out what really happened to the twins, it will put Waters out of business?"

Cull smiled. "Not completely, but it would hurt because he would have to go back to just being the family lawyer. We should get on up to the house. You're sure you're up to this?"

She was sore from her horseback ride and it was clear that he knew it. "I'm fine."

He smiled. "Yes, you are."

Everyone had already gathered outside the dining room when she and Cull came in from outside.

Travers McGraw saw her from his wheelchair and turned toward her, extending his hand. She took it in both of hers. "The wheelchair was doctor's orders. He wants me to rest, but I assure you I'm fine. Better than ever."

He did look better, she admitted. "I'm so glad. I was worried."

"No need. I'm just glad you're still here. Are you making progress?"

Before she could answer, Patricia interrupted to say that dinner was served. They filed into the dining room, Travers insisting they all go ahead of him. All Nikki could think about was the last time they were all in here.

A hush fell over the group after they were all seated at their places. Patricia stood and clinked her butter knife against her empty wineglass. "I just want to say how happy I am to have my husband home." She beamed down the table at him. "I'm glad you are all here to celebrate." Her gaze lit on Nikki, but quickly moved to attorney Jim Waters. She gave him a meaningful look before she sat down and Frieda began to pour the wine.

Nikki noticed that everyone but Travers was subdued. She could feel the tension. This was not a welcome-home celebration. It was exactly what Cull had suspected—a bushwhacking. Patricia wanted the lawyer and former ranch manager to talk Travers into forgetting about the kidnapping book.

She noticed that even Kitten wasn't her usual self. She fidgeted until the first course was brought out and then barely touched her food.

It wasn't until right before dessert that Jim Waters cleared his voice and said, "Travers, we're all glad you're all right. But I think we need to talk about the future."

Travers cut him off at once. "If this is about the book Nikki is researching here, please save your breath, Jim. I hope my heart attack will only make her that much more determined to find out the truth about that night."

Nikki smiled at him.

"I think you should hear them out," Patricia said, and smiled sweetly.

"We know what this means to you," Waters continued. "But at what cost? You have three sons, a wife and a stepdaughter to think about. If you were to—"

"I'm sorry, Jim, but I've made myself perfectly clear on this," Travers said, putting down his fork. "I won't hear any more about this subject from any of you." He looked pointedly at his wife.

"Then you need to know who this woman really is," Waters said, getting to his feet to point an accusing finger at Nikki.

She felt her heart drop as she saw the satisfaction in his gaze. He knew and now he was about to destroy her credibility with Travers and there was nothing she could do about it.

"She isn't here just to write a book about the kidnapping. She's—"

"We already know," Cull said, cutting Waters off.

"You *don't* know." Jim Waters looked furious that he'd been interrupted. "Nate Corwin—"

"Was her father," Cull said, finishing his sentence.

"What?" Patricia demanded, and looked to her hus-

band as if this was the first time she was hearing about it. No one at the table bought her act.

All the air rushed out of the attorney in a gush as he looked at Travers for confirmation. He'd been so sure he was about to drop a bombshell.

Nikki couldn't breathe. Her gaze was on Cull. How long had he known? She looked toward Travers. Did he know?

"Your *father* was Nate Corwin, the man who…?" Patricia acted as if it was so horrible she couldn't even finish.

Travers smiled at Nikki and reached over to pat her hand. "Cull told me everything."

"Well, it would have been nice if someone had bothered to tell me," Patricia said, her face flushed with anger. This hadn't gone at all as she'd planned. "So this was her plan from the beginning. She's writing a book that will make her father look innocent."

Cull didn't bother to respond to her accusation. "Nikki didn't know Nate was her father until recently," he said, still without looking at her. "I'm sure it's one reason she became interested in the case. But not the only reason."

She stared at him, speechless. How did he know that? *Her grandfather.* He'd talked to her grandfather, which meant he'd been investigating *her.* The irony of it didn't escape her. He'd warned that he would be digging into her life, but she'd thought it was an empty threat.

"Still you have to question her motives," Jim Waters said as he started to sit back down.

"Actually, it's your motives I'm more concerned about, Jim." Travers pushed his wheelchair away from the table. "Why don't we talk about that in my office?"

The attorney had just sat. Now he pushed back up and, looking like a hangdog, followed Travers out of the dining room.

"Why is it that I'm not allowed to mention anything distasteful and he gets to say things like that?" Kitten demanded, getting to her feet and leaving.

"I can't believe you and your father kept this from me," Patricia said to Cull as he tossed down his napkin and turned to Nikki.

"I would imagine you'll have to take that up with my father, Patty. You usually do," he said as he reached for Nikki's hand. "There's something I need to show you in the horse barn."

She stood on rubbery legs. His large hand was warm as it wrapped around hers. She felt that electric thrill at his touch even as she let him lead her out of the dining room. He was angry with her—she could feel it in the no-nonsense way he held her hand all the way to the back door.

"Cull, let me explain," she said as he opened the back door and waited for her to walk through it.

"Not here," was all he said in a low gruff voice.

She swallowed back whatever explanation she'd been about to give and went out the door. She could feel him behind her, hear his boots on the stone path, could almost feel the heat of his anger against her back.

CULL RUED THE day that Patricia had entered their lives for a second time. Their father had remained married to their mother even though she no longer seemed to know him—or her children. Then sixteen years ago, Patty had shown up at the ranch, a baby in her arms and no doubt a sad story to go with it.

Travers McGraw had not just taken her in, he'd divorced his wife and married her. She'd never been a mother to any of them, except Kitten. Admittedly, Cull and his brothers hadn't made it easy for her. He'd resented her intrusion into their lives—and still did.

He reached the barn and turned to find Nikki had followed him as far as the door. She stood silhouetted against it. In the dim light, he couldn't make out her expression, but something about the way she stood made him want to pull her into his arms and hold her.

"I know you're angry," she said quietly.

"Not at you. I knew Patricia had something planned at dinner. All my warnings about not upsetting Dad…" He shook his head.

"How long have you known about my father?" she asked.

"Did you really think I wouldn't check up on you? I made a few calls that first day when I went back into town to get your car."

She took a step toward him. "You talked to my grandfather."

He nodded.

"Why didn't you out me right away?"

Why hadn't he? He'd told his father, who'd taken the news even better than Cull had. "Then she is motivated to solve this even more, isn't she," his father had said. "Don't mention to her that you know. We'll keep it as our little secret for the time being."

"My father asked me not to say anything, but I wouldn't have anyway." He took a step toward her. "If my father had been Nate Corwin, I would try to clear his name, too. It's funny," he said, closing the distance between them. "You seemed…familiar the first time I saw you. There was just something about you. Now I realize what it is. You remind me of your father." He saw that his words pleased her.

"Then you understand why I don't want to believe that your mother and my father..." Her voice broke and she sounded close to tears.

"They were just friends." He brushed a lock of her hair back from her face, his fingertips grazing the soft smooth skin of her cheek. "I'm going to help you find out the truth."

Her eyes widened. "Why?" she asked on a breath.

"Because I liked your father—because I like you." His gaze dropped to her mouth and then his mouth was on hers. He dragged her to him, deepening the kiss as she came willingly into his arms.

Chapter Fifteen

Nikki woke the next morning to a knock on the pool house door. She quickly dressed and went to answer it, hoping it was Cull. She'd had a hard time getting to sleep after The Kiss. Unlike their first kiss, they'd both been into this one. It had sparked a fire to life inside them both. She shuddered to think what they might have done right there in the barn if they hadn't been interrupted.

The memory of that kiss sent a wave of need through her. She'd wanted Cull desperately, but they'd been interrupted by one of the ranch hands who'd apparently needed him more than she did. She hadn't seen him again last night.

Cull had unleashed a desire in her that she hadn't known existed. This morning she had to remind herself that she never mixed business and pleasure. But who was she kidding? She hadn't met anyone who made her interested in dating, let alone losing herself in pleasure.

She opened the door, a smile already on her lips, only to find it wasn't Cull on her doorstep looking worried.

"Ledger?" she said, unable to hide her surprise.

"My father sent me." From his expression, it was clear he wouldn't have been here on his own. "He was surprised you hadn't talked to me yet about the kidnapping."

"I was looking for you yesterday before Cull and I went for a horseback ride."

He nodded as if he'd made himself scarce knowing it was just a matter of time. "Is now a bad time?"

"No." She could see that he wanted to get it over with. "Let's go sit by the pool."

Once they were seated, Nikki put the recorder on the small end table between them. "Let's talk about that night."

"That's just it, I don't remember anything. I was only three."

Nikki nodded, then smiled. "I heard you loved to go outside at night after everyone was asleep." He said nothing. "In fact, when I spoke with Patricia, she told me that you had been outside that night."

His eyes widened in alarm. "Why would she say that? I was in bed asleep."

"I thought you didn't remember?"

"I'm just saying, I must have been in bed asleep." He looked flustered.

"I've already spoken with Cull. He said he awakened that night to find you weren't in your bed. He'd gotten up to go find you when he heard Patricia start screaming." It wasn't exactly what Cull had said, but it was close enough to the truth to hopefully jog Ledger's memory of that night.

He had a faraway, scared look in his eyes. "I told you, I don't remember. But it that's what Cull said..."

"Patricia also told me that when you showed up your bare feet were dirty. She had to wash them before she put you and your brothers into her bed." She let that sink in for a moment. "Does any of this bring back memories?"

He shook his head.

"You'd been outside that night. I think you saw something. Someone. Maybe the kidnapper. Maybe someone carrying away the twins."

He shook his head again and looked away as he shifted in his chair. "I told you—"

"But you saw someone, someone you recognized."

She watched him swallow and look toward the woods. Her heart began to pound. "Who did you see?"

He started to shake his head. The next words out of his mouth were so soft that she had to lean toward him to hear them. "I saw the bogeyman." He looked up at her, clearly embarrassed. "You see now why I never said anything. I was *three*. Who knows what I saw."

"You saw a man who scared you?"

He nodded. "He came out of the dark pines. He was big and scary."

"Did he see you?"

"No, I hid."

"Where did he go?" she asked, her voice cracking a little.

"Toward the house."

Toward the house. Nikki said nothing for a moment before she asked, "Was he carrying anything when you saw him?"

"No, not that I saw."

"Did you see him again?"

"Not that night," he said, and met her gaze. "I never told. I was too scared. I thought he would come back for me." That long-ago fear made his eyes shine with the terror he'd felt as that three-year-old.

"But you saw him some other time?"

He swallowed and avoided her gaze. "A few days before the kidnapping. He was standing on a street corner in town talking to our cook, Frieda. They seemed to be arguing. He looked up right at me." Ledger shivered. "It was the way he looked at me. But it might not even have been the same man. Another reason I never said anything."

"Did you ever see him again after the kidnapping?"

"No. Only in my nightmares."

"Did you say anything to Frieda?"

He shook his head. "Do you think he was the man who took the twins?"

"I don't know. He didn't have them when you saw him, so probably not," she said, realizing that she wanted to reassure him.

But her heart was pounding. She feared that Ledger's bogeyman had been the kidnapper—before he'd taken the twins.

NIKKI FOUND PATRICIA coming out of the kitchen.

"Whatever it is, I don't have time for it," the woman said in greeting.

As Nikki had come into the house, she'd heard mother and daughter arguing about shopping. Apparently, Patricia was going shopping and wasn't waiting until Kitten got out of school so she could go with her.

"I just need to ask you a few quick questions," she said. "I'm sure your shopping can wait that long."

Patricia gave her a haughty, irritated look, but then glanced toward Travers's office. He was behind his desk and he was watching their discussion. The woman's expression sweetened like saccharine. "I guess I could spare a few minutes."

"Use my office," her husband said and wheeled out from behind his desk. "I'll go see if I can make Kitten feel better."

Patricia let out a low growl as her husband passed, but kept a smile plastered on her face. She sighed as her husband disappeared into the back of the house. "I really don't have time for this."

From what Nikki had seen, all Patricia had was time. She was overdressed for a shopping trip into Whitehorse. Was that really why she was going into town, or was she headed somewhere else? Nikki wondered, catching the sweet scent of the woman's perfume.

"I'll make it quick," Nikki promised as Patty glanced at her watch in clear irritation. She walked behind her husband's desk, but didn't sit.

Nikki took a chair facing her and turned on the recorder and said, "After twenty-five years, maybe there are things you remember that you didn't that night."

"Well, there aren't. We already did this. And I don't want to relive all of it again. I'm sure you also have my testimony that I gave the FBI and sheriff at the time. That should be sufficient. It isn't going to change. Anyway, I don't understand what the point is since we already know what happened that night."

Nikki ignored that. "I can imagine how hard all this has been on you, living under the suspicion and the mystery of what happened to the twins," she said, trying another approach.

"You have no idea what it is has been like for me," Patricia said, her voice breaking. "It isn't just the suspicion. I live in *Marianne's* shadow." She put a world of contempt into that one word as she dropped her voice. "You think it doesn't bother me that Travers goes to see her every day? She's completely loony-bin nuts, doesn't speak, doesn't do anything but rock. Does it make any difference to him? No. He still loves her. He still misses her." She sniffed and looked away toward the window as she folded her arms over her chest. "There are days when I just want to get in my car and drive as far away from here as I can. But where would I go? What would I do? I have Kitten to think about."

Nikki had listened without interrupting, but now she asked, "Why *did* you come back?"

Patricia turned to look at her as if for a few minutes, she'd forgotten she was there. "I had nowhere to go and Travers had always been kind to me. When I'd left, he told me that I always had a home at Sundown Stallion Station."

"And now you're his wife."

"I didn't come back to marry him, if that's what you're thinking. I was…desperate, if you must know. I'd lost my job and with a baby to support… He was lonely."

"What about Kitten's father?"

"*Travers* is her father."

"Her *biological* father?"

"Of course not," Patricia snapped. "Her biological father was never involved."

Nikki could have argued that point since he was the one who got her pregnant. "You left here soon after the kidnapping."

"It wasn't like I could stay!" Her voice rose to shrill. "Even after Marianne went crazy and Nate Corwin was arrested, everyone still blamed me. I was the *nanny*. How had I let this happen?"

"It must have been hard to come back," Nikki said.

"I guess I thought after almost ten years that things would be different."

"And you had Kitten to think about."

Patricia narrowed her gaze. "You think I came back for Travers's money?"

"You're a lot younger than your husband."

The woman actually smiled. "You and the rest of the county can think whatever you want." She stretched to her full height. "I really don't care. But you'd better not write anything bad about me. If you defame me, I will sue you for everything you have."

"Yes, your husband employs his own lawyer. You must have known Jim Waters when you were the nanny, back when you were nineteen. You also knew Blake Ryan, the ranch manager and close family friend."

Patricia narrowed her eyes. "I don't know what you're getting at," she said, but Nikki was sure she did. "You should be careful making accusations. If I had my way, you wouldn't have gotten near my house, near me or my daughter. I personally am not going to do this anymore, no matter what my husband says." With that, she stalked out. A few moments later, Nikki heard her raising her voice in the kitchen, arguing with her husband and berating Frieda.

But Nikki was going to find out once and for all why Frieda put up with it.

AFTER THE KITCHEN cleared out, with Patricia storming off to town, Kitten taking Travers's car to school and Travers locking himself in his office, Nikki went into the kitchen.

Frieda was hard at work, but she seemed more beaten down than ever this morning.

"I thought Wednesday was your day off?" Nikki asked.

Frieda turned from what she'd been doing. "Patricia had a few things she wanted me to do before I left."

"One of the problems of living under the same roof," Nikki commented. "Well, I really want to go with you to your quilting group. If that's all right." She could see by Frieda's anxious look that it wasn't.

The woman glanced around as if frantically trying to come up with a way out of it. "I wasn't planning to quilt today."

Nikki took a step toward her. "Frieda, I thought it would be nice to get us both out of here. I'd love to see what everyone is working on. We can make it a quick trip."

Frieda looked resigned. "I can finish up here and leave in about thirty minutes then."

"Great, we can take my rental. You can just relax and enjoy the ride."

But even as she said it, Frieda looked anything but relaxed.

She'd just returned to the pool house when there was a knock at her door. She feared it might be Frieda with a better excuse for not going today, but when she opened the door, she found Cull standing there. One look at him and she could tell he was upset.

"You went to the sheriff without mentioning it to me?" he demanded as he pushed his way in, forcing her to step back.

"I'm worried about your father. I would think you would be, too. I didn't want to say anything to anyone else since it was just a suspicion and I knew you'd get upset."

He pulled off his Stetson to rake a hand through his

thick hair. All the fight seemed to go out of him. "My father just told me about the sheriff coming by the hospital before he was released to take a hair sample. You can't think that she's poisoning him."

Of course that was exactly what she thought. "It can't be much of a reach for you since you didn't even ask who I suspected—and neither did the sheriff."

"If true, Patty can't possibly think she can get away with it," he said.

"Why not, if she got away with it before?" Nikki said as she walked into the small pool house kitchen. "Coffee? I made a pot this morning."

He nodded and joined her in the small space. "What are you talking about—she did it before?"

"I don't just suspect she is poisoning your father. I think she did the same thing to your mother in the weeks leading up to the kidnapping."

He stared at her as she poured him a cup.

"Think about it. Your mother was acting…strangely. What if it wasn't postpartum depression at all? What if she was acting the way she was because she was being poisoned? I know it seems like a stretch but when I saw your father and how he looked…" She handed him his cup of coffee and poured one for herself.

"If what you're saying is true…"

"It's just a suspicion at this point. That's why I went to the sheriff. Hopefully when the lab test comes back, it will prove that I'm wrong."

"Or right."

Motioning to a chair, she sat down and Cull did the same.

He seemed lost in thought. "You do realize that if you're right, I'm going to kill her."

"No, you're not. You're not a killer."

He met her gaze. "You sure about that?"

"Yes." Was she basing that on the kiss? Or something more?

Cull swore under his breath. "You're right, but I'm going to want to."

"Did the sheriff say when they'd have lab results?"

"She said she'd marked them a priority and would get back to us."

"What did your father say?" Nikki had to ask.

"He was upset, of course. He defended her, but not very strongly. It made me wonder if he suspected something. What man wants to admit, though, that his spouse is poisoning him?"

"We don't know that's the case."

"Yet," Cull said. "McCall told me the symptoms of long-term arsenic poisoning. I can understand why you thought of it. I'm sorry I didn't."

"I have a suspicious mind, and murder is kind of my business."

He met her gaze. "I've noticed that. What now?"

"I continue gathering information. I still have to talk to Tilly and Frieda. They both were live-in staff at the time of the kidnapping." She didn't tell him that she especially wanted to talk to Frieda after what Ledger had told her about his "bogeyman."

THE SHERIFF HAD asked the lab to put a rush on the hair samples. She'd never been good at waiting. She especially wasn't now.

Her husband had called from Winchester Ranch to tell her that her grandmother and mother weren't at each other's throats and that their daughter was enjoying being around the grandmas.

"How are *you* doing?" she asked him.

"I forget how pretty it is out here. And lunch was good."

Luke always tried to see the good in everything. It was incredibly annoying. But she smiled in spite of herself.

"I'm waiting for the lab to bring me results. A case of a husband possibly being poisoned by his wife."

"Yikes. I'd better check your mother. I wouldn't put it past your grandmother to put something in her food."

She knew he was kidding, but still it worried her. Her grandmother wasn't the most patient person and the bad blood between her and McCall's mother, Ruby, ran blood-spilling deep.

"I'm kidding," her husband said. "You sound too serious on your end of the phone."

"You can hear that?"

"Because I know you so well," he said. "I love you."

"I love you."

"Hope you get the lab tests soon. What will you do if they come back positive for poison?" he asked. "Do you have enough for an arrest?"

"Not yet. The next step will be to get a warrant to search the house."

"Sounds like that's what you're expecting."

McCall realized it was. "If true, it gets complicated. This might not be the first time this woman has systematically poisoned someone to get rid of them."

Chapter Sixteen

Unable to sit still after Cull left, Nikki found Tilly running the vacuum in the off-limits wing. She called her name, but the older woman didn't hear her. Matilda "Tilly" Marks had been twenty-five, married and in debt the year the twins were kidnapped.

Now at fifty, she was divorced and still in debt. Nikki knew that the sheriff and FBI had done a thorough investigation of everyone in the house that night—including Tilly and her husband. They'd found nothing.

"Tilly?" Nikki raised her voice over the whine of the vacuum as she approached the woman. *"Tilly!"*

The sunlight coming in the window seemed to turn the woman's bleached blond hair white. With a start, she realized that it was this white-haired woman she'd seen at this window.

"Tilly?" When she still didn't hear her, she touched the housekeeper's arm.

The poor woman jumped a foot, making Nikki feel terrible.

"I'm sorry," she mouthed as Tilly fumbled to turn off the vacuum. In the silence that fell, she repeated, "I'm sorry. I didn't mean to scare you."

Tilly held her hand over her heart as if to still it. She

was a short thin nondescript woman with bottle blond hair and manicured nails. She moved through the house like a ghost, paying little attention to anyone and vice versa, from what Nikki had seen.

"I need to ask you about the night of the kidnapping. Could you take a break for a few minutes?"

Tilly nodded. "I could use a cigarette. Can we step outside?"

Nikki followed the woman to the end of the hall and down the stairs. If the kidnapper wasn't already in the house that night, he could have come in through this entrance. The stairs led down to a small patio next to the woods. Anyone coming in this way wouldn't have been seen.

But in order to get in, someone would have had to leave the door unlocked.

Nikki let the woman light her cigarette and take a drag before she asked, "What can you tell me about that night?"

"Not much. I had a cold and had taken some medicine so I could sleep. Plus I wear earplugs. I didn't hear a thing until I was awakened by someone pounding on my door. It was a sheriff's deputy. That's when I found out what had happened."

"Where was your room?"

"At the other end of the wing from where the twins were taken," she said, and tilted her head back as she blew out smoke.

"So you were in the room next to Frieda's."

Something in the way Tilly nodded caught her attention. "You would have been able to hear her leave her room."

"Under normal circumstances, but like I said, I took cold medicine that night."

"But you'd heard her come and go other nights," Nikki said, fishing for whatever it was Tilly wasn't saying.

"Sure. I heard her and whoever else come and go."

She took a not-so-wild guess. "A man?"

Tilly shrugged.

"Who was he?"

"A no 'count. I tried to warn her, but she didn't listen. I knew him. I told her he was going to break her heart."

Nikki was still reeling from the fact that Tilly was telling her that Frieda had a man visitor in her room. "Was it all right for her to have a man in her room?"

"Not hardly. Mrs. McGraw, the first Mrs., was very strict about that. Frieda could have been fired, but I wasn't about to tell on her. I got the impression that it was the first man she'd ever…dated, if you know what I mean. She was thirty-nine and never been kissed until him. So, of course, she fell hard."

"Was he a big man? Kind of scary looking?"

Tilly laughed. "Not exactly handsome or bright either."

"So Frieda snuck him in? Did you tell the sheriff and FBI about this?"

The housekeeper put out her cigarette in the dirt, pocketed the stub and lit another with trembling fingers. "He wasn't in her room that night, so why mention it?"

Nikki stared at her. "How do you know that if you were knocked out with cold medicine?"

Tilly sighed. "Because I had a talk with him. Like I said, I knew him. I knew he was using her. I didn't like him in the house at night. He was a bum. I thought he might steal something."

"Like the McGraws twins?"

"No, he wasn't that ambitious or that smart to pull something like that off. I was trying to protect Frieda. So I told him I was going to tell Mr. McGraw and the next time he snuck into the house, he'd be facing a shotgun. That did the trick. Never saw him again."

"Still you had taken the cold medicine—"

"Before I went to bed, before I took the medicine, I heard Frieda in her room pacing. It was late. He hadn't shown up. I knew she'd be disappointed, but it was for the best."

"He could have entered the house after you went to bed."

She shook her head as she took a drag on her cigarette and blew out smoke. "I made sure the door was locked. As I came back up, I saw that her light was out. I could hear her crying. She knew he wasn't going to come by."

Nikki took in this information. "What is this man's name?"

"Harold Cline, but like I said, I never saw him again and neither did Frieda. He left town."

"You don't think it's strange that he disappeared about the same time as the kidnapping?"

"He probably thought he'd be blamed for it once Frieda told the sheriff that she'd been letting him in at night."

"But Frieda must not have told, otherwise wouldn't she have been let go?"

Tilly seemed to consider that. "I suppose you're right."

"And that's the same reason *you* never told."

The housekeeper suddenly looked worried. "You aren't going to tell Mr. McGraw. At my age it's impossible to find another job." Was that what Frieda thought, as well?

"No." If there was something to this lead, then it could come out when the book did. In the meantime…

Tilly seemed to relax. "Like I said, Harold wasn't smart enough to pull off the kidnapping and if he had, he would have spent the money. The ransom money never turned up, right?"

"Right." Still, Nikki wanted to know more about Harold Cline.

CULL FOUND HIS father in his office. "I hope you aren't working."

Travers smiled up at him. "I'm not. I've always liked this room. I feel comfortable in here." The phone rang. He motioned to Cull to give him a minute and answered.

"No, Patricia, I can't tell Frieda that. It's her day off. She told me that she and Nikki are going to visit her quilting group. You have to stop making her work on her day off. Fine. Whatever." He hung up and sighed.

Cull saw that his father was upset. He wanted to wring Patricia's neck.

"I'm going to see Mother. I thought you might like to go with me."

"I can't. Jim Waters will be stopping by. I need to talk to him."

Cull studied his father. "Tell me you're going to fire him."

His father chuckled. "He's been with me a long time." Travers believed in rewarding loyalty. "Maybe too long." He turned toward the door. "I'll tell Mother hello for you."

"Thank you. Tell her…tell her I still love her."

Cull nodded and left, his thoughts veering from one to the next and always coming back to Nikki. He'd fought his attraction to her, but it was so much more than that. The woman fascinated him. He'd never met anyone like her. If only they had met under other circumstances.

AT THE HOSPITAL, he let a nurse lead him down to his mother's room. Marianne McGraw was right where he expected her to be—in her rocking chair holding the two worn dolls. She didn't react when he pulled up a chair and sat down in front of her. The blank eyes stared straight ahead, unseeing.

"Hello, Mother," he said. "It's Cull. Dad wanted me to tell you that he still loves you. Also I thought you'd want to know that he had a heart attack." Did her rocking change? "He's okay though. Weak, but recovering."

He listened to the steady creak of the rocker for a few moments. "I met someone." He let out a chuckle. "After all this time I meet someone who interests me and she ends up being a true crime writer doing a book on the kidnapping. But I guess we can't help the people we fall for, huh."

The admission surprised him, but had no effect on his mother.

He talked for another ten minutes, telling her about the ranch, the new stallion, her other children.

"Ledger is still in love with Abby," he said with a sigh. "I can't see any way that can have a happy ending." Just like his own situation, he thought. "Boone, well, he's ornery enough that it will take a special woman to turn his head."

He watched his mother's blank expression as she rocked back and forth, the rocker creaking with her movement. "This woman who's staying at the ranch, the true crime writer, she thinks she can find out what really happened that night. A part of me hopes it's true. But another part of me…" He swallowed, surprised at the fear that filled him. "What if she finds out that it was you? You and Nate? I don't believe it. But if it turns out I'm wrong… I can't let that happen, Mother. But I'm not sure I can stop her. I don't think anyone can."

THE SHERIFF HAD just gotten back from a meeting when she saw that she had a message from the lab. She quickly dialed the number and was handed off to the lab tech who'd taken the test.

"You have the results?" she said in the phone. McCall wasn't sure what she expected to hear. That Nikki St. James was wrong. Or that it was true and there was someone in that house systematically poisoning Travers McGraw. She'd been in law enforcement long enough that nothing should surprise her.

"We found arsenic in the hair follicles," the lab tech said.

McCall let out the breath she'd been holding. So it was true. "Thank you. Please have those results sent to my office." She started to hang up, but instead disconnected and dialed a judge she had a good working relationship with.

"I'm going to need a warrant," she told him and quickly informed him of the lab test. Poison had always been a woman's weapon throughout history.

"I'll have your warrant within the hour," the judge promised. "I'm assuming you have a suspect?"

Everyone in the county knew Patricia Owens McGraw. She could count the number of people who she'd befriended on one hand. "Let's just hope she doesn't know we're on to her. I'd like to wrap this one up quickly. The media is going to have a field day."

"Yes," the judge agreed. "Especially with the anniversary of the kidnapping only days away."

She hung up, thinking about Nikki St. James. The woman was sharp. She just might have saved Travers McGraw's life. But the irony didn't escape McCall. If Nikki discovered through her investigation for her book that the twins were dead, it might kill him given his condition.

NIKKI HAD FOUND out what she could about Harold Cline before she returned to the kitchen to find Frieda finishing her chores.

Just as Tilly had told her, Harold had been a ne'er-do-well with a sketchy background. He'd done poorly in school, had trouble holding jobs, had been married and divorced, but had never had a run-in with the law.

She had to agree with Tilly that he didn't look like someone who could engineer one of the most famous kidnappings in Montana history and get away with it. But whoever had taken the twins had help, and that person could have been the mastermind behind the kidnapping. Harold Cline could have just been the muscle.

The fact that Harold Cline seemed to have dropped off the face of the earth right after the kidnapping also made Nikki suspicious. She couldn't find anywhere in the information she'd gotten on the case that the sheriff or FBI had talked to Harold. Either they hadn't known about him or didn't consider him a suspect. She was betting it was the former.

Which was why she was anxious to talk to Frieda away from Patricia's prying eyes and ears.

The cook took off her apron and still seemed to hesitate. "I'm not staying at the Whitehorse Sewing Circle today. I'm just dropping off some fabric for future quilts. We make quilts for new babies in the area." She stopped short as if she hadn't meant to say that much.

"Great, I'll get my car. You can tell me where to go."

Frieda looked resigned as she climbed into the passenger side of the rental car a few minutes later, hugging the bag of fabric.

"I thought this would give us a chance to talk without any interruptions," Nikki said once they were on the road.

The cook said nothing as she looked out the side window.

She drove south, away from Whitehorse, deeper into the Missouri Breaks, following Frieda's directions. "I'm surprised they meet this far from Whitehorse."

"The first settlement of Whitehorse was actually nearer the Missouri River," Frieda said. "But when the railroad came through, the town migrated five miles to the north, taking the name with it. So now, it's called Old Town. It's little more than a ghost town, though some families have remained." Again she stopped abruptly.

Nikki drove through rolling prairie, the purple outline of the Little Rockies off to their right, before she dropped over a hill and slowed at a rusted sign warning there were children at play. A tumbleweed cartwheeled across the road in front of the rental. Frieda was right about Old Town being a ghost town. There were a few buildings still standing, including what appeared to have once been a country schoolhouse.

"It's that large building on the right," Frieda said as they passed the old school yard and she saw a weathered sign on the next building that read Old Town White-horse Community Center.

There were three pickups parked out front. Nikki pulled in next to the one on the end and shut off the engine.

"Looks like the whole group is here," Frieda said. She suddenly seemed even more nervous.

"If you prefer I not come in…" Nikki said.

"I just need to drop this fabric off." The cook looked conflicted. "You might as well come in and see what they're working on today."

As they stepped inside, Nikki was hit with a scent that reminded her of the old trunk in her mother's attic where she'd found the newspaper clippings about Nate Corwin.

It took a moment for her eyes to adjust to the cool dimness inside. Three older women sat around a quilting hoop. They all turned, their hands holding the needles and thread hovering above the fabric.

"I brought a guest," Frieda announced into the deathly silence.

The women quickly welcomed Nikki, though they seemed to watch her with interest.

"This is Nikki St. James. She's a true crime writer. She's doing a story on the McGraw kidnapping," Frieda blurted and took a breath.

"So we heard," said a small gray-haired woman with bright blue eyes. "It's a small town. Do you quilt?"

"No," Nikki said as she watched the woman make tiny perfect stitches in what appeared to be a baby quilt. "My neighbor does. I have one of her quilts. I love it."

"Did Frieda tell you that we have been quilting here for years? Used to make a quilt for every newborn in the area. Now not so much," the woman said almost wistfully. "Our numbers have dropped considerably."

Nikki had done her homework and found out that along with quilting the women of the Whitehorse Sewing Circle had also placed babies out for adoption illegally since the 1930s. No one had seen any jail time since most of the "leaders" behind the illegal adoptions were dead now.

"So tell us about your book," a large white-haired woman inquired.

"Not much to tell," Nikki admitted. "I've just begun my interviews."

Frieda hugged the bag of fabric she'd brought. "Has she interviewed you?" a sour-face dyed redhead asked Frieda.

"Why would she? I have nothing to add," Frieda said without looking at Nikki.

"I'm sure Frieda will help if she can. We all want to know what happened to the twins," Nikki said, hoping it was true.

"Well, most of us already know," the sour-faced one said. "One look at Marianne McGraw tells the whole story."

The three women who'd been at the table when Nikki had entered all shook their heads as if in condolence to poor Marianne. "Imagine the nightmares that woman has," the sweet little gray-haired woman said in sympathy.

"Of course there's a chance she wasn't involved," Nikki said.

Sour-face scoffed.

"There is always a chance that new information will surface," Nikki said and all the women gave her a look of pity.

"That good-looking horse trainer turned Marianne McGraw's head. It happens all the time and look how it ended," said the bottle redhead. "They both got what they had coming."

"But what about those sweet babies?" the little gray-haired woman said.

"They're long dead," sour-face snapped. "Someone will stumble onto their graves one of these days, you'll see. Lucky the kidnappers are dead or locked up. Otherwise, it would be dangerous digging around in the past for your book."

Next to Nikki, Frieda dropped the bag of fabric she'd been holding. "I'm so clumsy," she said, sounding close to tears.

They all turned to look at her as she quickly retrieved it from the floor and put it on a nearby table. All the color had washed from her face. For a moment Nikki was afraid the cook might faint. What had the women said that had upset her?

"We should go and let you ladies get back to work," Frieda said. She had regained some composure, but clearly didn't look well as they said their goodbyes and left.

Nikki thought about what Patricia had said to Frieda

about the quilt group, how the cook had gotten upset that day, as well. But what was it about this group of older women quilting?

"Are you all right?" Nikki had asked as she started the car.

"I just remembered something I promised Mrs. Mc-Graw I would do today."

"I thought it was your day off," Nikki reminded her.

"Since I started living on the ranch, Mrs. McGraw gets confused about what days I'm actually off," Frieda said, turning away to look out the side window.

Nikki backed out onto the dirt road. "Whose idea was it for you to move in?"

"The first Mrs. McGraw thought it would save me time driving back and forth from Whitehorse and save me money on a rental when I spent most of my time at the ranch anyway. It was a kind gesture on her part since my husband, George, is a truck driver who spends a lot of time on the road."

Unlike Patricia, who treated her like her private servant, Nikki thought. "I'm surprised you've stayed with the McGraws all these years," she said carefully as she drove away from Old Town.

She couldn't shake the feeling that Patricia was holding something over Frieda. Why else would the cook put up with the way the woman treated her?

Frieda remained quiet.

"Patricia must be a hard woman to work for." Still nothing. Nikki looked over at her. "Frieda, either you are working on sainthood or Patty is holding something over you. Which is it?"

All the color drained from Frieda's face again. "I don't know what...you're talking about," she stammered.

"Given the way she treats you and how wonderfully you cook, why haven't you quit? I know there are other ranches that would snatch you up in a heartbeat." Nikki looked over at the woman in her passenger seat.

"I can't leave Mr. McGraw. Or the boys," she mumbled, and looked embarrassed.

Nikki thought that might have something to do with it, but not everything. "You know what I think? I think the woman is holding something over your head. I think it might have something to do with a man. Wouldn't you feel better to get it off your chest? To get her off your back?"

She let out a bitter chuckle. "You have no idea."

"Let me help you," Nikki said.

Frieda merely stared out the side window.

Nikki's attention was drawn away from the woman as she caught movement in the rearview mirror. She'd been driving down the dirt road through the wild country and hadn't seen another car the whole way.

Now, though, an old rusty truck had come roaring up behind her. Nikki looked for a place to pull off, but there was nothing but a ditch on both sides of the road. She sped up a little since she had been going slow.

The truck stayed right with her, riding her bumper. She couldn't see the driver because of the glare off the cracked windshield of the truck.

Frieda had noticed something was wrong. She sat up and was watching in her side mirror. "I was afraid this would happen," she said, her voice breaking with fear. "He's going to kill us."

Nikki shot her a surprised look. What was she talking about? "No one's going to kill us."

"You have no idea what you've done by coming here,

asking all these questions, digging up the past," Frieda said, sounding close to tears.

"What have I done?" she asked, speeding up as she looked ahead for a place to pull over so the truck could pass.

The woman shook her head. She looked like a woman of seventy, her blonde hair appearing gray, worry making her face look haggard.

"Frieda, I've known something was wrong since I got here. You can tell me."

The woman turned to look at her, eyes shimmering with tears. "I knew it would come out one day. It isn't like I ever thought…" Her voice broke.

Nikki couldn't see a place to pull over and the truck driver seemed determined to get past even though there was only the one lane and no shoulder to pull off on.

"This has something to do with Harold Cline, doesn't it? The reason you let Patricia treat you so badly."

Frieda let out a cry and covered her face with both hands as the pickup slammed into the back of the rental car. "I told you he was going to kill us."

Fighting to keep the rental car on the narrow road, Nikki demanded, "Who is that driving the truck?"

Frieda said nothing and hunkered on her side of the car as the truck came up fast and crashed into them again.

The back of the rental fishtailed and for a moment Nikki feared she would lose control. "Get your cell phone out. Call the sheriff!" Frieda didn't move. "Frieda!"

They were coming to one of the rolling hills and a curve. Nikki hated to go any faster but she had no choice. She pushed down on the accelerator, hoping to outrun the truck. But the driver must have anticipated her plan.

The truck came up with so much speed that when it hit the back of the rental there was no controlling it any longer. The car tires caught a rut and the next thing Nikki knew they were sideways in the road. But not for long.

The tires caught another rut and she felt the car tilt.

"Hang on!" she cried as the rental car went off the road and over the edge of the hillside. It rolled once, then again and again until it came to rest at the bottom of the hill in a gully.

Chapter Seventeen

"Is there a problem?" Cull asked as he glanced to where Patricia was slamming pots and pans around in the kitchen, before he took a stool at the breakfast bar. Kitten had her head in the refrigerator.

"Frieda isn't back to make dinner. I'm going to fire her. I've put up with that woman long enough."

"It's her day off," Cull said, but Patricia didn't seem to hear. She appeared nervous and overly upset over something that happened once a week. Usually, though, Frieda gave in and cooked.

"Do we have any celery?" Kitten was asking. "You think it's true that it takes more calories to eat celery than it has in it?"

Cull didn't bother to respond. "Have you seen Nikki?" he asked even though he knew that would be a sore subject and the woman was already in a foul mood.

"She took off with Frieda," Kitten said, coming out from behind the refrigerator door with a stalk of celery in her hand.

Patricia slammed down a pot. "Who knows what that fool woman might tell her about all of us."

"I hope you aren't planning to cook or we are all

going to starve," Cull said. "Or wish we did," he added under his breath. "So where did Nikki go with Frieda?"

"To that old lady quilt group," Kitten said between bites of celery.

Patricia cussed under her breath and looked at her watch. "Shouldn't they be back by now?"

Having enough of this, Cull headed toward the living room. Looking up, he saw the sheriff and two deputies coming down the stairs. They headed toward his father's office. Travers McGraw was behind his desk. He looked as if he'd aged in the last few minutes.

"What's happened?" Cull demanded, his heart in his throat. Had there been an accident? Was it one of his brothers? Was it their mother? Was it... His pulse began to pound. Nikki? With a start he saw that one of the deputies was carrying what appeared to be an evidence bag. Cull realized that the lab tests must have come back—and that Nikki had been right.

"Where is your stepmother?" Travers asked as he came out of his office. McCall gave him a nod, and Cull saw the pain in his father's expression before he answered.

"She's in the kitchen with Kitten. I don't believe she heard you arrive." The sheriff and deputies started in that direction. "Please don't handcuff her. Not in front of her daughter," Travers said.

Cull turned to his father. "It's *true*? She's been poisoning you?"

He nodded. "Just as we suspect she did your mother twenty-five years ago."

"Patricia McGraw?" he heard the sheriff ask.

From his vantage point, Cull watched as Patty

turned. Her eyes widened as she looked from the sheriff to the deputies and past them to her husband.

"If you could step out into the living room," the sheriff said to her.

Patty looked as if she wanted to make a run for it. "What is this about?"

"If you could please ask your daughter to stay in here," the sheriff said as she took Patty's arm and led her out of the kitchen.

Kitten started to follow, but Travers wheeled past the deputy to keep her in the kitchen. "What is going on with Mother?" the teen demanded.

The sheriff was saying, "Patricia Owens McGraw, you're under arrest for attempted murder. You have the right to remain silent…" McCall continued reading the Miranda rights as Patty argued that she didn't know what the sheriff was talking about.

One of the deputies showed her something they'd found upstairs. Arsenic? Cull hoped they put her *under* the jail. If all of Nikki's suspicions were true… He fisted his hands at his side.

"Call my lawyer!" she barked at Cull as she was handcuffed, a lawman holding each of her elbows as they steered her toward the front door. "Call Jim. It's all a mistake. That poison was planted in my room."

"No one said we found it in your room," the sheriff said.

"It's all lies! I'm being framed! It's that writer. She did this!" Patricia looked over her shoulder at Cull. "Why would I poison your father? I love him."

"Where are they taking my mother?" Kitten cried as she tried to get past her stepfather's wheelchair. A moment later, the front door closed, car engines revved and Travers rolled out of the kitchen with a crying Kitten.

Ledger and Boone both came in then, both looking worried. No doubt they'd seen the sheriff's patrol cars out front and Patricia being led away.

"I'll explain everything," Travers said as he asked them all to sit down. Cull listened as his father explained that lab tests had been taken of his hair. Patricia had been poisoning him for some time, which no doubt was why he'd been so sick.

"Not just sick. She almost killed you!" Boone cried. "How did you figure it out?"

"Nikki St. James suspected it and went to the sheriff," their father said.

Cull glanced at his watch, worry burrowing in his belly. "Kitten said that Nikki and Frieda had gone out to Old Town." His father nodded. "Shouldn't they have been back by now? I'm going to drive down there. Let me know if you hear from Nikki," he said and he was out the door and driving toward Old Town Whitehorse.

NIKKI CAME TO SLOWLY, as if she'd either been stunned or knocked unconscious. For a moment, she didn't know where she was or what had happened. It came back to her in a rush. To her surprise, the car had landed right side up in a gully.

She looked over at Frieda, who thankfully appeared to be shaken but not injured. "Are you all right?"

The woman nodded. "You're bleeding."

Nikki touched her temple, her fingers coming away wet with blood. "I'm all right," she said, more to assure herself than Frieda as she dug out her cell phone. She prayed there would be enough coverage out here to get the sheriff. She looked back up the hillside they had rolled down, half expecting to see the pickup truck idling there.

The road above them appeared to be empty.

Nikki was glad to see she had a few bars on her phone and quickly tapped in 9-1-1. When the dispatcher answered, she told her what had happened. "I'm not sure exactly where we are."

"Near Alkali Creek," Frieda said.

She gave this information to the dispatcher. "No, I don't think we need an ambulance. But please hurry." She disconnected and tried to open her door. It was jammed. She thought she smelled gas. "Can you get your door open?"

Frieda didn't seem to hear her. She'd begun to cry.

Nikki reached across her to open the passenger-side door. "We need to get out of the car, Frieda."

As if in a fugue state, the cook climbed out, staggering against the hillside before sitting down hard. Nikki climbed out the passenger side and reached for Frieda's hand.

"We need to get away from the car. Gas is leaking out. I don't think it is going to blow, but it could catch fire. Do you hear me?" She stared at the woman, worried that maybe she was injured more than she'd first thought.

When she looked up at Nikki, there were tears in her eyes. "I told you he would kill us."

She took Frieda's hand and pulled her up, leading her away from the car to an outcropping of rock before letting her sit down again.

"He'll come back," Frieda said. "He can't let us live. He thinks we know too much."

"Who?"

The cook shook her head. She could see that the woman was terrified. Nikki had been so focused on making sure Frieda was all right and getting them away from the car that she hadn't let the full weight of what had happened register.

"Frieda, if you know who that was who ran us off the road, you need to tell me. Does this have something to do with the kidnapping? Frieda, talk to me. I can help you. Whatever is going on, you can't keep it to yourself anymore. This is serious."

"It's all my fault," the cook said and began to sob.

Nikki was trying to imagine Frieda being part of the kidnapping. The woman *had* been living in the house at the time of the kidnapping and could have drugged the babies and then handed them out the window to her boyfriend, Harold Cline. But that would mean that Frieda had been the mastermind behind the plot. That seemed doubtful.

"Frieda, please tell me. Whatever it is—"

"I was thirty-nine. *Thirty-nine!* Old enough to know better."

Nikki guessed at once that she was talking about Harold Cline. She felt her skin prickle. She tried to keep her voice calm, consoling. "You fell in love?"

She seemed surprised that Nikki had guessed. "He was funny, made me laugh, and he really seemed to like me."

Nikki feared what was coming. "You thought you'd found the man for you," she said instead of asking what the man had conned her into doing.

"I would have done anything for him."

And did, Nikki feared. She wanted to ask but waited

as patiently as she could for the rest of the story to come out. She could still smell gas leaking from the car nearby and wondered if they should move farther away, but didn't want to interrupt Frieda now that she had her talking.

"I would sneak him into the house at night," Frieda said between tearful jags. "He'd come to my room and…" She looked away. "He wasn't the only one sneaking in at night."

Nikki thought of her father.

"Patty had her own boyfriend."

She felt another wave of relief wash over her as she thought about the argument she'd witnessed the first night. "Jim Waters? Or Blake Ryan."

"Blake."

"Is it still going on?" she had to ask.

The older woman merely gave her a look.

"So you left the door open on the night of the kidnapping," Nikki guessed, still not sure yet where this was going.

Frieda began to cry again. "He didn't show up. I was so stupid. I really thought he was the one."

"Did you see him again after that night?" Nikki asked.

The woman only cried harder.

She took a breath, warning herself to tread softly. "Patty found out you'd been letting him in." It wasn't a question. It had to be what Patricia was now holding over the cook's head. Unless it had something to do with the kidnapping. "Did she tell the sheriff and FBI about your boyfriend?"

Another look that said she hadn't.

Nikki's heart began to pound. "I don't understand

why Patty didn't tell the sheriff and FBI. Unless she was already using it against you." She glanced over at Frieda and saw that was exactly what Patty had been doing.

Patty had known the man was sneaking in and was using it against Frieda even twenty-five years ago. But if the sheriff and FBI found out that Patty had known all this before the kidnapping, then she would be under even more suspicion than she had been at the time, so she'd kept her mouth shut and used it to keep Frieda under her thumb.

"She said she was protecting me and that I owed her," Frieda said between sobs.

Nikki had thought she couldn't dislike Patricia more, but she'd been wrong. How could Patricia keep something like that quiet all these years? Even now, it would be Frieda's word against the new Mrs. McGraw's.

"Was this man ever questioned by the authorities?" Nikki had to ask even though she knew the answer already, if indeed Frieda's lover had been Harold Cline, as Tilly had told her.

Frieda shook her head as she wiped at her tears. "I don't care what the sheriff does to me. I deserve it, but do you have to put it in your book?"

"I won't put in anything until I have the whole story."

That seemed to relieve Frieda. "I never told. Marianne was already locked up and so was the horse trainer. I figured they had the kidnappers and that it wasn't my…lover."

"I'm going to need to know the name of the man, Frieda."

She hesitated but only a moment. "Harold Cline."

Her mind was racing as she tried to understand what it was Frieda was telling her——and wasn't telling her.

"You'd want to know why he hadn't shown that night. Maybe he'd seen the horse trainer stealing the babies," Nikki said. "You would have gone to see him."

Frieda looked away again.

Nikki felt her heart sink. Tilly was wrong about one thing. Harold Cline had kidnapped the twins and Frieda knew it. Knew it because she'd seen him with the babies?

She was frantically trying to put the pieces together. Frieda had said it was all her fault. "Was there any reason to fear for the twins' safety in that house twenty-five years ago?"

"You don't know what the first Mrs. McGraw was like then. She was confused all the time. Often she couldn't remember the names of her children. I overheard her say that she didn't want the twins, wanted nothing to do with them and wished they would disappear."

A piece of the puzzle dropped into place. "You shared this information with your boyfriend."

Frieda let out a sob. "I had no idea he would kidnap the twins."

There it was. Harold Cline had taken the twins. "That's why you feel so guilty." But when she saw Frieda's expression, she knew that telling him about Marianne's state of mind wasn't the only reason Frieda felt guilty. Her heart dropped.

"Your boyfriend must have thought he was saving them," Nikki said, hoping to keep the cook talking. "That they would get better homes." But why not take the kidnapping ransom money and let the twins be found alive and well? Why make them disappear?

She thought about the broken rung on the ladder and

the concern that the kidnapper had fallen, injuring one or both of the babies.

What other reason would the kidnapper have for not returning the babies?

"He did plan to find them good homes, right?"

Frieda's eyes filled with tears again.

She heard the sound of a vehicle. Shouldn't the sheriff be here by now? What if Frieda was right and the man who'd tried to run them off the road had come back?

She looked around for a place they might hide and saw nothing but short scrub pine and sagebrush.

"Maybe I should call the sheriff again," she said to Frieda, but the woman didn't seem to hear her. Nikki realized that the key pieces of the puzzle were still missing.

"Where is Harold Cline now?" she asked as she started to dig her cell phone out of her pocket. Frieda had said that "he" would kill them. "Is Harold Cline the man who ran us off the road?"

"No," Frieda said her voice cold and hard. "He's dead. I killed him."

CULL TOOK A shortcut to Old Town and arrived at the Whitehorse Community Center as several older women were coming out.

He looked around for Nikki's rental car, but didn't see it. "Was Frieda here?" he asked a small gray-haired woman.

"Earlier, she and the writer. They left a long time ago, though."

He thanked her and headed down the main road thinking he must have missed them by taking the shortcut. Patricia's arrest had thrown him. He was still trying to process the fact that she'd been systematically poisoning his father—and might have done the same thing twenty-five years ago to his mother.

A feeling of doom had come over him when he'd realized that Frieda and Nikki should have been back to the ranch a good hour ago.

Maybe it was seeing his mother this morning, but he kept thinking that Nikki was right. If Patty had been poisoning his mother twenty-five years ago, it would explain her behavior more than postpartum depression. It could also explain her breakdown and how quickly she'd gone downhill. Losing the twins must have been the last straw.

But if it was true, would the sheriff be able to prove that Marianne was a victim of Patty's, and so was her husband? He wished he could get his hands around Patty's throat. He would choke the truth out of her.

The arrest had happened so quickly that he hadn't had time to think—let alone react. Now he was furious. Patty could have killed his father. Travers had taken it better than Cull would have. What wife poisoned her husband?

His cell phone rang. He answered, surprised he could get service this far out. "Hello?"

"A call just came in over the scanner," his brother Ledger told him. "A car was run off the road near Alkali Creek. Isn't that on the way to Old Town?"

"Who put in the call to the sheriff?" Cull asked and held his breath.

"Nikki St. James. She said she and Frieda weren't hurt. Deputies are on the way. They got held up because of Patricia's arrest. Where are you?"

"On my way to Alkali Creek," he said, and disconnected.

Cull hadn't gone far when he saw the tracks. He slowed. There was broken glass from a headlight at the edge of the road. Ahead he saw more tracks and in the distance, a dark green pickup parked off the road.

He had his window down as he drove toward the tracks. He hadn't gone far when he heard the gunshot.

NIKKI WAS STUNNED by Frieda's confession. So stunned that it took a moment to realize what was happening. There was a sound like something hard hitting stone. At the same time, Frieda flinched and let out a soft cry.

When she looked over at the woman sitting with her back against a large rock, Nikki saw that Frieda was holding a hand over her stomach. It took her a wild moment to realize that blood was oozing out from between her fingers.

The second rifle shot pinged off the rock above Nikki's head. She scrambled up, grabbed hold of Frieda and dragged her around the rock outcropping. Again she heard the sound of a vehicle engine.

She fumbled out her cell phone and quickly punched in 9-1-1 again, telling the dispatcher what had happened.

"An ambulance is on the way," she told Frieda as she disconnected.

The woman was still breathing, but her breaths were shallow and she was clearly in a lot of pain. Nikki had stanched the bleeding as much as she could with her jacket.

Her mind was racing.

"I can't die yet. I can't die with this on my conscience."

"You're not going to die."

A crooked smile curled her lips. "When I heard that someone had taken the twins, I knew."

"Frieda, you shouldn't try to talk."

The woman didn't seem to hear her. "I prayed it wasn't him. But when I couldn't reach him... There was an old cabin in the Little Rockies that Harold used during hunting season. I knew the ransom had been paid, but the babies still hadn't been returned." She grimaced in pain, her voice choked with tears as she said, "He was digging a hole to bury them when I found him."

Nikki felt her heart drop like a stone. She couldn't breathe, couldn't speak.

"He said it was my fault. I'm the one who said the twins weren't safe and he was just doing what I wanted him to do. The babies were in a burlap bag on the ground next to the hole he'd been digging. I begged him to take them back."

Hope soared at her words. "Take them back? They were still alive?"

Still Frieda didn't seem to hear her. She was lost in the past, lost in telling a secret hard kept all these years. "He said, 'Have you lost your mind? The place is crawling with cops. And what would I say? Yes, I took the little snots, but I've decided to return them because Frieda has changed her mind? You're in this as deep as I am. You'll go to prison with me. You think they will believe that I did this on my own?'"

She felt her blood run cold at Frieda's words. "Who did help him?"

Frieda shook her head. She took a ragged breath. "He never told me." Nikki could tell that she was in terrible pain. "All I cared about was the babies. I told him I was taking them and going to the authorities."

"'You're not doin' nothin' but goin' back to the ranch and keepin' your trap shut.' I told him I couldn't go back, not without the babies. 'You don't go back and you'll look guilty and I will be long gone and you can rot in prison.'"

Nikki couldn't bear to hear this and yet she hung on every word as she prayed for the sound of the ambulance and sheriff.

"I knew he was right. No one would believe me," Frieda said, her voice getting weaker. "He walked over to the babies. He was going to put them into that grave he'd dug. Put them in there still alive. I picked up the shovel." She began to cry again. "I dug the hole larger and buried him and the ransom money."

"What did you do with the babies, Frieda?" Nikki asked, her voice breaking.

The woman's eyes met hers. "I took them to the Whitehorse Sewing Circle. Pearl Cavanaugh was the only one there that night after everyone else had gone. I told her the same story I told Harold about Marianne. I begged her to find them good homes."

Relief rushed through her. "And did she?"

Frieda didn't answer. When Nikki looked into her eyes again, she saw that the woman was gone.

Chapter Eighteen

Across the ravine, Cull saw a man with a rifle run to his pickup. Something flashed in the sunlight as the man jumped behind the wheel. A moment later he took off in a cloud of dust. Was he going for help? What had he been doing with a rifle?

Cull pulled over to the side of the road and jumped out to look down into the ravine. In the distance he could hear the sound of sirens as he looked down to the bottom and saw the wrecked rental car. His heart dropped.

"Nikki!" he called. *"Nikki!"* He had already started down the hillside at a run when she came out from behind the rocks. His mouth went dry. He hadn't realized how terrified he'd been until he saw her—saw her injured and covered in blood.

He ran to her, weak with relief. "How badly are you hurt?" He could see that she had a scrape on the side of her face and there was dried blood on her temple, but it was the blood on the front of her shirt that had him shaking inside.

"It's not me. It's Frieda." She burst into tears. "She's been shot. She's dead."

He pulled her into his arms, the sound of sirens

growing closer. She felt so good in his arms that he never wanted to let her go. Relief gave way to realization. He'd seen the shooter leave in that old truck. "Did you get a look at the shooter?"

Nikki shook her head against his chest. "He ran us off the road, then came back…"

A sheriff's department patrol SUV stopped at the top of the hill followed by an ambulance, sirens blaring.

"Let's get you up to the road," he told Nikki.

She pulled back to wipe her eyes. "I can't leave Frieda."

"Let the EMTs take care of Frieda."

"But I'm the one who got her killed."

Chapter Nineteen

It rained the day of Frieda Holmes's funeral, but all of the McGraws were there standing under black umbrellas, listening to the preacher put her to rest. Frieda had no family except for the McGraws. But members of her quilting group had come to pay their respects.

Nikki stood next to Cull, the rain making a soft patter on the umbrella he held over them. Her heart still ached for Frieda. She'd paid a high price for what she'd done and the secret she'd kept all these years.

Still shaken by what had happened, Nikki questioned why she'd become a true crime writer. What drove this need of hers for the truth? Whatever it was, she'd gotten the woman killed. Her relentless need to dig in other people's tragedies had caused this. She would have to take that to her own grave.

As she looked around the cemetery, she thought of her father. She knew now that he had nothing to do with the kidnapping, but it would take more than that to clear his name. She had to find out who inside that house had helped Harold Cline. She would never believe it was Frieda.

The preacher was winding up his sermon. She looked to Travers McGraw, wondering how he was holding up given everything that had happened. He stood tall and erect beside the cook's grave, insisting he didn't need the wheelchair. In the days since Patricia's arrest, he'd improved. No doubt because he wasn't being poisoned, but it would take time for him to recover—if he ever fully did.

Cull had been afraid that the news about the twins would be the straw that finally broke him. But Nikki saw that he was filled with even more hope now. He was also stronger now that he knew why his health had deteriorated like it had. He would never be the man he'd been, but he was more determined than ever to find the twins.

The family gathered back at the ranch after the funeral. Tilly had made them all lunch, but no one was hungry. There were still so many questions, but now at least they knew that the babies had been saved. Unfortunately, Pearl Cavanaugh, the member of the Whitehorse Sewing Circle who Frieda had given the twins to, was dead. She'd died some years ago after having several strokes.

Travers had asked Nikki to tell them all what Frieda had confessed before she died. When she finished, the room fell silent.

"You believe Patty was poisoning our mother twenty-five years ago?" Ledger asked.

"It would explain your mother's behavior," Nikki said. "I'm not sure the sheriff will be able to prove it, though."

"We still don't know who helped this Harold Cline take the twins," Boone pointed out.

"But we do know that Frieda got them to Pearl Cavanaugh and that she probably found them good homes," Nikki said.

"But she is the only one who knows where they went and she's dead," Boone pointed out. "It's just another dead end."

"I have to wonder about the adoptive parents," Cull added. "They had to know about the McGraw kidnapping. It was on national news. Wouldn't they have questioned where their babies came from?"

Nikki had thought of that. "I'm sure Pearl had a story prepared. Remember, Frieda told her that Marianne wasn't stable, that the babies weren't safe here. I'm sure the new parents thought they were saving them."

"They were," Travers said.

"Which means they aren't together. Oakley and Jesse Rose had to have been adopted separately," Ledger said.

The room fell silent for a few moments.

"What now?" Boone asked, looking at Nikki, then his father.

"I'm sure Nikki is still planning to do the book," Travers said, and Nikki nodded. "I got a call from the sheriff earlier. They found the hunting cabin in the Little Rockies that Harold Cline used. They found his grave and the ransom money." His voice broke as he added, "The sheriff found a burlap bag in the cabin that had both Oakley's and Jesse Rose's DNA on it."

He turned to Nikki. "One of the things that was never released to the media was that when the twins were taken, so were their favorite animals that slept with them at night—and their blankets. Jesse Rose's blanket was found in the pool house. But Oakley's was never found. The small stuffed animals were horses with ribbons around their necks. Each twin had a different-colored ribbon."

Cull frowned. "So there is one blanket and two stuffed horses still missing. Let me guess. You're planning to release this information in hopes that the twins will see it."

Travers smiled at his son and nodded. "Just the information about the toy horses."

Boone got to his feet. "You're going to bring every nutcase out of the woodwork. Isn't it bad enough with all the publicity about Patricia?"

"The twins are alive," Travers said. "I've felt it soul deep since they were taken. What Nikki found out from Frieda only proves it. This is a chance I have to take. With Nikki's help, we'll put out the information and pray that the twins will find *us*."

Boone shook his head. "I have work to do. We are still a horse ranch, aren't we?" He walked out, mumbling, "This family is cursed."

"He's right. I still can't believe what Patty did," Cull said, looking over at his father.

"I suspect she got the idea from when she slowly poisoned your mother over twenty-five years ago and made her think she was crazy," Travers said.

Cull shook his head in disbelief. "She would have killed you and none of us would have suspected what she was doing. If Jim Waters gets her out of jail…"

"He won't," Travers said. "Patricia has no money of her own. She won't be able to make bail. Not only that, but also the judge thinks she is a flight risk and so do I."

"You're sure Waters isn't defending her?" Cull asked with disgust.

"He might have, before he realized she didn't have

any money to pay him. Before we got married, I made Patricia sign a prenuptial agreement. I worried that if we divorced she could force me to sell the ranch that I've built for my children."

"But she would get something. What happened if you died?" Nikki asked.

"She would have gotten a few acres so she could build a place for herself, if she so desired, and a large amount of money to live on the rest of her life. I'm sure she would have sold the land," Travers said. "Now we know that she couldn't wait for me to die." There was pain in his tone. He wasn't used to being betrayed.

"Nikki tells me that your mother kept a diary," Travers said to his sons. "One of the pages has turned up. Do you know anything about it?" he asked his family. There was a general shake of heads.

"The first I heard of it was when Nikki brought me the page someone had shoved under her door," Cull said. "Isn't it possible Patricia was involved? She seems to have been involved in everything else, including blackmailing Frieda."

"I'm going to go by the sheriff's office and see if Patty will talk to me," Nikki said. "If she has the diary hidden somewhere, I doubt she will give it up, though. But all I can do is try."

"Good luck with that," Cull piped up.

"Did the sheriff say if they've had any luck finding the person who ran us off the road and shot Frieda?" Nikki asked.

Travers shook his head. "They're looking for the pickup that both you and Cull provided a description for, but they've had no luck so far. There are so many old barns around here, not to mention thousands of ravines and ponds where it could have been dumped. That's what the sheriff thinks Frieda did with Harold Cline's old car he drove. She suspects it is rusting out in one of the ponds near the Little Rockies. It wouldn't be the first time a vehicle was hidden in one."

"Are you sure Patty wasn't in on the kidnapping?" Ledger asked.

Nikki shook her head. "Frieda didn't know who Harold Cline had helping him in the house. It could have been Patty, but I have my doubts. Yes, she wanted your mother's life, always did. The kidnapping I believe messed up her plans and forced her to leave. Also because of the large ransom demand, your father didn't have any money for a long while after that." Nikki shrugged. "It wasn't until she had her daughter and your father had recouped his losses that she doubled back."

"We still don't know who fathered her baby?" Ledger asked.

His father shook his head. "I never asked. Kitten has gone to stay with an aunt. Patricia insisted." He sounded sad. Travers had raised the child as his own and now she, too, had been taken from him.

Cull swore. "That coldhearted—"

"Patricia will get what's coming to her," Travers said as he got to his feet. "Boone's right. We have a horse ranch to run. Nikki will take care of releasing the information to the media. She tells me she can do that from back home while she's writing the book, so she'll be leaving tomorrow. Thank you again. If you hadn't come here..." He smiled at her, his eyes filling with tears.

"She can't finish her book until we find the twins," Ledger said. "So I hope that means you'll be back."

"We'll see what releasing the information about the

twins' stuffed animals turns up." She glanced over at
Cull. He seemed to be studying the toes of his worn
boots.

Ledger rose to his feet.

"Tell me you aren't going into town to the Whitehorse Café," Cull said, finally glancing up.

His younger brother shrugged. "You've never been
in love, so you couldn't possibly understand."

"Uh-huh," Cull said. "Just watch your back. I hope
I don't have to warn you about Wade Pierce."

"There is nothing you can tell me about him that I
don't already know," Ledger said, and headed for the
door.

"You're worried about him," Nikki said when she
and Cull were alone. She shared his concern.

"With good reason. My brother is in love with another man's wife. No good can come out of that." He
settled his gaze on her. "So you're leaving."

"I'll go home and start the book. I can do what your
father needs me to do from there. No reason for me to
stay now."

"I guess not." He lumbered to his feet. "Well, if I
don't see you before you leave, have a safe trip back
home."

NIKKI HAD TWO things she had to do before she left town
tomorrow. She had to see Marianne McGraw again and
then she would pay a visit to Patricia in jail.

This time she went through proper channels, and
having Travers's permission, she was taken down
the long hallway to the woman's room. Nothing had
changed since the last time she'd been here.

Marianne was in her rocker, the dolls clutched in her

arms, her slippered feet propelling her back and forth as she stared off into space.

Nikki dragged up the extra chair in the room and sat down in front of the woman. "You probably don't remember me. I came here to find out who kidnapped your children. I promised I would come back when I knew."

There was no change in expression or in the rocking motion.

"It was your cook Frieda Holmes's boyfriend. She wasn't involved. But the news I have to tell you is that her boyfriend is dead. She killed him and saved your babies. We suspect they went to good homes and eventually we will find them. So we believe that Oakley and Jesse Rose are alive."

Still nothing.

"You should also know that twenty-five years ago when you thought you were losing your mind? You were being *poisoned*. That's why you were confused. It's why you were having trouble bonding with the twins. Patty, your nanny, was poisoning you. She wanted your husband—and she finally got him. She's in jail for attempted murder because once she had Travers, she decided to get rid of him. Apparently what she really wanted was the ranch and you out of the way."

Marianne seemed to hug the dolls tighter as she rocked.

Nikki couldn't be sure any of this was getting through the walled-up dark place where the woman's mind had holed up all these years.

"Now everyone knows you had nothing to do with the kidnapping. Your name is cleared and soon, God willing, your twins will be found alive and well and Patty will be in her prison."

She looked into the woman's face for a moment, remembering the last time she was here. She'd gotten a reaction out of Marianne, but this time there was nothing.

Standing, Nikki pushed the chair back. "I'm so sorry you can't hear what I'm saying. I'd hoped it might free you." She turned and walked to the door to tap on it. A moment later, the door opened.

As she started to step out, she looked back, realizing that the rocking had stopped. Marianne was looking at her. Her arms opened and the tattered dolls tumbled to the floor. The woman let out a bloodcurdling cry that Nikki knew she would hear in her dreams the rest of her life.

"I CAN'T BELIEVE you'd have the nerve to come here," Patricia snapped as Nikki took the phone in the visitors' room and sat down on the safe side of the Plexiglas. "Your lies got me in here. But I'll get out. I have friends."

"I think lover more than friend," Nikki interrupted. "So which one of them were you arguing with the first night I arrived? Was it Blake Ryan or Jim Waters? I can see Kitten in either of them. I bet a DNA test would prove which one was her father. I'm also betting that whichever one it was, it was his idea for you to come back to Whitehorse and the McGraw ranch."

Patricia narrowed her eyes. "You think you know so much, don't you? Prove any of it."

"A simple DNA test will do that."

"Like I'm going to allow my daughter to be tested."

"You do realize that once the sheriff starts questioning Blake Ryan and Jim Waters, your…lover will turn on you and make a deal. Once the sheriff finds the old truck one of them used to force me and Frieda off the road… Once they find the man's DNA inside…I know he shot her to shut her up. If Travers had found out that you'd withheld information on the kidnapping… Well, he might have changed his will—before you killed him—and cut you off without a cent."

"You don't know what you're talking about."

"I know you don't want the twins to be found. You don't need two more McGraws turning up when you already have three stepsons watching you. But a little more poison and Travers's next heart attack would have probably killed him. You would have had some land to sell and money to do whatever you wanted. What did you plan to do, Patty?"

"Are you sure you aren't a fiction writer? It seems to me you just make things up as you go," the woman said. "What do you want?"

"To say goodbye. I'm leaving."

"Finally. Too bad you ever came here."

Nikki stared at her. She'd met others who lacked true compassion. Psychopaths who took pleasure in hurting others. People like Patty only felt pain when it was their own. She thought of the mousy nanny. No wonder no one had suspected what she was doing to poor Marianne. Not that the sheriff would ever be able to prove it.

"Did you ever have a dog?" Nikki asked.

"*What?* A dog? What does that have—"

"Just curious. I've found that people who can't love an animal are missing a part of their souls."

"I have no idea what you're trying to say," she said, looking away.

"I told Marianne that you were systematically poisoning her twenty-five years ago and that was why she thought she was losing her mind."

Patty laughed. "Marianne? She's a vegetable. You really can't believe she understood anything you said."

"You might be surprised." Nikki stood, still holding the phone. "By the way, what did you do with her diary?"

Was that surprise in her eyes? "Her life was so boring. Why would she bother to keep a diary?"

"Have it your way. I would imagine you'll produce it if you can find a way for it to help save you. But ultimately, you're going away for a very long time. I bet Blake is making a deal right now with the prosecuting attorney."

Patty looked scared. Nikki felt bad that she took pleasure in seeing the woman squirm. She thought of what Patty had done to Marianne, Frieda and Travers, and didn't feel so bad.

As she hung up the phone, she saw Patricia signal the guard that she was done.

Chapter Twenty

Nikki didn't see Cull when she went up to the house to say goodbye to Travers and tell him about both Marianne's and Patty's reactions to her visits.

"I'm sorry to see you go," the older man said. "You saved my life. I'll never forget that. Are sure you can't work from here?"

"This is best."

He nodded slowly. "My boys...well, they're gun-shy of relationships. Rightly so, given what they've been through. But you and Cull..."

She smiled. "There was a lot going on. I think we all need time."

"Maybe." He walked her out to her new rental car, which had been delivered that morning. "We'll talk soon."

Nikki held back the tears until she reached the ranch gate. She made the mistake of looking back. A half-dozen of the horses stood at the fence watching her leave. She thought of her father. He'd been innocent just as her mother had known, just as Nikki had prayed.

But what brought tears to her eyes was the pain in her heart. Cull had unlocked something in her. She could just hear what her grandfather would have said—if she was crazy enough to tell him.

She'd gotten too emotionally involved. With the family. With the story. With the oldest son. She and Cull had connected in a way that had scared them both. They were too young to feel this way, weren't they?

Look at Ledger. He'd fallen in love with Abby at the Whitehorse Café when they were teenagers—and nothing had changed even when she'd foolishly married another man. Nikki hoped they found their way back to each other. Ledger deserved a happy ending. So did Cull, but she figured it would be with some local girl now that the truth had come out about the kidnapping.

She drove away from the ranch, telling herself she'd be back but wondering if she ever would. Could she bear seeing Cull again? Bear seeing him with another woman? She thought not.

Tears blurred her eyes. She made a swipe at them as she drove, forcing her to slow down.

CULL WAS SADDLING his horse when his brothers found him. "What's up?" he asked, half-afraid something else had happened.

"We need to talk to you," Boone said. "What's going on between you and the writer?"

Cull almost laughed. This was it? "None of your damned business." He turned back to saddling the horse. He needed this ride more than either of them could imagine. Nikki was the only thing on his mind and he had to do something about that. He did his best thinking on the back of a horse.

"Are you serious about her?" Ledger asked.

Cull sighed and turned back to them. "Maybe I didn't make myself clear—" He frowned. "I thought you went into town?"

"Boone needed my help to make you see reason. We like Nikki. We think she's good for you," Ledger said, taking him by surprise. "She...challenges you. You need that."

Boone sighed. "You do realize that once she gets what she needs for her book she has no excuse to come back."

"I'm aware of that."

"Personally, I don't care what you do, but Ledger is convinced you're in love with her and too stupid to do anything about it."

"Thanks," he said to his youngest brother.

"Well, what *are* you going to do about it?" Ledger asked. "You going to let her get away?"

"She isn't some horse I can lasso and haul back to the corral," Cull said, annoyed that they were butting into his love life. His love life? Had he just thought that? "The woman has a mind of her own."

"So if you could lasso her and haul her back to the corral, you would?" Ledger demanded.

In a heartbeat. "I'm not discussing this with the two of you. Not one lovesick brother who lost his woman or a brother who's too ornery to ever lasso a woman."

"I don't want to see you make the mistake I did," Ledger said, obviously not taking offense at Cull's description of him.

"I could lasso any woman I want. I just haven't found one worth bringing back to the corral," Boone protested.

Cull shook his head. "What do you want from me?"

"If you love her, then go after her. Tell her how you feel," Ledger said.

"And if she leaves anyway?" he asked, hating how vulnerable he sounded.

"Then at least you tried," Boone said, surprising

him even more. "We already have one brother moping around here over a woman. I can't bear two. Fix it." With that his brother turned and stalked away.

"He's right," Ledger said. "Fix it or you'll regret it the rest of your life."

"She's already gone," he said.

"You might be able to catch her if you take the short-cut across the ranch," Ledger suggested. "Since you were going on a horseback ride anyway." He smiled.

Cull cuffed his brother on the shoulder as he swung up in the saddle. "I'll think about it."

CULL RODE HARD toward the cutoff road. It felt good, the wind in his face, the power of the horse under him, the freedom of escape that filled him.

He couldn't believe that his brothers had ganged up on him. Go after Nikki and what? Tell her he didn't want her to go? Even with Patricia out of the house, things were still too up in the air.

Not only that; he also told himself that he barely knew the woman. It wasn't like he could have fallen in love with her that quickly. It wasn't like it had been love at first sight. He thought of her lying on the street in front of his pickup and groaned.

She'd never admitted that she'd done that on purpose. What kind of woman would risk her life for...for what? To make him more sympathetic to the book she planned to write?

Pretty daring thing to do. He hated the admiration he felt. It had been a stupid thing to do. Too risky. She could have been killed. A woman like that...well, who knew what she'd do next.

He smiled to himself at the thought. He'd never met

anyone like her. He could see her fitting in just fine on the ranch now that Patricia was gone. He could see her just fine as his wife.

That thought hit him like a low limb.

He'd almost reached the road. In the distance he could make out her rental car. A tail of dust trailed behind it.

Cull brought his horse up short at the fence. Why had he let his brothers talk him into this? He had no idea what he was going to say to her. For all he knew she didn't feel the same way. She might even have a boyfriend back home.

Not the way she kissed you. He smiled to himself, remembering those kisses and hating the thought of never getting another one. He'd never told any woman that he loved her. He'd had crushes, even dated the same girl a couple of years in high school. He'd loved her, but he hadn't *loved* her. Not the kind of love that lasts a lifetime.

Nikki was getting closer. He could almost make out her face through the windshield.

Ride away now! You're just going to make a fool of yourself.

NIKKI COULDN'T BELIEVE what she was seeing. She squinted through the sun-dappled windshield. Was that Cull on a horse waiting for her by the ranch fence?

She touched the brakes, wondering what he wanted as she slowed and hurriedly wiped away the rest of her tears. Maybe she'd forgotten something. But he didn't seem to have anything in his hands. Or maybe Travers had sent him with a message.

Bringing the car to a stop next to him and his horse,

she lowered the passenger-side window. "Is something wrong?"

Cull nodded. She watched him slide out of the saddle. He hesitated for a moment, his gaze meeting hers before he vaulted over the fence. As he walked toward her new rental car, her heart lodged in her throat. She'd fallen so desperately in love with this man. How had she let that happen?

He leaned in the passenger-side window she'd lowered.

"I've been thinking," he said, and cleared his throat. "You're going to have to get over your fear of horses."

She frowned. Surely he hadn't ridden all this way to tell her that. "Really? I suppose you have something in mind?"

Cull's blue gaze locked with hers. "I have all kinds of things in mind." He let out a curse and drew back only to walk around to her side of the car. Opening the door, he reached for her hand.

Still mystified, she let him take it and pull her from behind the wheel. "Cull, what—"

"I don't want you to go."

"I'll be back to do more work on the book." It was a lie. She couldn't bear being this close to him and not being in his arms. She wouldn't be back.

"No," he said as if struggling to find the right words. Again his gaze met hers and held it. "I...I know it sounds crazy. It *is* crazy. I come riding out here like some kind of a fool being chased by the devil to tell you..." He faltered.

"To tell me...? Has something happened to your father?"

He shook his head. "I love you." He let out a breath and laughed. "I. *Love*. You."

She was so surprised that she didn't know what to say. She hadn't let herself admit her feelings until today. She'd blamed whatever it was between them on simple chemistry. She and Cull had been like fire and ice. But when they were fire...

"I just had to tell you how I feel." He took a step back from her. "I feel...better getting it out, how about that?" He grinned. "I think I've been wanting to say that for a while now." His blue eyes shone as they locked with hers. "I still can't believe it. I love you."

Nikki laughed. "That's it?"

He looked taken aback. "Hell, woman, you have no idea how hard that was to say. I've never told anyone... and you...you—" He blew out air as he stepped to her again. "*You* make me crazy." His fingers caught her hair at the nape of her neck and buried themselves in the long strands. "All I think about is kissing you. I want to make love to you slow and easy. I want to wake up every morning with you in my arms. I can't stop thinking about you. I don't think I can live without you."

She couldn't breathe at his words, at the look in his eyes. "Oh, Cull. From the moment I laid eyes on you... I felt..." She shook her head. "I've never felt like this before. I love you too."

He pulled her to him in a sizzling kiss that left her teetering on her high heels. As he drew back, he said, "The first thing we're going to do is buy you a pair of cowboy boots, woman."

She laughed. "*That's* the first thing?"

Cull dragged her into another kiss, this one hotter than the last. "Maybe not the first thing."

* * * * *

"I believe the feeling is mutual."

She looked at Cadell then, daring to meet his gaze directly without sliding quickly away. His gaze was warm, inviting, suggesting delights she could barely imagine. Yet he remained a perfect gentleman with her. He was getting past her guard, little by little.

An electric shock seemed to zing between them. Something invisible was trying to push her closer to him.

But then he broke their gaze and turned. "Wanna come inside and rummage through my fridge before I take you back?" He glanced at his watch. "I go on duty in a couple of hours."

Yup, in addition to sexual attraction, she was learning to like him a whole lot. Sexual attraction she could deal with. She'd sent away more than one guy over the years because she wasn't going to get that close to anyone.

But liking? That could be even more of a risk.

CORNERED IN
CONARD COUNTY

BY
RACHEL LEE

First Published in Great Britain 2017
By Mills & Boon, an imprint of HarperCollins*Publishers*
1 London Bridge Street, London, SE1 9GF

© 2017 Susan Civil Brown

ISBN: 978-0-263-92906-5

46-0817

Our policy is to use papers that are natural, renewable and recyclable products and made from wood grown in sustainable forests. The logging and manufacturing processes conform to the legal environmental regulations of the country of origin.

Printed and bound in Spain
by CPI, Barcelona

Rachel Lee was hooked on writing by the age of twelve and practiced her craft as she moved from place to place all over the United States. This *New York Times* bestselling author now resides in Florida and has the joy of writing full-time.

Prologue

Dory stirred from sleep and tried to cover her ears. Daddy was fighting with her big brother, George, again. But later she realized it sounded different. Voices shouted, but was Mommy laughing? It didn't sound like Mommy's fun laugh.

Curious, Dory climbed out of bed, picked up her favorite bunny and stood at the head of the stairs. Daddy was still shouting. Sticking her thumb in her mouth, she stared at the pool of light pouring out of the kitchen downstairs. Mommy made a strange sound, and curiosity pushed Dory to descend.

Before she was halfway down, things got very quiet and she stopped. She wondered if she'd get into trouble for being out of bed. Daddy and Mommy were very strict about that. Once in bed, stay in bed until morning. George laughed about it, but he said Mommy and Daddy needed grown-up time. But George was mostly grown-up and he got to go out at night. That was probably why they were yelling. Dory hesitated. The yelling was gone.

But then she heard a strange sound and came downstairs the rest of the way. Bunny tucked under her arm, thumb in her mouth, she turned toward the light spilling from the kitchen.

Everything was red. Like paint. It was everywhere and Mommy and Daddy were on the floor covered in the paint. George stood there, his face all tight and funny as he looked at her.

"It's okay, Dory. I made the bad man run away." He squatted and held out his arms to her.

Usually Dory ran straight toward him, but George was covered with the red paint, too, and she didn't like that.

"Dory? Come here, pumpkin."

She saw what was in his hand. A knife. It was all red, too. Why was everything so red?

Some instinct pierced her, and terror shook her out of her confusion. She didn't know what was going on, but she ceased to think. Something deep within her reacted, and she ran out the front door onto the street and started screaming...screaming...screaming.

Chapter One

Screaming.

Dory Lake awoke with her own screams ringing in her ears. The minute her eyes popped open, blessed lamplight greeted her, and for a moment, just a moment, she felt safe.

She remembered what she had seen, but over twenty-five years the nightmares had grown less frequent. Now they were coming back again, every night or several times a night.

Because her brother was about to be released from prison.

She sat up quickly, and was relieved when she didn't grow light-headed. She had low blood pressure, and sometimes it took her by surprise, causing her to faint briefly. A minor thing, a mere nuisance most of the time.

Drenched with sweat, she climbed from bed and walked into the small bathroom to shower. He wasn't out yet. Not yet. She was okay.

But the dream had brought that terrifying night back. All the intervening years hadn't expunged the memory, although it had been troubling her less and less. But ever since she had learned George was about to complete his sentence, the nightmares had returned. Every single night. No escape.

There was no reason to think George would have any interest in her when she'd never spoken about any of it, and he couldn't be convicted of the murder again anyway, she told herself repeatedly as the cold water pounded her. As she'd been telling herself ever since she got the news. He couldn't even be interested in her inheritance which was locked up in an unbreakable trust, a trust his lawyer had told him about.

Hell, he probably wouldn't even be able to find her. The last name Lake was an extremely common one.

At last she toweled off, climbed into a fresh nightgown and robe, and started downstairs. No more sleep tonight. Too bad, she was moving into her own place tomorrow... or was it today?

Downstairs the kitchen light was on. Her friend Betty made sure the house stayed reasonably well lit at night. For Dory, who couldn't stand waking in the dark.

But when she stepped into the gaily colored kitchen, she found Betty was already there with a fresh pot of coffee. Betty sat at the table, mugs, spoons and sugar at the ready, along with a plate of cookies. Her short graying hair looked tousled and, true to her taste, she wore a zip-up robe that was nearly psychedelic with cat faces. Betty was determined to become the cat lady. So far she'd acquired only three, all of whom were now swirling, wondering if it was time for breakfast.

"I heard the shower," Betty said. "Again?"

"Again. I'm sorry I woke you."

"What kind of friend would I be if I got annoyed by that? I don't have nightmares like yours, but I've had them. Nice to have someone near when they wake you." Betty bit her lower lip. "Are you *sure* you should move out? I can't stand thinking of you all alone."

Dory slid into one of the chairs. "I've been living on my own since college. I can't let George's release take my independence from me. Anyway, there's absolutely no reason he should want to find me. He served his time and I'm no threat. After all this time, we're strangers. And, as you know, I need to get back to my job."

Of course, those brave words ignored the fact that she'd run all the way to Conard County, Wyoming, from Kansas at Betty's invitation, when she'd learned her brother would soon be released and the nightmares had returned. Packed up and fled, if she was honest about it. Saying George wouldn't want to find her felt like whistling past the graveyard.

Betty, even back in the days when she taught Dory's high school English class, had been blunt, not one to pull her punches. So it bothered Dory that Betty had felt she should come here.

Apparently Betty didn't quite believe George wouldn't come looking for Dory. Or maybe she had just believed the move would ease Dory's nightmares. So much for that.

The coffee went down well, as did a cookie, and soon her fears eased enough that one of the cats, a ginger tabby called simply Ginger, was willing to leap on her lap and beg for pets.

Such a soothing scene, Dory thought as she rubbed the ginger cat's cheeks and elicited a surprisingly loud purr. Her relaxation deepened, and she thought that maybe she'd better get a cat herself.

"So therapy's out?" Betty asked quietly.

"I've been through years of it. I doubt they can do any more."

"Maybe not, but you're older now." Then Betty hesitated. "I have a friend I want you to meet this morning."

Dory stiffened a bit. She'd been here a week, and so far she'd avoided getting drawn into a social circle. She didn't know if she was ready for that, and anyway, she'd never been good at it.

"Oh, relax," Betty said, reading her reaction correctly. "Someday you'll want out of that shell, but I doubt it's going to be right away. You've been in it for too many years. No, this is a special kind of friend. He's the K-9 officer for the sheriff. He trains the dogs and other officers. Anyway, I want you to meet him."

"Why?"

"Well, apart from the fact that he's got two nasty ostriches he never wanted and can't get rid of, which I find hysterically funny and interesting, he has lots of dogs. I think you need a dog to keep you company."

Dory stared at her. "Why? I was thinking about a cat."

Betty smiled. "Think about it, Dory. What's going to make you feel safer? A guard dog or a guard cat?"

Almost in spite of herself, Dory laughed. "You make a point."

"I always have," Betty said.

Back in those long-ago days when Betty had been her sophomore English teacher, Betty alone had showed the infinite patience Dory needed to let someone become close to her. Betty's campaign had lasted well beyond high school until, finally, surprise of surprises, Dory realized she had a true friend.

No one else had come so close to her.

"Oh, and you're not moving today," Betty said, reaching for a cookie.

Dory preferred deciding things for herself. "Why?" she asked, a bit sharply.

Betty ignored her tone. "Because there was a voice mail message this morning. It'll be two more days before your high-speed internet is wired in. You need that to work, don't you?"

"They promised to do it today," she answered, but realized getting upset about it wouldn't help anything. Since she got here, Betty had offered to take her out to the community college to use the internet there. At home, Betty had little need for a high-speed connection. But her connection was good enough to pick up email, so Dory hadn't taken Betty up on her offer to go to the college. Anyway, the college didn't have what she needed.

But she couldn't stop working indefinitely and it had been too long already. Email sufficed for a short time only. "I need my connection," she said presently. "Two more days, huh?"

"What exactly do you do that keeps you online most of the day?" Betty asked. "I get the souped-up computer with all the whiz-bang gizmos, multiple monitors, a graphics card that would break anyone's bank account…but you can get your email here, right?"

Dory smiled faintly and poured herself a little more coffee. "I don't do graphic art all by myself. I work with a team most of the time. Being able to chat back and forth and share files is essential."

"I see." Betty furrowed her brow. "Well, I can call the company again and see if they can hop to it. I know Wil Gladston, and he should be able to pull a string or two."

Dory reached out to touch Betty's arm. "A couple of days more won't make or break my situation. Everyone knew I'd be off grid for a while. And everyone knows I'm moving. At least we're not under a tight deadline pressure right now."

"If you're sure," Betty said. "Things happen so differently in a small town, you know. Nobody's in a rush without a reason. I'm sure if I explained about your job…"

Dory shook her head. "It's all right," she insisted. "I've got more than enough to keep me busy, and I can check email on your connection, as you said."

She decided it was time to change the subject. She didn't want Betty worrying about her. "So this guy with the dogs? You said he has ostriches? Really?"

Betty's face smoothed, and a grin was born. "Two of 'em. Nasty critters."

"Then why does he have them?"

"He doesn't know." Betty laughed. "It's such a funny story. Cadell's dad died unexpectedly. When Cadell came home for the funeral, he found he'd not only inherited the ranch, but those damn ostriches, as well. No clue why or how they got there." She leaned forward a bit, still grinning. "Now I gotta tell you, that man is patient beyond belief and seldom cusses. But those birds can wind him up enough to cuss a blue streak. A very inventive blue streak. A show well worth watching."

Dory was smiling herself, verging on a laugh. "Why doesn't he get rid of them?"

"You think he hasn't tried? Oh, my." Betty threw her head back and laughed. "I'll let him tell you. It's a story and a half."

Several hours later as she dressed to go meet this K-9 guy with Betty, Dory wondered why she should need protection. Her brother always had been good to Dory before that night. More tolerant than most brothers that age with a girl of seven. Their relationship had been warm and loving.

Until that night. Every time she remembered him standing there drenched in blood, holding out his hand, holding a bloody knife, she wondered what his intentions had been. Would he have killed her, too? She still didn't understand why he'd killed her parents. Or how it was he hadn't gotten a life sentence.

But all those unanswered questions ate at her, and the nightmares proved that she was afraid of him to this day. Maybe that fear was groundless, but he *had* killed their parents and offered no good explanation for any of it that she had ever heard, not even much later when she was old enough to ask the questions.

Impatient with herself, she yanked on a polo shirt to go with her jeans and tried to look forward to seeing the nasty ostriches. And the dogs. She'd always liked dogs.

Just one step at a time, one day at a time, until her emotional upset settled once again. She'd be fine.

CADELL MARCUS STOOD near the ostrich pen, eyeing his pair of nemeses with restrained dislike. Except for some pretty feathers, these were the ugliest-looking birds he'd ever seen. He was a tall man, but they towered over him, a fact they never seemed to let him forget. Dinosaurs. Why weren't they extinct?

But there they stood, edged into the small pen he sometimes needed to use because, occasionally, despite ostrich demands, he needed his corral for things besides them.

Nor did he ever let himself forget those birds could kick him to death with a few blows. Not that they tried, but they'd sure given him the evil eye often enough, and when they stopped being scared of him and quit hunkering down, they had discovered great delight in pecking at his cowboy hats. Two expensive ones had bitten the dust before he'd realized what he really needed was a football helmet when he came within six feet.

He'd rounded them up into the small pen today, because Betty Cassell was bringing that friend of hers out to see about a guard dog. Betty had given him only the sketchiest of accounts as to why she felt it necessary, so he hoped he'd get more of the story when they arrived.

In the meantime…those damn ostriches would have to behave whether they liked it or not. At least the electrified fencing contained them. He couldn't imagine trying to catch them if they ever got out. He'd need Mike Windwalker, the veterinarian, with his magic dart gun.

They were glaring at him now. He glared back. "You two don't know how lucky you are that I don't send you to a boot factory."

He finally heard a motor approaching and the sound of tires on the gravel. Both birds redirected their attention and backed up, settling low to the ground in a protective posture. "Stay that way," he suggested, then went to greet his guests.

A smile lit his face the instant he saw Betty. Something about her always made him smile. But the woman who climbed out the other side of the car made him catch his breath. He wouldn't have thought a living woman could have the face of a Botticelli angel, complete with long blond hair, but this one did. She caught and held his gaze until he realized he was being rude.

Then he saw the rest of her. Oh, man, no angel could

have a body like that. Or at least shouldn't, because it caused an immediate firestorm in him, jeans and loose blue polo shirt notwithstanding.

"Hey, Cadell," Betty called with a wave.

Cadell gathered himself with effort, mentally whipped himself back into line and focused on her. He approached with outstretched hand. "Good to see you, Betty."

"Same here," she said, shaking his hand. "And this is my friend Dory Lake."

He turned and could no longer avoid looking at her. Simply breathtaking. With blue eyes the color of a summer sky. At one glance she made him feel dusty, unkempt and out of his league.

But she smiled warmly and extended her hand. When he reached for it, the touch was electric. "I heard about your ostriches."

"Not everything, I'm sure." Well, at least he could still talk, and the ostriches provided a bridge over his reaction to her. Never had a woman left him feeling so…well, hell, he was a cop. No one, male or female, ever left him gobsmacked.

Until now.

"Betty said you inherited the birds with the ranch?"

His grin returned. "Yup. I have no idea where they came from, just that apparently my dad had been taking care of them. Long enough to put in electrified fencing so they can't escape. So there they are." He turned and pointed to the pen. "Don't get too close—they peck."

She smiled, a beautiful expression. "Betty says you want to get rid of them?"

"To a good home somewhere the climate will suit them better. So far, no takers."

"I have to confess I had no idea how big they are," Dory said.

"Eight feet or so at maturity. Say, let's go look at the dogs. They make much better company."

He could feel the evil eyes following him as he led the ladies around his two-story ranch house to the dog run and kennels out back. At the moment he had six in various stages of training, mostly Belgian Malinois, but a German shepherd had joined the mix. In all he had ten kennels with access to fenced areas behind. It would have been unkind to expect them to live on concrete with their messes.

The dogs stood immediately, curious, ears pricked attentively. No barking, no crazy antics. Training showed.

He waited while the ladies looked them over, then Dory surprised him, pointing at the shepherd. "That's a different breed."

"Most people don't even notice," he answered. "Yeah, he's a German shepherd. The others are Belgian Malinois, sometimes called Belgian shepherds."

She looked at him with those blue eyes. "Do they behave differently?"

"A bit. The Malinois can be stubborn. He needs a good handler, but he's also more powerful than he looks. A great police dog. But the shepherd is more obedient, so…" He shrugged. "I've worked with both breeds over the last decade or so, and I love them both. Either breed would make you a good guard dog, but they're energetic. I hope you like to jog."

Her smiled dawned, and he felt his heart skip. Too much perfection?

"As it happens, I jog every day. Two or three miles. Would that be enough?"

"Like anything else, the faster you go, the faster they tire. They've got a lot of endurance, though, which is why they're such good working dogs. Both are also courageous to a fault."

He watched her look from dog to dog almost pensively. He pointed to two on the right end of the kennels. "Those two are almost ready to join the force as K-9s. Their handlers are about to finish training with them. But the other four are at various points in training, and any would make a good guard dog quite quickly."

She nodded. "Which would you recommend for a computer geek who can forget the time of day half the time?"

Cadell couldn't suppress a laugh. "The shepherd would lie at your feet and give you soulful looks. The Malinois might poke you with his nose to get your attention. But… they can all be mischievous. No guarantees on that."

He didn't expect her to decide just by looking, so he opened two of the kennels, freeing the shepherd and one Malinois. Far from racing away along the dog run, they stepped out, surveyed the newcomers, then politely sniffed both Betty and Dory. Once their immediate curiosity was satisfied, both sat on their haunches and waited expectantly.

"I've never seen dogs so well trained," Dory exclaimed.

"Most people don't want to be jumped on," Cadell replied. "They will if you want them to, but I don't recommend it. Hold out your hand palm up. Once they've sniffed it, you should be able to pet them."

DORY LOVED THE look of both dogs. Something about their eyes, at once alert and…empathetic? Did dogs feel empathy? She had no idea, but she was drawn to squat down so they were at eye level. Both dogs met her gaze steadily, which surprised her. She held out both hands, one to each dog, and as promised got nosed. Only then did she reach out to bury her fingers in their thick coats.

She'd never had a pet, she knew next to nothing about what she was getting into, but she knew in that instant that she very much wanted one of these dogs. She had the worst urge to wrap her arms around both their necks and hug them.

Amazed by her own response, one she almost never felt with people, she sat back on her heels and tried to regain her composure. "They're both beautiful. I have to decide right now?"

"Of course not," Cadell answered. "But it might help

if we went out in the paddock and played a bit with them. They have different personalities, just like people do. One of them will catch your eye more than the other."

So, for a little while, Dory forgot everything else as they played fetch with tennis balls and tug with a twisted rope. In the end she settled on the Malinois. Yeah, she could see the mischief in him, but she loved his coloration, a dark muzzle and legs that looked like they were cased in dark socks. There was something else, too, something that happened when their eyes met. It was almost as if the dog were saying, "I'm yours."

Crazy, she thought, but she announced her decision. A Malinois it would be. As she turned toward Cadell to tell him, a smile on her lips, she saw the heat in his gaze. Quickly shuttered, but not so quickly she didn't feel a responsive heat in herself.

She swiftly looked to the dog that had stapled itself to the side of her leg. Cadell Marcus was a very attractive man. Well built, a strong face and a great smile. He stood there in his sweatshirt, hands on narrow jean-clad hips, waiting, and she didn't dare look at him again.

These kinds of feelings frightened her almost as much as her nightmares. She was broken, she thought as she stroked the dog's head. Broken in so many ways, and all those ways led back to George. A spark of anger stiffened her spine.

"This one," she said to Cadell.

He smiled. "You're already a pair. He really likes you. Great choice. We can start training you right now, if you like."

"Training me?" she asked, surprised.

"Training you," he repeated. "All we're going to do is ask him to use his native personality and skills for your benefit. But you need to know how to bring that out of him."

Looking down at the dog, she felt a real eagerness to get started, to develop a relationship with him. "Sure. What's his name?"

"Flash. But you can call him something else if you want."

She smiled again. "Flash is a good name, especially since I'm a geek."

He laughed and turned toward Betty. "It'll be a couple of hours. If you want to stay, there's coffee and snacks in the kitchen."

Betty glanced at her watch. "I'll be back about twelve thirty, okay? You two have fun."

Cadell waved and returned his attention to Dory, leaving her inexplicably breathless. "Let's go," he said.

NEARLY A THOUSAND miles away in a Missouri state prison, George Lake sat in the yard enjoying the taste of sun. Two more days and he'd be out of here. He had to school himself to patience.

At least no one bothered him anymore. He'd grown strong and tough here, and he intended to take both away with him. He would also take distrust. He knew better than to tell even his friends here what he had in mind. Any one of them could blab, and this time no one was going to be able to link him to what he had planned.

So he sat there smiling, turning his face up to the welcome sun. Life was about to become so good. Just one little hitch ahead of him.

"Say, man," said a familiar voice. Ed Krank sat beside him.

"Hey," George answered, opening his eyes just briefly to assess the yard for building trouble. There were no warnings.

"So whatcha gonna do? Man, I can't believe you're getting out in two days. How can you stand waiting?"

"I've been waiting for twenty-five years. Two days look short." Which was a lie. Right now they looked endlessly long.

"They don't give you much when you leave here," Ed remarked. "You got something lined up?"

"Sure do."

"Good for you. Somebody said you had some money."

George managed not to stiffen. He knew where that came from. Even the oldest news got passed around here relentlessly, because there was so little new to talk about. Money had been mentioned in the papers long ago. "Anything I inherited they took away from me when I was convicted. No, man, nothing like that."

"Too bad."

Except that he'd been using the computers at the prison library when he could and had been tracking his little sister's life. She still had most of the life insurance, because she'd gotten money for the house, too. And she apparently had a tidy little business going.

If something happened to her, say, something deadly, he'd be her only heir. This time he'd get it, because this time he was determined that they weren't going to link him to any of it.

Oh, he'd learned a lot of lessons here, just listening, occasionally acting.

Dory might have disappeared a couple of weeks ago, but he'd find her. She had to surface online again, and he'd spent some time in classes learning how to use those skills, as well.

He'd find her. Then he just had to make it look like an accident.

"I'll be fine," he told Ed, not that he cared what Ed thought about it one way or another. "I made some plans."

Ed laughed. "Got plenty of time in here to make plans."

"No kidding," George answered, smiling. "There's work waiting for me." He just wasn't going to say what kind.

"Good for you," Ed said approvingly. "I'm getting out in eight months. Maybe you can set up a job for me."

"I'll see what I can do." But he had no intention of that. Remove Dory, get his inheritance and then get the hell out of this country.

Closing his eyes, he imagined himself sitting on a beach, with plenty of beautiful women wandering around.

Oh, yeah. Not much longer.

But between here and there lay Dory. Such a shame, he thought. If she'd just stayed in bed like she was supposed to, he could have slipped away and covered his tracks. Neither of them would have had to endure this hell.

But she had disobeyed a strict rule, had come down those stairs and walked in on him. She wouldn't even listen when he tried to tell her he'd gotten rid of the bad man.

Instead she had run screaming into the streets, and soon the night had been filled with lights spilling from houses, people running to help her, and cop cars. He'd tried to run, but it was too late to cover his tracks. She was to blame for that. Her and no one else.

So, she'd get what was coming to her. He'd paid for his crimes, and now he deserved the life he should have had all along. Instead she owned it all.

Well, he was just going to have to change that. Given the group she worked for, it wouldn't be long before he located her.

Then he'd have to figure out how to cause her a fatal accident.

He almost felt a twinge for the little girl she used to be, but the intervening years had hardened any softness that might have been left in him, and she was no longer a little girl who sat on his lap for a bedtime story. No, she was grown now, and not once had she written or tried to visit him.

It was all over between them. Well, except for ending her existence the way he'd ended their parents'. Only much more cleanly, making sure it didn't look like murder.

His smile widened a bit. He'd bet she thought he'd forgotten all about her. Stupid woman. She'd cost him everything.

Chapter Two

Two hours later, Dory sat in the middle of the dog run, laughing while Flash licked her face. "He doesn't wear out!"

"Not easily," Cadell agreed. "I guess he's chosen you, too. He needs a little more training with you to cement his role, but if you want you can take him back to Betty's with you."

"She has three cats!"

"They might not like it, but Flash will leave them alone. Okay, I'll keep him here for now. I wouldn't mind tightening up his training some more." He dropped down onto the ground beside her, knees up slightly, arms hanging loosely over them. "Betty told me a bit about what's going on. Want to talk a little?"

She tensed. Here she'd been having such a good time, and now this popped up. She wanted to resent him for it but could understand his curiosity. After all, he was training a guard dog for her. "Will it help?"

He caught her gaze and held it, an electric moment that conveyed compassion, as well. "Up to you, but I usually like to know what kind of threats my dogs will be working on. It allows me to hone their training. A bomb-sniffing dog doesn't always make a good attack dog."

She nodded slowly, looking down at her crossed legs and Flash's head, now settled comfortably on her lap. Her fingers were buried in his scruff, the massaging movement comforting him as well as her. Dang dog was magical, she thought.

Finally she sighed. "Betty probably told you the important parts. My older brother killed our parents. I was seven and I walked in on it. Anyway, somehow he only got twenty-five years, not life, and he's getting out soon."

She turned to look at him again, her voice becoming earnest. "I have no reason to think he'll be the least interested in finding me. I haven't seen or talked to him since that night. He never even wrote me from prison. But... I'm having a lot of nightmares at night, and no matter how much I tell myself..."

"You still can't quite believe he's not a threat to you," he completed. "Hardly surprising, given what you saw him do." He paused. "So he never once tried to get in touch with you all these years?"

She couldn't understand why that appeared to bother him. "No. Which means he isn't interested in me at all. He's probably all but forgotten me."

"Maybe so, but I guess your subconscious isn't buying it."

In spite of herself, she emitted a short laugh. "Apparently not. I feel so silly sometimes. Nightmares every night? And now a guard dog. That's over-the-top."

He shook his head a little. "I don't think it's over-the-top. Nothing wrong with having a guard dog around, not for anyone. At the very least, Flash will be good company."

She looked down at the dog she was petting. "He sure will be. He's wonderful. Petting him feels good."

"It feels good to him, too. But you'll have to work him every day so he doesn't turn couch potato on you."

Astonishment filled her. "Couch potato? Him?"

"Well, I don't mean he's going to get lazy. But he needs to remain sharp, so every day you're going to have to work with him for at least a half hour. Can you do that?"

"Sure. It'll be fun for both of us."

He smiled. "Good. You'll be a great handler for him. He likes the work, you know. For him it's a fun game. Now let's get busy on the attack training. I'm going to put on my padded suit, and you're going to make him attack me."

She felt perplexed. "But he knows you and likes you! Why would he attack you?"

"Because it doesn't matter that he knows me. Protecting you is all that's going to matter. When you tell him to attack, he'll attack. It's not his job to make decisions like that, but to take care of you. You'll see."

She still hesitated, concerned. "Does he know how to attack?"

"We've been practicing. Now it's time to get serious."

He rose in a single easy movement and went down the run to a shed at the end, disappearing inside. When he returned he wore thick padding on both arms.

Even so, that didn't seem like a whole lot of padding. Flash recognized it immediately and rose to his feet, tail wagging. Dory stood, too.

"He's been practicing on a dummy," Cadell said. "Now he gets the real thing."

They left the run and went out to a paddock, where the two ostriches stared at them over a fence. "Tell him what to do right now," Cadell said mildly.

Dory hesitated, then remembered. "Flash, heel."

The dog immediately came to stand alertly beside her. In all her life, she was sure she had never seen such an incredibly well-behaved dog. He was now still, watchful and right where she wanted him.

"Now you're not going to tell him to attack," Cadell said. "For that I don't like to use such an obvious word, one that he could hear in ordinary speech. It's not only tone that matters. They can pick words right out of a conversation. Now, some dog trainers don't worry about that, but I do. I don't want officers getting in trouble because someone is claiming to have been attacked and the dog reacts somehow."

She nodded, her heart beating nervously. "I understand." But she wasn't at all sure she wanted to command this dog to attack.

"The word I use is *fuss*. Long *u* sound. Like *foos*."

Her sense of humor poked its head up. "I hope I remember that when I need it."

"Well..." His eyes crinkled at the corners. "We'll practice until it becomes natural. But since you're going to start with a very simple command every night when you go to bed, or when you take him out, he'll know what to do even if he doesn't hear the word."

"Meaning?" She began to feel confused.

"If you tell him to guard, he will. And he won't always need an attack command to protect you. He's capable of evaluating a threat that gets too close. This is for when something is a little farther away and he might not see it as a threat to you immediately."

"Ah, okay." Now she was beginning to understand.

He patted her shoulder with his padded mitt. "It's about to all come together. I'm going to walk away about twenty feet. You're going to give the guard command. Then I'm going to turn around and point a toy gun at you. Pay attention to what happens as I approach you."

Okay, she thought. She could do this. "Flash, guard," she said. She felt the dog shift a little beside her but didn't look down at him.

About twenty paces away, Cadell turned around. He held a gun in right hand, but it was pointed down. Flash didn't stir a muscle. Step by step Cadell approached. At ten feet he raised the gun and pointed it at her. Flash didn't need another command. He took off like a shot and bit into the padding on Cadell's right forearm.

"My God," Dory whispered. She'd had no idea. The dog clung to that threatening arm and wouldn't let go even as Cadell tried to shake him off and whirled in circles, lifting Flash's feet from the ground.

"Stop him," Cadell finally said.

"Flash, release," Dory ordered, remembering the command he had taught her to make the dog drop his toy. Flash obeyed immediately, looking at her. "Heel."

He trotted over to her, looking quite pleased with himself. "Now the reward," Cadell said.

Which was the yellow tennis ball. She told him he was a good boy as she gave him the ball. Flash chewed on it a few times, then dropped it at her feet, begging for her to throw it, so she did. He raced happily after it.

"It's just that simple," Cadell said, watching her as much as he watched the dog. "A few more steps, a couple of days of practice and he'll do anything for you."

She squatted, encouraging Flash to come back to her. "How do I let him know it's okay not to be on guard?"

"Throw his ball. That means playtime."

So simple, she thought. And so amazingly complex all at the same time. Beautiful, too, she thought as she hugged the Malinois. The dog already made her feel safer. What's more, he made her feel as if she weren't quite as alone.

AFTER DORY LEFT with Betty, Cadell spent the afternoon working with two more officers who were training to become handlers. What they needed was more complex than what Dory needed, and the training was going to take a little longer. Simple fact was, while a civilian could get in some trouble for a misbehaving dog, a cop could have his career ruined. Or the department could be sued. Plus, these guys went into a wider variety of situations, situations that required tracking, rescuing and so on. Dory wouldn't need all those skills.

When he finished that up, he ate a quick dinner, then headed into the sheriff's office to do his shortened shift. On training days, he worked as a deputy for no more than four hours.

Before he left, he took time to feed the ostriches their very expensive feed and open up their pen so they had more room for roaming. Neither of them appeared appreciative.

He and his dog Dasher, also a Malinois, drove into town in his official vehicle and parked near the office. Inside, they found the place quietly humming. Another placid night in Conard County, evidently. He was surprised sometimes how much he enjoyed the relief from the much higher activity level of Seattle. Must be getting old, he thought with an inward smile. Yeah, like thirty-five was ancient.

Dasher settled beside his desk, tucked his nose between his paws and just watched. Since nothing seemed to be happening, he used the computer on his desk to look up the story of Dory Lake and her brother. He felt no qualms about discovering what he could from public records about that incident. He wasn't snooping, but he'd be learning what she had faced and would get a much better threat assessment than Dory's, which seemed to be somewhere between terror and dismissal.

He wasn't surprised to find a twenty-five-year-old case still accessible. The basic police report would be available for many years to come in case George Lake ever got into trouble again. It *was* nice, however, to find it had all been digitized. Newspaper archives were also ready and waiting.

So Dory, just turned seven, had been found screaming in the middle of the street at nearly 2:00 a.m. Neighbors had come running and called the police, who arrived in time to catch George Lake trying to flee the scene. Open-and-shut as far as George was concerned. He'd wiped the murder weapon, but he was far too drenched in blood to claim innocence. For some reason, not clearly explained, he'd been offered a plea bargain for twenty-five years. Drugs appeared to be involved, and the father had been abusive. He guessed the prosecutor couldn't pull together enough to uphold a first-degree murder charge, so George had accepted a bargain down to twenty-five. Without a trial, there was very little in the record to explain any of this.

But what stuck with him was a newspaper account. Apparently, when Dory had stopped screaming, the only words she had said for nearly a year were *red paint*.

God. He sat back in his chair and closed his eyes, seeing

it all too clearly. The child had been well and truly traumatized. There was even a mention of hysterical blindness,
a conversion disorder, but that hadn't lasted as long as her
refusal to speak.

She'd been taken in by her godparents and raised by
them, so no additional trauma from foster care, but what
difference did that make after what she'd seen? No one, at
least in these files, knew exactly how much she had seen,
but it was clearly enough to be shrieking in the middle of
the road and rendered dumb for nearly a year.

Except for *red paint*.

He'd seen a lot of bad stuff during his career, but the
thought of little Dory in the middle of the street…well, the
story was enough to break his heart.

As for her mixture of feelings about George…well, that
was settled in his mind when he read that Dory had received the entire—very large—insurance payout and all
the rest of the property. George might be feeling cheated.
In fact, Cadell was inclined to believe he was. He'd lost his
entire inheritance because he'd been convicted of killing
his parents. He might be thinking he could get some of that
back. Make Dory pay him to leave her alone.

Or maybe worse. Because it occurred to him that if Dory
died, her only heir would be her brother…and if he weren't
linked to her death…

Hell. He switched over to the reports menu and tried to
shake the ugly feelings.

Being a cop had made him a much more suspicious man
by nature. Sometimes he had to pull himself back and take
a colder view, stifle his feelings and use his brain.

But his gut was telling him this wasn't good at all.

DORY WAS ALL excited about Flash when she saw Betty
again that afternoon. "I feel like a kid at Christmas," she
confided. "That dog is wonderful. I fell in love instantly."

Betty laughed and poured the coffee. "I knew a dog was

a good idea. He'll brighten your days even if you never need him."

"I need him already," Dory admitted. "I'm so used to living in a world that exists only on my computer I'd forgotten a few other things might be nice. A friend like you, a dog like Flash."

"A man like Cadell," Betty remarked casually.

It took a second for Dory to catch on. "Betty! Are you trying to matchmake?"

"Never." Betty grinned at her. "I just meant you should give him a chance to be a friend. He's been in town for a year now, and I haven't heard anything but kind words about him. So I'm fairly certain you can trust him...as a friend. But I ought to warn you—grapevine has it that he had a messy divorce and he doesn't even date."

Dory shifted uncomfortably. She was well aware that Betty felt she cut herself off too much from the real world. And not just because of her job.

But trust didn't come easily to her. It hadn't since that night. It had even taken her godparents a while to get past the barriers that had slammed in place back then. If she hadn't already known and loved them, it might never have happened. Betty was the unique exception, worming her way past ice and stone and into Dory's heart.

"I'll try, Betty," she said eventually. "But I tend to get stubborn if I feel pushed." And anyway, she hadn't missed Betty's warning about Cadell's aversion to women. Which suited her fine.

"Tell me about it, girl." Then Betty laughed. "No pushing. Just saying Cadell's a nice guy and you can trust him. I'd never advise you to reach for more than that. Anyway, I've got some women friends you'd probably like, too, but you notice I haven't invited them over since you arrived."

Instantly Dory felt ashamed. "I'm sorry. I don't want to disrupt your life. You should just keep living the way you always do. If I get uncomfortable, I can take a walk. And I'll be in my new place soon. I can go tonight if you want."

Betty sat straight up. "What makes you think I want you to go? Cut it out. I love having you here. Anyway, you're not moving until Cadell gives you a dog." Pause. "When is George getting out?"

"Tomorrow, I think. Or maybe the next day." She looked down. "You'd think the date would be engraved in my memory, considering what it's doing to me."

Betty's face tightened. "Then you're definitely staying with me. You need someone around when the nightmares disturb you. Maybe the dog will help once you have him. I hope so. But in the meantime, you're not going anywhere."

"They're just dreams," Dory protested, although neither her heart nor her gut entirely believed it. Her brother was a living, breathing monster, not some fantasy creature. She might never see him again. In fact, she hoped she never did. But as long as she was alive, he rode in the cold seas of her memory, a very real threat.

Later, as she helped Betty make dinner, she made up her mind. She was moving tomorrow. She'd dealt with the nightmares all her life. Maybe not as bad as they were right now, but she'd dealt with them. She could continue to deal with them.

But she wasn't going to turn Betty into some kind of shut-in for her own benefit. No way. The woman had a life here and deserved to enjoy it. As for herself, well, even though George might be released tomorrow, there was no possible way for him to get here tomorrow. Or even the next day.

And she still couldn't imagine any reason why he'd ever want to see her again. They'd been close when she was little. He'd held her on his lap and read to her to distract her from their parents' fighting. But that had been a very long time ago. After twenty-five years, there was nothing left to put back together. Nothing.

Besides, whoever she had thought her brother was when she was little, he'd shattered all that one night in the kitchen. No way those shards would ever fit together again.

IN THE MORNING she drove herself out to Cadell's ranch for another training session. Betty had a meeting to attend, but having been to the ranch once, Dory didn't have any trouble finding the place. She loved driving down the battered county roads in the open places, looking at the mountains that appeared to jut up suddenly from nowhere. The land rolled, hinting at foothills, but these mountains looked as if they had been dropped there, not developed slowly over eons. Maybe that was just perspective, but she stored it in her mind for use someday in her art.

Cadell was waiting for her when she pulled up. He sat in a rocker on his wide front porch and stood immediately. The day was exquisite, Dory thought as she climbed out of her car. Warm but not hot, tickled by a gentle breeze. The kind of day where it was possible just to feel good to be alive.

"Howdy," he said from the top of the steps. Today he wore a long-sleeved tan work shirt, sleeves rolled up, and jeans. "You want to get straight to work or do you have time for some coffee first?"

He probably wanted coffee himself, and while she *was* in a hurry, wanting to get her move taken care of during the afternoon, she decided to be polite. The man was doing her a big favor, after all.

Inside, his house was welcoming, showing signs that he was doing some renovation.

"Excuse my mess," he said as they went to the kitchen. "My dad kind of let things go the last few years, and I couldn't get away for long enough to really take this place in hand."

"I don't mind. So you grew up here?"

"Yup. Left when I was twenty for the law enforcement academy, then I took a job in Seattle."

She sat at the table and watched him as he moved around digging out mugs and pouring coffee. Man, was he built. She wished he'd just sit down so her eyes wouldn't be drawn like a magnet.

"This must seem awfully tame after Seattle."

"I like that part." Smiling, he brought her coffee. Sugar and milk were already on the table. "I get to spend more time with the dogs."

"And ostriches," she dared to tease.

He laughed and sat across from her. "And ostriches," he agreed.

"So no idea how they came to be here?"

He shook his head. "Dad had enough time to set up the electrified fencing, but the vet, Mike Windwalker, tells me he only had them a couple of months before he passed. Mike had no idea where they came from, either—Dad just asked for his advice on keeping them healthy. Once. I wish he'd mentioned them when we talked on the phone, but he never did."

"Maybe he thought he wouldn't have them for long."

He shook his head a little. "Possible, I suppose, but that fencing…well, yeah, he'd have needed to do something quick to keep them from escaping. I'd love to know where they came from, but when I ask around, nobody seems to know a thing."

A smile suddenly split his face. "In a way it was funny. I got the call that Dad had passed, and as I was packing to get out here, I got a second call that left me floored. It was from Mike, the vet. He said he'd take care of the ostriches for a few days so not to worry. I'm standing there holding the phone with my jaw dropped. Ostriches?"

A giggle escaped Dory. "That'd be a shocker."

"Believe it. And I was no less shocked when I got here and found out how ornery they are." He paused. "Okay, maybe that's just my feeling and I ought to give them more of a chance. But they've already killed two of my favorite hats, and I don't much like being pecked whenever they feel like it. I'm hoping we can eventually reach a truce."

She glanced out his window and saw the two ostriches in the small pen not far away. They weren't especially cuddly looking, even now when they were just looking around. "Are they hard to care for?"

"I have to special-order feed for them. One of the big pet food companies also makes food for zoos, so that helps. Special ostrich blend. And in the winter when it gets too cold, I need to keep them in the barn."

"So they don't have to be in a warm climate all the time?"

"Evidently not." He sighed, half smiling, an attractive man comfortable in his own skin. She envied him that. Had she ever felt comfortable within herself, apart from her work? "I really would like to give them to someone who actually wants them."

"Wants them as pets?"

"Not likely. As far as I can tell, they weren't hand raised as babies. Or maybe they just don't like me." He shrugged. "But I won't sell them for meat or leather. Betty keeps reminding me that ostriches are worth thousands of dollars, but I'm not looking for that. There's a market for their eggs, though, a very expensive market, so I'm just trying to find someone who wants them for that, or for breeding. Although some days I think they'd make fine boots."

She laughed, delighted by his self-deprecating humor. "Are they really troublesome?"

He leaned back, turning his coffee cup slowly on the table with one hand. "In all fairness, no. If they were parakeet-sized, they'd be cool. They're not doing a darn thing birds don't do. They're just doing it in a *much* bigger way."

She laughed again. "I had a parakeet when I was ten. You have my sympathy. My bird liked to peck."

"These like to peck, too. It can be painful."

"And costly in terms of hats, you said?"

"Two of my favorites, gone." He suddenly grinned. "Come on, let's go work with Flash."

Her own eagerness surprised her, but it shouldn't have. Since she awoke this morning, she'd been impatient to see Flash again. She was already coming to love that dog, she realized. She hoped Cadell judged her ready to take him with her soon.

Then it struck her: she had no way yet to care for Flash. No food, no bowls, no bed, no leash…wow. She needed to take care of that fast.

She mentioned that to Cadell as they stepped out back through his mudroom. "I feel silly for not taking care of it yesterday."

He shook his head. "Every dog here has his own bowls and leashes, and they go with him. Same with his favorite toy. As for a bed…he'll sleep just about anywhere you let him, but I'm warning you, if you invite him onto the bed, he may claim possession."

That elicited another laugh from her, and amazement wafted through her again. She hadn't felt this good since she got the news about George. Her spirits were up, her confidence was high—all because of one dog trainer and a dog named Flash.

She wondered how long that would last.

He paused halfway to the dog run and faced her. "You can love him, Dory. Just don't spoil him. Remember, he's a working dog, and working makes him happy. Keep his training fresh and establish your boundaries. Then you'll have a great relationship."

She nodded and followed him, thinking that was probably good advice for people, too.

Flash's tail wagged fast, and she could have sworn he grinned at her as they approached. Excited or not, however, he didn't misbehave, and when released from his kennel, he merely nosed her hand in greeting. Dory, however, was a little more exuberant, squatting to rub his neck and sides. "You're a beautiful boy," she heard herself saying. Talking to a dog?

But as she looked into Flash's warm brown eyes, it suddenly felt right. She suspected this dog understood more than she would ever know.

She looked up at Cadell and found him smiling affectionately down at her and the dog. "Okay," he said, "let's go. Maybe you can take him home with you today."

CADELL REALIZED HE was developing a problem. His attraction to Dory wouldn't quit. Yes, she'd caught his eye with her almost ethereal beauty, but that should have worn off quickly. It wasn't as if she was the only beautiful woman he had ever seen.

No, something about her was reaching deeper than mere superficial attraction, and that wasn't good. He had years of experience in a lousy marriage to teach him that even cop groupies didn't necessarily like being married to a cop. The endless complaints that had assaulted him after the first six months of marriage should have been lesson enough. If something kept him late and he missed dinner, an explosion would result. If he had to break a date because of his job, he found no understanding. Sometimes he'd wondered if the woman would be glad if he never came home from one of his shifts.

It wasn't his safety that had worried her. No, she was annoyed that his job interfered with her life, and that was not a happy way to live, for either of them.

In the process he'd learned that love could die fast with the wrong person, and that was painful all by itself. Since his divorce, finally agreed to when the fighting became almost constant after a few years, he'd avoided entanglements. He didn't know whether he was guilty of lousy judgment—although as a cop his judgment was usually pretty good—or whether he was just poison. Brenda had turned into a woman he didn't recognize, and he wondered if that was his doing.

Anyway, even in his new job the unexpected happened. A search for a missing person could keep him from home for days, often without warning. And that was only one example. So...he judged it best to avoid long-term affairs. Maybe later in life, he told himself. Maybe when he retired from being a cop and devoted himself to the dog-training school he was slowly starting. Maybe after he got rid of those dang ostriches.

He enjoyed helping Dory run Flash through his paces, though. As the sun rose higher, with frequent breaks for Flash to lap water, he watched the woman and dog bond more securely. From his perspective, Flash had totally given his loyalty to Dory. He was already crazy about her.

There was no better protection than that. But there was still her brother. Unease niggled at Cadell. While a trained dog was great, it wasn't a perfect solution. There were always ways around a dog if you thought about it—usually a bullet.

When they were done with training and Dory sat on the hard ground to play tug with Flash for a little while, Cadell dropped beside her and stretched out, propping himself on an elbow.

"You ever marry?" he asked, mainly because if she told him she'd had a lousy marriage he could hope she'd have as many reasons to avoid involvement as he had. One thing for sure—with this woman he was going to need a lot of protection for himself. Everything about her appealed to him.

"No," she answered as she threw the knotted rope and Flash leaped into the air to catch it. Her reply was remarkable in its brevity. Interestingly, she didn't ask him, which would have been the usual conversational flow.

He decided to plunge in anyway. An understated warning to both of them. "I was," he said.

Her attention returned to him as Flash brought the rope back to her and dropped it in her lap. "Flash, down," she said. All of this was coming naturally to her, and he smiled. Flash obeyed immediately, head still high and curious. "Not good?" she asked.

"Awful," he said frankly.

"I'm sorry."

He wondered if he should tell her more, then decided to go for it. She'd gotten his attention enough in so many ways that he was going to be checking up on her frequently. Officer Friendly, as long as George might be a threat.

"My wife, Brenda, was a cop groupie." He watched her eyes widen. "Now, a smart cop knows that's dangerous, that most of those women just want a notch on the headboard. But Brenda seemed different. Maybe she was. I never heard of her sleeping with any of the other guys. But she used to sit there in the bar with big eyes, encouraging us to talk, basking in as much of the camaraderie as we were willing to share with her."

Dory nodded slowly. "I'm picturing it, but probably all wrong."

"Probably not. Some women love the uniform, not what's inside it. And some cops want brief affairs and one-night stands, just like the women. Consenting adults and all that. But Brenda seemed different. Unfortunately, she was."

Dory looked down and scratched Flash behind one ear. "How so?"

"I felt drawn to her, so I started sitting with her more and more often. As we got to know each other better, I decided she was genuine and I liked her. So we started dating. Long story short, I fell in love, we got married, and six months later I started to learn how wrong I was."

He plucked a blade of dried grass, shaking his head, then stared away from her out over the pasture to the nearby mountains. He'd had mountains in Seattle, but here...these were already special to him somehow.

"Anyway, it turned out she couldn't stand my job. Irregular hours, broken plans. She started in on me for being unreliable, demanding I find a regular job."

She drew an audible breath. "She called a police officer unreliable? Really?"

"In all fairness, from her perspective I probably was. I lost count of the times I missed dinner or a movie date with her. She wanted a very different kind of life, and I wanted to remain in law enforcement. So then it got truly ugly. No reason to rake it up. But I learned something."

"Yes?"

He looked up and found her blue eyes on him. "That maybe I should just avoid marrying anyone. I sure as hell was doing something wrong, something I never seemed able to fix unless I gave up part of myself."

Now it was her turn to look away toward the mountains. Whatever she was thinking, Flash sensed something and stirred a bit, raising his gaze to her face. Almost instinctively, she petted him.

"I never got that close to anyone," she said after a minute or two. "I couldn't tell you whether either or both of you were at fault."

"I'm not asking for that," he said quickly. "But since we're probably going to be seeing each other quite a bit because of Flash, I thought..."

"We could be friends," she finished for him. She turned her face toward him. "I don't make friends, Cadell. Except for Betty. She's the lone exception." She closed her eyes briefly, then snapped them open. "I'm incapable of real trust. Even years of therapy didn't help with that. So... consider me broken, which I guess I am."

Then she rose to her feet. Flash stood, too.

Cadell gave up on trying to reach her. He'd issued the warning he'd wanted to, but evidently she didn't need it.

Closed up, walled in, all because of something she saw as a child. He wished he could say that surprised him.

He stood, too. "Want to take Flash home with you today?"

"Betty's cats might object."

"I thought you were moving?"

"I almost decided to, then changed my mind. Tomorrow, when the internet is installed."

Everything settled, returning to normal. Back to business. "Okay," he said. "I'll keep him for you and bring him over tomorrow."

Flash wanted to go with her when she started toward her car, but she told him to stay. Looking forlorn, he settled on his belly and put his snout between his paws.

Dory didn't miss the expression. "Tomorrow, Flash. I promise."

Cadell watched her drive away, forgetting himself and standing too close to the penned ostriches. He ducked just in time and stepped away.

"Dang birds," he said, but his mind was elsewhere. He'd just learned a lot about Dory Lake, and far from putting him off, it made him hurt for her.

Damn her brother. If that guy showed up in this county, Cadell was going to feed him to the birds. The big birds.

Chapter Three

The next morning, Betty insisted on helping Dory move many of her belongings. Most of it was computer equipment, some very heavy, but Betty brought the clothes and lighter items for the kitchen.

The house was partially furnished, which made Dory's life easier, and already contained the items she'd had shipped here, mostly work related office furniture, including the extra battered old chair that tipped back farther than the new one. She loved to sit in it sometimes just to think. Eventually she could spiff the house or her office up if she wanted, but with most of her attention on her job, on creating graphics with her team, she was seldom more than half-aware of her surroundings.

The pile of clothes on her bed amused Betty, however. Jeans. T-shirts. More jeans. Sweatshirts. "Lord, girl, don't you ever dress up?"

"I don't have any need." But Dory laughed, too. It did look odd, all together like that. Add the plain undies and the three pairs of jogging shoes and she was sure she would appall most women.

"We have to do something about your fashion sense," Betty remarked.

"Why?" Dory asked. And that really *was* the question. She worked long days, she had no desire to socialize and the one man who'd managed to pierce her desire for isolation had told her he wasn't interested because he'd had a bad marriage. She didn't need a neon sign.

Betty followed her into her office and watched as Dory unpacked the real center of her life. "You know I love you," she said as Dory pulled out the first of six monitors.

"I know." She braced herself for what she was certain was coming.

"You need more of a life than your job. Won't you at least meet one or two people I think you'd like?"

"I met Cadell," she reminded Betty. "Nice guy. Also seriously burned by life."

Betty sighed, then said a bit sarcastically, "Well, at least you're a pair, then."

"Nope," said Dory. "Nice and all that, great dog trainer..."

"And gorgeous as hell," Betty said bluntly. "At least tell me you're not blind."

Dory paused, a power cord in her hand. "Betty? Please tell me you're not going to keep pushing me this way. Because if that's your goal, I'll stop unpacking right now."

The room nearly turned to ice as Betty stared at her. Then almost as quickly as it came, the ice thawed. "No, that's not my goal. I just worry about you. None of my business, I guess."

Betty turned and went to get some more items from the car. Dory stared after her, realizing she had just hurt her only friend in the world.

Well, take that as a warning, she told herself. All she brought was pain. Whatever lay at her core, it was locked away forever. And that hurt other people.

She returned to setting up her office, glad to know that soon she'd been in touch with her team, the nerds who were fun and smart and never demanded she get personal about anything. A meeting of minds. Who needed a meeting of hearts?

As she turned back to her desk and began to connect more cables, she felt herself easing back into her comfortable world where she could control everything she needed to. Even her desk, shipped from her old home, seemed like a warm greeting, encouraging a new life.

Her life. Then she thought of Flash. Okay, so maybe there was more to it than the digital world she lived in.

Betty returned, her voice announcing her. She was speaking with someone, and Dory instinctively stiffened.

She pivoted quickly to see Betty enter the office space with a woman wearing a tool belt.

"Dory, this is Rhonda, your cable man."

Rhonda laughed. "I'm your cable tech person."

Dory couldn't help grinning. "You get that, too?"

"All the time. Say, I hear you're into graphics design?"

Dory nodded.

"Then I'll make sure you have the best connection this company can offer. I'm a gamer. So what graphics cards do you use?"

Betty rolled her eyes. "I'll go get the last few things, then make some coffee. I can see what's coming."

Dory and Rhonda both laughed but soon were involved in the nuts and bolts of computing and bandwidth and a whole range of technical subjects. While they gabbed, Rhonda busied herself putting the connectors in the wall, testing them and then adding the routers. "The best we have," she said, placing the two routers on the desk. "Betty kind of rattled some bars, you know? So you'll have two broadband connections. That's what you wanted, right?"

"As long as they're not piggybacking and sucking up the bandwidth from each other."

"I'll take care of that at the junction outside. It's wonderful how far we're coming. A federal grant is making it possible, you know. High-speed connections in rural areas. You wouldn't have been able to stand it here a few years ago. We were still with the dinosaurs and dial-up."

"Oh, man, dial-up was a nightmare."

Rhonda finished quickly, considering all she had to do inside, including hooking up Dory's TV and converter box, and that was just the beginning. A lot more to do outside. But she took time for a quick cup of coffee with Dory and Betty before getting to it.

"Hope to see you again," she said cheerfully to Dory before she zipped out the door.

"Nice woman," Dory remarked and went back screwing, snapping, plugging and otherwise turning a collection of expensive hardware into two expensive, smoothly running workstations. Everything top-of-the-line. The max.

At last, though, she was able to turn everything on and test it. All good. She sent an email blast letting her team know she was back on the grid. Almost immediately her computer pinged with the arrival of emails.

She was home.

CADELL LEFT FOR work a couple of hours early, carting two dogs with him, Flash and Dasher. Dasher was eager to get to work, recognizing the backseat cage of the sheriff's department SUV as the beginning of adventure. Flash didn't see it that way, but he was glad to take a car ride.

He hoped he didn't unnerve Dory, dressed as he was in his khaki uniform, gun belt and tan Stetson. Not the guy she was used to seeing in shirts with rolled-up sleeves and jeans.

He pulled into Dory's driveway, behind a blue Honda sedan that had seen better years. The house was small and old in the way of many in this part of town, but it had been recently painted white. The driveway was two wheel paths of concrete, the sidewalk cracked but not heaving yet, and the porch from a time when porches were inviting.

Not that Dory would probably care about that. Betty had mentioned that Dory wasn't very sociable, and that she worried about her being too deeply mired in her work.

Being mired in work was something Cadell understood perfectly, so he didn't hold that against her. Given the woman's background, he wasn't even surprised that she had told him she couldn't trust. He figured Flash would be the best therapy he could offer her. Dogs had a way of getting past defenses.

He left Dasher in the car with the engine running so the air-conditioning would keep him cool and walked Flash on a leash to the front door.

"Your new home, Flash. You take good care of it."

He knocked. There was a doorbell, but cops never used them and the habit was impossible to break. At least he didn't use the heel of his fist or his big flashlight to resound through the house. A normal type of knock that shouldn't startle her.

A couple of minutes passed while he looked around the neighborhood and wondered if she had decided to take a walk. Clearly her car was here.

Then the door opened, and Dory was blinking at him. "Oh! You look so different in uniform, I almost didn't recognize you. I'm sorry, I forgot you were coming this afternoon."

He smiled. "Not a problem. If you want to take Flash's leash, I'll go get his supplies. Can't stay— my dog's in the car, and while it's specially built with heavy-duty air-conditioning to keep him cool...well, I never trust it too far."

He hesitated, holding the leash out to her. She bit her lower lip, then blurted, "Can you bring Dasher inside, too?"

He glanced at his watch and saw that he still had plenty of time to grab a bite at Maude's Diner and get to the station. "Sure. It might help Flash feel a little more at home."

She smiled then, a faint smile, but it reached her eyes as she accepted the leash. "These dogs are practically people to you," she remarked.

He had turned and now looked over his shoulder. "Nah. They're nicer than a lot of people."

That made her laugh quietly, and the sound followed him as he went to turn off his vehicle and get Dasher. He liked her, he realized. It wasn't just that she was beautiful. Oh, hell, he didn't need the trouble.

But he brought Dasher inside anyway and left him with Dory while he returned to the back of his car. Two bowls, a large padded bed, several tennis balls, chew toys and forty pounds of dry dog food later, he was sitting at her rickety kitchen table, watching her search her fridge for a soft drink to give him.

"So it's true computer types drink a lot of soda?" he asked casually.

"As long as it has caffeine. I can do a good job with a pot of coffee, as well. Orange, cola or lime?"

"Orange," he decided. "Cheetos?"

"Now that's a stereotype too far," she said with humor as she passed him the bottle of soda. Evidently it didn't come with a glass in her world. "Although," she said as she slid into the one other chair, "I did have a friend in college who loved to eat them sometimes, but she didn't like the grit on her keyboard. So she ate them with chopsticks."

The image drew a hearty laugh from him, and her smile deepened.

She spoke again. "Thanks for bringing all the doggy stuff. You never said, but how much do I owe you? You're giving me a well-trained guard dog that you must have spent a lot of time on."

He shook his head slowly. "I'm kinda thinking of Flash as an extension of my oath to serve and protect. He's a gift, Dory, if that won't offend you."

Her eyes widened. "But, Cadell..."

"No *but*s. You can be my advertising around town, how's that?"

Both dogs, trailing their leads, were sniffing their way around the house, checking out everything. Dory watched them for several minutes, the faint smile still on her face. After a bit she said, "I've never received a better gift."

"I hope you'll never need his finer skills."

"Me, too."

Silence fell. He glanced at his watch and saw he had a little longer. Somehow it didn't feel right to just walk out.

Then Dory surprised him by asking, "What else do you teach the dogs to do? There must be a lot involved in police work."

"Apart from what we taught Flash to do? Plenty. A dog has a wonderful nose, hundreds of times more sensitive than ours. It can follow scents that are weeks old, and even those that are high in the air. That's an extremely useful tool in searching, particularly search and rescue."

"Do you do a lot of search and rescue?"

"Around here? In the mountains, quite enough. Hikers, mainly. Then there are elderly people who sometimes ramble and forget where they are. Earlier this summer we had to hunt for an autistic girl. She'd wandered off, become frightened and hid in a culvert out of sight."

"Her parents must have been terrified. My word, *she* must have been terrified!"

He smiled. "She didn't trust us, but she trusted the dog."

He watched her smile again. For a woman who had come here to escape a possible threat, and who, according to Betty, suffered from a lot of nightmares, she smiled easily. Props to her, he thought.

"Anyway," he continued, "it's possible to train the dogs to hunt only for specific scents, too. Like explosives. Or drugs. Or cadavers."

Her smile faded. "Dead tissue?"

"We train them to distinguish human tissue from animal tissue, and their success rate is about ninety-five percent. They can find buried bodies a century old. And they can smell them down to at least fifteen feet, and some say up to thirty."

Her eyes had grown wider. "So they don't get confused?"

"No." But he didn't want to get into the details. Some things just didn't need to be talked about.

She looked down, then lifted her head and drank from her own bottle of orange soda. "How do they learn all this stuff? I mean, isn't it hard to teach them?"

"A little patience and they pick it up pretty quickly. They're remarkable, and they're eager to please." Dasher came over and laid his head on Cadell's thigh. "I think he's ready to go to work."

Dory popped to her feet immediately. "I'm sorry, I've been holding you up."

"Actually, no. I allowed some extra time." He reached into his breast pocket and pulled out a folded slip of paper. "Feeding directions and all that. If you have any questions, call me. And if you don't mind, I'll drop by every day or so to see how you two are getting on."

Holding the paper, she looked at him. "I'll never be able to thank you enough, Cadell."

He chuckled. "Tell me that again when you have fur all over the place. He doesn't shed a lot, but he's going to shed. See you tomorrow afternoon."

He headed for the door with Dasher and heard Dory behind him telling Flash to stay. The dog needed to learn his new home. He figured Dory was going to make it easy on him.

As he climbed into his vehicle with Dasher in the cage behind him, he realized something. Betty unintentionally had painted Dory unfairly. She might not be prepared to trust people and allow them within her circle; she might be scared to death of her brother's imminent release from prison; she might be haunted by terrible nightmares.

But Dory had grit. Real inner strength.

He liked her. He respected her. And he needed to watch his step, because he sure as hell didn't ever want to make another woman miserable.

DORY AND FLASH regarded each other in the kitchen. She'd removed his leash, but he sat there staring up at her as if he were pleading.

She tapped the piece of paper Cadell had given her. "It says here you don't get supper for another two hours."

Flash lowered his head a bit.

Feeling like the wicked witch, Dory scanned the paper again. "But you can have your dental chew. What the heck is that?"

She looked at the heap of supplies in one corner of her

kitchen, then rose to look through it. She discovered a plastic bag behind the huge bag of food. In it was a nubby nylon or plastic bone of some kind. Unzipping the bag, she pulled it out and turned to hold it out to Flash. "Is this what you want?"

He stared at it and licked his lips.

There could be a minor problem with a dog so well trained, she thought. Was he just going to sit there like a statue or let her know what he wanted? "Take it, Flash," she said finally in desperation.

He apparently understood that. In one leap he reached the bone and took it from her hand with amazing delicacy before settling down to gnaw on it.

"Well, cool," she said. "We have communication!"

Flash barely glanced at her. Almost grinning, she sat down at the table to read the directions from Cadell more carefully. From the other room she heard her email dinging, but she ignored it. Flash was more important.

She nearly giggled when she read what Cadell had typed at the top of the page: *The care and feeding of your personal K-9.* She wondered if he gave that to all his trainees.

Flash looked up at her, forgetting his bone for a few seconds as he wagged his tail at her. He seemed so happy right now, it was impossible not to feel the same.

LATER, AFTER SHE had caught up on email and reopened her participation in the project, she felt a nose gently prod her thigh. A glance at the clock told her it was after eleven… and she hadn't walked Flash since he arrived.

She put her conference on hold, explaining she needed to walk her dog. Hoping she didn't get the slew of jokes she half expected, she found Flash's leash. The dog gave one joyful bark, then stood perfectly still while she hooked it to his collar.

That was when it struck her how late it was. Ordinarily she worked well into the night, but before she hadn't been afraid of anything. Now she was afraid. Her brother might already be out of prison. They'd given her the exact date, but she'd run the letter through the shredder as soon as the shock had passed. She wanted nothing with his name on it.

So today. Maybe tomorrow, but most probably today. Betty knew for sure because Dory had told her, but it was too late to call and verify it.

Point was…she was suddenly frightened of the night and its secrets, a fear she hadn't felt in a long time.

She looked at Flash and saw him watching her, not a muscle twitching. He must have felt her abrupt burst of dread.

"I shouldn't be silly about this," she said aloud, not entirely believing herself. "I have you, after all."

The slightest wag of Flash's tail. God, the dog seemed to be reading her like an open book. Could he do that?

"I promised to take good care of you. I'm sorry I didn't walk you sooner, but do you think you could manage with just a short trip to the backyard?"

He looked agreeable, but he probably didn't understand a word of her prattle. God, she had grown so completely unnerved for no good reason. George, even if he wanted to find her, couldn't have located her yet. She hadn't even needed to leave a forwarding address, because she paid all her bills online and the rest was junk. She'd established no real connections here yet except the broadband and that didn't have her full name on it. She was truly off the grid as far as the world was concerned.

She would be very hard to find, she assured herself as she began to walk toward the back door. "Flash, heel," she said quietly, and he walked right beside her.

Besides, she had a guard dog. Flash would make George's life hell. So she was safe, yeah?

She just wished she could believe it.

The night beyond the door felt pregnant with threat. But it was the same backyard that had been there when she rented the place. With a locked six-foot wooden privacy fence around it. She'd know if anybody tried to get past that.

And there was Flash, of course. Oddly, however, as impressed as she was by the dog, she didn't know if she was prepared to put her life in his paws.

God, she was losing it. Stiffening her back, she pulled the door open and let herself out with the dog. Should she unleash him?

But Flash seemed to be reading the situation well. As soon as they reached grass near a shrub, he did his business, then turned around to face the house again. He sensed she wanted to get back behind locked doors.

Tonight she was in no mood to disagree, or to even try to reason through her probably unreasonable fear. Just get back inside and give Flash a treat. Tomorrow in the daylight she could give him a longer walk, even work with him.

But not tonight. She felt as if evil lurked out there, and she didn't want to find out if she was right.

GEORGE NEEDED MONEY to travel. Everything else was on hold until he had more than the pittance he'd received at his release late that afternoon, fourteen hours earlier than he'd expected. But then, he'd been a model prisoner, and he noticed they'd dated the paperwork for the next morning.

But he didn't have enough money to travel on or eat while he figured out exactly how he was going to deal with Dory. The bus ticket they'd given him was nonrefundable, meant only to take him back to the place where he'd originally lived—a small suburb of Saint Louis.

He'd been given the address of a halfway house, so he went there, arriving late at night, and resigned himself to spending some time figuring out how to get his hands on some money quickly. He sure as hell didn't intend to work any of the low-paying menial jobs they probably would point him to. He had bigger things to hunt.

Even though it was late, with his release papers he got inside the door. They showed him to a bedroom and didn't seem particularly worried that he asked to use a computer. The residents had one in a public room downstairs. Help himself.

So he did. He was too keyed up to just go to sleep. He'd dozed on the bus anyway. The only thing about this that shocked him was his surprising discomfort at not being surrounded by walls when he'd walked from the bus to this place. Not having his every movement watched or directed.

He'd never imagined the world could feel so big, and he suspected that once tomorrow began and life resumed out there, it was going to overwhelm him with chaos. He wasn't used to chaos anymore. The order of his days had become deeply embedded over twenty-five years.

But so had sitting at a computer and hunting for information about his sister. She had vanished from the town where she had grown up. She was reputed to be a partner in a graphics business that had no address other than a web URL and email. The godparents who had raised her were dead.

He needed to know more about her than this, but he suspected if he called people around here in their old hometown he'd meet a brick wall. Well, unless he could somehow convince them he was someone else. Not likely. He feared too many local people might remember him. Maybe not young people, but the older ones who had probably devoured all the lurid details in the newspaper and on the evening news.

With that thought in mind, he headed upstairs to his room, where his bed was ready to be made. His own room. It had been a while. Not big, but bigger than a cell, without a cell mate.

For a little while the space bothered him, but then he settled down. Room was a good thing. If he thought back very hard to his early days in the slammer, he remembered how claustrophobic he had felt. No more of that.

Now there was infinite freedom.

He needed to remember how to enjoy it. To use it.

Chapter Four

Dan Casey dropped by Cadell's place in the morning. Dan had recently married a woman with a young daughter and was now expecting an addition to the family. Fellow deputies, he and Cadell had built a good friendship.

"So," said Dan, pausing near the ostrich pen. The birds had been let out into the larger corral but didn't seem interested in taking advantage of the space. They regarded Dan with the same glare they gave Cadell. Dan shook his head.

"So?" Cadell asked.

"Krys wants to come out and see the birds," Dan remarked, referring to his five-year-old stepdaughter.

"Krys would be snack-sized for those demons," Cadell said with a wink. "Bring her anytime I'm home."

"And then there's the puppy she wants."

"Ah. Come on in, if you have time. Is she thinking young puppy? The vet has plenty for adoption."

"I know." Dan shrugged. "She likes the police dogs."

A chuckle escaped Cadell. "You're in for it. And I don't mean from the dog."

"I didn't figure."

They walked into the house together. The morning's coffee had just finished brewing, so Cadell poured a couple of cups and they settled at his trestle table, left over from the days when hired hands ate with the family.

Cadell asked, "So what's happening with Krys and what does her mother think?"

"Well, that's the other question. Vicki has mixed feelings. She thinks a dog would teach Krys some responsibility but that in the end the two of us would be taking care of most of it. The idea of a puppy is irresistible, but every time Vicki mentions it, Krys gets a very mulish look and says she wants a police dog."

Cadell nodded slowly. "Her birth father was a cop, wasn't he?"

"Yeah, and Vicki's wondering how much that has to do with this. It's hard to tell, but maybe Krys has some lingering fears because of her father's death."

Cadell pondered that as he sipped his first cup of coffee for the day. A lot more would probably follow. "Well, I can give her a well-trained dog that would protect her and obey her. But you or Vicki are going to have to keep the training fresh or you'll wind up with just another dog. Which might be okay."

Dan sighed and rapped his fingers on the table. "The problem is, Krys isn't being very clear about exactly what she means by a police dog. Does she just want to know it's a police dog? Does she want it to be able to do certain things? One thing for sure, I am not giving that child a dog that will attack on command."

Cadell had to laugh. "I wouldn't dream of it. A kid that young? One temper tantrum…"

"Exactly." Dan grinned. "I don't think she'd tell the dog to hold us at bay, but by the time she's a teen that could change."

Both men laughed then.

Cadell spoke as his laughter faded. "I can make sure the dog recognizes certain people as friends, no problem. And I can train it to protect her without an attack command." He paused and lifted one brow. "You *do* understand that if the dog perceives a threat to her, he *will* attack without a command?"

Dan frowned. "Depends on what kind of threat. I mean, the mailman holding out an envelope…"

Cadell shook his head. "No, more like a stranger takes her by her arm or hand. Or tries to get her in a car. Come on, Dan, you've worked with these dogs before. You must have some idea of how well they can discriminate."

"Most of the ones I've worked with haven't been that

finely tuned. I didn't know if they could be. So, okay. I'll leave it to you."

Cadell hesitated. "Wait a sec. I have an idea. I just gave a guard dog to a new friend in town."

"Dory Lake? I heard about her from Betty, I think it was." Dan was suddenly all cop. "What's the problem?"

"Her older brother killed their parents. He just finished a twenty-five-year sentence, and Dory is naturally nervous about him being on the loose again." He didn't offer anything more than that. Not his place. Dan could look up the same files, if he wanted to.

Dan frowned. "She might have a reason to be worried." Then he returned to the subject at hand. "So what's your idea?"

"I just thought that with Dory's permission maybe you and Vicki and I could bring Krys to see Dory's dog, Flash. He's a youngster, just two, and trained only to protect. Krys might discover she wants something very different."

"I like that idea," Dan agreed. "It might settle Vicki some, too. I think she's concerned about putting a potentially lethal K-9 in the hands of a five-year-old."

"I wouldn't do that," Cadell said. "I hope you know that. But I'd really like to meet Krys again and talk about it. See if we can find out what's going on in the child's head."

"I'd love to know that, too. It's not like her dad was a K-9 handler. I don't know where this came from. But," Dan said with a shrug, "I often don't know where Krys gets some of her ideas. She's a mystery at times."

AROUND TWO THAT AFTERNOON, Dory stretched and turned off her computer monitors, allowing her recent construct for the graphics scene to render into a high-definition, nearly realistic image. It wouldn't take long, given the power and number of graphics cards she had, but it did remind her that she needed to take Flash on a longer walk than just around her backyard. She'd also promised to work with him to keep him fresh

Perfect time to do her part by the dog and grab something to eat, maybe a sandwich. She and Betty had stocked her freezer with easy-to-prepare foods, although Betty had tsked quite a bit and said Dory had to promise to come over every Sunday for a decent meal.

Amused, shaking her head, she said aloud, "Flash, walk." She heard the scrabble of his claws on the wood floor in the hall, and by the time she reached the front door he was standing there with his leash in his mouth.

Smart dog, she thought. Also probably desperate by now. She was sure he was used to a whole lot more activity.

"I guess nobody warned you that I forget time when I work," she said to Flash as she bent to connect his leash. "Sorry about that, boy." She ruffled his fur and scratched between his ears, but there was no mistaking his eagerness. He moved from paw to paw as if he could barely contain his excitement.

Maybe she should set an alarm to remind her that she needed to make dog time now. She stuffed a plastic bag in her pocket for cleaning up after him.

"Ready?" she asked. Stupid question. The dog was over-ready. "Flash, heel."

They stepped out the front door together in time to see Cadell pull into her driveway. Once again the official vehicle and the uniform. Dory had never been keen on uniforms, but this guy...well, he filled that khaki uniform exceptionally well.

She waved, and he waved back as he climbed out. "Going somewhere?" he called.

"Flash and I are taking a walk."

"I'll bring Dasher along, too, if you don't mind some company."

Dory didn't even hesitate. For once she was glad of company. The world around her seemed to be growing more threatening by the day, and no amount of internal argument could change the feeling. George was on the streets again. George blamed her for his conviction. She'd heard that clear enough, even though she hadn't testified and had still been in a state of utter shock. "Great. You can tell me if I'm doing it right."

They reached the corner without either of them speaking. Dasher and Flash were completely well behaved, waiting patiently to learn which direction they were supposed to take.

"Any preference about where you want to walk?" Cadell asked.

"Honestly, I've been out jogging nearly every day, but I'm totally unaware of my surroundings. My head is on my projects, and everything else goes away when I run."

Cadell hesitated, then said, "Right now that's not wise, Dory. Yes, you'll have Flash with you, but you need to be aware of your surroundings. Not to mention learning your way around."

She flushed faintly, knowing he was right. Scared as she was of her brother, she couldn't afford to be off in her own world when she was outside. But running cut her free, let her mind wander in ways that could be extremely useful and creative.

She frowned down at the pavement, trying to figure out how to balance this. Just how afraid was she of George? Afraid enough to pay attention? To relinquish some of her best thinking time?

She lifted her head and looked around the quiet neighborhood. It seemed so benign, her fears so out of place. Yet the neighborhood she had lived in as a child hadn't been much different. Quiet. Benign. And then a monster had emerged in her own house.

"Okay," she said finally. "You're right. I don't like it, but you're absolutely right."

"You don't have to be hyperalert," he said. "You *will* have Flash keeping an eye out. But you at least have to know where you are and develop a sense for when something isn't right. For your own peace of mind, really."

He had a point. She'd skipped jogging yesterday because of George, all the while telling herself how ridiculous she was being. Even if George knew where she was—highly doubtful—it would take him at least some time to get here.

She turned to the right, and they resumed walking. Soon she admitted something that was hard to say out loud. "I think I've endowed my brother with some of the qualities of a supervillain."

"How so?"

"Oh, you know. Finding me. Getting here in an instant, walking through walls...I don't know, exactly. Even if he knew I was here, it would take time for him to arrive. Yet yesterday I skipped my run."

"I'm sorry you skipped your run. But I understand the rest."

She glanced up at him. "How could you possibly understand that kind of insanity?"

"Because I've seen what a truly horrible experience can do to the human mind and heart. The impossible has become possible. Why not all the rest, as well? That's not insanity."

"Maybe not." She couldn't believe she had just revealed that to him. But Cadell seemed like an honestly nice guy, and he'd been understanding of her fears from the outset. Maybe she needed more than one person to talk to. Betty had heard most of it more than once. Maybe all she wanted was a fresh perspective.

"So," he said two blocks later, during which she had tried to pay attention to everything around her, "do you think you might do me a favor?"

Everything inside her tensed. That would depend, she thought, although she stopped herself from saying it out loud. Heavens, the man had given her a beautiful guard dog. She owed him...if she was capable of providing what he wanted.

"What's that?" she asked cautiously.

"One of my friends—also a deputy, by the way—has a five-year-old stepdaughter, almost six. Her dad was a cop who was killed. Anyway, he says she's lately become determined to get a police dog. Neither of us is sure why or what she really wants. So…could I bring her over to see Flash? He hasn't got the kind of training that would make her parents nervous, but he might be exactly what she needs. I don't know. How could I?" He laughed quietly. "I'm not sure where this demand is coming from, but she's adamant. Not a puppy, but a police dog."

Dory felt torn. A little girl who'd lost her dad. She identified with that. But she didn't want to sink social roots in this town. She didn't want to socialize at all. Life was so much clearer when she kept to herself and simply worked. Trust never became an issue.

But a little girl? One not so very different than Dory herself had been once. Some string in her heart began to knit a connection of some kind, like it or not.

"All right," she said. She was sure she didn't sound enthusiastic.

"If it's too much trouble…"

She whirled then. Flash stopped walking and came to stand right beside her, but she hardly noticed. "It's not a matter of trouble. It's a matter of me. I'd rather be a hermit, if you haven't heard. Bring the child over. At least I can trust *her*."

She resumed her walk with Flash, leaving Cadell and Dasher behind. Well, that was a lunatic sort of thing to have said, she thought irritably. People around here were evidently going to insist on pushing into her life. She needed that to stop.

But then she remembered the gift of the dog trotting beside her and felt like an absolute ingrate. A sleaze. Couldn't she at least put a pleasant veneer over her scarred personality?

Abruptly she halted and pivoted on one foot. Cadell was right there behind her, his face revealing nothing.

"I'm sorry," she said.

"You're under a lot of stress," he replied. "I guess I'm adding to it."

Aw, heck, she thought as they resumed their walk. Now she was making *him* feel like a problem when all he had done was be incredibly kind and understanding. Flash scooted over onto some grass to do his business, and she pulled the plastic bag out of her pocket, picking up the mess, then knotting off the bag.

"You're not adding to anything," she said after a bit. "You've been great to me. The problems are all my own. I'm not usually like this, but…"

"Well, you've moved, your brother is out of prison, you're having problems with that…I'd say that's not usual by any means."

"I don't deserve excuses. I need to learn to handle all this. It's the way life is, now."

And this version of life evidently didn't include her hiding out with her computers and her projects except when she had to emerge to buy groceries. Nope. Now there was Betty nearby, and Cadell, who seemed determined to keep an eye on her, and some little girl who'd lost her daddy.

The idea of the little girl wormed past her defenses, and she felt an ache in her heart. Their stories might be different, but she understood the loss that child must feel, and for the girl it was relatively recent.

"What's your friend's daughter's name?"

"Krystal. Everyone calls her Krys."

"How long ago did she lose her father?"

"Two years now. About anyway."

"How sad." Dory sighed. "Sorry for my outburst. By all means, bring her over to meet Flash. Just call and let me know first."

CADELL SPENT A little time in the backyard with Dory and Flash, refreshing him, but Dory didn't show her usual joy in the exercise. She looked pensive, and he hoped he wasn't responsible for that.

So she wanted to be a hermit. Well, some people were built that way. Completely introverted. The thing was, Dory didn't act introverted. Avoidance was something else altogether. And he gathered from what Betty said that she worked with a team online, chatting with them around the clock.

Now that might not be face time, but it was still a group of relationships she'd built. Did she feel safer because of the distance? Because if there was one thing he'd noted, it was that people could become very close online and could be seriously hurt by people they never set eyes on.

So Dory's fortress might not be as safe as she believed.

But he shoved that aside, thinking of her fears about her brother and how they must be pushing her right now. She'd come here to hide out, and by now she might very much want a hole to disappear into.

Instead he was bringing some new people into her life, one of them a little girl he was sure wouldn't allow her to remain detached. He sensed that Dory was identifying with Krys already.

Now he had to wonder if he'd made a huge mistake by trying to help a friend. But the simple fact was he didn't want Krys to become attached to one of his nearly trained police dogs. They were already assigned. Which left Flash as an example of the dog he could train for her. Even as young as Krys was, she would certainly understand that Flash was Dory's dog, something not as easy to explain at his kennels, where he had a number of dogs and worked individually with their handlers most of the time. Out there it might not be clear that a dog wasn't adoptable.

So that left Dory. And maybe a bit of him trying to get in deeper than he should. He had this little niggle that Krys might be able to pierce Dory's barriers in a way no one else could.

He didn't bother asking why he should care. He just did. Which, he reminded himself, ought to be a huge warning. Klaxons ought to be going off in his head. Time to turn around and walk away.

But he didn't. He was, however, disappointed when she said all too soon, "I've got to get back to work. I have a team waiting on me. They know I went out with the dog, but they're probably wondering if I got kidnapped."

He managed a faint smile. "Do they know about your brother?"

Her face closed instantly. "No."

She headed toward her house, leaving him to find his way out of the fenced backyard. "I'll call before I bring Krys over," he said.

She barely glanced back. "Thanks. Thanks for everything, Cadell."

Thanks for what? he wondered as he let himself and Dasher out the gate and walked to his car. He hadn't done anything. Well, except for giving her a dog she desperately needed.

Shaking his head a little as he put Dasher in the backseat, he wondered at himself. He'd probably way overstepped himself by asking her to let Krys come over. Because it wouldn't just be Krys, and she knew it. It would be Krys and at least one parent.

People she evidently didn't care to meet. Interrupting the life she'd worked long and hard to build for herself.

He snorted at his own folly as he backed out of her driveway. He was acting like a stupid moth, coming back to the flame again and again. But she wasn't a flame. The sight of her might ignite his own fires, but he'd seen enough to know that Dory might singe him with cold. Bitter cold.

DORY SLIPPED BACK into her chair at her desk and soon forgot everything else as she dived into working on her part of the animation they were creating, and chatting with the other members of her team. Mostly they talked business, tools, ways to solve problems and new ideas. Once in a while they became more personal, but she hid herself well. She doubted any of them guessed that D. K. Lake was a woman. Given the harassment of women online, she wanted to keep it that way. Not that any of her colleagues would dump on her, but if word got out that one of Major Animation's creative team was a woman? No, thanks.

After a couple of hours, concentration escaped her and she realized that her thoughts were drifting to other things. God, she been nearly rude to Cadell, if not outright rude.

No, she wasn't thrilled about meeting this little girl, because caring was such a dangerous thing. But a five-year-old? Yeah, she'd have to meet at least one of the parents, but that didn't have to go beyond a half hour or so. The kid wanted a dog. Cadell had thought one trained like Flash, rather than his other dogs, would be best.

Would it kill her to be helpful? Being helpful didn't mean she had to become involved.

Except for Betty, only her godparents had gotten inside the walls erected by one horrific night in her family kitchen. Of course she knew people. She'd made friends all the way through high school and college. But she'd never let those people close. They never met the real Dory Lake, because she never let them. She skimmed the surface with them while holding herself apart.

She'd had enough therapy to know exactly what she was doing, and she had absolutely no desire to change that about herself. That shell she kept around her innermost being was all that protected her. She'd learned that the hard way.

As Flash rested his head on her thigh, and she looked down at him, she realized her wall might have been penetrated. Just a little bit.

Sighing, she patted the dog and returned to work.

Chapter Five

More than a week later, on a Saturday morning, Cadell joined Dan and little Krystal at Dory's house. Last night he'd checked up on George Lake and had found some disturbing news. He didn't know whether to share it or not, but this morning he was determined to let no shadow hover over Krys's meeting with Flash and her desire for a police dog. Maybe later, he'd tell Dory what he'd learned.

She greeted both him and Dan pleasantly at the door, but he noticed circles under her eyes. She wore a burgundy sweatshirt labeled Heidelberg, as if she were chilled on this summer morning, and jeans. Her feet were covered with socks. Beside her, alert, stood Flash, his head cocked inquiringly.

"Come on in," she said, swinging the door wide. "I was just about to put my shoes on."

Once inside her small foyer, introductions were made. She shook hands with Dan, giving him a pleasant smile, then squatted down until she was at eye level with Krys. "I heard about you, Krys. So you want a police dog?"

Krys nodded quickly. "Dan says you have one. Is that him?"

"That's Flash. He's beautiful, isn't he?"

"He's big," came the response. "Can I touch him?"

"Sure. Flash, sit. Shake." That was her own addition to Flash's repertoire, surprisingly easy to teach to this very bright dog. Flash obediently sat and extended his right front paw.

Krys giggled and reached for it. "I like him!"

Flash apparently liked her, too. If dogs could grin, he was grinning now.

"But is he a *real* police dog?" Krys asked. Apparently,

she wasn't about to be snowed. Cadell caught the smile on Dory's face as she stood up. She looked at him.

"I trained him," said Cadell. "He's a good guard."

Krys looked up at him. "No biting?"

"No biting." Not exactly true but true enough. "He only bites if you tell him to."

"Mommy says I can't have a dog that bites."

Cadell looked at Dan. Dan half shrugged, then said, "I don't think she meant a dog that wouldn't bite a bad man. Does that worry you, Krys?"

"Not if it's only bad men." Her face grew serious. "There are bad men. One killed my daddy. I wish he had a dog."

Three adults exchanged looks, but as soon as the cloud appeared, it blew away, and Krys asked, "Can I play with him, too?"

"Of course you can," Dan said. He looked at Dory and Cadell. Dory smiled and waved toward the back door. "You guys take him out. I need to finish up something."

BUT INSTEAD OF returning to her computers, Dory wound up standing at the back window of her bedroom, watching the two men and the little girl play with Flash.

God, Krys tugged at her heart. Another child's life forever scarred by someone murderous. She could easily imagine some of what that little girl was living with.

The window was open a few inches to let the summery breeze in, and she heard some of the conversation.

"Flash won't let you tell him what to do," Cadell was explaining. "He only listens to me and Dory. So your dog would only listen to you and your parents, okay? That's part of what makes a police dog different."

So Cadell was going to give that little girl a version of Flash. Dory wondered if the child was haunted by nightmares, or by fears she didn't know how to express.

None of her business, she told herself. Not a thing she could do about it. Returning to her office, she buried her head in her work. Work was her salvation. Creating artificial worlds made her happy.

Little enough else did.

A HALF HOUR LATER, she heard Krys's piping voice go out the front door and assumed she was once again alone. She wished she knew how to reach out better, especially to that little girl. Everything inside her seemed to freeze up, though, leaving her basically useless. God, it would be easy to hate herself.

She heard Flash trotting toward her, and soon his head rested on her thigh. She reached out automatically to scratch his neck while she watched her latest animation unfold on her screen.

Water was rushing into the ground floor of a building, sweeping furniture and other debris before it. As she watched, she was keeping an eye out for ways to improve it.

"That's cool," said a voice behind her.

She nearly jumped out of her skin. Whirling around, she saw Cadell standing in the doorway of her office. Her heart had nearly climbed into her throat, making it impossible for her to speak.

"Very cool," he repeated. "Did you make that?"

She gave a stiff nod.

"I'm impressed. Sorry I startled you—I thought you heard me heading this way. I wanted to thank you for letting Dan and Krys see Flash."

"No problem," she mumbled, waiting for her heartbeat to slow. "Krys can come again, if she wants."

"That's generous of you. I could tell you were uneasy about it. And the way you looked at Krys... At least she didn't see anything, Dory. She was at home in bed when her father was killed."

"Does it matter?" she asked stiffly.

"Sorry?"

It was as if a wrench turned inside her, loosening a

huge bolt. Before she knew what she was going to do, she started talking.

"There was this little girl," she said, looking down at her lap. Flash had settled at her feet. "She was just seven years old. She thought her big brother was the best person in the whole world. She worshipped him."

Glancing up, she saw Cadell nodding, his expression utterly grave.

"Her big brother used to play games with her," she continued. "Read her stories. Carry her around on his shoulders. He made her laugh a lot. Their parents were strict, but he made it seem not so bad. Sometimes he said he'd done something when the little girl had really done it so she didn't get punished. And when the little girl couldn't sleep at night because of the fighting, he sometimes came into her room in the dark and told her stories. Safe stories. Stories without people arguing."

"I'm listening," Cadell said quietly.

"Their parents didn't fight a lot. It wasn't often. But then they started fighting with her big brother, and the little girl was bothered. She knew her big brother was staying out too late, and that her parents thought he was doing things he shouldn't, but she thought her big brother was a good guy."

She drew a shaky breath. "She loved her big brother. Until one night. The fighting was loud, bad, scary. They were fighting with her brother. She knew she wasn't supposed to go downstairs, but she was worried about him. So she crept down the stairs and…" Her voice broke. She panted the last words, struggling for the breath to get them out. "She discovered her brother had turned into a monster."

CADELL DIDN'T MOVE for long moments. His chest felt as if steel bands had wrapped around it and were tightening with every breath. For the first time in his life, he absolutely did not know what to do.

Touching her, even to offer comfort, might send her

into flight. This was the woman who wanted to be a hermit. Part of him was amazed that she'd told him her story in such an intimate way. Another part of him was alarmed that she was so vulnerable now—a wrong word or movement could lock her down forever.

Something about Krys had drawn this out of Dory, because he was sure he'd done nothing to make it possible for her to drop her guard this way. To open up. Hesitantly, he finally said, "What about Krys?"

At that she seemed to snap into focus and looked at him. Whatever emotions had been rising out of her depths suddenly backed off—swallowed, he thought, by her cultured distance. "Krys? So what if she didn't see anything bad? She went to bed one night and woke up in the morning to learn that her dad was never coming home again. That's hard to deal with."

"I'm sure." He took a tentative step toward her, wishing the tension would leave her face. "So you think the dog will help her?"

"Flash helps *me*."

Well, that sure as hell made him feel good. Finally he reached her and squatted right in front of her chair. The news he'd learned that morning was going to have to wait.

"Can you get away?" he asked.

"Get away?"

"Out of here for a while. For a drive, a walk, whatever."

Perplexity awoke on her face, dispelling some of the tension. "You're in uniform. Don't you have to work?"

"I need to stop by the ranger station for a few minutes. They want some K-9s, too, but it won't take long to sort out. You might enjoy meeting Desi Jenks. She's a pistol. Anyway, can you take some time?"

He watched her hesitate, turning her head to the loop of flooding waters that was repeating on her monitor, almost like she wanted to dive into it. Then he watched a shudder pass through her, as if she were releasing tension. "Okay," she said finally. "I guess I do need to get out for a little while. It'd do me some good. Give me a minute to let my team know I'll be back later."

"What?" he said lightly. "You mean you don't carry them with you on a cell phone?"

At that her demeanor changed entirely, and she smiled faintly. "I've noticed there are a few dead zones around this town."

"We all have that problem. It's getting better but not perfect." He straightened and turned toward her door. "I'll be out front, but I need to get to Desi over her lunch hour." He glanced at his watch. "Which is very soon."

"Okay," she said briskly, once again all business. She turned to her computer, and he watched words popping up on one of the screens not displaying the flood or grids of some kind. "How long should we be?"

"Not long for Desi, probably, but if you want to see a little of the area, give us a couple of hours."

"Okay." She tapped away, chuckled quietly and then faced him again. "Let me get my shoes. Is Flash coming?"

"I hope you don't consider going anywhere without Flash."

"The supermarket might object," she said lightly.

"Then I'll get him a vest. Get your shoes."

DORY FELT ODD, and she acknowledged it as she went to get her jogging shoes. First that unexpected dump about what had happened to her as a child. She wasn't sure what had brought that on, but she had a feeling it very much had to do with Krys. Identification. A need to make it clear to at least one person that losing a parent left wounds behind, no matter whether you saw any part of it.

But she'd never told her story quite that way to anyone. She also hadn't finished it. She wondered if she should. She gave Cadell marks for not reacting as if there was anything he could do. Her experience was in the past, beyond changing, beyond reaching. Long ago she'd grown tired of those who upon hearing about her past wanted to make it better with a hug or trite phrases. She understood everyone had meant well, but it had all been useless. Her soul had been twisted and hammered into a different shape by what she had seen, and nothing was ever going to wrench it back into shape.

At last she left the house, locking it up behind her although she'd once asked Betty why she never locked her house.

Betty had laughed. "Around here? Nobody does."

But not everyone had the kind of expensive computer equipment Dory used. Hers might look just slightly larger than usual towers, but she had several four-thousand-dollar graphics cards in there, not to mention all the add-ons. If she had to replace much of that stuff—never mind her work—she could easily spend twenty thousand dollars or more. So she locked the door and kept the curtains closed all the time to conceal what was inside. Betty might say theft was rare around here, but why hang the temptation out for all to see?

She and Flash climbed into the car with Cadell. Dasher was in the backseat and woofed a greeting. Flash answered.

Dory felt relieved when her sense of humor began to awaken. "They're like best buddies."

"They'll probably have a great conversation with their noses back there. By the time we get to the station, they'll know all about what each has been doing since their last meeting."

Dory smiled, thinking it was very likely possible. "So we're going to meet a ranger?"

"Well, not a ranger, per se. She's the local senior game warden, otherwise known as a redshirt."

"Why redshirt? Or is that obvious?"

He laughed. "Obvious. They all wear red shirts. Mostly

with jeans, boots and cowboy hats, although ball caps are creeping in. Very laid-back approach to uniforms."

She thought it would seem that way to him. His khakis were pressed and even had military creases in the shirt. "Well, with shirts that distinctive, they probably don't have to worry about the rest."

"Nope. They're pretty readily identified."

"I've never met a game warden before."

"You'll like Desi. No nonsense and damn good at what she does. She broke up a ring of unlicensed outfitters last fall. Pretty risky business. But then, her job has its own set of risks. I'm not the one heading out into the woods during hunting season when everyone is armed."

That drew a laugh from her. It felt good to be out, she realized. Sunshine, warm air blowing through the window. She spent too much time in her cave. Seasons could go by almost unnoticed. She averted her head, looking out the window at the small houses they passed, then the open areas. The drive to the station wasn't long, but long enough for her to start wondering if she was in love with her work or if she was hiding in it.

The question made her uncomfortable, and she shoved it aside. George was out of prison. Soul-searching was going to have to wait until she was sure he wanted nothing to do with her.

No reason he should. The words had become almost a mantra inside her head: *No reason George should want to find her.*

Now all she needed to do was believe it.

GEORGE FOUND HIS sister in remarkably short order. Yeah, it took a few days, but she was a presence on the web because of her design work, no matter how hard she tried to hide behind her initials. Besides, he'd found out about her job years ago.

As for the money he needed...well, that was easy enough

to pick up. No rotten job necessary. He'd sweet-talked a woman in her fifties, giving her a sob story that made her invite him to stay with her. It wasn't long before she'd given him all the money he needed, and he was quite sure she'd be too ashamed to tell the cops what had happened.

So he was able to vanish from the halfway house. He told them he'd found a job in another town. None of their concern, since he was a free man and the halfway house was only supposed to be temporary.

He hung around for another week, treating the woman like a queen, feeling sickened every time he made her titter like a girl. At her age. Really.

After that he left for a "job interview" and never went back. Even if she decided to call the cops, she didn't know his real name, she'd never taken a photo of him and he'd been very careful about what he touched...except her. Wiping up after himself had been nearly automatic.

Then he discovered he hadn't found Dory at all. Her old address had been abandoned a few weeks ago, and her neighbors hardly knew her. No one could say where she'd gone. From the looks on most of the faces of the people he talked to, he gathered they hardly cared about her disappearance and that they really didn't have any idea where she was now.

He cussed and spent some time at the local library using their computers. She had to have left a trail of some kind. She was still working. The only thing was, he'd learned from hard experience that her company didn't release detailed information about the whereabouts of the people who worked for it. The most they gave on their lead designers was a geographic region. Over the phone it became apparent they didn't answer questions about one of their team and they'd never met her. They thought she was a guy.

That amused him a bit. So she was living a pretense. Gutless.

Sighing, needing to put more miles between him and

the woman he'd just conned—he couldn't be *positive* she'd be too embarrassed to report him—he left the library and headed down the road.

He'd find her. He knew enough about her from keeping tabs over the years to know her head would poke up eventually. Once she reappeared in one of the chat rooms she had used in the past, he'd be able to find her. Amazing how many details those social sites kept on people even after a decade or more.

When he was in prison, he'd watched plenty of his fellow inmates go to those same rooms because they wanted company. Mostly they wanted some girl to get sweet on them.

He'd avoided all of that. Leaving online traces could be a big mistake. Anyway, as long as he kept moving now and created different email addresses or log-ins at each new location, nobody would be able to track *him*.

But Dory... Dory might be smart about some things, but she probably thought she was safe behind the wall of her company and her alias. No reason for her to imagine, either, that George could find her online. After all, he'd been in prison, and she probably had absolutely no idea just how much you could learn about computers and the internet in prison.

He savored the fact that she probably thought she was perfectly safe where she was now.

She was in for a shock.

DORY FORGOT HER fears for a little while as she met Desi Jenks, a lovely woman with a nimbus of dark curls and a very strong personality. She was clearly in charge, at least as involved her job, and both crisp and clear about what she hoped for in a couple of dogs from Cadell.

"Basically police dogs," she told him. "We'll probably be using them mostly for search and rescue, but I also need them to be able to find shells and bullets so we can triangulate a scene, sniff for drugs..." She paused and laughed.

"You know all of this, don't you, Cadell? What I want isn't so very different from the dogs you train for the sheriff."

"Not really, no," he answered with a smile. "You might make a few additional demands. We'll have to see as we work through it. Will you have vests for them?"

"Orange," she answered properly. "Already on their way."

"At night, hook some glow sticks to them, okay?"

She nodded. "I don't want them mistaken for game, either. You can count on it."

"How many are you thinking?"

"Two for now. Any more and I'll bust my budget."

Cadell's eyes crinkled at the corners. "We'll see what we can do about that."

Then Desi turned to Dory, who was standing silently to the side. "So you're a graphics designer? What kind, exactly?"

"I make animations for films and ads."

Desi's eyes widened. "You mean like that stuff I see in the movies?"

"Some of it. The bigger animation studios do the work on the major films, but we get some thrown our way, and we work on independent productions."

"If I ever find time to get away from here, would you show me something?"

Dory hesitated almost imperceptibly. "Sure."

"Not that I have much free time," Desi said drily. "Kell and I are still trying to find time to get married and fit in a honeymoon."

"Elope," Cadell suggested. "Call in sick and run away."

Desi laughed loudly. "Sure. As it is we hardly see each other."

Such normal concerns, Dory thought, watching the two of them laugh and chat easily. Maybe hiding in her work all the time was depriving her of something.

But to be that relaxed with other people…it would require more trust than she seemed capable of giving. No, she was better off staying within the world she had created for herself. Just because Betty had turned out to be special didn't mean anyone else would.

"So what breed of dogs do you want?" Cadell asked Desi a few minutes later.

"Whatever works. I'm not particular, and I wouldn't usually need my dogs to be frightening. Most of the time I need them to track. Whatever you can give me that will be willing to traipse through the woods."

Cadell nodded. "I got it. I'll call next week and tell you what kind of selection I can come up with. When I've got a few, you can come out and see what you think."

Cadell seemed lost in thought as they drove away with the dogs in the seat behind them. "I guess I need to let those two take a walk," he said eventually.

"Probably."

He looked over at her. "You okay, Dory?"

"I'm fine. Why?"

He paused. "Well, you said you wanted to be a hermit, and I've been dragging people into your life all day. Not very considerate of me."

"You asked first," she answered. Yeah, it was fatiguing when she wasn't used to being around new people, but she could have said no. However, she wouldn't have missed meeting Krys for anything. That little girl had something special about her and Dory wished she'd been able to escape her own internal frost to spend more time with her. And Desi was nice enough and hadn't pressed Dory in any way that made her uncomfortable.

"I know I asked. I'm just wondering if you felt you couldn't say no."

She was oddly touched by his concern. Most people wouldn't even have thought of that.

They stopped somewhere along a dirt road on a turnout

near what appeared to be a stock gate, and Cadell let both dogs off leash to race around and work off energy.

He had a lot of confidence in them, Dory realized. More than she had in Flash. She never walked out the front door with him unless he was leashed.

The dogs were clearly in heaven. Cut loose with no orders to follow, they raced through the grasses like the waves of a sea.

"I know some guys who are going to need a bath when we get home," Cadell remarked. All of a sudden, he barked, "Flash! Dasher! No digging."

Whether they knew that particular command, both dogs immediately raised their heads and stopped working at the ground.

"Come," he said.

With tongues lolling happily, both of them came trotting back. Cadell went to the rear of his SUV and lifted up the tailgate, pulling out a gallon bottle of water and a large metal dog bowl. He set it down while the dogs sat and waited politely. When he'd filled it with water, he said, "Go ahead, guys."

They didn't need further permission. Dory felt another bubble of amusement. "These fellows understand a whole lot more than you told me."

He smiled, still holding the plastic bottle while he waited to see if the dogs wanted more. "There's some disagreement about how much verbal language dogs understand. Some say about hundred words, some say closer to six hundred. They're also very acutely aware of other signals. Think about it, Dory. They talk to each other with sounds, postures, tails, ears…but clearly they understand some verbal commands, so they must have language centers. Given that, they probably understand a whole lot more than we think."

"I'm seeing that right now."

"Maybe." He laughed. "Or maybe you're seeing the fact that we've done this before and they know the drill."

She nodded, watching the dogs splash water everywhere with their tongues. "That would make it hard to figure out."

"Very. But one thing I'm sure of—they're a lot smarter than we give them credit for."

When they were back in the truck, Cadell said, "Let's take them to my place to clean them up. I've got a doggy shower, a whole lot easier than you trying to deal with it in a bathtub. Although I'm sure you could."

She twisted and looked back at two very happy dogs, now flopped on the backseat. "I'm more concerned about the burs than the mud."

"Burs are always fun. And I'll show you how to check them for ticks."

Ticks? Oh, man, she hadn't even thought of that. The notion made her squeamish. "Do I have to?" she asked finally.

That made Cadell laugh. "Well, if you want I can come over and do a tick check every day."

In an instant she realized that she wouldn't at all mind him dropping by every day. Something else to worry about? Because she found it almost impossible to build real connections with other people. The last thing she wanted to do was make Cadell feel bad when he'd been so good to her.

She squared her shoulders and told herself that she *would* learn how to deal with the ticks. She hoped.

"Let's go by my place," he said. "I'll wash the boys up, we can grab a small bite and then I'll take you home."

"Thanks." Then with effort, "How are the ostriches doing?"

"As usual. They're worth a lot of money, as Betty keeps saying, but I can't sell them. Some inheritance, huh? They hate me, they're expensive to maintain and they drive me nuts. I wish my dad had given me some clue as to what he was thinking when he got them. But none of his friends seem to know, either."

"That's strange."

He shrugged. "My dad was an interesting guy. He would

get big ideas of one kind or another, then nothing would happen. Like the time he traded a shortwave radio for a telescope mirror. Admittedly he didn't use the radio, but he never used the mirror, either. It's still sitting on his workbench."

After a minute he said, "I wonder if I could trade two ostriches for a couple of horses."

A giggle bubbled out of Dory. "The horses might be friendlier."

"Oh, there's no question of that."

They drove through miles of open rangeland on the way to Cadell's ranch. The land rolled gently, hinting at the mountains that rose to one side like a huge, distant wall. Herds of deer or antelope grazed alongside cattle, and she wondered if the ranchers minded.

But slowly, ever so slowly, the bigness of the space around her planted uneasiness inside her. Out here there was no place to hide. You could run forever and still be visible.

Why was she having these thoughts? George. But George had no idea where she was. She tried to shake the creeping sense of unease but was failing miserably. She needed the protection of small spaces, walls, locked doors and windows. She needed to keep the bogeyman out.

That drew her up short. The bogeyman? Her brother was no bogeyman. He was a murderer, yes, but for all that he was human. She had no idea why he'd killed their parents, whether it had been born of a rage that caused him to lose control or if he was a seriously broken man. But either way, he wasn't some mythical beast. Just a man.

But the uneasiness wouldn't leave her. The skin on the back of her neck crawled, although there was no reason for it. She had enough scars, she scolded herself. Was she going to live in terror for the rest of her life because George was out of prison? That didn't impress her as a great way to spend the next forty or fifty years.

She was relieved when they reached Cadell's ranch. He had buildings she could run into. Lots of dogs that were being trained to be protective. And two ostriches that would probably love to peck George's eyes out.

That last thought at last made her laugh as tension seeped away.

"What?" asked Cadell.

"I was imagining your ostriches pecking out George's eyes."

As he switched off the engine and set the brake, he gave her one of those smiles that crinkled the corners of his eyes. "Feeling bloodthirsty?" he asked lightly.

"I guess. Better than feeling afraid."

His expression sobered instantly, but he didn't reply directly. "You can go inside if you want and hunt through my fridge for something. The thing is full of leftovers, and there are some soft drinks. I'll just take the dogs to the shower."

"You were going to show me how to check for ticks."

"Actually not difficult if you pet your dog a lot. But yeah, come along and I'll show you."

He *did* have a doggy shower, a concrete room with a sprayer attached to a long hose. Both dogs appeared to be used to the drill and didn't put up a fuss. One by one they stepped in to be shampooed and rinsed. Cadell ran his hands over them as he washed and told her she needed to pay attention to any little bump.

Even as he spoke, a tick fell off Dasher and disappeared down the drain. "Not attached yet," he remarked.

"What do I do if they've already burrowed in?"

"I like nail polish."

Her voice broke on a surprised laugh. "You like what?"

"Nail polish. Once their heads are buried, they have to breathe out the back end. You cover that with polish, and they'll back out real fast. I also don't want to chance leaving a head embedded by pulling on them. It could get infected. So a dab of nail polish, they back out, I grab with tweezers and dump them down the nearest drain or toilet."

"Seems like a good idea to me. I've heard of using something hot."

"Well, you can do that, too. But I figure why risk burning the dogs? Just be careful not to get the polish all over their coats. It only takes the thinnest smear to conquer a tick."

When he finished rinsing Dasher, he said, "Stand back."

She soon learned why. The dog began to shake out his coat, and water flew everywhere. Then he dashed out of the shower and up and down the run, shaking himself again at every kennel he passed.

"He's sharing the shower," Cadell remarked. "Flash, get in."

Dory would have almost sworn that Flash sighed, but he did as he was told, standing perfectly still. This time Cadell handed her the shampoo and spray. "He needs to know you can do this, too."

Well, she couldn't argue with that, and anyway, it was better than thinking about creepy things that could watch her across the open miles out there. Not for the first time she wondered if she were losing her mind.

Flash proved mercifully tick-free, and he seemed to like the warm water rinse the best of all. Then she got to watch him shake out and run up and down as if full of excitement.

Cadell spoke. "I've never been able to decide if they do that because they're so glad to be done with the shower, or if they're just happy."

"They look happy to me." And they did. For a few minutes, Dory forgot everything else. Flash did that for her. Even if he never did another thing, he released her inside, if only for a short while.

"I love that dog," she announced.

"I believe the feeling is mutual."

She looked at Cadell then, daring to meet his gaze directly without sliding quickly away. His gaze was warm, inviting, suggesting delights she could barely imagine. Yet he remained a perfect gentleman with her. He was getting past her guard, little by little. Just as Betty had. She tried to tell herself that wasn't a bad thing. A man who'd give her a dog like Flash had to be special. All the hours of training...she'd bet he didn't do that for free very often. Yet, he'd insisted Flash was merely an extension of his job as a lawman.

Um, wow?

An electric shock seemed to zing between them. Something invisible was trying to push her closer to him. Was he magnetic or something?

But then he broke their gaze and turned. "Wanna come inside and rummage through my fridge before I take you back?" He glanced at his watch. "I go on duty in a couple of hours."

The moment broken, she tried to find steady ground in the practical. "After the shower I think you're going to need a fresh uniform."

He looked down at himself and laughed. "What's a little water?"

Yup, in addition to sexual attraction she was learning to like him a whole lot. Sexual attraction she could deal with. She'd sent more than one guy away over the years, because she wasn't going to get that close to anyone.

But liking? That could be even more of a risk. Sex she could refuse, because she didn't want to be vulnerable and couldn't trust a guy that much. But liking...well, it grew of its own accord, and she had no idea how to prevent it. Nor did she know if she should. She didn't have to let him that far inside.

Although telling him part of her story earlier, reaching back to the little girl who had been terrorized for life by what she'd seen...well, that had involved trust, hadn't it? Trust that he wouldn't minimize it or tell her to get over

it. No, he'd accepted her confidence in silence, not judging at all.

Maybe she was more afraid of judgment than trust. After
all, her brother had done something inexplicable. Maybe
she thought others judged her to be as bad. Or maybe it
was herself she couldn't trust.

Hell. It was a mess, and she didn't want to think about it
now. She needed to get back to work. Flash made her feel
safe. Just leave it all at that.

They passed the ostrich pen on their way to the house.
For once the ostriches didn't even look at them. Instead
they stared out over the open fields, away from the mountains. Longing to run free?

But as she was about to cross the threshold behind
Cadell, something stopped her. She pivoted sharply and
looked out over the endless grasslands. The back of her
neck prickled. No reason. Nothing out there.

Maybe she was just reacting to the ostriches' behavior.
Or to her own fears.

Shrugging, she followed Cadell inside. Leftovers were
beginning to sound good.

BEFORE LEAVING ON his patrol, Cadell checked to see if he'd
gotten any pings on the whereabouts of George Lake. Nothing. After a bit of internal argument earlier, he'd decided
not to tell Dory that her brother had left the halfway house.
It was probably meaningless; the guy wasn't required to
stay there since he'd finished his sentence. It might only
mean he'd gotten a job offer in another town.

Odd, though, that nobody at the house had any idea
where he'd gone or why. All they could tell him about
George was that he'd spent a lot of time on their computer
when he first arrived.

That made Cadell uneasy, but he'd need a warrant to get
a cop out there to look at the computer and find out what
George had been so interested in. Unfortunately, uneasi-

ness was not a valid reason to get a warrant. He was lucky the people at the halfway house had told him as much as they had.

No one else in town was likely to know anything anyway. Dory had moved from there with her godparents before she reached middle school, so she had no connections in that town at all. After twenty-five years, there probably weren't even many people who remembered those long-ago murders, or would care that George Lake was hanging around town briefly.

Dead end. So it was good he hadn't said anything to Dory about George's whereabouts. All he'd do was make Dory even more anxious, and she was already anxious enough.

Being a cop had made him acutely aware of people's unspoken reactions. He'd detected her uneasiness in the open spaces. He'd even picked up on the sudden fright that had made her turn around on his doorstep and look out over empty fields.

He wished he could ease her mind, but all he could do was try to pinpoint one man among millions. Not likely unless the guy crossed the law somehow.

Well, if this was all he could do, he'd do it. And he'd keep an eye on her, too, as unobtrusively as possible.

Because he truly didn't think her fears were unfounded. Not with that inheritance hanging out there.

Chapter Six

George didn't especially want to be found—not yet, at least—but he faced a conundrum anyway. Yeah, he'd taken that woman for quite a bit of money he could get by on, but it was difficult to get by anywhere when you didn't have identification.

He'd been told to take his release papers and his prisoner ID to a Social Security office to try to obtain a Social Security card. He wondered if anyone in the prison system had looked lately at how many proofs of identity were required to achieve that. He hadn't had a driver's license in twenty-five years and didn't think anyone would just hand him one. Getting a birth certificate turned into another set of hurdles.

Not that he wanted to put himself back on the map just yet, but although he had the cash to do it, he couldn't even buy a beater of a car without some ID. That meant he'd have to steal one and hope he didn't get stopped on a road somewhere.

In all his dreaming about what he was going to do to Dory and how rich he was going to be once he got his rightful inheritance, he'd never once considered that even though he was outside the gates, he might as well still be inside. Every avenue seemed blocked—except committing crimes.

There was an irony that he was far from appreciating.

It fueled an old rage in him, but that wasn't helping anything. Not one bit. There was only one crime he wanted to commit, and he sure as hell didn't want to leave a trail of smaller crimes over a wide swath of the country. That would draw as much attention as getting himself a valid ID.

He knew of a guy who made fake IDs, but he wasn't cheap. George hadn't soaked the woman for enough to cover that *and* still be able to travel. Hell, he should have thought all this through better.

But he did have one breakthrough. He noticed a fresh change at the website of the animation business Dory worked for. One of the designers was now listed as living in Conard County, Wyoming. Seemed a stupid thing to put up, but the feeling he got was that the group was trying to make it clear they could work from all over the country. How that was helpful, he had no idea. He knew how it helped him, though. Well, sort of. A county was a big place.

He was sure it was Dory, though. The timing of the change was too close to his release. Evidently she never wanted to see him again, but that was fine by him. Now that he knew where to look, he just had to get there and scope the situation.

Then he spent some time enjoying daydreams. Did she guess he was coming? Did she even remotely understand that he needed her dead or why? How surprised she was going to look when she saw him.

He remembered the kid sister, the one he had read to and played with, but that kid, the one who had loved him, had died the night she'd run screaming from the house before he could clean up, make it look like someone had broken in. It was her fault he'd gone to prison.

He wondered if she remembered that.

DORY ERUPTED ON the conference. All caps got attention, and she was typing them to her cohort.

WHO THE HELL PUT MY WHEREABOUTS ON THE WEBSITE?

We always do.

THE VICINITY OF KANSAS CITY IS A WHOLE LOT DIFFERENT THAN WHAT YOU'VE PUT UP THERE.

But it's a whole county.

IT'S A COUNTY WITH HARDLY ANY PEOPLE!

The team leader stepped in. Do we need to take this to Skype?

Dory drew deep breaths, steadying herself. Did she want her team members to know she was a woman? Did she want them to see her face? How many people might they tell?

No, she typed, forcing herself to be calmer. Please take that information down immediately. My brother's a murderer. He just got out of prison. I don't want him to find me.

Consider it done, the team leader typed back. I just removed it. We didn't know. I'm sorry, D.K.

She refreshed the webpage and saw that Reggie was as good as his word. It was gone already. She just hoped it hadn't been there for long. And why the hell had she even told them where she going? Because she'd had to explain why it would take her so long to get back on the grid? Because at the time it had seemed innocent enough? Because she hadn't been paying attention to what they put on the webpage?

Because in her panic she hadn't been thinking clearly enough. There was no other reason. She'd let slip some information because she'd been too afraid to realize that it might be unsafe to share with her coworkers. Because all she'd been concerned about was getting away from her last known address as Dory Lake.

Brilliant. She wanted to kick her own butt.

A whimper drew her attention, and she looked down. Flash was lying right beside her, but as he stared up at her without lifting his head, she got the distinct impression he was unhappy. He must be picking up on her anxiety.

He needed something to do, she decided, some purpose. She'd given him little enough, and right now she was in no mood to take a walk or a jog. Heck, right now she didn't even want to step out her front door.

Because she couldn't escape the feeling that George might have found out who she worked for. It wasn't exactly the biggest secret on the planet. And if he knew that, what if he'd found that change on the webpage? She had no idea at all how long that change had been up.

God!

She looked into Flash's soulful eyes and took pity on him. He needed something to do, and she needed something from him. "Flash, guard."

At once he was on his feet, tail wagging. Then, as if he understood, he left her side to check out the other rooms in the tiny house. When he returned a short while later, he lay down with his back to her, head erect, ears alert. He was definitely on duty.

That should have made her feel better. After all, she *had* seen what he could do. But a dog as her only protection?

How was she to continue? Bad things could happen no matter what. She knew that indelibly. But nobody could live in the constant expectation that something bad waited around every corner. Her therapist had tried to hammer that home.

But that was also a kind of trust that Dory found difficult to gain. Trust that nothing bad would happen? Yeah, right.

A ping drew her attention back to one of her monitors. It was Reggie on private chat. You dropped out. Everything okay?

Yeah. Just taking some time to cool off.

She was grateful that he let it go. So how's that flood simulation going?

I'll have the roughed-out version ready for you in a few days.

Great. Ping me if you need anything.

Work, she told herself. *Just get to work.* She could bury herself in the intricacies of bringing a writer's idea to vivid full-dimensional life. An endlessly fascinating process, and no matter how much of it she did, there was still more to learn.

She started up the flood sequence again, looking for any points that would give it away as animation. Animations of human beings were nearly impossible to make so real that you couldn't tell it was an animation. But the stuff like this? It could fool just about anyone if she did it right.

She turned her viewing angle around slowly, seeking any hitches in the way the water moved. Just as she thought she might have found a problem, the doorbell rang.

Part of her wanted to ignore it, but then she noticed Flash had risen to his feet and was wagging his tail excitedly. He glanced back over his shoulder as if to say, "Hurry up!"

So it was someone he knew. She could guess who that was. Much as she wasn't eager to admit it, she wanted to see Cadell again. It had been over a week. Betty had only popped in once. For a hermit, she was starting to feel a bit lonely.

She was right. She opened the door to find Cadell standing there holding a big brown bag, dressed casually in jeans and a black T-shirt. "Hey," he said. "I brought dinner if you have time."

Flash was sitting obediently beside her, but his hindquarters were twitching as if he wanted to jump up on Cadell.

Trying to shake away the fog in her head, she stepped back. "You'd better come in and pet Flash before he decides to jump on you. I guess he's been missing you." Then she remembered her last command to Flash had been to guard. Quickly she squatted down, catching his head in both hands and rubbing him. "It's okay. Playtime."

Happily he danced away, following Cadell into the kitchen. "I guess you've taught him a new command," Cadell remarked as he began to remove foam containers from the bag. "Maude's finest," he added as he put things on her shaky table. "I'm assuming you're a carnivore?"

"Absolutely."

"Thank goodness. If you'd said you were vegan, I'd be looking through here trying to find something you can eat. I'm not even sure the salad would be safe. I think Maude puts blue cheese in it."

She wished she could laugh, when he was trying so hard to be lighthearted, but laughter felt far away.

"I hope I didn't disturb your work."

"No." Truthful as far as it went. Concentration seemed to have escaped her since the shock earlier of finding her whereabouts on the website. She vaguely knew they listed her general vicinity but hadn't really paid it much attention. Why the heck hadn't she thought to tell them not to change it, or just not tell them exactly where she was going?

They were seated across from one another at the table when he spoke again. He pushed a tall coffee her way, then popped open the boxes for her to choose. "I'm not fancy. Just dig into whatever looks good." He passed her plastic utensils.

She should get out some of her few dishes, she thought. Not that she had many. She'd never needed more than one person could use.

But then Cadell rattled her. "What's wrong?" he asked bluntly.

"Wrong?" she repeated. She hadn't said anything.

"It was written all over your face when you opened the door. You had Flash on guard, I could tell. What's going on?"

She forgot the delicious-looking spread in front of her, any possible appetite disappearing. "Probably nothing." God, she hated being always afraid, and most likely afraid of an eventuality that would never happen. How many times did she have to ask herself why in the world George would ever want to find her? Was there something wrong with her?

Cadell surprised her with a sudden change in tack. "Did you testify against your brother?"

She drew a sharp breath, her vision narrowing until she was looking down a long, dark tunnel. All of a sudden she was standing in that street again, screaming, screaming and not really knowing why, just knowing in her child's heart that everything in her world was broken forever.

"Dory? Dory!" A hand gripped her upper arm gently. Cadell's voice reached her through the darkness. "Tell me," he said. A quiet command.

"Red paint," she said. "Red paint." She sagged into him, dimly feeling his arms close around her. It all came back, every bit of it, worse than the nightmares. Then everything went black.

THERE WAS A rickety couch in the front room, and Cadell carried Dory there, settling her on his lap.

What had he said? What had he done? He'd sent this woman into flight deep within herself, so deep it might be worse than a faint. All he'd asked was if she'd testified against her brother. If she had, she might have some real reasons to be afraid. She might not have even considered that her inheritance could be a threat. He'd found during his law enforcement career that most people didn't have naturally suspicious minds. They didn't think like criminals. Those kinds of ideas just didn't occur to them.

He hadn't even told her that her brother had disappeared from the halfway house after only two days. He had every right to move on, and leaving a place like that was understandable, especially if you hooked up with someone who could help you get on your feet. Lots of prisoners had contacts on the outside, some cultivated in prison. How else did they manage? Family, friends, a few agencies...

He felt a shudder pass through Dory. Looking down, he saw her eyes, as blue and deep as a cloudless sky, open. A Botticelli angel.

Only this angel was feeling like no angel. She squirmed, struggling to get off his lap. He refused to let her go. "Easy, Dory. Easy. It's just me."

It was then he saw Flash. Staring at him. His lip slightly curled. Ready to attack to protect her, but unsure because it was Cadell.

"Dory, snap out of it before your dog rips off half my face."

That reached her. Those amazing eyes abruptly focused. She looked up at him, then over at the dog. "Flash, stay." Then back to Cadell. "I don't know what happened, but you'd better let go of me."

Wow, talk about feeling as if he'd been slapped in the face. He released her immediately, ignoring his body's natural response to her wriggling off his lap. "I was worried about you," he muttered. "You all but fell out of your chair."

An eternity passed before she spoke. Flash, at least, settled at her feet, but he kept eyes on Cadell. "I'm sorry," she said finally.

"You don't have to be. I just don't understand what happened. I asked a simple question, then you said something like 'red paint,' and you were gone. Collapsing. Like you'd fainted."

When she didn't speak, he asked, "Do you need some water or something?"

"Water, please. My mouth feels like cotton."

He rose, went to the kitchen and found one of her two glasses in a cupboard beside the sink. He filled it with water and returned, saying lightly, "You could use a few more dishes."

She nodded but didn't look at him. At least she didn't object when he sat beside her. She took the glass and drained it, leaving little droplets of water on her lip that he'd have loved to lick away. Then he caught himself. Damn, was he losing his mind? This was neither the time nor the place, and most likely not the right woman. Besides, having been badly burned once, he wasn't about to volunteer for another round.

"I'm sorry," she said again.

"Dory..." He gave up. She wouldn't even look at him now, and he'd already told her she didn't need to apologize.

"Red paint." She spoke in a voice so tight it sounded as if it were ready to snap. "I never told you. I don't know if I ever even told Betty. But for a time after the...murder, I was blind and couldn't speak except for two words. *Red paint.* I thought all that blood was red paint."

A seven-year-old girl? Of course she would have no other way to explain it. It also gave him a very clear idea of just how much blood she'd seen. Man, he ached for her. For the child who had been exposed to such horror.

"Anyway," she said, her voice a little steadier, "they said it was a conversion disorder. Someone explained it to me years later. I couldn't handle what I'd seen, so I shut down. My vision came back after a couple of months, but for a year I could speak only two words."

"Red paint."

"Exactly." She let go of a long breath. "All of a sudden, when you asked me if I'd testified against George, I was back there. On that street, screaming. I don't know how long I screamed. I vaguely remember the neighbors running up, the cop cars, the lady police officer who took me away. After that, I don't remember much except my godparents taking me home with them. I was terrified because I couldn't see. As for talking... I never really wanted to talk again."

Taking a risk, Cadell reached out and covered her small hand with one of his much bigger ones. He was relieved when she didn't pull away. He felt the faintest of tremors in her hand.

"Anyway," she said eventually, "I have nightmares about that night. They'd almost stopped, but they've come back big-time since I heard George was being released. Why did he get only twenty-five years? I've never understood that."

"Lots of things play into charging and sentencing," he said carefully. "You could talk to our local judge, Wyatt Carter, if you want. I'm sure he could give you an in-depth answer. All I can tell you is from my own experience. First-degree murder is very hard to prove, for one thing. Intent isn't always easy to prove in a courtroom, and that's the only way he would have gotten a life sentence unless there were aggravating circumstances. If you want my guess..."

"Yes, please."

"An argument with your parents. Tension for some time, from what you said. Your brother lost his temper and saw red. A crime of passion, without premeditation. That weighs into the charges a prosecutor thinks she can sell to the jury. It would certainly play into his defense. Basically, I guess what I'm saying is your brother's sentence wasn't unusual given the circumstances and his youth, being only fifteen at the time. I know that doesn't make you feel any better..."

"No, it doesn't," she interrupted. "Not at all. He butchered them, Cadell. *Butchered* them."

He dared to squeeze her hand and was relieved when she turned hers over and wrapped her slender fingers around his.

"So," she asked on a shaky breath, "how likely is he to do something like that again?"

He couldn't answer that truthfully. A quarter century in prison could straighten out a man's head, or twist it more. "I don't know," he admitted.

"No one can know," she said quietly. "No one." Then she switched course. "That dinner you brought is getting ruined and I'm suddenly hungry."

He watched her stand and leave the room, Flash at her side. Each new thing he learned about Dory filled him with more respect for her. She'd built a life for herself on some very brutal ashes. He knew well enough that kids all over the world had to survive as she'd survived because of war and natural disaster, but that didn't make her any less remarkable.

Before he followed her, he allowed himself to reflect on his marriage, on the woman whose unceasing demands had left them both so unhappy. What a difference. Somehow he didn't think Brenda could have survived half of what Dory had been through, or at least not with as much grace.

"Cadell? Are you coming?"

He rose and went to join the angel who hadn't fully spread her wings for a quarter century.

THE FOOD WASN'T that cold. Neither of them opted to microwave the steak sandwiches.

"I like cold beef," Dory announced. "Cold roast beef sandwiches are at the top of my list."

"Mine, too. Although the way I live, I seldom cook at home, so no roast beef."

"I should make one," she said. "We can share it. The only reason I don't do it more often is that to get a well-cooked roast, you need more than I could ever eat by myself. And I don't like it as much if I freeze it for later."

"Well, that's one job you can expect my help with. Let me buy the roast. You cook, I'll carve."

She laughed, a small one, but enough to ease his heart a bit. She was looking forward again, at least for now. It wouldn't last forever. In fact he'd probably have to be the one who shattered her hard-won peace.

While they were putting the leftovers away, he said, "You looked upset when I got here. You never said why."

She shook her head a little, drying her hands on a dish towel. "I was furious because my company put my whereabouts on their webpage. They thought it was vague enough. I had to explain that Conard County is underpopulated."

"Wait," he said almost sharply. "Back up. Why do they include anything about where you live?"

"I guess it's felt that since we don't have a central office we might make an advantage out of being scattered all over the country but still working together. Major Animation has three teams like mine. And we *are* scattered all over."

"Okay. I suppose I can get that. Centralized without being located in one place. So how detailed are the locations?" His heart had sped up a bit. He didn't like the way he was feeling right now. Worry had begun to gnaw at him like a hungry rat.

"Well, for example, they used to have me listed as being in the vicinity of Kansas City. There are a lot of people there, and nobody could have found me easily. But I screwed up. I guess I wasn't thinking clearly. Anyway, I told someone on my team where I was moving, and today I saw it on the webpage. Conard County, Wyoming. They thought listing an entire county was vague enough."

"Not if it's this county," he agreed. "So what then?"

"They took it down. I doubt anyone noticed it."

He wished he was sure of that. "Does it have your full name?"

She shook her head. "I go by D. K. Lake. It's not even my real middle initial."

Good enough, he thought sourly, even with a wrong middle initial. If he'd discovered somehow that she was working for this company, he'd have no trouble finding her now no matter how common the last name Lake was—and it was. "So nobody's thinking about personal security for you guys?" He found that hard to stomach.

"We're just a bunch of graphics designers. Most of the people we deal with are ad companies, indie filmmakers... it's not like we're putting our life stories out there." She looked down. "Except today. I raised Cain. I had to tell them about my brother."

He took a step closer. "And you didn't like that."

"Of course I didn't!" She rubbed her arms from shoulder to wrists, one after the other as of trying to push something away. "It's like an invisible stain. My brother is a murderer. Worse, he killed our parents. What does that say about him, about me, about our family?"

Oh, God, he was going to be wishing he had a graduate degree in psychology before much longer. Opening and closing his hands, he tried to find something to say, something that might actually comfort her.

The only thing that occurred to him was a question. "Do you really believe that, Dory? Do you think you could ever have done what your brother did?"

Her entire face froze, grew still and motionless. For a few seconds, he feared he'd pushed her back into the horror, but then she shook her head. "No," she said. "I don't think I could have, ever. But who can know that, Cadell? Perfectly ordinary people go over the edge all the time."

"I'm a cop," he reminded her. He nudged her back to one of the chairs at the table and brought her one of those orange soft drinks she seemed to like so much. He unscrewed the cap before he put it on the table.

"So?" she said. "You're a cop. What's that mean?"

"I like this town because it's pretty peaceful most of the time. But I've worked in much bigger towns. What you saw your brother do? I've seen that and a helluva lot more. There's no limit to what human beings are capable of."

She tilted her head, looking up at him. "And that's comforting why?"

"I'm not sure it's comforting. But I can tell you something—there were warning signs in every one of those cases. Something askew. Maybe nobody noticed it in time, but those signs were there. Tensions building. Things being said or hinted at. A withdrawal, maybe. But by the time an investigation was complete, we almost invariably had a profile of someone who'd been sending out warnings like invisible flares for months, maybe years. Very, very few cases erupted out of nowhere, and when they did drugs were often involved."

She nodded slowly. He slid into the other chair across from her. "The thing is," he continued, "the vast majority of people never kill, and even fewer of them kill in the way your brother did. He's in a very small group. There's no reason to even wonder if you could do what he did. To feel like it's a taint of some kind. Your parents weren't murderers, were they? Have *you* ever wanted to do something like that?"

"God, no!" She shuddered as her eyes widened.

"You have no reason to be ashamed because your brother went off the rails. One of the cops I used to work with back in Seattle had a brother who was a con man. You couldn't ask for two more different guys, and they came out of the same genetic stock into the same environment. Ralph hated it, though. He was frustrated, he couldn't talk sense to his brother, and occasionally we'd arrest the guy and put him away for a few years. Ralph took some ribbing, but if ever anyone had an excuse to want to kill someone it was Ralph. His brother was good at preying on people, but as angry as it made Ralph feel, he'd put his brother in handcuffs and bring him in. He never tried to hurt him."

"Wow," she said quietly. "That's awful."

"It sure was for Ralph. He was convinced it was holding him back in his career. I don't know if it was. I mean, the higher you go, the harder it is to move up because there are fewer slots. But Ralph believed the department never quite trusted him. I know all us guys who worked with him trusted him completely."

Deciding he'd said enough for now, and feeling thirsty himself, he helped himself to a soft drink from her fridge, choosing cola.

When he came back to the table and sat, Dory had reached for a paper napkin and was creasing it absently. "I've always felt that something must be wrong with me," she admitted. Then she raised her head and smiled faintly. "Well, obviously there are some things wrong with me by other people's estimation. I'm mostly a hermit, I don't trust people much at all...but I'm talking about something else."

"I know you are."

She compressed her lips and nodded. "When something like that happens so close to you, especially in your own family, maybe you always feel different."

"Maybe." He tilted the bottle to his lips and drank deeply, figuring he'd said as much as he could or should. From what she'd mentioned, he gathered she'd had plenty of therapy. He had no business mucking around with whatever peace she'd managed to make.

"I'm sorry if I'm interrupting your work," he said. It suddenly occurred to him that he'd come over uninvited, meaning only to stay about a half hour, but with what had happened he'd been here much longer.

"Not really," she said. "I put in most of a day before I erupted at my team about the website."

"Well, I'd still better go." He glanced at his watch and realized it was getting late. Flash dozed near Dory, but he'd wake at the slightest sound. She was in good paws, he decided. He also decided not to tell her about George yet. She'd been through hell tonight, all because of his question.

Dory sighed and went back into her office. He and Flash followed her, and as soon as she sat Dory seemed to be watching her simulation intently, was probably at least halfway back into her work. Time to go. Cadell opened his mouth to say good-night.

But then she spoke, surprising him. "So your wife couldn't handle being married to a cop?"

Astonished, he didn't answer immediately, but then tried for lightness. "Please be sure to include the *ex* part when calling her my wife. And her name was Brenda."

She turned from her screen, her hand still on her mouse,

and her eyes danced a bit. In that instant she looked posi-
tively edible. "Kinda bitter?"

"That isn't the word I'd use. Not anymore anyway. I was
certainly angry, back then. I felt as if she'd been lying to me
from the moment we met, although that probably wasn't a
fair feeling. She just had no concept of what she was getting into, and once she got there she didn't like it. A longer
engagement might have been wise. In that case it probably
would have helped." He shrugged. "But you never know.
It only lasted two years, but that was plenty for both of us.
I'm just glad we didn't have kids, because that would have
made it a tragedy."

"It would indeed," she said quietly, her face shadowing. Well, of course. He'd reminded her of what it was like
to lose parents.

For a half minute he actually contemplated just keeping
his mouth shut around her. Then he realized that walking
on eggshells would be unsettling for both of them. He decided to offer her another nugget of truth before he left.

"With Brenda," he said, "I learned something. At the
time I just wanted to be with her, and I didn't think about
giving her the wrong idea. I switched quite a few of my
shifts with my buddies so Brenda and I could have a night
out, do something she wanted to do, whatever. So if she expected that to continue, it was my fault and nobody else's."

She nodded slowly, her face smoothing again. Dang,
she was beautiful. Hard to believe that so much ugliness
resided in her memory and haunted her life.

"So it couldn't continue?" she asked.

"Nope. My buddies were great, but eventually it became
a problem. The brass started objecting, I got a few sarcastic comments about why I didn't just tell them when I'd be
available to work…"

"Ouch." She winced, then smiled. "That would do it."

"It sure did. So I have to take a measure of responsibility
for Brenda's disappointment." It had a taken him a while

to face that, but it was a lesson well learned, and one good reason not to tiptoe around Dory. Only honesty could build her trust. If she ever built any real trust in him.

He stirred. "Anyway, I've taken up your entire evening, and that wasn't my intention. I'll be off now."

Something in the way her blue eyes looked at him seemed almost like an appeal. But what kind of appeal? He couldn't imagine what she might want from him. This was a woman who'd told him at least twice that she preferred to be a hermit.

Suddenly, moved by an impulse that even to him seemed to come out of nowhere, he squatted before her, not touching her. "You're beautiful, you know," he murmured. "You remind me of a Botticelli angel."

She blinked, looking uncertain. Enough, he thought. He could kick his behind when he got home. Straightening, he turned toward the door.

"Cadell?"

He half turned. "Yeah?"

"You're a hunk."

Startled, he looked directly at her, then began to laugh. "Imagine the painting that would come out of that." Then he resumed his exit, pausing only to say good-night to Flash.

DORY LAUGHED QUIETLY. The painting that would come out of that? An angel and a cop? Or a cowboy? It was humorous, all right.

But gradually her humor faded. The night had closed in around the house, and she felt it as an almost physical pressure. "Flash, guard."

He obeyed, sitting beside her, alert.

Alone but not alone. Who would have thought she'd be so grateful for a dog? And what had happened just now with Cadell? She'd revealed things to him during her flashback that she was sure she'd never told anyone but her therapist. She could hear her own voice as she told the story of that night in third person, as if she were removed from it, yet still sounding a bit childlike.

He'd handled it well. Why not? He was a cop—he'd probably seen it all. Part of her was surprised that when all that had burst out the triggers of memory had made her turn to him, a near stranger. She didn't *do* that.

She tried to lose herself in work, but her mind refused to cooperate. The door to the past had opened tonight, and she felt it was as fresh as yesterday.

Damn.

Then, turning to her other computer, she brought up an image she had constructed of that terrible night. She didn't know why she had felt compelled to render it with near photo realism, but she had done it a few years ago. There it sat, just as she had seen it as a child.

What good did that do? What earthly use could it have? What part of her mind needed it? Did she think that by looking at it over and over again that she'd become de-sensitized?

Did she really want to become desensitized to such horrific violence?

No.

But she sat staring at it as if mesmerized. Her brother, they had said later when she could understand such things, had evidently been a drug user. Cocaine could wreck the mind and turn some people violent. Blame it on cocaine?

Hitting a key, she made the image vanish and considered just erasing it. It held no answers for her. There could be no real answer to what had happened that night. No satisfactory explanation for that kind of act.

She heard a ping and turned to see that Reggie, the team leader, had reentered the chat. Looking for her.

D. K. You there?

She hesitated then typed her answer. Yeah.

I'm really sorry about the mess up on the website. I just want to be sure you're okay.

Yeah, she replied. Like she was ever really okay.

The webmaster fixed your location. You're back to where you used to be.

Thanks, Reggie.

No problem. Countable seconds passed before he typed something else. Look, we're all worried about you. You need anything at all, ping me or Skype me. I'm usually within a few feet of this damn machine.

Me, too. Played any good games lately? Anything to get off this subject.

Nothing new, he admitted. I'm still trying to beat the goblin at the gate so I can get to the reward. Damn smart goblin.

Her spirits lifted more as they chatted about the game they sometimes played together, although she wasn't really into spending hours gaming the way some were. The advanced games that might hold her attention involved teaming up, and that made her as uneasy on the computer as it did in real life.

After a few more minutes, she signed off the chat claiming fatigue, but she didn't feel fatigued at all.

She didn't want to go to sleep. She didn't want another nightmare.

Closing her eyes, she thought about Cadell, surprised that she'd told him he was a hunk. Even more surprised that he thought she looked like an angel.

Forget Cadell, she told herself. How could she be sure he wouldn't rip her heart to shreds the way George had? Maybe not with violence, but in some other way.

She sighed, rested her chin in her hand and tried to study her scene. It sat there frozen, waiting for her attention to the misplaced vortex. There were a lot of items she needed to add, all of them listed in a file she'd received from Reggie. Every one of them had to be constructed. They weren't, unfortunately, items that the team had in its library from previous builds.

De novo. From scratch. She usually loved the challenge. Tonight she wasn't loving much of anything.

Flash stood, stretched and shook himself out before resuming his position at her side. Life with her must be boring for that poor dog, she thought.

Time to take him into the backyard for a walk. Maybe she should bring his tennis ball and let him chase it a few times. It'd sure make him feel better. Maybe it would even help her shake off the cobwebs of horror, grief and fear that kept brushing her soul and making her want to shiver.

As soon as she picked up the ball, Flash leaped to his feet, wagging his tail like mad. Oh, yeah, he knew what was coming, and the sight of his eagerness made her smile.

"Let's go," she said and headed for the back door. It was nearing midnight, but Flash was good about not barking, so running around for ten minutes or so wouldn't disturb the neighbors.

It was not until she reached the back door and opened it that she realized something had changed tonight. She could not make herself cross the threshold. The night seemed like a huge, solid wall, holding her back.

Panic attack, her mind registered. God, it had been a while. What the hell was going on with her this evening? It was as if whatever progress she had made over time had been stripped from her.

Then Flash, right beside her, growled into the darkness.

Chapter Seven

Cadell heard the call come in when he was halfway home. He turned his vehicle around immediately, lit the roof lights and hit unsafe speeds.

When he pulled up near Dory's house, there were two other cars, lights swirling around the neighborhood. They were collecting a crowd on the surrounding porches. He ignored them, only one thought on his mind.

They let him through and into the house. Dory sat rigidly on her couch, Flash on guard in front of her, holding two city cops and a deputy at bay. No one was going to get near her as far as Flash was concerned.

"Hey, Cadell," said Dan Casey, the deputy. "Ms. Lake said her dog growled at something in the backyard. We didn't find any sign of intrusion."

"Dory. Dory!"

She looked at him, and a shudder ran through her.

"Tell Flash to play. We're here."

She nodded jerkily. "Flash. Play."

At once the dog eased up but remained watchful. Damn, that one had been well trained, Cadell thought. Thoroughly attached to Dory, too.

As Flash relaxed, so did the other officers. They all had a healthy respect for a trained guard dog.

"So what happened?" he asked Dory.

"I don't know. I was taking Flash out back. I figured he needed a walk and a little play. Almost as soon as I opened the back door, he started growling. I figured I shouldn't ignore him."

"Good decision," Cadell agreed.

"But I didn't mean to cause so much trouble."

"No trouble at all," said one of the city cops, Matt Hamilton. "That's what we're here for. Besides, I agree with Deputy Marcus here. Never ignore your watchdog."

A short while later, the others left, promising to take another turn around the backyard and the alley behind before they left.

Cadell remained. Dory looked at him. "I'm sorry," she said again. "You must have been nearly home."

"Doesn't matter." There was an ancient wood rocker across from the dubious sofa, and he decided to sit in it. "Would Flash have reacted that way to an animal? Maybe a cat or another dog?"

"He shouldn't, but I could test it for you tomorrow if you want."

She shook her head. "I'm sure you have a life to take care of, and not just me. You've been wonderful, but…"

"But what?" he said. "I don't get to choose how I spend my time? Or are you telling me to get lost, that I'm bothering you?"

She gasped. "I didn't mean that at all."

He smiled. "Good, because I'm going to look around out back myself, then I'm camping here tonight. Got an extra blanket?"

He watched her struggle before she answered, and he guessed she was struggling with herself.

"Kind of an overreaction?" she said finally.

"I don't think so." Unfortunately, he figured he was going to have to tell her about George before long. Problem was, how much did it mean that one convict had dropped off the radar? He was quite sure it happened all the time. The fact that he couldn't get tabs on George's whereabouts didn't mean he was headed this way.

But tonight…tonight he was feeling that a little more honesty was needed from him. She had a right to know what he knew and what he suspected. She'd already set off the red alert when Flash growled, and he was quite sure Flash hadn't growled without a damn good reason.

That was what was getting to him. He looked at Flash, a dog he knew intimately and had been training for a while. The dog's growl wasn't meaningless, and he didn't ever want Dory to think it was, no matter what it signified.

"Lock the front door," he said finally. "I'm going to get my flashlight and look around."

"But the other police already did that."

"I'm sure they did." He pulled up one corner of his mouth in a half smile. "I'm also sure they did a good job. They're all fine officers. This is for me, okay?"

He guessed she got it, because she nodded and locked the front door behind him when he went out to his car. For now he didn't pull it into her driveway, just got his flashlight and other gear.

Because something had disturbed Flash.

FLASH HADN'T BEEN the only one disturbed by something out back. Dory still felt the way the night had seemed like an almost physical wall when she'd tried to walk him. How she froze on the threshold and couldn't move.

She wondered if Flash had been reacting to her and her swift change of mood. Maybe her apprehension had leaped to him. He seemed amazingly sensitive to her moods.

She looked at him now as she sat on the couch waiting, and he wagged his tail lazily, just once. He appeared relaxed.

"Maybe I imagined it," she said to him. "It was the weirdest thing I've ever felt. I wish you could tell me why you growled."

But he couldn't talk to her, although his gaze never wandered from her and his ears were at attention, twitching this way and that as if he were gauging every sound. Probably even sounds she couldn't hear. How could he look so relaxed yet still be so alert?

"You spooked me as much as that crazy feeling," she told him. He didn't seem the least abashed.

She sighed and leaned back on the sofa. Okay, so something had troubled him, too, but it probably wasn't that weird feeling she'd had. Cadell might believe he wouldn't react that way to another dog or a cat, but what about a coyote? They probably came into town sometimes. Or even a rabbit or snake.

As for her, she'd probably smelled something. A faint odor she'd noticed only subconsciously. Something that put her off. A whiff on the breeze. Maybe Flash had smelled the same thing.

Regardless, she was fairly certain that Cadell wasn't going to find anything amiss any more than the earlier cops had. She wondered if she were losing her marbles at last, then realized the dog had backed up her experience.

Okay, she wasn't crazy. So what the hell had happened?

A car pulled into her driveway, and Flash stood. Apparently he didn't need to be told to guard constantly. Except when he was chasing his ball or playing tug with her, he seemed to be on duty all the time. Quietly, but always alert for trouble.

Which, she guessed, was probably why people had taken up with dogs in the first place.

The knock on her front door brought her to her feet. She twitched the curtain back a bit and saw Cadell, so she unlocked the door and opened it.

He stepped inside, his big flashlight still in hand. He just shook his head as he closed the door behind him and locked it.

"Nothing?" she asked.

"Nothing anyone needs to worry about." He looked at Flash. "I'd be happier if I knew what made him growl, though."

She hesitated, fearful of the response she might get. For so long after her parents had been killed, people had regarded her with pity and had openly talked about how she wasn't right and might never be right again. Even at that age, they were talking about her mind. Her mental state. Unfortunately that had lingered with her as another fear, making her distrust *herself.*

"Let's go get something to drink," she said. "Maybe leftovers if you're hungry. If you plan to spend the night, I may do some talking."

She was surprised to see the warm smile spread over his face. "I'd like to listen."

As simple as that. She just wondered if she'd have the guts to speak.

THANK GOODNESS FOR MICROWAVES, Dory thought as she began reheating the leftovers from the dinner he'd brought. She'd probably have starved without one as often as she forgot to prepare a meal for herself. Sometimes weeks went by while she lived on raw veggies and frozen egg rolls. Some diet. Maybe Betty was right to be concerned about her.

Cadell put the remains of the two salads together on the inside top of a foam container. It could have been embarrassing to expose how little she actually had—a couple of plates, a few mugs, two glasses, cheap flatware—but Cadell didn't seem the least disturbed.

Maybe he'd roughed it when he was younger, she thought. But she had no excuse for this except disinterest. She made enough money, she had plenty socked away... she didn't have to live like someone who was just starting out. But she really didn't care most of the time. She wanted only what she truly needed.

Her extravagance, and it was a big one, was technology. Yes, she needed most of it for work, but not all of it. Some of it was purely for fun, or to satisfy her interest in the technology. Which, she supposed, made her a geek or nerd or whatever the current name was.

They sat at the table, and Dory started out by avoiding the things she'd been thinking about. Her usual style. Even she recognized her misdirection for what it was.

Cadell probably did, too. He'd certainly proved to be very savvy so far.

"So how are the ostriches doing?" she asked.

"They're fine. I'm beginning to think they're indestructible."

She glanced up from her plate, forgetting that she was almost afraid to look at him because of the strong response he evoked in her. Longings, feminine longings buried for most of her life, stirred around him with increasing pressure. "Why?"

He shrugged. "Because they're an exotic species I know next to nothing about. Sure, the vet gave me some instructions, but they're even out of the usual for him. It's amazing that my ignorance doesn't seemed to have harmed them any."

"So they're tough."

"Like you."

The words caught her between one breath and the next, and for a few seconds she simply could not inhale. Tough? "I'm not tough," she insisted when she could find her voice. "I'm a wimp. I'm so scared you and Betty decided I needed a guard dog so I could sleep at night. And there's probably no good reason for me to feel this way."

He stabbed his fork into a cherry tomato but didn't say a word. Giving her time to find her own way, pressuring her not at all. His hands looked so powerful, like all the rest of him. She hated to imagine what he must really think of her. He was a kind enough person to try to help her out, but he probably figured her for a nut. And maybe she was.

Taking what was left of her courage in her hands, she blurted, "It wasn't only Flash's growl."

His head snapped up, his dark gaze fixing on her with total attention. "What do you mean?"

"It's crazy."

"Everything about this, all the way back to the murder of your parents, is crazy. I'm not dismissing anything. What happened?"

"Me," she admitted. "I may be the reason Flash growled. I mean…" God, how could she explain this? Words didn't seem to fit it right. "I couldn't make myself go out that door. I was taking Flash out to do his business, maybe run around the backyard a bit, and I froze. It was like…like…" The words at last forced themselves past her resistance, past the tightness in her throat. "Like the night turned solid. Into a wall. I couldn't move."

His gaze narrowed slightly. "Did you hear something? See something?"

"Not that I was aware of. It was just as if this force held me back. Then before I could fight it or push past it, Flash growled. I turned tail and called the police. But maybe he growled because of me. Maybe my crazy fear reached him."

She swallowed hard. There, she'd said it. If he suggested a butterfly net, she wouldn't blame him. She studied her plate, unwilling to read his reaction in his face.

"Has the night scared you before?" he asked calmly.

"Occasionally. Sometimes it seems threatening, but not all the time. Because running out into the night was what saved me back then. It's not like the night itself was ever a source of my terror. At least not enough to worry me or anyone else."

He pushed the salad aside and reached for his drink. "The night frightens lots of people. Understandably. We're vulnerable then. Atavistic response that probably goes back to our cave days, if not earlier. As a species, we're not night dwellers."

"You make it sound so ordinary," she protested. She didn't feel what had happened at the door was ordinary. As a measure of her mental state, it was probably a big red flag.

"I'm just saying that all by itself, fear of the dark is common, and it can become very strong sometimes. We might not even realize what triggers it. But it's not crazy."

"Maybe not," she answered, hearing the flatness of her

own voice. She wondered why she was fighting his kindness. Did she *want* someone to tell her she was nuts?

"When you were really little, did you ever wonder if there might be something under your bed?"

She sighed, thinking it wasn't the same thing at all. "Of course."

"I'm pretty sure there was something under *my* bed."

His choice of words startled her. "You still think that?"

He smiled faintly, and she glimpsed it when she darted a quick look his way. "Not anymore. But for a long time, I jumped out of my bed. Far enough away that nothing could grab me. Now, just because there wasn't anything there in the daylight doesn't mean there wasn't in the dark. Reason doesn't work on that one, because we're programmed to have a sensible fear of the night."

"But this was different!" she protested.

"I believe you." He sighed and shook his head. "I guess I'm not being clear. I used to *jump* out of my bed so nothing could grab me. Nothing on earth could have convinced me to put my foot on the floor right beside my bed. It was *real*. What you felt when you tried to go out the back door was real. I don't know what triggered it, but something did, since this isn't common for you. Maybe it's being in a new place. Maybe it's knowing George is out there free now. I can't tell you, but I *believe* you and what you felt."

She swallowed again, then reached for her soda to wet her dry mouth. Her tongue and lips kept sticking. Then she came back to the important question. "Could my fear have made Flash growl?"

"It's possible. Not likely, but possible. Sensing your fear should have put him on high alert, and he should have remained quiet. No, something else bothered him, but it's anyone's guess."

She faced the grim possibility yet again. "So something out there disturbed us both."

"Evidently." He rose and began to gather up the remains of the meal. "Do you want to save any of this?"

It had been pretty well picked over. She shook her head and watched him cross the small kitchen to her wastebasket as he dumped in everything that was left. Then he rinsed their plates and flatware she had brought out for the leftovers, placing them beside the sink.

Drying his hands on the towel she kept hanging from the oven door handle, he leaned back against the small counter. "I'd suggest you move your equipment to my place, but that would only isolate you more if something worries you. I can hardly say you won't be alone there, can I? But I can put my bedroll here and be around when I'm not on duty. There are always the neighbors to help out here."

She knew the offer was meant kindly, but she stiffened anyway. "I've been living on my own since college."

"I'm sure. But George was in prison then. Things have changed a bit. I wish there was some way I could assure you that he's on his way to Brazil or some desert island, but I can't. So you're going to be worrying for a while."

"But it's so *stupid*!" she said vehemently. "*Stupid!* There's no reason for him to look for me. I know that. All these years he never tried to get in touch with me. Not even a letter from prison. Why would that change now? My fears are irrational. Even I know that."

"I don't know about that." He tossed the towel on the counter, then pulled his chair around the table so he could sit closer and take her hand. His grip was gentle, holding hers on his denim-clad thigh. "You saw your brother in the midst of an act so heinous that most people can't even adequately imagine it. You found the monster—it wasn't under your bed, and it wasn't your imagination. Why wouldn't you be frightened of him? You know what he's capable of."

She shook her head a little, although she wasn't disagreeing. His grip felt so reassuring, like a warm, strong lifeline. She'd like to bury herself in that grip.

"Then top it off with finding your whereabouts on your company's website today... That was hardly reassuring."

It was true. Seeing that had not only infuriated her, but it had frightened her. She'd come here to hide from George, not to have him directed practically to her doorstep. "Maybe I should leave. It's probably too easy to find someone around here."

But as soon as the words escaped her, she felt craven. Run? Again? She'd run once, but she still had as many fears, as many nightmares. She couldn't run from herself. She needed to face down the monster that had been pursuing her in her dreams for a quarter century.

Cadell hadn't spoken a word, but she squeezed his hand tightly and hung on. "I'm not running again. It won't do a damn bit of good. I'm carrying my brother around inside me. No escape."

"I don't have any idea how you get that monkey off your back," he said. Gently, he squeezed her hand in return. "But I agree about not running again. And we may be a small town and a sparsely populated county, but people notice strangers. People have noticed your arrival, but it was clear you're a friend of Betty's. He wouldn't have that going for him if he shows up here."

She looked at him, sinking into his dark eyes. They offered something warm and reassuring, welcoming. He made her feel as if he cared about her. Which she guessed he did, since he'd been talking about spreading his bedroll here indefinitely. "If you stay here, won't that cause talk?"

"Nothing that worries me. If it worries you..."

She quickly shook her head. "No. I was actually thinking about you, not myself for a change."

That made his eyes dance a bit. "Just keep your dog in line, lady. I really think he'd have gone for me earlier if you had resisted me holding you in any way."

She blinked, surprised. "But you trained him!"

"Which may be the only reason he didn't spring. He was

certainly thinking about it." He nodded toward Flash, who appeared to be snoozing across the kitchen doorway. "He knows he's yours now. Pretty happy about it, too, from what I see."

Then he turned back toward her and astonished her into complete stillness by leaning into her and brushing a kiss on her lips. "More where that came from, if you ever want it," he murmured as he pulled back.

The maelstrom that had been whipping her about was nothing compared to what he unleashed in her with that butterfly touch of his lips. All her life, because she couldn't trust, she'd refused to let anyone get close to her. When an attraction began to grow in her, she had squelched it mercilessly.

"Cadell," she breathed. God, she wanted more, a whole lot more.

He shook his head slowly. "Not now. Not when you've been feeling like a punching bag. Besides, I want you to be sure it's what *you* really want. I don't think you know right now."

She could have felt rejected, but she didn't. Much as she wished it otherwise, he was taking care of her yet again. Remembering what he'd said about his marriage, she guessed he had some trust issues, too. What a pair.

He thought waiting was better. Given her current state of mind, she couldn't disagree. She really did feel all mixed up inside. Strong as her desire for him seemed to be, she couldn't be sure it wasn't just part of the tangled mess she'd become since she'd heard that George was going to be released.

"I'll hold you to that," she said, feeling spunky for the first time since she'd seen the website and read the riot act to her fellow team members.

He smiled. "I'm counting on it."

SHE DID HAVE an extra pillow and a couple of blankets, and she gave them to Cadell, although she couldn't imagine how he would sleep comfortably even on the rag rug on the living room floor. He seemed dubious about using the couch, and she didn't blame him. Every time she sat on it she was aware of how it creaked.

"You know," she said, "I'm going to stay up and work tonight. You could use my bed."

"Nope. I'll be just fine, and you might actually want to sleep at some point."

She should have been exhausted after the emotional turmoil of this day, but she felt keyed up, almost antsy. Maybe she wasn't really sure the monster hadn't been in her backyard. Although he couldn't possibly have gotten here this soon, could he?

She paused as she started to leave the living room on her way to her office. Cadell was spreading a folded blanket on the floor for his mattress. Dimly aware that despite the food she had just eaten, she was growing light-headed, she ignored that for a moment. More important things concerned her than her routine low blood pressure.

"Cadell?"

"Yeah?"

"How fast could George get here?"

He finished laying out the blanket, then straightened, standing with his hands on his narrow hips. "Depends."

"On what?"

"Well, when a prisoner is released, he's got nothing. And by nothing, I mean *nothing*. They give him a bus ticket to get back to the town where he was arrested. It's nonrefundable. If he has any ID at all, it's his inmate ID. They may give him the address of a halfway house, but basically…" He hesitated. "Unless a prisoner has a friend or family member on the outside, he's going to find life pretty hard for a while. A few bucks in his pocket, maybe a place to lay his head, and no real way to get a job or help. Hell, they can't even get temporary assistance without ID of some kind."

She faced him, leaning against the doorjamb. "That sounds brutal."

"It can be. Those who don't have someone to turn to often wind up sleeping under bridges or at a shelter. If they're lucky, someone will be willing to help them get all the paperwork together to get a new Social Security card, a state ID. Only then can they really start to look for work."

"That sounds like a great recipe for recidivism."

"It is, for long-term inmates. You go in for two years, you might well have access to all that stuff. But after twenty-five...it's hard. Most of them weren't arrested with a Social Security card to begin with. It's gone. Driver's license? It expires, and these days thanks to the new Homeland Security rules, to get it replaced or renewed, you need a birth certificate, proof of residence, Social Security card...you get the idea. It's definitely not easy."

Part of her was seriously disturbed by that news, in a general sense, but when she thought of her brother, she was glad it wouldn't be easy for him to get going. "So it might take George a while before he can even buy another bus ticket?"

"Maybe. Like I said, I don't know his resources. Maybe he made a friend or two on the inside who are willing to help him right now. Or he might find another way to get his hands on money."

From the way he said it, she suspected it wouldn't be legal. And she needed to get to a chair soon. She gripped the doorjamb.

"I'm sorry I can't offer more reassurance," he said after a few beats. "If he's resourceful, he'll manage somehow."

"But there's still no reason he would want to find me."

She saw him hesitate visibly. "Dory?"

"Yeah?"

"Have you considered that half of your inheritance would have been his if he hadn't been convicted?"

"Of course I have," she nearly snapped. "My godparents

put it in a trust. They set aside everything but the proceeds of the house, which were used for me to go to college. They told me the rest was my retirement fund, or for help if I ever got disabled. They set me up well for the future, but I can't touch it."

"But does he know that?"

"He should. My godparents told his lawyer when they did it. I think they thought it might protect me from constant pleas for money from him. If he thinks he'll get his hands on a dime, he's in for a shock. Even if I die, he can't have it."

"Maybe he thinks he can make you change that."

And that, she thought, would indeed be enough for him to hunt her down. It was her last cogent thought. Too much, too weary, too light-headed, and the last flare of anger did her in.

WHEN SHE CAME TO, she was lying on her bed, Cadell hovering over her. Flash had jumped up to lie right beside her. Tentatively he licked her cheek.

"Welcome back," Cadell remarked. "Are you eating enough? Should you see a doctor?"

She shook her head a little. "I've always had low blood pressure. Good for my health, but I can pass out easily."

"Well, that was scary," he said frankly. "I almost didn't catch you in time. Pet your damn dog, please. He's worried."

He sounded aggravated, but she didn't feel it was directed at her as much as the whole situation. Cadell struck her as a protector by nature, and right now he must be feeling next to useless.

The inheritance. She'd believed she was protected by the trust, but in an instant she realized that could be a reason for George to want to find her. What if he thought he could make her change it? To demand his share. She rolled over, wrapping her arms around Flash. "Cadell? Is there some way I could just send him money?"

"Yeah, if anyone had any idea where on earth he's gone. And what if it's not enough?"

Her mouth turned even drier and she closed her eyes, holding onto Flash for dear life. She didn't need Cadell to spell it out, but she said it anyway. "He probably thinks he's my legal heir."

"Unless you did something to change that."

"He isn't. The way the trust is set up, he can never have a dime. But what if he doesn't realize that?" Fear seized her then, running across every nerve in her body like a horde of stinging ants. She'd never know why George had killed her parents, but now she knew why he might want to kill her.

The monster was coming for her. There was no longer any doubt in her mind.

ANY HOPE OF sleep had fled. Her blood pressure had returned to normal. Dory tried to push herself into working, but instead she remained on the bed, Flash stapled to her. Across Flash, on the other side of the bed, Cadell had stretched out. Flash kept himself firmly between them, as if he'd made up his mind. Cadell had even had to negotiate permission to lie down.

But now here the three of them were: man, woman and dog, the humans staring at the ceiling, the dog watching everything. His eyes roved restlessly, remaining on duty although there was no need.

Dory rubbed his neck. "Sleep, Flash. No point in you staying up worrying with me."

Not that he seemed to understand. If he did, he didn't care. She sighed, letting the evening sink in the rest of the way. So George *did* have a reason to seek her out. Given what he'd done to their parents, it didn't require much imagination to think what he could do to her if he thought he could get money.

"He used to love me," Dory said quietly, little more than a murmur.

"George?" Cadell asked.

"Yes. He always took such good care of me. Unlike many older brothers, he never treated me like a pest. When he was out for the evening, he'd come back and sneak into my bedroom to leave some little treat on my pillow. Sometimes I'd wake and see him and he'd smile and put his finger over his lips. No noise."

Closing her eyes, she could see that so clearly, and the memory tore at her heart. She'd loved him so much, as much as a seven-year-old could. What had gone wrong?

"Why no noise?" Cadell asked when she didn't speak for a while.

"Our parents were strict. At the time I assumed he didn't want me to get into trouble for making noise when I was supposed to be sleeping. But maybe he was protecting himself, too. I don't know. I wasn't supposed to come downstairs after I was sent to bed. But that night... God, I wish I hadn't broken the rule!"

"Me, too," he said. "I wish you'd never seen that."

She felt the bed move, and the next thing she knew he'd reached across Flash to lay one of his large hands on her upper arm.

"This dog may be good at his job, but right now he's an impediment," Cadell remarked, a tremor of amusement in his voice, surprising her. "So consider this the best hug I can give you."

"He's hugging me, too," she answered, feeling a slight lift to her spirits. A lot of hugs, something she'd been missing in her life since her godparents had died. Almost immediately, her mood sank again.

"Do you really think he'd come after me for the inheritance? Even though his lawyer should have told him it was in trust? That when I die it goes to a charity?" she asked, figuring that, like it or not, she needed to address the possibility directly. Hiding from it wouldn't help anything, and she'd been hiding from a lot for a long time.

"I don't know what he knows," he said honestly. "It's possible he thinks you can change the trust. Or that he'd be the heir anyway. It's mostly still there from what you said."

"Even if I could access the trust I wouldn't. Another way I'm weird, I guess. I didn't want to..."

"Profit from the murder of your parents. I get it."

She sighed. "Like I said, weird. They had insurance policies to make sure their kids were taken care of if anything happened. Would I feel the same if it had been a car accident?"

"I don't know," he answered honestly. "That's a question for you, but I don't know how you could answer it. That isn't what happened."

She turned onto her side, throwing her arm across the dog, too, and her hand landed on his waist. "Flash sandwich," she remarked. Not that the dog seemed to mind a bit. "You're a cop," she said a little later, her mind flea-hopping around from one item to the next. No rhyme or reason that she could determine yet.

"It's been rumored."

"You know something about people like George."

His answer was clearly cautious. "Something."

"I don't expect you to explain what he did to our parents. I'm just wondering...what did all those years in prison do to him? Could he be worse now? More dangerous?"

"I don't know," he answered frankly. "That long in prison...I can't say. I *do* know that as men get older, they're less likely to commit crimes. Less recidivism among men who are past their midthirties. On the other hand..." He just let it trail there.

"He could have gotten angrier," she said, feeling as if a stone were settling into her heart. "Meaner. It could have made him worse."

He didn't reply.

She spoke again after a minute. "You don't have any idea how much time I've spent trying to figure that night out, to understand what made George do that. It wasn't the George I thought I knew, but I was so little. I knew he was fighting with our parents, but my mother told me once that it was just his age, and he'd grow out of it."

"Often true," he said quietly.

"So what made him so different?" The question seemed to erupt from her very soul. Sitting up slowly, testing whether she'd get light-headed again, she found her feet and headed for her office, Flash right on her heels. Cadell wasn't far behind.

Then she did something she'd never done before: she shared her 3-D rendering of the murder scene that night.

"My God," Cadell whispered.

"This is what I saw. The thing is, once I put all this stuff in, I can turn it around. I can see it from different angles. It doesn't help me to understand anything, but I keep looking for answers. There aren't any. What do I expect? That some ugly demon will suddenly appear in my rendering and I can tell myself that my brother was possessed?"

She closed the image and swiveled the chair to look up at him. "I need to learn to let it go. I thought I had, until word came about George's release. It's like someone opened the floodgates on a dam. It's all coming back as if it were yesterday." She twisted her hands together. "The brother I used to love is gone. I need to face that. I need to face the fact that if he could do that once, he could do it again."

"Dory…"

She shook her head. "My brother is a murderer. I have no reason to think he's not the same person who stabbed our parents. Who cut my mother's throat. And you're right, if he thinks I still have some of that inheritance, he'll want his share. Because if there's one other thing I remember clearly about him, it's how frequently he snuck into Mom's purse or Dad's wallet and took money. Probably for drugs,

I don't know. But he was never above stealing. I didn't like to think about it then, and I guess I lost that in the detritus of what came later. He was a thief. Never to be trusted to begin with."

She shook her head as if trying to wake herself up. "I've been trying to connect two pieces of a different puzzle. Trying to fit parts together that never fit to begin with. I don't know why he was often so kind to me when I was little, but that was only a piece of him."

Cadell cleared his throat. "Would you have tattled about his thievery if you hadn't liked him so much?"

She drew a sharp, long breath that seemed to carry ice all the way to her soul. "Maybe. I knew it was wrong."

He didn't say any more, but he didn't need to. Suddenly those pieces snapped into place, and it was painful. Those cherished memories of the before time, as she thought of it, turned black and drifted away like dead leaves.

In an instant it all became painfully clear. She *did* have a reason to be afraid. Her brother was capable of using her and God knew what else if he didn't get what he wanted.

Her breathing broke, and scalding tears filled her eyes, trickling down her cheeks. "Years ago," she said brokenly, "my therapist tried to tell me that he was a manipulative psychopath. I refused to believe it. I should have. I should have!"

When Cadell's arms closed around her, she grabbed his shirt with her hands and hung on for dear life. Adrift in a sea of ugly discovery, she needed an anchor in the storm.

CADELL HELD DORY for a long time. While he'd been suspicious that she might have valid reasons to be afraid, he hadn't expected anything like this to emerge. For her to suddenly see her childhood in a very different light had to be wrenching in the extreme. He'd heard the love in her voice when she'd spoken of how George had treated her before the murders. That had just blown up in her face.

How much can one woman take? he wondered. He also wondered if she needed a lot more help than he could provide. Maybe he should call Betty in the morning, get Dory to talk to her.

Damn, Dory was isolated. He understood it was by choice. She was a self-proclaimed hermit. But it remained there were times in life when you needed someone else, someone to lean on and talk to. He had buddies he could share almost anything with, but this woman had no one except Betty. Maybe that was enough, but after tonight he wasn't at all sure.

She had warned him she didn't trust, but she had trusted him with an amazing amount of information about herself and her brother. Because he was a cop and might understand?

Being a cop didn't make the horrors understandable. All it did was build necessary walls of self-protection.

But another question seriously troubled him, and when her tears quieted and began to dry, he kept his arms tight around her, as if he expected her to try to escape. Maybe he did. But he had to ask.

"Why'd you make that graphic of the murder scene?"

At once she stiffened against him. As he'd suspected, she pressed a hand against his chest, trying to push him away.

"Do you think I'm sick?" she asked, her voice raw. "Is that what you think?"

"I just want to understand." Not exactly true. He'd heard her say she studied it trying to find some answer, but it was frankly macabre, and he needed to know the reason behind it. It would tell him so much about Dory.

She breathed rapidly but stopped pushing against him. "Why? Because my psychologist taught me to do it."

"What?" He was startled.

"You heard me." Her thickened voice managed to grow angry and a bit sharp. "I couldn't talk, remember? So she had me draw pictures. Any kind of pictures. I drew that night over and over again. It seemed to help. So she encouraged me to keep doing it as long as I felt a need."

"Apparently you're still feeling a need."

He felt her shudder, and her hand, flattened against his chest from pushing at him, fisted and grabbed his shirt. "It's a different kind of need now. And I don't keep redrawing it. I finished that rendering over five years ago. It's a snapshot of what's stamped in my mind forever. When I was a kid, it was a way to express. You have no idea how many sheets of drawing paper got torn by crayons as I expressed my feelings from anger to terror to sorrow. It was a violent expression for a while."

He rocked a little, wishing she weren't still in her chair. The floor was hard beneath his knees, and this certainly wasn't the world's most comfortable hug. He wasn't ready to let go yet, though. Something was happening tonight. Something inside Dory had opened up. He damn well wasn't going to make any move that might shut her down.

"Police wish they had such good renderings of what a person saw at a crime scene," he remarked after a while.

"It's what I saw. What I *think* I saw." She relaxed a bit against him, tension easing out of her. "Who knows how accurate it is. I don't. Even though I think I couldn't possibly have forgotten or changed a single detail, I probably did. Memory is a funny thing."

"Yeah," he said quietly. Five witnesses could tell five different stories and believe them, even when disputed.

"Anyway," she went on, "until recently I hardly ever looked at it anymore. Then there I was beating my head on the question that didn't have an answer. Looking into my memory for some clue by looking at the image. I don't think I need it anymore."

"Really?" That startled him, and inadvertently he loosened his grip on her. At once she pivoted away from him, facing the computer where just a few minutes ago bloody horror had been displayed. She brought up a list that looked like file names, highlighted a few then hit a key. Another key, confirming the deletion, and they were gone.

"I don't need it anymore," she said quietly. "Problem solved. The psychologist was right. He's a manipulative psychopath. He manipulated me when I was a kid, and given that psychopaths don't outgrow it, he probably hasn't changed for the better. Maybe he got smoother, but nobody could supply him with empathy. It's impossible."

He stood, wincing as his knees shouted at him, then pulled the other, more battered, desk chair over from the corner so he could sit beside her. He didn't know whether all this was a good sign or a bad one for her. Her psychologist had diagnosed George as a psychopath, but had her psychologist ever interviewed George? Was the diagnosis simply based on the things Dory told her? What if it was wrong?

But cautious as he might be about things like that, it remained they couldn't afford to assume George wasn't exactly that: a manipulative psychopath. He'd met plenty of them in the course of his career, people who were simply incapable of any genuine feeling for another human being. Some were good at pretending. Quite a few never got in trouble with the law and were very successful because they were also very smart.

Then there were the others. The stone-cold rip-off artists and killers. Oh, so charming, but dead inside.

She turned her head toward him and said abruptly, "How did you know about my inheritance?"

He stiffened, watching the matchsticks of the bridge of trust they had just started building waver and maybe begin to tumble. "I looked up the murder after I gave you Flash."

"Why didn't you mention it before tonight?"

Yup, he thought, he'd blown it. So he might as well light the final fuse. "I also checked on George's whereabouts. He vanished from the halfway house two nights after he arrived there, and his whereabouts are currently unknown."

"And you didn't think I should know that?"

"Honestly," he said, rising, "I wasn't sure you needed to know. Why add to your fear unless it became necessary?"

"Then what changed your mind? Why should I trust you enough to let you sleep in my house?"

He'd shattered their fragile trust, but he didn't want to add to it by getting into a fight about it. Time to go. "What you told me about him. Good night, Dory. I'll keep watch from my car out front. You know where to find me."

With every step away, he kept hoping to hear her call him back. She didn't.

A PSYCHOPATH. As suspicious as Cadell was of long-distance diagnoses, the more he thought about it, the more he thought that psychologist had been right. As Dory had said, it brought the puzzle pieces together, matching at last.

If George was indeed a psychopath, then trouble was on its way. Standing on her front porch, he considered what he and the rest of law enforcement around here might be able to do. Sure, strangers stuck out. But George might be smart enough to stay in the shadows once he saw how small this place was. Heck, he could probably figure it out by looking up this area online.

Being a psychopath, he had no limits on what he would do. He'd proved that once before. Now, if he felt Dory had taken his inheritance, he'd do anything necessary to get it back. Coming out of prison with nothing might have exacerbated an old resentment, a feeling he'd been robbed. While Dory wasn't responsible for that, she still held his entitlement. What if he believed her death would leave it all to him, trust or no trust?

If they were lucky, he'd call and demand his share. But Cadell's neck itched with a certainty that he wouldn't do that. Whatever he'd been denied by his parents that had brought him to the point of a vicious murder, he had showed his stripes. If murder was the easy way, he'd take it.

Wishing vainly that he could locate George was a waste of time. The guy had finished his sentence. Nobody now had a reason to keep tabs on him, so unless he crossed paths with law enforcement because of a misdeed, he might never pop up on the radar again.

Damn it! What the hell had he been thinking? Sure, he wanted Dory to feel safe. She desperately needed it, and that's why he'd given her Flash. The woman had been terrified, and while at the time he'd thought she'd never really need Flash, the dog would be a comforting presence and protector to have around.

Now here he was standing in the ruins of a budding relationship with a woman who'd quite frankly told him she couldn't trust and preferred to be a hermit.

Well, he'd pushed himself into her life, and now it was time to back out. Let her be. She had Flash to look out for her.

Forgetting Dory for the moment, he sat on the top step, wished he hadn't quit smoking ten years ago, and thought about everything he knew.

The image on her computer was stamped into his brain now, like a piece of evidence, and he wasn't particularly concerned about whether her memory had been faulty. It still told him things.

So, George had been stealing from their parents and subtly manipulating Dory to keep her quiet about it. He might have taken more than money out of a purse or wallet, leading to the fights Dory had mentioned. Creating tension.

But that scene in the kitchen, the wounds Cadell had read about…that was no impulsive murder. The heat-of-passion argument had been enough to prevent a life sentence, but Cadell was no longer buying it.

Rising, he climbed the step and rapped on Dory's door. "Dory, it's me." Then he opened the door and stepped in.

Flash came charging at him.

Chapter Eight

"Flash, no," Dory snapped just before the dog reached Cadell. She hadn't put him on guard, but she honestly wasn't sure if he was attacking or greeting. "Stay."

Flash immediately halted, and only then did she note that his tail was wagging happily. Then she looked at Cadell, part of her still burning angrily and part of her honestly glad to see him.

She was annoyed that he hadn't told her he knew something about George that she didn't, but on the other hand... well, Cadell was obviously protective.

"I thought you'd gone," she said.

"I didn't get all the way off your porch. The cop kicked in. Is there any chance you can recover that image of the murder? Because I'd like to look at it."

She hesitated. She'd had the sense that he'd been horrified that she'd drawn such an image in so much detail. "What changed?"

"Like I said, the cop kicked in. Some things struck me, so I'd really like to study it."

She nodded slowly. "I can recover it." She paused, then asked, "Want a soda?"

"Any chance of coffee?"

The faintest of smiles lightened her face. "Of course. Just let me start the recovery and then I'll make it."

WHEN SHE REACHED the kitchen, she had to grip the edge of the counter and lean on it. Her knees felt weak, and she was shaking from head to toe. Had it mattered so much to her that he'd walked out? That he'd come back? Hadn't she been mad at him?

But all of that had vanished in the contradictory realization that he hadn't left. Now he wanted to see her rendering of the murder scene. Maybe she'd been wrong in thinking that she had repelled him with it.

Drawing several deep breaths, telling herself she was overreacting, whether to Cadell's return or the idea that there was a good reason for George to seek her out, she didn't know. Too much. She'd lived with too much for a long time.

The coffee didn't take long. She seemed to remember that he took it black, so she carried a mug to him. She didn't want any herself. She was already wound up and simply relieved to have stopped shaking.

The picture once again filled the screen, every detail clear.

"You can turn it?" he asked, then thanked her for the coffee.

"Yeah, but you have to understand I couldn't see it from any other direction, so you get the reverse of what you see here, plus the other side of the kitchen as I recall it."

"Every little bit helps. Can I rotate it myself?"

"Not easily." She pulled a chair over, and he scooted to one side while she called up a menu. She highlighted a box from the graphics software. "The problem with this is you're not really moving the picture, you're moving cameras around it. It can get awkward."

He nodded and picked up the mug, drinking, his gaze intent on the screen. "Turn it ninety degrees, if you can."

Well, that was easy enough. She hated this view, though, looking straight at her brother as he stood over their parents. It didn't look like him, of course. He was a morph, but she knew exactly who it was—an unrealistic face didn't change that.

He spoke. "The kitchen behind him. That's what you remember should have been there?"

"Yes."

"Okay, give me another ninety in the same direction."

She did. There was the dining table, the doorway, the

little girl standing at the foot of the stairs. Her brother partially blocked the view, though.

"Do you have a drawing of the kitchen without him in it?"

"Of course. That's where I had to start."

"Can I see it?"

At least the shakes were gone, she thought as she reached for the mouse and switched to another image. The kitchen. Empty. The way it should have been that night at that hour.

"A back door," he muttered. "A knife block all the way over there, with the table in between."

"In between what?" she asked. Her heart was accelerating as she wondered if he'd seen something there that she hadn't.

He rubbed his chin and leaned back in the chair. It creaked, but he said nothing as he continued to stare. Finally he stabbed his finger at the screen, pointing out the knife block. "All the knives are there."

"Well, of course," she said. "Until he used one."

"I want you to look at this whole picture, Dory. The whole thing. For now just use your imagination to put the figures in it."

"Okay." That wasn't hard to do, considering that she'd looked at it until she hardly needed it anymore.

Her parents lying on the floor between the table and a wall of dish cabinets. George standing over them.

"The police report said he killed them with a ten-inch chef's knife," he said.

"Yes," she whispered, then opened her eyes in spite of his instructions.

"From that butcher's block."

"Yes."

He swiveled, and suddenly she was fixed by his gaze. "This was premeditated."

IT HAD TURNED into a night of shocking revelations. She didn't even want to know how he'd reached that conclusion, not at first. Giving up all thought of sleep and peace, she headed for the kitchen and got herself a cup of coffee. Cadell wasn't far behind, refreshing his own mug.

"I'm sorry, Dory. But the more we know about him…"

"I get it," she interrupted, not caring if she was rude. "I get it."

Oh, yeah, she got it. He was saying that her brother hadn't been overcome by a blind rage, driven to an act he might never otherwise have committed. He was saying George had intended to kill them. That he'd planned it. Who knew how long he might have been planning it? Subtly bribing her and making her love him, then reinforcing their parents' dictum that she mustn't come downstairs after she was sent to bed.

Considering how many rules he'd broken, it was weird that he hadn't wanted her to break any.

"God," she whispered.

"Maybe you should sit down. I don't want you to faint again."

"I don't know if I can, and anyway I think my blood pressure is through the roof right now. Cadell, how can you be sure?"

He nudged her over to the table until she was sitting. "If you can stand to, think about that kitchen. How likely is it that he could have taken both your parents by surprise if he'd gone to get a knife? He'd have had to round the table, go to the knife block and come back around that table… Don't you think at least one of them would have run at that point? Getting the knife was a deadly threat, not some innocent act like getting a glass. The fact that they're lying beside one another… He was already armed. He took them utterly by surprise, and he knew exactly how he was going to do it."

Somehow she had moved past feeling shocked. In place of all her fears was the feeling that she was receiving repeated blows yet again, anger surging in her. Fury at George. Fury at what he had done and the scars and terrors he had left her with.

She closed her eyes, clenched her fists and wished he was there to scream at, to pound, to tell him once and for all that he'd killed part of her, too.

But George didn't care. He'd never cared. *Manipulative psychopath*. The brother who'd been so sweet to her had merely been using her. Then a strange calm came over her, leaving her feeling as if she were standing outside herself, observing from miles away.

"I have my answers now," she whispered.

"So it seems." He was quiet a moment, then said, "I guess I should leave. I've given you enough shocks and bad news for one night. You're going to hate the very sight of me."

Her eyes snapped open. Her voice emerged tonelessly. "I'm going to have nightmares if I sleep. I'm going to wake up screaming."

He stood there, his face creased with concern, his hands opening and closing as if he didn't know what to do. "Do you do that often?"

"A lot since I heard about George's release. I can feel it coming, almost like I'm already half-asleep. He's going to stalk my dreams."

"God," he muttered.

She looked down as she felt something on her thigh. Flash. He'd rested his head on her, his eyes peering up at her.

"Cadell?"

"Yeah?"

"I can't stand to be alone in the dark when I wake up screaming."

He shifted, then slid into the chair he'd pulled closer earlier. "I'll stay. I told you I'd stay tonight. I just figured after what's happened, you might want me gone. Being the bearer of bad news and all."

Still feeling oddly detached, she lifted her gaze and studied his face. "You didn't tell me anything new. Not really. Well, I *did* get angry when I found out you hadn't told me those things. Then you left."

"Not exactly," he admitted. "Didn't make it three steps. But I reckoned you felt betrayed, and for someone who says she can't trust...I figured all the bridges between us had been burned."

She shook her head slowly. "For a minute or two... Well, I'm glad you came back. And I'm glad to know for sure now about George. No questions left. You answered them. All the time I stared at my representation of that awful scene, I felt like there was an answer there somewhere. You found it."

"I'm sure that's thrilling you," he said tautly. "Good old Cadell, bringer of more bad news. I'm a great one for making people feel worse."

Her head jerked up at that. A sliver of feeling pierced the cold detachment that had overtaken her. "Brenda?"

"What?"

"Did your ex make you feel that way?"

She watched him consider it for a few minutes. "Yeah, in part. But being a cop brings a lot of that on, too. How many times have I had good news to deliver? Not many."

"I never thought about that," she confessed. "Never thought about what it could do to you and other police officers. My memory of the police is all warm and good. They took such good care of me back then. All of them. I've never forgotten it."

"I'm glad you feel that way."

Impulsively, surprising herself, she reached out for his hand and wrapped hers around it. "You're a good man. I keep thinking about how awful all this has been for me, but tonight can't have been fun for you, either. I'm surprised you came back after the way I reacted earlier."

He shrugged slightly. "Like I said, the cop kicked in. You

told me you'd been looking for answers in that graphic, and while I was out on the porch doing a decent job of beating myself up for sacrificing your trust, I thought about what you'd said about seeking answers in that picture. You have an artist's eye, but I have a set of cop's eyes, and a thought occurred to me. I'm sorry it was so bad."

"The whole thing was bad." Some of her detachment was easing, and she wished she could hang on to it. She doubted she was ready to start feeling anything yet. Unfortunately, she knew she would. She always did. That night had been haunting her for over a quarter century. If she could have become ice, she certainly would have done it by now.

"Look," he said after a moment, "you really need some sleep. For that matter, so do I. It's awfully late."

So much had happened since he'd arrived with dinner that time had flown. Looking at the clock, she started. "Wow. Don't you have to work in the morning?"

"I'm off tomorrow. Maybe, if you can find time, you and Flash could come out and check on the ostriches with me. I'm certainly going to need a shower and a change."

The smallest of smiles cracked her frozen face. "Sure. Why haven't you named them?"

"The birds? Because I don't want to get attached. I'm trying to get rid of their ornery butts, remember?"

He turned his hand over and tugged her gently. "Bed. Flash will keep me in line. If you have a bad dream, I'll be right there."

At last, she nodded and felt the tension that had been building for hours let go. She wouldn't be alone. And while she was sure Flash would protect her, he wasn't the same as having someone right there she could talk to. During the time with Betty, she had learned how much that could mean. Since moving into this house, she had realized how much she missed having someone there.

Then his words struck her. "Why should Flash have to keep you in line?"

He just laughed. She felt a few more cracks in the ice that was encasing her, because she understood that laugh.

For the first time in a long time, she hugged something special close to her heart.

GEORGE CUSSED HIMSELF for a fool. He'd gotten all the money he needed off that woman, and she hadn't slowed him down much. It was everything else that was slowing him down.

Things had changed since he'd gone to prison. He'd been shocked to discover that he couldn't even buy a bus ticket without ID. The last thing he wanted was a record of where he'd been. The bus company might have accepted his prison ID—they had when the prison sent him home—but even if they would, he didn't want anyone to be able to trace his movements. Not with what he had in mind.

Of course, that gave him an idea. Walking boldly into the bus station, he asked for a ticket to Miami, and while the clerk hesitated a moment when seeing his prison ID, she didn't hesitate long. He walked out with a ticket to Miami, a false trail already started.

Now he just had to figure out how to get to that place in Wyoming. Once again, he walked to a different town. The outdoors still felt too big to him. He wondered if he'd get past that. Anyway, he felt better when surrounded by houses and trees. They cut the sight lines to something more reasonable. But from what he knew of Wyoming, he was going to have to get used to wide-open spaces quickly.

The next town had a small library, but that didn't mean they were without computers or the internet. He made his way to one of them without having to show a card or other ID and set to work. If they didn't want people to walk in and just use the machines, if they hassled him…well, they had books, and he was pretty sure they didn't have a problem with people browsing the books.

But no one harassed him the least little bit, and he began to do his research on Conard County.

An hour later he was wondering what had drawn Dory to a place like that. It was the ends of the earth. Hardly any people, nothing to do, really. The main town, Conrad City, was a cow town, if that. The plus was that she'd stick out and be easy to find. The minus was that so would he.

Leaning back as far as the chair would let him, keeping his hand on the mouse, he tabbed between pages. One gave him the stats about the place. Another gave him a reasonable map, although he was sure plenty of minor roads probably didn't show up. The third gave him photos. Beautiful mountains, a worn-out town and plenty of wide-open spaces.

He had no way to know if Dory had moved there on her own or if some guy had drawn her there. Her personal life was a closed book to him. Crap, she didn't even have a social media account under any possible name he could cobble together for her.

It hadn't always been like that. That was how he'd learned she'd become a graphic artist and worked for some company. Then everything had shut down ten years ago. As if she'd gone underground and wanted to stay there.

It didn't make any sense. What was she afraid of? He'd still been in prison, and anyway, he'd given her absolutely no reason to fear him.

If only she hadn't come downstairs that night. She'd loved him back then. He'd made sure of it. Made sure that she worshipped him more than their parents, that she was his ally and kept his secrets. Then she'd broken the rule and come downstairs.

Even so, she had no reason to fear *him*. No reason to think that her loving brother would come after her with murder in his heart. He'd *always* been good to her.

It did seem suspicious that her location had changed on the company's website right around the time he was released. But it had changed back. What if it was just a mistake? Because why the hell would she go so far out of the way?

"Sir?"

George looked up. A middle-aged woman smiled at him. "I'm sorry, but you've been using that computer for over an hour, and we have other people waiting."

He smiled, calling on every bit of charm and sexiness he owned. No point in making himself memorable. "I'm sorry. Let me just shut down my search."

"Oh, take a few more minutes," she said, smiling in answer. Her cheeks even flushed a little. "I'll explain you're almost done."

As she walked away, he wondered if he should chat her up a bit, maybe spend the night with her. Then his memory flashed the image of the wedding ring she wore.

Nope. He'd have to find a different flophouse.

He closed out his search, erased the search history and rose, heading for the door. He gave the librarian another smile before he stepped out into the sunny morning. The library was on a wide boulevard, and for a moment he froze, overwhelmed by the space. Then he gathered himself and began to stroll down the sidewalk, glancing in shop windows, a handsome man just past forty. He liked seeing his reflection.

All the while his mind kept ticking things over. The change of address, changed back. Too coincidental. Why the middle of nowhere? Because she was afraid, after all?

When he'd seen her standing in the kitchen, he'd tried to reassure her, telling her he'd gotten rid of the bad man. Had she believed him? She should have, but a lot of years had passed, and he'd spent them in prison. Maybe she believed his conviction more than she had believed him. Certainly something in her had snapped. He'd never forget the way she ran from him and stood in the street screaming her fool head off. The sound had frozen him, had thrown all his plans into a mixer, and in the end he hadn't had the time he had planned on to clean himself up, get rid of the weapon and lay a false trail.

If she'd just stayed in bed... She'd never told their parents that he was stealing from them, even though she'd seen it. In the end she'd never told anyone anything about that night, as far as he could tell. Hell, she'd stopped talking entirely. His lawyer had been good about keeping him informed. The freaking lawyer thought he was worried about his sister. Idiot.

He'd kept tabs through that guy, loosely, of course. The years she spent with her godparents, a couple he'd never cared for. The trip to college when briefly he'd been able to follow her on social media. But then, for no apparent reason, she'd dropped out. Gone. Canceled her accounts.

He still wondered what the hell had brought that on. Maybe someone had been bothering her. Anyway, she'd apparently never picked it up again. She was almost as far off the radar as he was.

The idea made George smile. Maybe he could just make her disappear. Who'd be worried about it? Her coworkers? If she had friends, he hadn't been able to find out. Not even that damn lawyer could tell him, and finally the guy had gotten impatient, reminding George that he was not on retainer and while he'd been doing favors out of kindness all these years, he was through.

Bastard. George sometimes thought he'd take care of that lawyer once he'd settled matters with Dory.

With a start, he understood he'd reached the end of town. He hesitated only a minute before deciding to just keep going, heading west. He'd been warned that hitchhiking was illegal, but that didn't mean someone wouldn't pick him up. He looked innocuous enough, clean, not too big, carrying a backpack over his shoulder. No one would guess that a slender guy like him could be trouble.

Which was just how he wanted it. He'd used his exercise periods to stay lean. Fit, but lean. Bulking up like so many of the guys did only made a man look like potential trouble. George didn't want to frighten anyone.

For now the only weapons he needed were his good looks, his smile and his tongue.

EVEN THOUGH IT was late, the morning sunlight almost hurt Dory's eyes as she opened them. She needed to get some curtains in here.

Then she realized she was alone. At once she turned over and saw that both Flash and Cadell were absent. Reaching out, she touched the covers and felt warmth. They hadn't been gone long. Then she heard sounds from the backyard and saw that Cadell was running Flash through his paces.

She sat up and stretched until joints popped. No nightmares. None. Not even a hint. She'd just had the best sleep she'd had in weeks, maybe a month.

Feeling better than she had in quite a while, she slipped out of bed and headed for a shower that would make her feel even better.

When she emerged freshly dressed in a light T-shirt and jeans with a towel around her blond hair, she stepped outside to watch Cadell and Flash. They'd passed the work stage and were now at the play stage. She smiled as she watched the dog jump for joy each time Cadell threw the ball. To be so happy...

Before her thoughts could take a downward spiral, Cadell called Flash to heel and came toward her. "You slept well?"

"Like a rock. It was amazing. That hasn't happened in a while."

"Good news, then. When you're ready, we'll go out to my place. I *do* have something there besides two ostriches and a dog kennel."

Her smile started to widen, then hitched. "Who's taking care of the dogs?"

"They are," he said simply. "I never know when I might

have to be away for an extended period, so I have a very modern kennel. It feeds and waters them."

"And the ostriches?"

He laughed. "I hope they got all the insects out of the corral."

His cheer was contagious, and she liked it. Before long they were heading out to his ranch with Flash in the cage in back. He seemed excited, as if he knew he was going to visit his dog friends.

Dory wondered what was happening inside her. After last night's shocks, shouldn't she be more upset? Instead she felt as if she had been freed in some way. Maybe Cadell had given her some of the answers she'd been looking for. Maybe now she felt she knew what she was facing, rather than wondering.

But she was sick of her own fears this morning, and she shoved them aside. George's release didn't mean she couldn't still have an enjoyable day. In fact, now that she thought about it, she was appalled at how much power she'd given her brother over her. She'd allowed him to haunt her for years. Allowed him to terrorize her sleep and dreams. He didn't deserve that right.

Lifting her head, she looked to her left and drank in the mountains. At midday they looked a little hazy, the greens very dark except for lighter patches here and there. She wondered if she was looking at different trees or if that was the dappling of sunlight.

"Cadell?"

"Yeah?"

"After your divorce...did you find it hard to trust?"

He snorted. "Oh, yeah. I got distrustful of women, and I got distrustful of myself."

"Why yourself?"

"Because before that I thought was a fairly decent judge of character. Afterward, not so much. Which was probably a good thing for a cop."

She turned a little in her seat so she could look at the side of his face. "How so?"

He paused as he steered them into his rutted driveway. The truck began to jolt. "Because it's not possible to really judge a book by its cover. In my line of work, making that mistake can be deadly. I guess I figured out that before you can trust someone, you need to get to know them. You need to see them in stressful situations, not just dates where everything is fine. If I ever marry again, I'll want to know how a woman reacts when the toilet overflows."

The quiver began deep inside Dory, and seconds later emerged as the heartiest belly laugh she'd had in ages. "The toilet?" she gasped finally, wiping an errant tear from laughing so hard.

"Well, it could be something else," he allowed. "But I think you get my drift."

She did indeed, but it was still funny, and she couldn't stop grinning. She imagined him with a clipboard ticking off boxes as a harried woman worked on a toilet.

"Are you keeping a checklist?" she asked.

"Not consciously. But that's the best way I can explain it. People change under stress. I kind of think it's important to know how they change. Every life has problems that have to be dealt with. I'd prefer someone who can deal."

Which ruled her out, Dory thought, wondering why it should matter. He'd seen her under stress, and she didn't think she was getting any gold stars from him. Afraid of nightmares, of being alone? Afraid of her brother? Turning herself into a hermit because she trusted no one easily? How was that truly coping with anything? She was a mass of defense mechanisms.

She sighed, imagining him filling out his checklist when it came to her, or worse, writing "Failed" across the sheet.

Oh, well. She might not pass his tests, but that didn't mean she couldn't enjoy the day. Even if George were somewhere close, he'd never find her out here.

Chapter Nine

Cadell had left the ostriches in the corral, which was also electrically fenced. They'd done a good job of scratching up the place looking for food. Leaving Dory to get out of his vehicle in her own time, he headed for the pen. The two birds came running.

"Yeah, you guys know who feeds you," he said. Before he let them in, though, he had to dump feed in their trough. No way was he going to let them get close. He'd learned his lesson.

He opened the gate into the pen and stepped back as the two birds entered. He didn't know if he wanted to confine them again just yet, so he left the gate open.

Dory had joined him, Flash at her side. "Man," she said. "They moved fast!"

"They didn't even get up to full speed. Quite amazing birds...at a distance."

He was pleased when she laughed again. He'd gotten the feeling just before they finished the drive that something had darkened her mood. Well, not really darkened. Not that bad. Just a kind of sadness, he guessed.

Which under the circumstances needed no explanation. He was pretty impressed with how well she'd handled last night's revelations, especially the one about the murder being premeditated. She probably had been fighting that thought for years, unwilling to believe that her beloved brother was capable of it. Much easier to believe he'd lost his temper in a big way than to imagine him plotting the entire thing.

He led her along the fence. "See the wire fencing inside the wooden corral? Courtesy of my father and the ostriches."

"What was your dad like?"

"An honest, decent, hardworking, churchgoing man. Respected by his neighbors. A good example for any kid."

She looked toward him. "Why'd you leave?"

"Youthful wanderlust, I guess." He sighed and shook his head a little. "I didn't think I was cut out to be a rancher. It about wore my dad to a nub. Same thing every day and worries that never quit." He shook his head a bit, leaned his arms on the fence and lifted one booted foot to the lower railing.

"It's hard to remember what I was thinking back then," he said. "I'm sure it made perfect sense to me. I tried staying for a couple of years, but my dad didn't stop me when I took off. He was already winding down the operation here. Cattle are expensive to raise, and he wasn't getting enough when he sold them. I sometimes wonder if he didn't think I'd be better off doing something else."

"Maybe he did," she said quietly. The breeze was blowing, tossing her hair, caressing her skin gently. A beautiful day. "Then you come home to the ostriches."

He laughed easily. "Yup. And don't think I don't wonder if he planned that. He knew me well. I wouldn't leave animals uncared for, and he probably knew just how much difficulty I'd have getting rid of this pair. What a way to get me back to my roots, but he sometimes had a strange sense of humor."

"They're quite a joke," she remarked, watching the two strange-looking birds eat ravenously. "I know they're birds, but…"

"Too big," he agreed. "Dinosaurs."

"I've heard people can ride them."

He laughed again. "No, thanks."

He studied her for a few minutes before turning his attention back to the mountains that loomed over one side of his ranch. She seemed tentative. After starting the day in a mood so good it surprised him, she had retreated a little.

"I wish I could have met your father," she said.

"Why?" It occurred to him that she'd never really had a chance to know her own father or mother. After all, a child of that age would have only a few memories and very little knowledge about the adults in her life.

"Because the person you are tells me something about him." She astonished him with a small smile. "I'm sure he was every bit as good a man as you said."

Quite a compliment coming from a woman who'd frankly told him she didn't trust easily. Although saying something like that was hardly a matter of trust.

A bark from the kennel area drew his attention.

"Flash!" Dory said and then laughed. "He must be feeling forgotten. He wants to play with his buddies."

"Let's go let them out, then." He paused only to lock the ostriches in their pen.

The summer-baked ground was hard beneath their feet, the remaining grasses dry and crackly. Out back where the kennels resided, however, the ground softened and greened because of how often he had to spray down the concrete. Each kennel opened onto a small, individual outdoor space so the dogs didn't start feeling too cooped up, but right now they were all at the front, watching Flash, who was prancing right up the middle of the dog run.

"I could almost swear he's taunting them," Cadell remarked.

"That dog is capable of more expressions and feelings than I would have believed," she answered. "You have a lot more cages than dogs. How come?"

"It varies, actually. I don't just train police dogs. I work with service dogs and even family pets. But mainly my job is being the lead K-9 officer and trainer. Anyway, every now and then I might have eight or ten dogs here."

"That'd keep you busy."

"It sure does. Some training is far more intensive and time-consuming that other types." He walked down the row, opening the kennels and letting the dogs free. At once they entered a joyous chase all over the unfenced acreage, to the ramshackle barn and back. Their joy was infectious, and both Cadell and Dory smiled as they watched.

"So," he said, risking it, "who took care of you afterward?"

He watched her suck her lip between her teeth, and he regretted spoiling the mood. Still, he needed to know her better. Wanted to know her better. He had not the least doubt there was more to this woman than the graphics designer and the frightened little girl.

"My godparents," she said after a moment. "They'd been good friends of my parents for a long time, and I knew them somewhat. Better than foster care, I imagine."

"The only judge is you. Did you feel loved?"

"They tried. I can't have been easy. Like I said, I didn't talk for over a year. They took me to therapists and doctors. But even when I started speaking again…well, I told you I don't trust people. All the way back then, I lost my trust. It had to be hard on them. They gave me so much, and when I look back I realize I gave them very little in return."

"I doubt they were doing it for what they could get out of it, Dory. I'm sure it was more about what they could do for you. Anyway, Betty became your friend. How did that happen?"

Dory's face lightened. Relief flooded him. He hadn't ruined today for her. Enough that he'd ruined last night.

"She was my English teacher my sophomore year of high school. How well do you know Betty?"

"In passing. We're not tight, but we talk from time to time. Why?"

"I just wondered if you had any idea of how persistent she can be."

At that he laughed. "I've heard about it."

Dory's smile grew. "She was persistent with me. I don't know why, but for some reason she wouldn't let go. She kept working on me, talking to me in odd moments. Finally she started inviting me and my godparents to have dinner at her house, and then they reciprocated and... Well, she never gave up on me. Even after I went to college, she'd drive over on a Saturday and take me out to lunch. Like water dripping on stone, I guess." She gave a little laugh, and her gaze met his. "I don't know when or how it happened, but she became my friend. My only friend. After my godparents died, Betty was the only person I had left."

He nodded. He was beginning to get a real clue about how truly alone this woman was. "What happened to them? Your godparents?"

"A tornado," she said simply, then directed her attention back to the mountains.

God, he thought. She'd been through a hell of a lot. The murder of her parents, the betrayal by her brother, then the loss of her godparents in an extreme act of nature? Without giving it a thought, he stretched out an arm, wrapped it around her shoulders and drew her to his side.

He wanted to find a way to express how bad he felt for her, but he suspected she wouldn't want that. She had made peace with most of her life, as far as he could tell. With everything except her brother. Anyway, sympathy didn't make up for the losses. So he offered what comfort he could with his touch.

After a couple of minutes, she surprised him by turning toward him and resting her cheek on his chest. "I'm such a mess," she said. "I don't know why anyone puts up with me."

"I don't think you're a mess."

She shifted a little against him. "How can you say that? I told you I can't trust. I'm afraid so much of the time..."

"I don't blame you for either. What your brother did would make it hard for anyone to trust again. As for being afraid... Well, he's a coldhearted murderer, isn't he? I wouldn't want to run into him any more than you do."

A thin laugh escaped her. "No machismo?"

"I'm not going to promise you something I have no right to promise," he said firmly. "I'm here for you, but that doesn't mean I can guarantee anything about your brother or your safety. All I can promise is that I'll do my damnedest."

Slowly her arms wrapped around his waist. He had to close his eyes against the sudden surge of passion. It had been simmering since he'd met her, and he'd been dumping cold water on it because that was probably the last thing she needed or wanted. Some problems were too big to be answered with a roll in the hay.

"Thank you," she said. "Thank you."

"For what?" He couldn't imagine.

"For being honest with me. Last night you told me things you knew I didn't want to hear, and now today you're not making wild promises. Not that I'd believe them."

The dogs were beginning to tire from their romp but weren't quite ready to quit yet. He stood there with one of the most beautiful women he'd ever met and wondered if he were capable of letting his own guard down enough. She freely said she found it hard to trust. Well, he did, too.

They made quite a pair. A hopeless one.

THE SURPRISE HE had promised her came in the form of Betty. She arrived midafternoon while Cadell was still checking the dogs for ticks.

"I need some help," she announced.

"Betty!" A smile bubbled up in Dory. "What's wrong?"

"Nothing. I just have a car full of food this young man asked me to buy, and I'm danged if I'm going to carry it all myself."

"One more dog," said Cadell, looking up. "What did you do? Shop for an army?"

Betty put a hand on her hip. "Clearly you don't shop for groceries here often. Shopping for two or three is impossible. So I hope you have some freezer space."

Dory felt a spark of curiosity. "Why is it hard to shop for small numbers?"

"Because an awful lot of people hereabouts have large families or shop for a couple of weeks at a time so they don't have to drive into town."

"Then what do you do?"

Betty's eyes twinkled. "I flirt with the butcher. He'll give me a single steak or chicken breast when that's all I want. However, he wasn't there today, so I had to get what's available. We could feed six or eight easily."

"I've got the freezer space," was all that Cadell said.

For a second, Dory had feared one of them would suggest inviting others over. She knew Betty wanted her to meet people, but not right now. Please, not right now. She was still feeling too stirred up.

"I'll help you," she said, ready to follow Betty to her car. She could at least do that much.

"I'll be along in just a minute," Cadell said. "Just go ahead and put everything on the table. You know your way, Betty, right?"

"That house isn't so big I could get lost," Betty answered drily. "Yes, I've been here before, that time you had that barbecue." She eyed Dory. "The man is popular. I think a couple of hundred people showed up for that one. He had to send runners to the store for more burgers."

Cadell's laugh followed them. "It was the free barbecue," he called.

"More like the ostriches," Betty commented as she led the way around to the trunk. "They're the talk of the whole damn county."

"I've been missing you," Dory said truthfully as she helped Betty pulled the reusable bags from the trunk.

"You'd miss me a whole lot less if you weren't always working," Betty retorted. "Those times I dropped in, I felt like I was interrupting."

"You probably were, but that doesn't mean I minded."

Betty laughed. "I'll keep that in mind." They climbed the front steps together. The house had a wide porch, and the front door was unlocked. "How are you and that dog making out?"

"I love him," Dory said simply. "I hardly have to tell him what to do. He seems to know."

"Cadell's a great dog trainer, from all I've heard." Betty turned left into the kitchen. She'd been right: the house wasn't big enough to get lost in. They put the bags on the kitchen table—much bigger and sturdier than Dory's— and began unpacking.

"You sure went to town," Dory remarked as she began to stack items. "You could feed an army!"

"Hardly," Betty said. "But I figured you could take some of this home with you. What have you got in your refrigerator? Soda. In your cupboard? Popcorn. Really, Dory."

"Hey, it's not as bad as all that."

"Right," Betty drawled.

Cadell joined them and separated out the three steaks, the potato salad and the bag of frozen broccoli. "For our meal?" he asked.

"Yeah," said Betty. "Then I'm thinking Dory can take home most of the rest. I just don't want it to spoil in the meantime. Have you seen her refrigerator?"

Cadell grinned at her. "An awful lot of raw vegetables. And soda pop."

"Ha."

Dory smiled. "What is this, a conspiracy to feed me?"

"Somebody has to. You'd forget to go to sleep if you could."

Being here with the two of them made Dory feel even better than she had upon awakening that morning. The not knowing must have been making her feel worse than knowing. Cadell had certainly answered one of her most pressing questions about the murder, and that was a relief, too. The whole thing had been so horrific. Facing her brother's capacity for such acts removed all the doubt that had plagued her over the years.

He'd never loved her. He'd used her. And he'd use her again if he could. Strange as it seemed, that made her feel stronger. Made her feel that she could face the moment when he came for her. If he came for her.

Or maybe it had simply taken love out of the equation, relieving her of the torment of wanting to understand because she still remembered loving George. Her unwillingness to face what he really was in the hope that he wasn't that bad. Yet terrified of him at the same time.

A royal emotional mess, she thought as she helped make dinner. Clarity, after all that, was welcome.

Not that it killed her fears. She suspected they'd always be there if George was on the loose. But at least she didn't have to feel guilty and confused because he'd loved her as a child. He'd never loved her at all.

AFTER A DELICIOUS DINNER, they settled on the front porch with cups of coffee to enjoy the late-afternoon breeze.

"So," Betty asked after a while, "any news on George?"

"Not exactly," Cadell answered when Dory remained silent. He looked at her, not Betty, as he spoke, hoping he wouldn't see shadows chasing across her face again. So far her face remained untroubled. "He went to a halfway house in his hometown, then vanished from it after only two days. There's been no trace of him since. I'm keeping my ears and eyes on it, though."

"Good," said Betty. "Although if that man has a lick of sense, he'll stay far away from her."

Dory turned her head. "Why do you say that?"

"Because you're the one person he can reasonably be expected to contact. Does he think no one would be watching out for you?"

Betty had a point, Cadell thought, but she was reckoning without knowledge of the inheritance. George had been willing to steal to get what he wanted, to lie to keep it secret. And to kill when something went wrong. Right now he was out there with nothing. Why would he pass up a chance to go for all that money if he thought there was any way to get it? Cadell seriously doubted he would just show up and ask for it. After all, Dory knew who had murdered their parents. Why would she turn all that money over to him?

If he'd been keeping tabs on Dory, he probably knew she hadn't married and didn't have children. But even if he hadn't, he wasn't above taking out her whole family to get what he wanted. Of that Cadell had not the least doubt. He'd seen it in that graphic Dory had made. Clear as crystal.

Dory spoke, surprising him. "Cadell says the murder was premeditated."

Betty drew a shocked breath. "How can he know that?"

"Because I made a three-dimensional graphic of the kitchen and murder scene."

"Oh, my God," Betty breathed. "Why? Didn't it just make everything worse?"

"No. I was using it to try to understand. My therapist taught me to draw things I couldn't cope with. It just continued. So I had this graphic."

"Amazing," Cadell intervened smoothly. "She wanted her answers, and it was right there in her drawing or whatever it's called. Clear as day if you knew what to look for. The man's a psychopath, Betty. And yes, as a cop, I would call the murder impossible unless it was premeditated."

Betty leaned over and seized Dory's hand. "How are you coping with this? Are you okay?"

"I'm fine, actually. Knowing is better than not knowing. Especially now that I don't have to wonder any longer if George loved me. He never did. He used me. I can't tell you why, but that makes this easier somehow."

"But you're still afraid?"

"Of course." Dory regarded her from eyes that suddenly looked hollow. "At least there's nothing left to muddy the waters if he shows up, but I think I'll be living with fear for a long, long time."

Cadell ached for the woman. He hadn't thought her good mood could survive the day, not as last night's blows began to sink in. But he *did* understand what she meant about it being easier knowing George had plotted the murder and had used her. It gave her permission to throw out her last lingering hopes about her brother. It gave her permission to hate him if she needed to.

It gave her permission to do whatever was necessary to protect herself.

He stared out over the rolling plain, the dry summer grasses, the tumbleweed caught on his neighbor's fence, feeling the weight of the mountains behind almost like a physical force. An energy. If they had lived and breathed, he wouldn't have been surprised.

Part of him hoped George Lake would show up here. Part of him wanted to wring the man's neck for all the suffering he had caused Dory.

Another, more sensible part of him hoped George was next seen somewhere in South America.

He didn't feel a lot of hope.

A little while later, Betty stood up. "I've got to get home. Dory, do you want to come with me?"

"I'll take her," Cadell said. "Her dog is here, too."

"Well, don't forget the food. I mean it, girl, you need to eat better. You're too thin already."

Dory gave a little laugh. "That's a matter of opinion."

Betty simply shook her head. "I don't know how anyone can stay that thin sitting at a desk all day and evening. Which means you're not eating enough. I'll say no more... until next time. So it's okay if I drop in?"

"Absolutely."

A short while later, Cadell watched the dust cloud rise behind Betty's small sport utility vehicle. It sat high enough to get over the rough roads around here but was just big enough to carry her, one passenger and her groceries. Putting Flash in there would have been ridiculous. A seventy-five-pound dog wasn't exactly small.

"It'll start getting dark soon," Cadell remarked. "The mountains really suck the light out of the afternoon."

"I kinda like it. Anyway, let me know when you want to head home. You seemed to enjoy the day."

"I did." She gave him the full force of her lovely smile. "I really did. I didn't expect to, but…well, it was a relief. I suppose it won't last long."

"You never know. You could move your stuff out here if you think you'd feel more comfortable. The thing that bothers me, though, is that you'd be really isolated out here when I'm at work. In town, you can always get help."

All of a sudden, maybe because of the words *in town*, she slammed back to the little girl standing in the street screaming. She'd gotten plenty of help. Out here, no one would hear her scream.

"Thanks, but I'll stay where I am. Generous offer, though."

"Not entirely without ulterior motive," he admitted.

Startled, her eyes widened and she uttered a totally uncharacteristic "Huh?"

He chuckled quietly. "You know I'm attracted to you. Admit it. I've even let you know. From the first moment I saw you, I thought you were the most beautiful woman I'd ever seen."

He could see her cheeks redden. "Don't exaggerate."

"I'm not. It's my personal opinion. You're absolutely beautiful. But it's more than that. The better I get to know you, the more I want you."

He paused, watching a rapid play of emotions run across her face, too quickly to read.

"Anyway," he said, rising. "I don't want to scare you

more. Let's pack up the groceries and the dog and get you home. You can decide if you want me around tonight."

"I'd like you to stay with me," she said.

Well, his heart leaped a little at that. *Down, boy,* he said to himself, as if he were one of his dogs. "Okay. Let me pack what I need for tomorrow, check the dogs one last time and then we'll load up."

DORY WONDERED WHY she'd asked him to stay. Flash was a great protector, but for some reason she felt safer with Cadell around. Crazy, since the last people in her life to make her feel at all safe had been her godparents, and it had taken them years.

Cadell brought out his uniform in plastic from a dry cleaner, neatly pressed on a hanger. His gun belt and all those accoutrements went in the back end with what looked like a whole bunch of other law enforcement stuff.

She peered in. "I never saw what was in a policeman's trunk before." About the only thing she recognized was the body armor.

"Not nearly as much as I used to cart in Seattle. There's actually room for the groceries."

He brought Dasher as well as Flash, probably because he needed his dog for work the next day. He'd also brought a sleeping bag.

She couldn't have begun to say why that made her feel cheated. She wanted no involvements, she didn't trust anyone except Betty and she was just beginning to trust Cadell.

No, it was best this way. Having him there would make her feel safer. Any more than that was a risk she didn't yet dare take.

Even if she felt the constant irritant of desire when he was around.

OVER THE NEXT DAYS, Dory and Cadell settled into a routine of sorts. She began working a little less during the daylight hours, instead driving herself out to spend time with him at his ranch as he trained dogs and tended the ostriches.

She thought he'd die of laughter when she told him she'd named the birds Itsy and Bitsy. Well, she was smiling more, too.

Except when she looked out over the wide-open spaces. Deep in her bones, she felt George was coming, that her fear was no figment of her imagination. Not since Cadell had mentioned her inheritance. People had killed for a lot less money.

A nugget of real anger had begun to burn in her, however. That man had destroyed her childhood, had blighted her life, and now he wanted to steal more. She was sure of it. If he'd cared about her at all, he'd have left instead of killing their parents. He wouldn't have taken them from her.

Ergo, he didn't care. Not at all. It was all about George.

The anger felt empowering, reducing her fear bit by bit. She knew the terror would return; it always had. But for now anger was a great reprieve. When she was out at the ranch with Cadell, she channeled that energy into working with the dogs, helping where she could. Daily she grew increasingly impressed with how much labor and patience went into training the dogs. Cadell wouldn't settle for half measures. These dogs would be walking with someone carrying a badge, and no one could afford the least miscalculation or misbehavior.

Most of the dogs were simply eager to please and did what was required of them. They were happy knowing their good behavior would be rewarded by playtime.

But one, a week later, failed the course.

"It's killing me," he told her as they watched a Malinois dash around the backyard. "He's going to have to go."

"Why? Are you going to put him down?" A new kind of horror filled her. She had grown attached to all these dogs.

"Of course I'm not going to put him down." He spoke almost sharply, then softened his tone. "No, nothing like that. But I can't curb his energy sufficiently. He's stubborn, and while all the things I teach these dogs should be fun for them, he keeps rewriting the rules. I'll wind him down a bit, and then he'll be suitable for a pet."

Considering she had been consistently amazed by how hard these dogs tried to please, she was surprised that any of them would fail the course. But when she thought about it, it made sense. One of the other things she'd learned from working beside Cadell was that the dogs had their own quite distinct personalities.

Cadell touched her arm, and a ribbon of pleasure ran through her. "It's okay, Dory. Not every dog is cut out for police work. Or rescue work. Just like some aren't cut out to be service dogs."

That sparked interest in her. "Do you teach service dogs, too?"

"Sometimes. That's a really special skill, though, so I don't do it often."

"I don't get it."

"It's simple. Service dogs need a lot of in-depth special training, and they have to be individually trained to serve a particular kind of companion. It's better to have someone familiar with all that do the job. But service dogs are expensive. Not everybody can afford one, and not everyone can be supplied by a charity. So occasionally, I do it. It's a hell of a lot bigger job than what I usually do. In many cases it's a matter of teaching dogs to do things they don't normally do. Whereas a police or rescue dog…the talent is pretty much innate for that kind of work. It's mostly a matter of directing it."

She laughed then. "And making sure they listen."

He winked and looked back at the corral. The dog was still running around, chasing and tossing the tennis ball for his own amusement. Itsy and Bitsy watched from their pen, their huge dark eyes intent.

"Now watch," Cadell said. "This is part of the problem."

He whistled and called the dog's name. The animal looked at him, then went back to the tennis ball. "See? Two months and I still can't get him to come reliably. He'll make a couple of kids happy, but I can't send him out with an officer. *Most of the time* just won't work for them."

Later he persuaded her to stop at the diner for supper, although she wasn't entirely comfortable with being out in public. Dang, she thought, this man was pulling her out of her comfortable hidey-hole whether she wanted it or not.

But she felt safe going with Cadell, which worried her. Was she turning him into another bubble around herself, a safe place that held everything else at bay?

Troubled, she hardly said anything throughout the meal. She put down a hamburger and fries and didn't taste a thing.

She was a psychological mess. Nothing had ever completely sorted her out, but so far she'd managed not to hurt anyone else with it.

After dinner, he insisted on paying the bill, then surprised her again. "Let's go over to the sheriff's office."

She balked on the sidewalk. "Why?"

"You don't think I'm the only one trying to track down your brother, do you? I've asked for some help. I don't know about you, but I'd feel a whole lot better if we could pinpoint his location. Come on, nobody bites, and everyone would like to be sure you're safe."

Her temper flared. "Who gave you the right to discuss me with anyone?"

He put his hands on his hips, tilted his head and simply looked at her. God, he looked good in that blue shirt, jeans snug on his narrow hips, a cowboy hat shadowing his head. So good. Why the hell was she trying to start a fight?

But she hadn't given him permission to make her problems public, and it troubled her that other people knew. Even police officers.

"If you want me to apologize for protecting you," he

said, "then I will. But I won't mean it, and you'll know it. So what's the point, Dory?"

"It's having so many people know about me! I don't like it."

"They're cops," he said, an edge of frustration creeping into his voice. "They know how to keep things secret. Not a one of them is going to gossip about you or your brother. Not here, not ever. Unlike the rest of this town, they know how to zip their lips about matters like this."

She couldn't speak, the turmoil inside her was so great. She felt as if she'd been left exposed in plain sight, tied out like a goat.

"Dory, you can't face this alone. You don't need to."

She'd had enough. She never should have come to this benighted town. Letting Betty talk her into coming here had been a huge mistake. Painful layers had been stripped from her once again. Her privacy. Her small sense of security. Even her coworkers had helped expose her.

George. She should have just hit the road and kept moving on a regular basis. The idea that she could now ever stay in one place seemed like insanity.

Without a word, she opened the back door of Cadell's truck and took Flash out. He'd been sitting in there in a wire cage with the windows open. Now, glad to be free, he jumped down eagerly.

"Flash, heel." She grabbed his leash and hooked it to his collar, then started walking home.

Alone.

Because alone was the safest way to be. The only way to survive.

Chapter Ten

"Damn it," Cadell said under his breath. Had he really done something wrong by trying to trace her brother? Evidently she thought so. But it was the kind of thing he'd have done for anyone as a cop, and usually people were grateful for the interest and possible help.

She was one confusing woman. Life had seriously wounded her, and he wasn't sure that she was able to be truly rational when it came to George. Well, of course she wasn't. None of this was about reason. It was about gut feelings. He ought to know that.

After a moment's debate, he hopped into his vehicle and drove the half block to the sheriff's offices on the corner. A parking space awaited him, and he slid into it a little too fast. Then he walked into the station, where he was greeted by the dispatcher, a new hire who'd started only the month before over the old dispatcher's objections. He gathered that Velma, who'd been with the department longer than anyone could remember, felt she was the only one who knew how to do the job properly, which had caused a parade of new hires to quit over the years. Duty officers had often had to fill in the excess hours. Harriet, the new woman, was at least adequate, although Cadell was already wondering how long she'd last with Velma constant carping at her.

"Gage?" he asked.

"In his office," Harriet answered. "Getting ready to leave."

Gage had an open-door policy, so Cadell didn't hesitate to walk himself back and knock. Gage looked up from the papers he was straightening, his burn-scarred face offering a crooked smile. "Hey. What's going on?"

"Apart from me stepping knee-deep into a pile of manure, nothing. I've got one less dog I'm going to train—wrong temperament. I'll have a couple more sometime next week."

Gage pointed to the chair. "And?"

"The manure, you mean?"

"Obviously."

Cadell didn't want to sit. "Dory Lake is furious with me for bringing you in on her problem, and she's walking home alone with her dog, Flash."

"The one you trained?"

"Yes."

Gage nodded. "Then she should be safe enough." But that didn't keep him from reaching for a radio. Five minutes later he had both deputies and city police officers advised to keep an unobtrusive eye on Dory Lake as she walked home. "Make sure she doesn't know."

The tension inside Cadell eased.

After a moment, Gage spoke. "She doesn't have any reason to trust us, you know. I read her case. Sure, cops took care of her after she ran out of that abattoir that had been her home, but I gather she hasn't trusted much since."

"No," Cadell admitted. "I may have blown it entirely, but I'll head over there in a little while and try to mend the fences."

Gage rocked back in his chair. "That's up to you."

"Meaning?"

"Exactly what I said. If you want to mend fences, mend them. I tried to call earlier, but you didn't answer. It seems her brother bought a bus ticket to Miami. Last week."

"So he's headed the other way."

"Uh, not yet. He never used the ticket."

Cadell closed his eyes. "Hell."

"Misdirection? Maybe. I've asked my counterpart in Florida to keep an eye out for him, but if he never went there…"

"I get it." Cadell stood up. "Thanks, Gage."

"You might not want to wait," Gage said as Cadell was walking out. "Don't give her time to raise the drawbridge over the moat."

Cadell paused and looked back. "You're troubled, too?"

"Let's just say from what I read, I wouldn't put anything past George Lake. Not even murdering his sister. She may have every reason to be terrified."

DORY DIDN'T WANT to answer the knock at her door. She'd been vaguely aware that there seemed to be more than the usual number of police cars on the streets, and one corner of her mind wondered what was coming down.

But Flash's tail told her who was at the door. At the moment she wouldn't have opened it for anyone without knowing who was there. She needed to get a peephole installed, she thought vaguely, but right now there was no threat outside, simply Cadell.

She wasn't sure she wanted to see him ever again. She felt exposed, like a raw nerve ending, and it was his fault. Her past haunted her, not only within her own mind and heart, but everywhere else, it seemed. She'd had to tell her coworkers about her brother, which she'd never wanted to do, and now Cadell had broadcast it. So what if only other officers knew about it? She couldn't manage to hide from it, no matter what she did.

Flash danced a little from side to side, impatient. The slightest begging whimper escaped him. Damn it.

She opened the door at last. Flash did a little happy dance, then immediately sat, realizing he was in danger of breaking his rules. Not that Dory cared. She hadn't put him on duty yet.

Cadell looked somber, standing there with his hands at his sides. "May I come in?"

She wanted to slam the door in his face but caught herself in time. Just because the rest of the world was going insane around her didn't mean she had to, as well. Anyway, she was already crazy enough.

"Sure." She stepped back, letting him pass. Flash wiggled a bit in his seated position, hoping for a pat. He got one from Cadell as she closed the door.

She led the way to the shoddy living room and let him have the couch. She had her doubts about the wooden rocking chair holding him for long. It barely held her.

"I ran into your neighbor out front. Marissa Tremaine. Have you met her?"

What did this have to do with anything? "Not yet." And with the urge to pack up and move on growing stronger in her, she doubted she was going to meet anyone.

"Her first husband was killed overseas a few years ago. She lives in that big house across the street with her new husband and child. It's nice to see her happy again."

Point? She wondered where he was going with all of this. So what if that woman was happy again? Happiness had eluded Dory most of her life. Oh, here and there she'd run into it, but it didn't last long. Somehow it felt disrespectful. All the therapy hadn't changed that, either.

"Look," he said, "I'm sorry I upset you, but I'm not sorry that I spoke to the sheriff about this. All he can access is public records."

Her lips tightened a bit, but she nodded. Public records? Anyone could get those if they looked.

"Anyway, it turned out to be useful. He found that your brother purchased a bus ticket last week from Saint Louis to Miami."

Tension hissed out of her like the leaking of a balloon. "He's headed away."

"We don't know that. The ticket hasn't been used."

That was all it took. Tension once again gripped her, winding around her every nerve ending. "Damn it," she muttered. "Damn him." She looked at Cadell. "He's not stupid."

"Nobody's counting on him being stupid. The sheriff has someone in Miami keeping an eye out for him, but if he uses the bus ticket, we should hear quickly."

"But he could give the ticket to anyone!"

"These days you can't travel by bus without ID. I doubt his prison ID would pass muster for anyone else unless he can find a near-identical twin. Regardless, he found the money to buy the ticket. I'm wondering what else he's been up to."

"Stealing," she snapped. "What he used to do all the time. I'm surprised he's not leaving a string of police reports in his wake. Oh, wait…he's probably being careful not to be noticed. So we really don't know anything."

"I'm afraid not."

But she saw that he didn't really believe this was nothing. No. She closed her eyes. "He tried to lay a false trail. He's coming here."

Cadell didn't immediately answer her. When he did, it was clear he was choosing his words carefully. "We can't know that based on just one thing."

Her eyes snapped open. "Tell me you don't really believe that."

His frown deepened, and he rose from the couch, pacing the small room, seeming to nearly fill it with his presence. She easily imagined that everywhere he went he made rooms feel small. "We can't know that," he repeated. "But it's suspicious enough to put me on alert. I'm sure the sheriff feels the same."

"Well, thank you for that."

He stopped and stared directly at her. "Meaning?"

She'd been extremely sarcastic, and she really hadn't meant to be. Or maybe she had. "Sometimes I feel as if people just dismiss me as crazy. I've felt that way for years. Well, I am a little crazy, I suppose. Untrusting, afraid of shadows…even when George was in prison, I didn't feel entirely safe. It just wasn't something I could explain. I guess I don't need to explain it anymore."

"Of course not. Anyway, I don't think you're crazy. What happened to you as a child was bound to have a long-term impact. I'd be amazed if it hadn't. *Then* there'd be something wrong with you."

Unexpected gratitude filled her, washing away the last of her irritation with him. "I'm sorry," she said finally.

"For what?"

"For getting so mad at you. You were right, you were only trying to protect me. I'm not used to that."

He shook his head a little. "I should have asked you first. I was high-handed, and I know it."

"The cop?" she said, allowing a little amusement to slip into her dark internal places.

He smiled faintly. "The cop," he agreed. "I have this thing about taking charge."

She rose from the rocker. There was little room to put between them, and other feelings began to niggle at her. Among them an overpowering desire for him, to put aside everything for just one night. She'd given in to that urge only a couple of times in her life and had learned how rarely it turned out well. But Cadell...since the beginning something about him had been calling to her on multiple levels. She wanted his friendship, though, and after what he'd said about his marriage, she doubted he'd be interested in anything more. Even though he'd mentioned it...

Her thoughts stuttered between one breath and the next. He'd told her he wanted her. What kind of delusion was she feeding herself now?

"I need a drink," she said and marched to the kitchen for a bottle of soda.

"I could do with something strong," he remarked, following her.

"I don't have anything. I don't like liquor."

"I meant coffee," he retorted. "I'm not much of a drinker myself. I've seen too many problems arise from alcohol. So call me an occasional one-beer man."

She screwed up her face. "No beer for me. I don't like the taste."

"Tsk," he said, but she could tell he was teasing. Someone teasing her was a relatively rare experience. Probably her own fault. After all, she was far from the easiest person to get along with. So many hot buttons, who would dare?

She started the coffee and got herself a cola. She was oranged out for the day. Settling in at the table, with Flash beside her, she sipped from the bottle and thought about her reactions that day. One minute she was enjoying Cadell's company, enjoying the dogs and—dare she admit it—amused by the ostriches, Itsy and Bitsy. Then she'd gone off like a rocket because he'd asked his colleagues to keep an eye out for developments with George.

"Why do you put up with me?" she asked bluntly. "I'm a pain."

"True." He leaned back against the corner while the coffeemaker hissed and streamed black brew. The corners of his eyes, however, were crinkled. "You don't come close to Itsy and Bitsy, however."

"What have those ostriches ever done to you?" Once again, amusement was trying to creep in. She decided to let it.

"They ate two of my favorite hats. Felt. Leather hat bands. Stretched just right to fit my head perfectly. I'm ashamed to admit that not until after they grabbed the second one did I realize it was going to be a continuing problem. I thought about getting a football helmet."

At that she cracked a helpless laugh. "Why did they want the hats?"

"Ask them." He shrugged. "Didn't take them long to shred them, though. The goats aren't nearly so bad."

She straightened. "You have *goats*?"

"Sorta, but not exactly. I pasture them farther from the house for one of my neighbors. I don't need them arguing with the birds or the dogs."

"But the dogs could hurt them, too."

He shook his head. "One of the ways I finish up training is by taking the dogs out to the goat pasture. A new distraction. If they can follow orders despite the goats, they pass."

She shook head, feeling a smile tickle the edges of her lips. "I thought you weren't ranching."

"I'm not. I've got two birds and I provide grazing for a neighbor's goats. That's not ranching. Ask anyone." The coffee had finished brewing and he snagged a cup from the cupboard to pour himself some. Then, at last, he gave her room to breathe again by coming to the table and sitting.

"The goats amuse me," he said. "Last spring I headed out there with one of my dogs. There were lots of little kids gamboling about, but one of those damn adult goats had jumped up on the roof of the hay shed. I still can't figure out how he got up there. I wonder if he was sick of all those noisy, excited kids. Or maybe he thought he was on guard duty. Anyway, I called my neighbor, asked what he wanted me to do about it."

"And?" She was loving this.

"He said, 'Damn goat got up there, he can get hisself down.' Which he did by the next day."

This was a whole part of the world she'd never been exposed to before, and it delighted her. Most of her life she'd lived in suburban or urban areas, and the last decade or so she'd pretty much become a troglodyte. Her graphics work endlessly fascinated her. It always offered a fresh challenge, and the amount of detail required kept her fully engaged.

But goats and ostriches? Her exposure had been one trip to a local zoo when she was ten, and she didn't remember any ostriches.

For the very first time, she considered the possibility of remaining here, once her problems with George were behind her. There seemed to be a whole wealth of new experiences awaiting her, something she hadn't thought about in a long time, if ever.

"You know," she said slowly, wondering how she had come to trust him this much, "I've let George deprive me of too much. Even when he was in prison, he controlled my choices in a lot of ways. Made me avoid other people.

Made me distrustful." She paused then hit on the underlying truth. "It's time I realized that he hasn't been the one depriving me. I've made all the choices since he went to prison. He's no Svengali, controlling me at a distance."

She sighed and stared down at the table, at the familiar bottle of cola, and took a hard look at herself. "Plenty of people go through terrible things that leave deep and abiding scars. That doesn't mean they quit. I've quit, Cadell."

The chair creaked as he leaned forward and stretched out a hand, palm up. Uncertainly, she placed her hand in his. "You haven't given up," he said.

"What do you call it when I want to be a hermit? Betty's the only person I've let get close to me in my entire life."

"Including your godparents?"

"Including them. God, they gave me so much, and I gave almost nothing back, and now it's too late. There were people in college who tried to be my friends, but I always pushed them back until they quit trying. I've made myself a nice, safe little world, but it's far from complete."

A few beats passed before he responded. "What made you think of that?"

"Goats. Ostriches. Dogs." She shook her head and lifted her gaze to his. "It just struck me—I'm missing so many things by living in my little cave. It's not that I don't enjoy what I'm doing, because actually I do. But there's so much more out there. Maybe I ought to make a little time for it."

"You've been coming out to the ranch and working with me and the dogs," he reminded her.

"It's true. But that's a baby step. Maybe I should meet my neighbors. Talk to that Marissa you mentioned earlier. Meet other people."

"I'm not opposed to that, but I'd suggest you take it slowly."

"But why?"

"You don't want to overload yourself. You're not used to a big social life, are you?"

"I'm used to words on a screen," she admitted. "But maybe that's not enough anymore." Then she sighed. "Anyway, George."

"George?"

"All these ideas about changing my life would be easier to implement if I didn't have him hanging out there like an albatross around my neck." The part of her that had been trying to expand pinched a little. She felt it happen. "He's coming, Cadell. I think we both know that."

He didn't disagree.

"So all plans are on hold for now," she said. "I've got to deal with him somehow. If he just wants money, he can have it. If he wants me dead...well, I don't think I'm going to let that happen. So I'm going to stop hassling you about everything you do to try to help. I'm just sorry I'm taking over your life."

His hand tightened around hers. "You're not taking over anything. I'm exactly where I want to be."

She half smiled without humor. "Cop?"

"Cop," he answered. "But only partly. I also happen to like you. And yeah, you can be difficult, but who can't? I'm the take-charge guy who'll probably annoy you again. But unless you want to throw me out, this is where I'm staying."

A warm rush of gratitude filled her. "You're a nice guy, you know."

"Don't feed my ego." Then he grew serious. "I mean it, Dory. I'm here because I want to be. And I *do* like you, thorns and all."

"Why is that the sweetest thing anyone's ever said to me?"

"I can't imagine. But it's not sweet, it's just true." He paused. "I'm not one to shine people on. Never have been. If I have a problem with you, you'll know it. And if I say I like you, I mean it."

"Thank you." But even as the warmth continued to remain with her, her mind insisted on jumping around, which wasn't a usual state for her. She could summon a laser-like focus for hours when she needed it, and had long ago learned a reasonable control of her thoughts. That was what cognitive therapy was all about. Which was not to say she never slipped, and the news of George's release had caused a big-time slip. She'd come running to the first offer of a haven like a scared mouse.

But now she was glad she had, because she would have missed a lot if she hadn't.

"You're never going to believe this," she remarked, "but I like Itsy and Bitsy."

He didn't seem disturbed by her change of subject away from him liking her—a pregnant statement, full of possibilities she wasn't ready to consider. Possibilities she somehow knew she was going to hug to herself, because she liked him, too.

"I don't *dislike* them," he answered. "We have a mutually irritable relationship."

"Well, I'm not saying I want to pet either of them." She summoned a smile. "What happened to your mother? You never mentioned her."

"Where did that come from?" But he didn't wait for an answer. "She died shortly after I was born. Some kind of infection."

"I'm really sorry."

He shook his head a little. "I never knew her, never knew what it was like to have a mother. Sometimes I wished I was like other kids, but mostly I just accepted it. My father took good care of me. He worked me hard on the ranch. But he still made space for me to have a social life when I was in high school. I guess I never thought about the work he must have been doing when I wasn't there."

"But he didn't have a problem with you becoming a policeman?"

"If he did, he never let on. I may have mentioned it already, but by then he was winding the ranch down. Swore the land had more value than the livestock."

"Did it?"

"I lease a lot of it, so yeah, I guess. But then I look at those dang ostriches and wonder if they weren't a plot on his part to keep me rooted here. He was a great believer in roots. So am I, I guess. No regrets at all about coming back here."

"Roots." She spoke the word, feeling around it in her mind. "I'm not sure I really had any. Even when I was with my godparents. Uncle Bill, as I called him, was always being transferred. Sometimes we went with him if it was going to be a long stay, and sometimes Auntie Jane and I remained where we were. They did more of that when I was in high school. I guess they thought that was important."

"Wasn't it?"

She shrugged. "I don't know. Like I said, I don't make friends. Well, except for Betty. I met her in the high school in Saint Louis."

"Well, I'm your friend now, so live with it."

He was teasing her again, and she liked it. There was something so normal about it, a normalcy she'd avoided for years. Now that she was trying it on, a piece at a time, she was discovering that it was good.

She was acutely aware that these feelings were just a house of cards that would tumble the instant George arrived, but she couldn't give up these moments.

"He stole too much from me," she announced. Then, with a boldness she exhibited in her work, she rose and came to his side. "You busy tonight, Deputy?"

He looked up at her, his eyes narrowing. "I was planning on being here."

"That's not what I meant." Then she opened the dam she'd built to avoid thinking about what she truly wanted and let the needs pour through her for the first time. She was done holding them at bay. Good experience or bad experience, she didn't care. She was damn well going to have the experience.

"Come to bed with me," she murmured. "Now."

Chapter Eleven

Cadell froze, conflicting emotions welling up in him. He wanted this woman, no secret there, but he was also afraid of hurting her in some way. He wasn't even sure why she was asking so boldly. Every time he'd thought he glimpsed heat in her gaze, she'd concealed it quickly. Even so, just a short time ago she'd been furious with him, and now this? What had brought it on?

Rising, he slipped his arms around her waist and felt a tremor pass through her. There was only one way to know. "Why?"

She closed her eyes and shook her head a little but didn't draw away. "Is this the time for analysis?"

"I'm not asking for analysis. I want a reason. I'd like to know that you don't want to use me to make you forget. I need to be more than that."

"Nothing can make me forget," she whispered. "But I've missed a whole hell of a lot because of that. I want you. I've wanted you for a while, but I kept coming up with reasons to tell myself no. I tried to bury it." Her blue eyes opened and met his straightly. "I can't bury it, Cadell."

He supposed that was honest enough. And from the tightness of her whispered words, he sensed this honesty wasn't easy for her. Why should it be? People talked easily about a lot of things, but sex seemed to be different. He'd also gathered that it was never easy for her to admit her own desires and needs, whatever they were.

Living in a cave hadn't helped her to blossom in many ways. She was a flower in desperate need of some sunshine.

He leaned closer and brushed his lips against hers. "You should know I want you, too. I've mentioned it more than once. But it has to be good, Dory. Are you sure this is the right time for you?"

"There'll never be a right time if I think about it too much. Cadell…"

These could be the tenderest moments between two human beings or they could become an ugly mistake. He wanted her more than he could say, but he needed to protect her, too.

So do that and quit being a jerk. See where it leads. Satisfy her in every way.

And to hell with his qualms. If regret were coming, it was going to have to wait a few hours.

He kissed her again, pushing his tongue a little past her lips until it met the gate of her teeth. Another shiver passed through her, then she let her head fall back and her mouth open. She hadn't changed her mind.

For right now, that was all he needed.

Flash stood up as Cadell swept Dory up into his arms. "Darlin', could you tell your watchdog to stay?"

Dory quickly clasped her arms around Cadell's neck and spoke thickly. "Flash, stay. Guard."

"You could sound like you mean it," Cadell remarked as he easily carried Dory the short distance to her bedroom.

"He better not get in the way," Dory mumbled. "You'd think he'd understand he doesn't need to guard against you."

"He does." He'd made sure of that over the past week. He just hadn't wanted the dog in here, where he might misinterpret something as play to join.

He set Dory down slowly, sliding her along the entire length of his body. She inhaled sharply as she felt him hard against her. No secret about his desire anymore. The pressure even through his jeans made him want to groan. He reminded himself to take his time, to make sure she could savor every sensation. Then thought started to slip from his grasp as she reached down and touched him through the denim.

"Mmm," she murmured.

He had this thing in his head, where he undressed a woman, then himself. Where it had come from, he had no idea, but it now completely vanished. She reached for the snaps on the front of his shirt and ripped them open ruthlessly. Then her soft, small hands began to explore his chest, sending shafts of pleasure through him with each stroke, each caress, even each pause as she learned his contours.

When she brushed over his small nipples, he was unable to repress a shudder.

"You, too?" she murmured. Before he could respond in any way, she'd leaned forward and taken him into her mouth, licking and sucking until the drumbeat in his head grew deafening.

Not only was this woman an angel, she was also a witch. A very talented witch with her tongue. Then she gave him a gentle nip, and he jerked.

He looked down at her, and there was no mistaking that pleased, sleepy smile. "Happy with yourself, huh?" he asked, his voice low. He was now sure he wasn't dealing with a totally inexperienced woman, which removed his last inhibition.

Oh, this was going to be good.

Reaching out, he grabbed the bottom of her T-shirt and pulled it over her head. Amazement grabbed him as he discovered a lacy bra, not at all what he would have expected. Delightfully, it pushed up the globes of her breasts invitingly.

Bending his head, he kissed the top of each breast, then ran his tongue lightly over her skin. A soft moan escaped her. Then, with a twist of his hand, he found the back clasp and released it.

At once the bra gave up its control, but before he could slide it away, Dory did so. She stood before him in the dim light from the hallway, making no attempt to conceal herself from his gaze. Instead she took his hands and pressed them to her breasts, then leaned in again to suck on his small nipples.

As he massaged her breasts, trying to judge her response by her soft moans, he felt her hands reach for the snap on his jeans. So that was how it was going to be?

Thrilled, he reached for her jeans, too. With almost surprising speed, underwear and denim fell to the floor.

Now the damn shoes. He pushed her down so that she sat on the edge of the bed, then squatted to remove her tennis shoes, her socks and the last of her jeans.

A giggle escaped her, surprising him.

"What?" he asked, looking up before attending to his own problem.

"Is there any graceful way to do this?" she asked.

"Yeah. Robes. Negligees. Nudity." But a smile creased his face as he sat beside her on the bed and fought his way out of his work boots and all the rest. He even remembered to grab a condom and roll it on. "Kind of a punctuation mark."

But then she stole his breath by reaching out to close her hand around his erection. "Dory..." Her name escaped him on a choked breath.

"You're a beautiful hunk," she murmured, her own breath beginning to come rapidly. "Can we..."

"Anything," he promised, caught in a consuming fire.

"Hurry," she gasped. "Rerun later."

He couldn't pass that up. All the finesse he'd been planning ceased to matter as the firestorm took over. As soon as she lay back, he slid over her, her delicious curves melding with his angles in all the best ways possible.

For an instant he couldn't even move because it felt so good. Catching her face between his hands, he looked down into her blue eyes. Botticelli angel. His for now.

Then he slid himself into her, feeling her rise up to meet him. Her legs twined around his hips, holding him as close as she could, and her body arched in response to his every thrust.

Almost too soon, she stiffened and cried out, a shudder running through her from head to foot. He couldn't contain himself another minute and joined her, erupting into her as if he were turning inside out.

When he collapsed on her, her hands settled lightly on his shoulders. A welcome. The most beautiful welcome of all.

GEORGE FINALLY HITCHED a long ride on a big rig headed in the right direction. This one had pulled up alongside him as he'd been walking down the shoulder in the dark, unwilling to risk sticking his thumb out for fear the law would take an interest.

But this guy seemed bored with his long haul and wanted someone to chat with. The radio was unusually quiet. Well, George was a good talker, able to readily make up entertaining tales, and it was a small price to pay for getting to the truck stop just outside Conard City.

He cast himself in the role of a down-on-his-luck bartender who was heading home to see his sick mother. That one always brought sympathy his way. But he didn't linger over those details, instead coming up with amusing stories about things he'd supposedly experienced while tending bar. Soon enough, the driver was chuckling, and with the laughter the guy decided he liked George. George knew how to read people, and this one was in his pocket. Now he was assured the guy wouldn't drop him off at a crossroads in the middle of nowhere.

Eventually the driver asked him about being out of work. "I thought a bartender could always get a job."

"I will eventually, after I look in on my mother. But I was stupid, man. This woman looked thirty years old at least, and I served her without asking for ID. Bitch got me canned because she was working for the state. Trying to catch ordinary joes like me."

"That stinks," the truck driver said.

"Ah, my fault," George said. "It's getting harder and harder to tell how old a person is by looking. Always check the ID."

The driver snorted. "She must have been pretty."

George laughed. "Believe it. But I was still stupid."

"I make it a rule never to pick up riders," the driver remarked. "But I picked you up. I figured, what's the harm? I dumped my load in Omaha, couldn't find a return load anywhere, so I'm driving an empty trailer and burning gas. I ain't got nothin' to steal."

"What about your truck?" George asked.

"Not likely. This baby is old. She keeps going because I hold her together. Besides, she's got LoJack. I don't get home on time, my wife will be calling the cops."

"Tight rein, huh?" George asked. "No time for a little fun on the road?"

The driver laughed again. "Not for me."

Satisfied he had the driver exactly where he wanted him, George began to consider his plans for the days ahead. This guy would leave him at the truck stop, but he had no idea where Dory was in relation to that. She might have settled into a log cabin in the middle of nowhere.

Naw, probably not, he decided. He gathered from what little he knew of her work that she must need a great internet connection. Those generally didn't reach isolated cabins.

So she'd be somewhere in or near one of the towns. There were a bunch of really small ones, then the big one where he'd be dropped off.

He rubbed his chin, feeling the beard he'd begun growing almost as soon as he'd been freed. Right now he didn't look a whole lot like himself, which was exactly what he wanted. The gray streaks in it helped, too, making him look a lot older.

But this town he was going to wasn't that big. It might be best to lie low as much as possible. Maybe people minded their own business, and maybe they didn't. He couldn't risk the latter, couldn't risk people commenting on a stranger who didn't have a job and didn't seem to be passing through. The last thing he wanted was anyone's attention.

The truck stop would probably be a reasonably safe place to hang on and off, with a constant turnover of clientele. But apart from that?

He needed to keep low.

Which multiplied the problem of locating Dory.

Around five in the morning, he gave up his comfortable ride with the trucker, asking to be let out in a larger town, away from his destination. A town that would give him the freedom to plan and the tools he might need.

And that sign about Rodeo Days meant there'd be a lot of strangers around. Good. Not a soul would notice him unless he wanted it.

He waved goodbye to the trucker as he stood beside the road. He'd long ago learned not to do anything that might make someone remember him, so he was always polite and friendly but not too much so.

Smiling, he started to whistle. He was on his way, getting it together.

LIMP WITH PLEASURE and fatigue, Dory could hardly move. She lay on the bed waiting for Cadell to return and felt Flash lick her hand. The air was filled with the musky aroma of their lovemaking, delicious to her.

"Down," she said, barely able to muster the energy for that one word. She had forgotten that she could feel so good, so sated, so complete…if she ever had before. She felt the corners of her mouth curve, as if she couldn't stop smiling. Heck, her whole body was smiling.

She just hoped her impatience hadn't turned off Cadell. Well, she didn't know how to be a lady. She was a woman, and nothing in her life had made her feel she needed to take a backseat, although she'd learned online that there were plenty of men out there who wanted just that. Hence her secrecy about her identity.

Well, that and George. She knew he was coming. She could feel it. Somehow she would have to face him down, get him to move on and leave her alone. Money. With him it had always been about money. She'd gladly give him her last dime if he'd move to another continent.

The bed dipped as Cadell returned. She was surprised she'd delved so deeply into her thoughts that she hadn't heard him coming. The light was still dim, coming from the bathroom, but she could see he was smiling. She reached up a hand and cupped his cheek.

"I'm limp," she told him.

His smile widened. "You're not the only one. And we're not done."

Her heart leaped. "We're not?"

"Oh, no. I hardly got to explore you. That needs a bit of correction." He stretched out and propped his head on his hand, still smiling. "Close your eyes. Just *feel*."

Excitement was already galloping through her veins, though just a minute ago she would have thought it impossible. She obliged, closing her eyes, nearly holding her breath in anticipation.

First came the featherlight touch of his fingertips, tracing the shell of her ear, the line of her jaw. Passing sweetly over her lips until they parted and she drew a long, quivering breath. With each moment, every nerve in her body felt as if it were growing more sensitive.

Then his touch trailed lower, remaining light, offering no pressure. Across her shoulders, her collarbones, down to her fingertips and then back up the inside of her arm. Now a helpless shiver raced through her.

"Easy," he murmured. "Just enjoy."

Oh, man, was she enjoying. When he found her breasts at last, she bit her lip, hoping…and his fingertips moved on. She could have cried out.

He trailed his hand down, tracing the most fragile of ribbons across her midriff, then lower, making circles around her navel, moving side to side but taking ever so long to dip lower.

Just as she thought he would, his hand slipped down her thigh, stroking the outside first, then the inside, but coming no nearer to her most sensitive places.

He was driving her out of her mind with an impatient

excitement like none she had ever known. Then her other leg, down the outside then up until he returned to her belly.

Now! Please, now! Her thoughts had turned into a stew of boiling need and even some fear that he might leave her like this, hungry but unsated. She felt as if she were vibrating from head to toe, like a stringed instrument that he was playing skillfully.

Oh, so skillfully.

Then, causing her to suck air between her teeth, his fingers slid downward and found her moist cleft. She could no longer hold still but arched upward against his touch, needing so much more.

For a little while, he indulged her, stroking her with gentle fingers, but then it stopped.

She couldn't even open her eyes, she couldn't stand it. "Cadell..."

"Easy."

She felt him part her legs, felt him settle between them, then the most exquisite sensation in the world, almost painful in its intense pleasure. With his tongue, he drove her upward until she mindlessly dug her fingers into the sheets and hung on for dear life.

When at last she reached the pinnacle and shattered into a million flaming pieces, all that was left of her was woman, flying free among stars.

CADELL'S ARMS WRAPPED her in warmth and strength. He'd pulled the blanket up over them and held her close, close enough that she could feel his hard contours, the slightest movement as he breathed. The whisper of his breath on her hair. Her own arm lay over his waist, feeling more of his warmth, more of his skin.

The intimacy of the moment pierced her. She'd taken a couple of lovers before, never for more than a single night or two, but those experiences had been nothing like this.

She'd walked away from both of them thinking she was really not missing much by avoiding men.

All that had changed in an earthquake named Cadell. The intimacy. The closeness. Again, the understanding floated through her. She had never felt this close to anyone, at least not since her childhood.

She should have run from it. Where had love and trust gotten her the last time? But she could not quell it. It filled her, altering her, changing her, and she didn't want to fight it.

Come what may, she thought sleepily, she was going to be a different person. Maybe a better person. Now if only they could get rid of the threat.

Then, safe in the arms of a man who had taken it on himself to protect her, she drifted off into the happiest dreams she had enjoyed for years.

CADELL AWOKE FIRST in the morning. Slipping carefully out of bed, he pulled on his jeans and boots, then took Flash for a run in the backyard. When they came back in, he started a pot of coffee for himself and began looking for something to use to make a breakfast for the two of them.

After last night, he had the appetite of a lumberjack.

Then he paused, realization setting in almost hard enough to knock the wind from him. The woman who had warned him that she didn't trust anyone had trusted *him*.

And not just last night. Little by little she'd been opening herself, sharing herself, talking about herself, her feelings, her thoughts. No longer was it all about George. No, it was sometimes about the changes in her, her personal growth.

She'd shared herself in so many ways over the last couple of weeks. Even announced she was thinking about meeting other people.

Dory had come a long way.

And so had he. He sat abruptly, waiting for the coffee, waiting for the changes inside him to settle. He'd tried to help a woman who had good reason to be afraid. He'd thought at the outset he'd give her the dog, maybe check up on her from time to time. Instead his days had steadily become more and more entwined with hers. Especially since the moment when she had shared her graphic of the murder with him. He'd looked into a small child's heart and seen how it had affected the woman she'd become.

With that, all distance on his part had vanished. All thoughts of forever avoiding another debacle like Brenda went away. He'd crossed his own personal barriers with Dory, and he wasn't at all sure he wanted to put them back in place.

What he did know was he wanted more than a one-night stand with her. Whether it grew into anything more than casual, only time could tell, but for the first time since Brenda, he was willing to give it a chance.

Besides, he was growing very fond of Dory. As she emerged from her shell, he saw more than a Botticelli angel who took his breath away. He saw a rose blossoming into fullness, no longer a cramped bud hiding in work and her computers. She was showing strength. Fortitude. Determination. She was no longer talking of running.

For his part, he felt truly alive in every way this morning. He kind of hoped the feeling would last.

He'd rediscovered the man he used to be. What could be wrong with that? It felt good.

Smiling, he went back to trying to devise a breakfast from the slim pickings in her fridge. He guessed he was going to have to be the cook as long as they stayed together.

"I thought I smelled coffee," Dory said from the kitchen doorway. She wore a blue robe and slippers.

He looked over his shoulder and smiled at her. "It's there if you want some. I hope you don't mind, but I was looking through your fridge and cupboards trying to find something to make for breakfast."

She arched a brow at him. "You don't eat cereal?"

"Not often. Most of what you have in there is too sweet."

A slow smile spread across her face. "Try it at 3:00 a.m. after working for ten hours. It's the absolute greatest energizer." She started to move past him, but he snagged her around her waist and drew her down onto his lap. At once she wrapped her arms around his neck.

He smiled into those blue, blue eyes of hers. "Good morning, darlin'." Then he kissed her soundly, feeling his body stir in response. This, he thought dimly, was not likely to lead to breakfast.

He pulled his head back reluctantly, enjoying the way her eyes had closed, the way her mouth looked slightly swollen. Beautiful. "But this won't feed us," he said gruffly.

"Depends," she answered pertly, her eyes opening. Then with a little laugh, she slid off his lap. "You're too distracting. So no cereal, huh?"

Then she pulled a can of soup out of the cupboard. "Will you eat lunch for breakfast? Because I can make a mean grilled cheese sandwich, and with a little tomato soup, I think we can top the tanks."

Why hadn't he thought of that? Dang, was he getting too mired in his routine?

What made the breakfast wonderful, however, was the woman sitting across from him, smiling and chatting as if she hadn't a care in the world.

He knew that wouldn't last. It couldn't.

"I need to go in to work for a couple of hours today," he told her as he ate his second sandwich. "But then, if you can spare the time, we can go out to my place. Doc Windwalker is bringing me a young dog he thinks might be perfect to train as a companion for a little autistic boy."

"I thought you didn't do that kind of thing."

"I don't do it often. I can call on help if I need it, but this has landed in my lap. The family can't afford to go elsewhere, so..." He shrugged. "We'll see what we can do."

The smile she gave him then made him feel about ten feet tall.

By the time Dory showered, dressed and went to her computers, she found a raft of messages awaiting her. The team was discussing a potential new project and whether they could accomplish what the client wanted in the time allotted. Dory read the specs, such as they were, and the comments from the rest of the team. It was clear everyone wanted to do it, but it was going to be a huge challenge, something they'd never done before. Almost like going back to the very beginning of graphics design. It intrigued her, too, as she thought about it.

Then a private message popped up from Reggie.

Where you been?

Busy. Sorry. Life.

Yeah, I know about the whole life thing. Was getting worried because of your brother.

I'm fine. Pretty protected, too, by a trained guard dog. She didn't want to mention Cadell. Not their business.

Well, good. But I needed to let you know something. We had a hack attempt from a library in Nebraska a few days ago. Our webmaster didn't think a whole lot about it, just put it in his report. Anyway, I'm telling you because the hacker was trying to get into our personnel files. He failed, but...

Thanks, Dory typed back quickly, even as her heart slammed into high gear. How many days ago?

There was a pause and she could imagine Reggie switching to another file. Then came the answer.

Five days.

Five days was long enough to get here from Nebraska. Plenty long enough. All of a sudden the day didn't seem as beautiful as it had just a few minutes ago.

Then another ping. Reggie typing more.

If there's anything at all we can do, just ask. Nobody's happy about this.

Thanks, she typed again. I really appreciate it.

Now about that new project...

She was glad to think about the project. Work had been her salvation for a long time, and it was again that morning. The less room she made in her thoughts for her brother, the better she felt.

Heck, she hadn't even had a nightmare last night. That made her smile even though she felt as if a dark cloud were steadily moving her way.

But then it occurred to her that she needed to let Cadell know about this. It might be nothing. Or it might be George.

DORY'S PHONE CALL blew up Cadell's plan for the day. Or at least delayed things a bit. He called Mike Windwalker and asked him to postpone bringing the family and the dog to his place for a couple of hours. Mike thought he could manage that, but if not what about tomorrow?

"Tomorrow would be fine, too, but I'm pretty sure I can look over the situation this afternoon. I'm just sorry about the holdup."

"I know all about that," Mike responded drily. "I'm a veterinarian, remember?"

A vet with a wife and a daughter in a wheelchair. He probably hated it when he couldn't get home on time.

Then he headed for Gage's office. The sheriff looked up expectantly.

"I'm not sure this means anything," Cadell began, "but I think we need to check it out. Dory's coworker told her that someone attempted to hack the company's personnel files from a library in Nebraska."

"Maybe nothing," Gage said, but as he straightened, it was clear he didn't believe it. "Can we find out which library?"

"I'll call Dory right now."

It took Dory a few minutes to realize how many times her cell phone rang. Persistent, whoever it was. She surfaced from her study of the new program specs and reached for it. Cadell? And for once she felt as if her heart smiled.

"Hey," he said warmly. "Got a question for you."

"Sure."

"Is there any way to find out which library that hack attempt came from?"

"Hang on while I message Reggie. It might take a few if he's busy. Would it be better if I called you back?"

"I'll wait." There was no mistaking the resolve in Cadell's voice. The hack attempt, which she had been trying so hard to forget, surged back to the foreground, and with it her level of anxiety. Clearly Cadell didn't think it was innocent.

"God, what next," she muttered as she typed rapidly to Reggie.

Cadell answered her. "Next I'm going to come over and get you, and we're going to meet a family with an autistic child and try to make him happy. In the meantime..."

In the meantime. Yeah. She drummed her fingers impatiently, waiting for Reggie. When nearly five minutes had passed, she got his familiar Yo.

I need to know which library that hack attempt came from.

What I got is an IP.

Give it to me, I'll look it up.

K.

Another pause, then a string of numbers, three at a time with a decimal between them.

Thanks, she typed. I'm liking the project, btw.

Great!

Then she picked up her cell. "I've got the IP address. For nongeeks, that means it can lead you right to the computer that was used, as long as he didn't use an anonymous server."

"I'll take it."

"I can also look it up for you."

He gave a quiet laugh. "Maybe you should do that. We could use a more advanced IT department here, but who has the funds?"

"I hear a lot of police departments have that problem and hence still use fax machines."

"You'd be right."

"So last century," she remarked, trying to sound light when she didn't feel good about this at all. It could be a random hacker, though. It always amazed her how many brains wasted themselves on trying to disrupt other people's computers just for kicks.

It didn't take long to trace the IP. The internet was decent about keeping track of itself, or it would have blown up and become useless from the start. "Okay," she said to Cadell. "It's one of four computers assigned to a library in Landoun, Nebraska. Small, like Conard City."

"So maybe the librarian will remember someone. Okay, thanks. I'll get back to you shortly."

She wondered if she would survive waiting even a few

minutes. Then, with determination, she pushed all thoughts of George aside. Focus on her job. She was good at burying everything else.

Soon she was lost in a world of storyboards the team had begun to build, offering a few opinions, making some changes that would be a little less difficult to carry out.

But then her phone rang, and all hope of distraction fled. It was Cadell.

"Okay," he said. "The librarian didn't recognize George's inmate photo when we emailed it to her. But she did say a few days ago a man she didn't know used the computer for several hours. He had a thick beard, though. So I'm sending George's inmate photo to the state to have them put a beard on it. Just in case. I'll pass it by the librarian and see if we come up with someone who resembles her unknown man."

Dory sagged in her chair. "Thank you," she answered. "I have the software to put a beard on him, too, if it would save time." She needed to know. Even as she sagged, a vise had gripped her heart. She was sure it was George. Who else would be trying to penetrate Animation's personnel files?

"Dory? You know this is slim."

"Then why am I having so much trouble believing it?" she snapped.

He paused. "So you've got software that can do this? I'll be right over with his faxed photo."

She disconnected, staring at her screen, knowing full well that she wasn't going to be able to focus until she'd dealt with the photograph. It was as if everything had moved out of the realm of possibility and into the realm of reality.

She felt a poke on her leg and saw Flash nudging her and looking up at her. Almost automatically she reached out to pet him. "Can you hold it until Cadell gets here?"

Because all of sudden she didn't even want to walk into her backyard alone.

GEORGE HEISTED A pickup and switched the plates with a similar vehicle before pulling it out of the dirt parking lot from among a great many others. Rodeo Days must be a big thing around here. Once he was safely out of town, he hit the state highway, and at the first opportunity in the middle of nowhere, he pulled onto the shoulder and began to check what was in the truck. Registration and insurance. Good, but he still had no license. He'd better not get stopped.

And a gun? That might be useful. Although guns made a mess, and he wanted Dory's death to look accidental. In the back of the truck, which was dirty enough to convince him it was used for some serious work, he found other items that could be useful, from rope to barbed wire, regular tools and then something he couldn't at first identify.

Curious, he pulled out the three-foot-long rod by its handle, then noticed the two tines on the end. It looked like a Taser. An awfully big Taser. He pressed the button and saw the spark with satisfaction. A cattle prod. He smiled. That could be useful. He just wished it were smaller in size so it could be more easily hidden.

He climbed back into the cab and drove toward Conard City. Not much longer now. He had plenty of tools in this truck that could be useful. Now all he had to do was find his sister without being seen himself.

There was a battered, misshapen cowboy hat on the seat beside him, looking like someone's castoff. He put it on, pulling it low over his brow. Beard or no beard, the less anyone could see of his face, the better. He whistled tunelessly, thinking that it was a beautiful day. The wide-open spaces didn't even bother him as much anymore.

Life was finally going his way.

Chapter Twelve

The photo Cadell brought Dory was from a fax machine. Not the highest resolution, but she put it through her scanner and some software to enhance the clarity. Then she plugged it into the software that would add a beard.

"Did the librarian say what kind of beard?"

"Full. Not terribly long."

"Okay. This is going to take a while, though."

"How long do you think?"

"A few hours."

"Then let's go see an autistic child about a dog."

"Sounds good to me." The last thing she wanted to do was hang around here wondering and worrying. Keeping busy had always been her salvation. But then she found she couldn't stand up.

"Oh, God," she whispered.

"What?"

"I just looked at my brother for the first time in a quarter century. He could be a stranger, Cadell. I barely recognize him."

"Let's hope he has the same problem with you." He squatted. "You going to be all right?"

"I always am," she said irritably. But her legs still felt like noodles, and she reached for the fax again, staring at a face that had changed an awful lot but still belonged to the brother she had once loved.

"It's a shame," she said presently.

"What is?"

"That he was never the person I thought he was. That person could have done wonderful things with his life. Instead…" She didn't finish. She tossed the photo to one side.

He straightened and touched her shoulder. "Put George

on the back burner while your software works. And remember, if he really is looking for you, he has to find you first."

"Maybe I need a wig and some big sunglasses."

He looked at her, then his eyes twinkled.

On the ride out to Cadell's place, she once again drank in the countryside. At first it had been so different from anything she'd known before that it had looked dry and scrubby to her, not especially attractive except for the mountains.

But time had taught her to see differently. All that space, dotted occasionally with copses of trees, a lot of scrub and the tumbleweeds, fascinated her. She loved to see the wind catch a tumbleweed and carry it along.

"Every place has its charms," she remarked. "It took me a while to see them here."

Cadell tossed her a grin before returning his attention to the roads. "I was overwhelmed when I first moved to Seattle. All the green seemed suffocating—there were no long lines of sight. Kinda claustrophobic at first. But it didn't take long before I began to see it differently. Anyway, when I came home here to visit, *this* place looked bad to me. I used to run up into the mountains just to see the forest. So yeah, I get what you mean."

"Well, I'm beginning to appreciate it. Mostly I love the mountains, though."

"One of these days soon I'll take you up there. Some great vistas overlooking the valley. And lots of trees."

She laughed, feeling the last remnants of her concern about George slip away. He could wait, at least for a few hours. Being with Cadell was more important.

And certainly a whole lot more pleasant.

CADELL HAD JUST enough time to make some coffee to offer to Mike when the vet arrived in his fully equipped van. The man had to be ready at a moment's notice to provide care to livestock almost anywhere around here, and he had half a clinic in the back of his vehicle.

A tall Cheyenne with black hair he refused to cut short, Mike was a great guy. Over the last couple of years his practice had grown by leaps and bounds. So had his kennels and the number of dogs and cats he had for adoption.

He greeted Cadell warmly, asking after the ostriches.

"Itsy and Bitsy are doing fine, as far as I can tell."

"Itsy and Bitsy?" Mike's eyes widened.

"Blame her," Cadell said with a grin, indicating Dory with his thumb. Then he introduced the two of them. "So now, what kind of dog did you bring me?"

"A good one, I think," Mike said, walking around to the back of the van. "He's a mutt, already neutered. Near as I can tell he's got some golden Lab in him and something much smaller. Regardless, he's just about two, so he's lost some of the puppy energy, he's smart and he listens. So we'll see."

Mike opened the carrier in the back of his van, grabbed a lead already attached to the dog's collar, then let the animal jump down.

Cadell thought he looked like a somewhat miniaturized golden Lab, good-looking but probably not big enough to intimidate a child of about six. "Great choice," he said. "Listen, you know where the coffee is. Go on in and help yourself. I want to run him around the corral and get to know him. Does he have a name?"

"I've been trying to avoid that."

Cadell arched a brow. "So what have you been calling him?"

"Dog."

"Ha!" Cadell laughed, and Dory joined in.

"But why avoid a name?" she asked Mike.

"Because I'll get attached. Because whoever adopts my animals is going to want to name them. I realize that's ridiculous, because I've found you can change a dog's name a dozen times and he'll still answer. But…" He shrugged.

"Okay, I don't want to get attached. Sooner or later I've got to let them go."

At that moment, Flash, who'd been allowed his freedom in the kennels and fenced yard, came dashing up to sit beside Dory. He regarded the new dog inquisitively, tilting his head a little to one side, his tail sweeping the ground in a friendly manner.

"Test one," remarked Cadell. The small golden came trotting over and began to sniff Flash from top to bottom. Flash lay down as if to make it easier, and soon the golden was lying right beside him. Friends, it seemed.

"Okay, no dog aggression," remarked Cadell. "Dory, keep Flash beside you while I take Dog into the corral."

DORY NOTICED AS she and Mike walked to the back of the house that the ostriches leaned over their pen's fence as if they wanted a better look.

"I don't think they've forgotten me," Mike remarked. "Or the injections I gave them. I'm not a popular person with them."

"Is anyone?" Dory asked.

Mike chuckled. "They're really not so bad, usually. They'd rather run than fight. But getting into a fight with one…well, I wouldn't recommend it. They may not have teeth, but they can peck with a lot of force. Then, while the nail on their single clawed toe on each foot isn't the sharpest, they pack a hell of a kick. Bones could break. If they're trapped and feel threatened, a human might not survive it."

Good to know, Dory thought. Not that she ever intended to get into the pen with them.

Cadell was already at work with Dog, and from his face and posture, Dory thought he was pleased. In almost no time at all, the dog was following commands to sit and stay. When Cadell saw Mike and Dory approach the corral fence, he called out, "Good one. Smart and eager to please. That's what we want, right? A companion."

"As far as I know, they don't have any other needs for their son. Just that he be perfectly safe with the animal because…well, I guess the child can get rough and loud sometimes."

"What child can't?" Cadell asked rhetorically. Then he turned his head. "I guess that's them."

Dory peered in the direction he was looking and saw a dust cloud just beginning to come up the long drive.

Soon a family of three, one of whom was a thin boy of about six, were coming around the house to the back. The boy was incredibly silent, Dory thought. Sadly so. He walked past the kennels of dogs, looking at them but not making a sound.

His parents were young, dressed like a hardworking ranch couple, in jeans and somewhat faded shirts. Neither of them held the boy's hand.

"Brad doesn't like to be touched," the woman said. "I'm Letty Embrow, and this is my husband, Jase." She looked at Mike. "What do you think?"

"I picked the one I think is best. Cadell's pleased with him."

Her eyes trailed to Cadell. She seemed like a pleasant woman, but right now there was a deep tension riding her. Because she didn't know how her son was going to react? Or was she afraid the dog might do something?

They walked together, with the Embrows in the rear, until they reached the gate into the training yard. Cadell looked at the parents. "Can I talk to him, or do you need to do that?"

"Let's see what happens," Letty answered.

So Cadell squatted and looked at the child from about five feet away. "I hear you want a dog."

Dory thought the boy's gaze fixated for the first time since he'd arrived. His attention was fastened to Cadell.

"I have one I think you'll like, Brad. But you and I have to go inside the fence to meet him. If you like him, I'll get him ready to go home with you."

Cadell glanced up. "I may need a couple of days to be sure he's well trained, but I'd like you to bring Brad every afternoon to work with him. Doable?"

Both parents nodded, and Cadell returned his attention to the boy. "Want to come through the fence and meet the dog, Brad?"

For the first time, the boy became animated. He bobbed his head in the affirmative. Dog was waiting on the other side of the fence a few feet away. The instant Cadell opened it wide enough, the little boy slipped through and ran right up to the dog.

Dory heard everyone's breath catch. Then Brad threw his arms around Dog's neck and crowed, "Doggy! Doggy!"

And Dog didn't seem to mind it one bit.

Magic, thought Dory. There was still magic in the world.

THE LONG SUMMER twilight covered the world when Cadell and Dory got back to her house. They'd taken time to care for the animals, cleaning kennels, letting the ostriches into the larger corral so they could clean up their small pen, then putting them back in the pen and feeding them again.

They stopped at Maude's on the way back for carryout, because Dory was concerned about her work. "I keep taking time off," she told Cadell frankly. "I've got to make up for at least some of it."

"Yeah, for me working with the canines is the largest part of my job. I appreciate all your help, though."

"I've enjoyed doing it. I never really had the chance to find out before, but I like animals. Someday I want to meet the goats."

"That's easy enough."

They pulled into the driveway behind her car, then climbed out with the bags and started for the front door.

The evening suddenly changed for Dory. "God," she whispered.

Cadell stopped and faced her. "What?"

"I feel watched. That's ridiculous." She tried to brush it away, but the feeling was an icy one, just awful.

Cadell set the bags on the rickety porch bench. "Unlock the door, but stay here. I'm going to make sure no one got into your house."

"Why would…"

"I'm just going to make sure. Meanwhile, you look around and see if something has changed right around the house, something minor that troubled you, okay?"

So she stood there with Flash sitting at her side. Foolish as it felt, the feeling would not go away, and she put him on guard. The dog missed little, but when she ordered Flash to guard her, his attention grew more intense.

She studied the house as Cadell had told her to but didn't see anything amiss. Not that she'd paid that much attention. The house had never been intended to be more than a way station for her.

Although maybe… But she pushed the thought aside. She and Cadell might be having sex now, but that didn't necessarily mean anything about next week.

She watched as lights turned on inside the house. He was going room by room. Like someone could hide in her very few rooms. She might have been amused if the itchy feeling of being watched hadn't persisted.

She studied the street, looking for another human being, but most humans were probably indoors eating dinner, or maybe in their backyards having a picnic. The street was as silent as it was empty.

She heard an engine start way down toward the edge of town. A battered old red pickup appeared eventually, and she watched it approach. Before it got near, however, Cadell opened the door.

"All clear inside. Did you note anything?"

"Nope." She stepped in beside him, hardly noticing as the pickup rolled by behind her. "I guess I was just feeling too good most of the day. God forbid I should forget George for too long."

His eyes crinkled as he smiled, but she didn't miss the way he locked the door behind them.

"Do you want to check your computer for the image of that guy first, or do you want to eat? I'd hate for the food to get cold. Maude's a master with steak."

"Let's eat." Honestly, right now she didn't want to see her brother's face again, bearded or not.

Cadell carried the bags into the kitchen. Flash followed along hopefully, but he got dry food and a fresh bowl of water. Dory wondered what Cadell would think if she fed the dog people food. Sometimes she was tempted.

They sat facing each other, Cadell with a tall coffee from Maude's, she with another one of her inevitable soft drinks. The sandwiches were perfect, the steak tender enough to melt in the mouth, and still warm. He'd been right not to wait.

"I'm surprised you didn't dismiss my feeling," she said when her appetite settled into more reasonable proportions. She had no idea what had made her so hungry. Must have been all that fresh air, because it wasn't unusual for her to miss lunch.

"I never discount the feeling of being watched. Plenty of people get it sometimes, and the amazing thing is that plenty of people are right. It's not always important, of course, but when you're a cop and you get the feeling someone is focused on you? You don't ignore it."

"I just want you to know I appreciated it. It's not a sensation I've had very often. Besides, there was no reason to be afraid of it with you right there."

Again that smile danced in his dark eyes. "I'm no superhero, but thanks for the vote of confidence."

He really was a nice guy, she thought as she continued eating. She'd have grown impatient with herself long ago. Amorphous fears about a brother who might never want to see her again. She wished she could just erase him from her memory.

But erasure had proved impossible, and Cadell wasn't about to dismiss the possibility that George might feel he had business with her. Money business. Well, that wouldn't surprise her.

She shifted a little in her chair. "Do you have any idea how much I inherited?"

He swallowed and took a drink of coffee. "Not really. The news articles from back then suggested a million-dollar insurance policy."

She snorted. "So much more sensational, huh? No, actually it was about half of that, including what my godparents got for me from the sale of the house. That's a lot of money—it might have grown over the years sitting in CDs and bank accounts, but I don't know. You see, I have a vice."

His brows rose. "Tell me it's not cocaine."

If she'd felt more comfortable, she would have laughed. "No. I can't touch it, I told you. But when I turned twenty-one I made just one change to the trust with my godparents' permission…I started donating half the interest."

"That's a *vice*?"

She shrugged faintly. "Some financial advisers think so, but not me. They handle the trust and apparently keep it growing. Anyway, the interest goes to various causes, mostly those helping children. Which brings me around to today. Brad couldn't have afforded a companion dog without you and Mike Windwalker stepping up, right?"

"I don't believe so."

She nodded. "Maybe that'll be my next charity. Kids like Brad who need companion animals. They shouldn't be out of anyone's reach."

A warm smile spread across his face. "I like the way you think, Dory Lake."

"George wouldn't agree. When my godparents set up

the trust they made it clear that they wanted me to save it for the future. I didn't have any reason to disagree, but when I turned twenty-one, ownership passed to me. I left everything the way they'd made it except the use of the interest. And that's when I made it irrevocable. If George had ever tried to contact me for money, I wouldn't have responded. Not by then."

"Theoretically he didn't know where you were to contact you."

"Probably not. My godparents moved a lot because of Uncle Bill's job." She sighed and pushed her dinner to one side. "I'm tired of every discussion coming back to him. I want him gone. Out of my life. Not constantly hanging over my head." She closed her eyes briefly, then opened them so she could see his face. "The thing is, I think I create that threat myself more than anything. He might be headed to the opposite end of the country. He might not want to see me any more than I want to see him."

"It's possible."

She didn't miss the doubt in his tone. He believed George was going to show up. Her biggest fear was going to materialize. And Cadell intended to be at her side as much as he could. Gratitude filled her.

She looked down at Flash. "He'll take care of George."

"He'll certainly try."

The word hovered in the air along with her fears. Flash would try. No guarantees.

"Will you stay tonight?" she asked, trying to sound casual.

"I wouldn't be anywhere else in the world."

GEORGE NEVER WOULD have dreamed it would finally be so easy to find his sister. Changing license plates on the truck had made him think of something that hadn't occurred to him before: she had a car, and that was information he could get for a fee from a private company online. The library in the place he thought of as "Rodeo Town" along with a prepaid debit card, had made it possible for him to find out what kind of vehicle she was driving. It still bore Kansas plates, the site claimed, which would stick out in Wyoming, even though the site wouldn't give him the plate number or VIN.

And lo and behold, when he drove through Conard City late last night, he'd seen it. There she was. The only problem was that parked behind her car was a police SUV. Sheriff's department. K-9 Unit blazoned on its side.

Curious, he'd parked up the street and waited until it was evident that cop wasn't going anywhere else.

Hell. She'd hooked up with a guy—fast work, he thought—and worse, she'd hooked up with a cop. A freaking cop.

Anger shook him to his core, and he cleared out of town before he blew his stack. Pounding on a steering wheel and cussing loudly would only have drawn unwanted attention.

It wasn't long, though, before he regained his self control and came back to town. Rage was a tool to be used, not something he should ever let control him. He knew that.

He kept watch from a safe distance. And what he'd seen had both given him ideas and frustrated him more.

The cop never left her side. When they came out of her house in the late morning, it was together and with a dog. Probably the cop's K-9, although he had to wonder why Dory was holding the leash.

He also had to admire his sister. She'd been a cute kid, everyone said so, but she'd grown into a stunning woman. Too bad he had to get rid of her. If he'd thought he could have talked her into working with him, she'd have been a great asset. But from everything he could tell about her—which wasn't a whole lot—she had chosen to live on the right side of the law.

What a waste.

He watched them drive out of town toward the mountains and hung a safe distance back. If he lost them...well, there was always tomorrow.

He trailed behind, but not so far he didn't see them turn in to a ranch. He kept going for another couple of miles and then headed back. In the distance, near a two-story white house, the cop's vehicle was still parked. It must be his place.

Ideas were beginning to swim again. Once he was sure the two of them were safely tucked in for the night at her place, he was going to come back out here and see what kind of opportunity he could create.

Because opportunities were always there, just waiting for a clear enough eye to see them.

He'd waited a long time to put an end to Dory and get what he truly deserved. He could wait a little longer.

"I'VE GOT WORK in the morning," Cadell told her later that night. Lovemaking had once again left her feeling limp and good all over. She wondered if she had been missing something all these years or if she had been missing Cadell.

She rolled lazily toward him. "No one's ever made me feel this wonderful."

He turned his head on the pillow and gave her a smile. "Now that's a great thing to hear."

"Truth."

He stirred until he was on his side, too, and draped his arm over her waist. He lifted it briefly to brush a strand of her blond hair back from her face. "Truth," he agreed. "You make me feel wonderful, too."

She sighed happily and buried her face in his shoulder.

"Work in the morning," he said again.

"I heard," she mumbled.

"Are you going to be okay?"

"I've got my work, too."

"You know I wasn't referring to that."

She did, but she didn't want to think about it. "Let's not ruin this by thinking about tomorrow. If I get uneasy, I'll run over to Betty's, okay? But don't forget, I have Flash. I wouldn't want to argue with him."

"He *does* have a lot of teeth," Cadell said, allowing the mood to lighten.

But she felt the concern in him and knew he was right. Until George was dealt with somehow, there *was* a threat. She sought a way to reassure him. "You know, I'm not exactly in the middle of nowhere. It'll be daytime, people are around, I'll have Flash, and if I scream for help, I think someone will call for it."

"You're right," he admitted. "Everyone around here would call for help and probably come running, too."

"So I'll be fine. But if you're worried about it, I'll go to Betty's."

After a moment he shook his head. "You have to work, too."

"What are you doing?"

"I've got patrol duty. I don't just train the dogs, you know." He tightened his hold on her, and she snuggled closer. "Four hours. I'll be back in four hours."

"Okay." But she didn't feel okay. Long after she felt his breathing deepen and steady, she stared into the dark and shared her mind and heart with a little girl who was still traumatized.

She doubted any number of years would entirely get her past that. It was better now, much better, even if George's release had awakened long-buried fears. But that little girl? Sometimes she needed attention, too.

BEFORE CADELL LEFT in the morning, he suggested she drive out to his place. He could meet her there shortly after noon, but he needed to check on the animals again. Maybe work with them some.

She was happy to agree. Plenty of time to work, a nice afternoon break, and then some more work this evening. Or something else, she thought with a private smile. Something else with Cadell had become the high point of her days.

Maybe a dangerous place to go, but she was going anyway. It kept hitting her that life as a hermit might provide safety, but it sure hadn't given her a lot of good times. Not good times like Cadell gave her. However long it lasted, she wanted as much as he'd give her.

She spent a little time with her eyes closed, remembering last night, remembering Cadell's smile, thinking about the way he looked striding around his ranch. Incredibly male, yet incredibly kind. She wasn't used to men who were so kind. Heck, she worked with kind men, but she didn't allow them to know she was a woman. Women weren't welcome in the men's world of computers. Although maybe she wasn't being fair to the guys she worked with.

Then she laughed. For all she knew, some of them might be women, too.

Sometime later as she was finishing up her work, she ran into a mental hitch and couldn't quite get her finger on it. Something was wrong.

Sighing, she heard an answering sigh and looked over to see Flash, his head on the floor, looking up at her as if to say, "Have you forgotten I need exercise?"

"Okay," she said. "We'll go for a run." It would clear her head about work and allow her a good excuse to let her mind wander over Cadell and all his attractive attributes. He made her body sing, true. But he was bringing long-cold parts of her back to warmth and light.

It was probably going to hurt, but right now she didn't care. She was willing to take whatever this slice of life offered her and pay the cost later.

She knew all about costs. And she knew she could survive them.

GEORGE WATCHED HER come out of the house with that dog of hers. He'd learned a little about her boyfriend last night when he'd explored the guy's ranch. Dog trainer? K-9s? Cop dogs? He looked at the dog trotting beside Dory on a leash and suspected it had been trained by that man. An extra wrinkle, but one he could deal with.

What he'd found at the ranch was the perfect way to get rid of Dory and keep himself out of it. Ostriches had a kick worse than a boxer's punch. All he had to do was get Dory in with them and then stir them up. That'd look like an accident, especially since he planned to break the lock on the pen when it was over. At worst it would look like she'd been trying to round them up after the lock failed.

But nobody would think they'd been used as a murder weapon. And thanks to the electric fencing, she wouldn't be able to climb out.

Man, sometimes his own brilliance blinded him.

CADELL SPENT HIS morning missing Dory. Not a good sign. He'd vowed a long time ago not to get into another deep relationship, and here he was violating his own oath. Dory wasn't the best bet, either. He doubted she fully trusted him, and that meant he'd be wise not to trust her completely, either.

Nor could he be sure she wouldn't just pack up and leave. She'd been avoiding real human contact for a long time and had said as much. She preferred being a hermit. This was an interlude for her, a bit of entertainment by helping him with his dogs, a change of pace. But soon she'd probably feel it was interfering with her work, and she'd want to crawl back into her safe emotional cave. Especially if they couldn't somehow put the issue of George to rest for good.

He sighed and prowled the roads, filling in for Carter Birch, whose wife had just had a baby. He hated patrolling. Yeah, he'd done thousands of miles of it over the years, but back in Seattle at least he was likely to see something or do something, even if it was only writing a traffic ticket.

Out here on the prairie and the foot of the mountains, there was almost nothing to do unless he got a call.

It was important, of course. If a call came, the idea was that a patrol wouldn't be too far away. Distance could cost a life in an emergency. But he vastly preferred training the dogs and K-9 officers, and he often wondered just how he could expand his business so it would become full-time.

Again his thoughts trailed back to Dory, and he glanced at his watch. Another hour, then he could start heading toward his place to meet her. Another hour.

He pulled over to the side of the road and poured himself a cup of coffee from the thermos bottle he'd had Maude fill for him that morning. Still hot, still good.

He scanned the wide-open spaces that led up the mountains. A beautiful summer day easing slowly into autumn. The air was dry, the breeze steady.

And he wished he could ignore the sense that Dory needed him. She was fine. She had Flash, she was at work, she'd have called if she needed help and the department would have called him.

Everything was fine.

So why couldn't he believe it?

Chapter Thirteen

Dory figured she could give Flash a good thirty-minute run before she'd need to shower and head out to Cadell's ranch. She was eagerly looking forward to seeing him again, and not all her good reasons for avoiding those feelings would get rid of that.

Oh, well, she thought as she ran down the sidewalk, her jogging shoes slapping on pavement. She passed a couple in their front yard, and they exchanged waves and smiles. Maybe getting out of her shell wasn't so bad.

Her run took her to the edge of town, where a vacant lot with a brook running through it covered several acres. Tall trees grew there, and she loved the way they dappled the light. No houses were nearby, but that was okay. She had Flash.

When she reached the end of the trees, she sometimes paused to watch the brook, but today she didn't have time. "No stops today, Flash," she told him. He didn't appear to mind. Tongue lolling, he was galloping along happily at her side.

A truck pulled up, and she barely spared it a glance until a voice called to her, chilling her to her bones.

"Dory? Get in."

Turning, ice running through her veins, she saw a gun pointed at her. Then she saw the man behind it, leaning out of a battered red truck. George. *Oh, my God, George.*

"Make that dog behave or he gets the first bullet."

Neck stiff, she looked down at Flash. He was at full attention, his gaze fixed on George and the gun. Cadell had said he would recognize a threat when he saw it.

"I'm warning you, Dory. You think I won't kill that dog?"

She never doubted it. But there was only one way to take Flash off guard. Shoving her hand into her pocket, she pulled out a tennis ball.

His entire demeanor changed. His tail wagged, and for

an instant she thought he was going to get down and gnaw the ball. But instead he dropped it and lowered his head as he stared at George.

"Okay, then," George said. "Bring him a few steps closer."

"No."

"I won't shoot him unless you don't do what I say. Get him closer."

Step by agonizing step, she approached, feeling Flash start to pull at the leash. He wanted to go after George.

But when they stood a few feet away, the barrel of that gun still leveled at her, George thrust the truck door open and stuck out a yellow pole. What the...

Then she heard the sizzle and Flash's yelp. He fell to the ground, jerking.

"More than one way to deal with you and that dog. Now get your behind into this truck."

She dropped the leash, looking down at Flash, relieved to see he was still breathing. It was the last relief she was able to feel.

Then, almost numb, past fear, she climbed into the passenger side of the truck. He kept the pistol aimed at her every second.

"I'll give you money," she said stiffly as he shoved the truck into gear.

"You bet your sweet butt you will. Now shut up or I'll use that prod on you."

CADELL GOT A radio call just before he was scheduled to get off duty. It was the sheriff, Gage Dalton.

"We've got Dory Lake's dog here. He's fine, but Dory's missing. Not at her house. I've put out a county-wide alert."

Just as Gage finished speaking, the alert popped up on Cadell's mobile unit, along with the rendered photo of a bearded George Lake.

Cadell jammed on the brakes, closed his eyes and gripped the steering wheel so hard his hands cramped. He didn't need to know the odds against finding someone in all these hundreds of square miles of open space.

"We're doing a door to door," Gage said. "Meantime, we've started the phone tree with the ranches. Get yourself home, Cadell."

"Home? What the hell can I do there?"

"Get us a bunch of search dogs."

THE OLD PICKUP rattled down roads that Dory recognized. A smidgen of hope awoke in her. Either she'd be able to talk her brother into taking money, or she'd find another way to deal with him. Because when they turned in to Cadell's ranch, it was well-known territory to her. She guessed that Cadell would be there in about an hour, as he'd planned... as long as the job didn't delay him. But she refused to consider that possibility. He'd come and he'd come on time. She just had to make it for one hour. Surely she could do that.

"I never did anything to you," she said trying to make herself sound small, almost childlike.

"You should have stayed in bed."

"I wish I had." She closed her eyes briefly. "I wish I'd never seen. But I never did anything to *you*."

"You took away my escape time. You ran screaming out onto the street. I thought you loved me."

"I did."

"Then why did you run, Dory. Why?"

She shook her head a little, watching Cadell's house grow closer. Soon she could see the ostriches. Dog pens out back. If she could manage to let the dogs out somehow...

Why was he bringing her here, of all places?

"I ran because I was terrified. George...I didn't even understand what I was seeing! For more than a year I could only speak two words, *red paint*. That's all I could compare it to."

He said nothing more. She struggled to think about how she could distract him. Thought of Flash and hoped he would be okay, because her poor dog hadn't done anything to deserve that shock.

And mile by mile, she had felt her fear of George transforming into hatred. Then she remembered what Cadell had said about George being her only heir.

Her heart slammed, and she realized for absolute certain, all the way to her very core, that she was not going to survive this. Far from weakening her, the knowledge pumped strength into her. If she was going to die, she wasn't going to make it easy.

"You know," she said, watching the house grow closer, "I didn't take the inheritance away from you. The court did. You can have it all if you want. I'll turn it over to you." A lie, but he wouldn't know that.

"A little late, don't you think? Twenty-five years in prison. I need to even the score more than that. Anyway, my lawyer told me that it's in a trust you can't break. You couldn't pay me enough to leave you alone now."

Her hands clenched. "I didn't put you in prison, George. I didn't testify. Hell, I couldn't even tell anyone what had happened. Conversion disorder, they called it. For more than a year I only spoke two words, and for over three months I was blind."

That caught his attention as the house rolled closer. "Blind, huh?"

"Blind," she said. "I didn't even understand what had happened. I couldn't. I had nightmares, though. Plenty of nightmares."

"You should have stayed in bed," he said again. But this time his voice was stony cold. Whatever charm he exerted on the rest of the world, he wasn't going to waste any on her. Not anymore.

They pulled up to one side of the house. The familiarity of the scene jarred Dory, contrasting as it did with George's abduction of her. This was a place where she'd always found peace and welcome. Just having George here seemed to shatter all that.

"Dory."

Reluctantly she looked at her brother. The gun was pointing at her again.

"Get out."

"Just shoot me here." Yeah, the anger was growing huge, and a mental voice warned her to rein it in. Now was not the time to stop thinking. But oh, the things she wanted to do to George right now would get her thrown in prison herself. Flash popped into her mind's eye, and a little crack broke through the anger. Her beloved Flash. This man had taken everything from her. Her parents. Her childhood. Her trust. Now even her dog.

Oh, yeah, she wanted him to pay. He hadn't paid nearly enough.

But she had to be smart, await her chance. Right now all she'd get for her efforts was a gunshot wound. So she climbed out of the truck, scanning the area, looking for anything she could use.

Curious, the ostriches watched them with those inscrutable dark eyes, but they had backed up in their pen, getting as far away as they could, unlike when Cadell showed up.

"Ostriches seem like a weird thing to have out here," George remarked.

Dory didn't answer, still trying to figure out what she could do. If she ran toward the kennels to let the dogs out, he'd probably put a bullet in her back before she got halfway around the house.

"I like those birds," her brother continued conversationally. "Big, beautiful and scaredy-cats."

She glanced at him, wondering how he could know that. But clearly he'd been out here before. When? Last night?

He motioned with the gun. "Let's go get a closer look at those birds. I hear their feathers are worth a fortune."

Was he going to kill the birds and steal their feathers?

But then she realized he was still carrying that long yellow stick, the one that had zapped Flash. What the hell was he up to?

As they drew closer to the cage, the birds pulled back to the farthest side, then hunkered down, making themselves as small as possible. They didn't seem to like the strangers. Or at least George.

"That's how they protect themselves," George remarked. "They either try to become invisible or they run. Did you know they can run nearly forty miles an hour? Only a cheetah can catch one."

She wondered why the hell he was talking about this and taking her ever closer to the pen. Maybe he had gone crazy. This was making no sense.

"Now here's the deal," George said when they reached the pen, watched by suspicious birds. "You can either go into that pen with them, or I'll zap you with this prod and put you in there myself."

Dory's heart nearly stopped. For a few seconds, her anger drained completely, leaving her filled with terror. Her knees weakened, and the urge to run nearly overwhelmed her. A sane voice in her head shouted it would do no good to run. She needed to buy time. She stiffened inwardly, feeling a crazy rush of strength. One thing became clear to her: if she was going to be in the pen with those birds, she didn't want to be paralyzed for even a few minutes. No way.

She couldn't scale the wire fence because it was electrified at the top, but maybe she could soothe the birds, keep them from getting too agitated. Just become small and inoffensive, she told herself. Maybe they'd leave her alone.

Her mouth turned dry, but she ignored it. Her hands moistened, making it difficult to work the latch. The birds remained hunkered down, watching.

And all the while, she wondered at the point of this. Was he going to shoot her inside the pen with the birds? What

good would that do? Why not just leave her corpse somewhere along the roadside?

Eventually, with fumbling fingers, she opened the latch.
The gate dragged on the ground as she pulled it open then
slid inside, moving very slowly. Behind her, she heard
George latch it once again. Then she heard an unmistak-
able *snick*. He'd added a padlock. From inside this pen, she
didn't think it was possible to open the other gate into the
corral. Whenever Cadell did it, he opened it with a mech-
anism on the outside.

She was breathing too heavily, in danger of becoming
light-headed. She couldn't afford to faint again. Not now.
So far the birds had offered no protest at her presence but
stayed hunkered down.

Maybe she should imitate them. Slowly, she lowered
herself to the ground, wrapping her arms around her knees.

"What do you want, George?" she asked, keeping her
voice steady, beginning to hope that the birds would remain
calm. God, she knew how huge they were, and she didn't
like being in here with them, with those enormous feet.
They didn't have talons like ordinary birds, but they each
had one toe that grew a nail so large it looked like a weapon.

Anger toward George was surging again, erasing her
fear, making her scan the enclosure for just one item she
could use to get out of here, or to attack George once he'd
finished enjoying torturing her.

The birds, though. She just couldn't figure out why he
wanted her in here with the birds.

Then he told her. "I left out one interesting fact about
these birds, dear sister. They have a powerful kick. If they
can't run and feel threatened, they kick with enough power
to break bones."

She caught her breath. If anyone could think of something like this…her brother had. But how could he make
that happen?

And then she saw. Walking around the pen, he poked

his rod through the wire, and she heard the snap and sizzle. One of the birds screamed and rose to its full height.

For the first time, anger began to give way to despair. Those birds had nowhere to run. If he kept torturing them...

She closed her eyes. Cadell should be here soon, she thought. The only question was whether he'd arrive before she was kicked to death by frantic, tortured ostriches. She desperately hoped nothing would delay him.

CADELL RACED so fast over the back roads that when he hit a rut, he literally went airborne, killing the suspension. He didn't care. As long as he didn't break an axle.

Dory was missing. Her worst nightmare had come true. Only now did he realize it was his own worst nightmare, as well.

He keyed his radio. "Nobody saw a thing?"

"Not a thing," answered Gage. "One of Jake's city cops saw the dog trailing its leash back toward her house. He recognized Flash immediately. That's all we know."

There was hope in that, Cadell tried to tell himself. At least George hadn't killed the dog. Maybe all he wanted from Dory was money, after all.

He wished he believed it.

Dasher whimpered from the backseat, voicing a protest at the rough ride. Cadell couldn't bring himself to slow down. The dog would be fine. His crate was belted in and not so big that that he was being thrown all over the back.

He pounded his fist against the steering wheel. How in hell were they going to find one woman who could be anywhere in these vast, open spaces? Hope a ranch hand came upon her before it was too late? Even with the phone tree operating, there was no way the folks on these huge ranches could check every acre. They'd have to catch sight of something by sheer chance.

No, all the phone tree would do was serve notice to be

watching for anything unusual. Better than nothing, but not by much.

Then he heard the *whop* of helicopter blades pass over. So they'd taken to the air, as well. That might help. Maybe. But you couldn't tell who was driving a car from above.

Then, when he was ten minutes away from his place, the radio crackled. "Cadell? You read?"

"I read."

"There's a truck parked beside your house. An old red pickup. Anyone you know?"

"Damn it, no!" He floored the vehicle even more, hardly hearing the call for units to head toward his ranch.

LYING ON THE ground curled up with her arms over her head, Dory awaited the blow that might kill her. Except that things weren't going according to George's plan. The ostriches were growing increasingly frantic, but they didn't seem to regard the small ball of human at their feet as a threat. Or anything they even wanted to step on. When she dared to open her eyes, she saw those ostrich feet racing around, coming close, but never striking her.

She heard George cussing, heard the awful sound and smelled the terrible smell of singed feathers every time he prodded one of those poor ostriches. She just wished she had a gun so she could put an end to this. So she could save those birds from more terror and pain.

But she didn't have a weapon and didn't dare move.

Then, wonder of wonders, she heard helicopter rotors overhead. She desperately wanted to look but didn't chance it. She heard George start cussing even more viciously, though. Soon the rotors passed on into the distance.

The cops? Had the cops already discovered she was missing?

Oh, God, please let help come soon. Those birds couldn't take much more, and she hated feeling so helpless to put a stop to George's hatefulness.

George spoke, his voice tight with fury. "I'll get you later, *sis*."

Then the truck engine started. Risking a kick, she lifted her head a little and saw George taking off. It must have been the cops.

She waited, hoping the birds would settle soon. As they began to quiet, she eased herself into a sitting position and looked at them. Each was pecking at its own feathers, as if to remove the singed ones. And neither of them showed the least interest in her.

CADELL WHEELED INTO his driveway, nearly losing his traction on the gravel and headed straight up it. One lane, a ditch to either side, invisible beneath the cut grasses. No place for anyone to go.

Then he saw the red truck bearing down on him. It, too, appeared to be moving at top speed. Cadell gripped the wheel tighter, his mind made up. He was not going into the ditch. Either that so-and-so would swerve or they were going to meet head-on. He had not the least difficulty imagining who would get the worst of a head-on, and it wasn't going to be his official vehicle with the heavy-duty front bumper, strengthened frame and roll bar.

He had one moment when hesitation pierced him. One moment when terror rose as he realized that Dory could be in that truck. But as it came closer, he could see only one head.

His heart and chest tightened. She might already be dead. Well, if so, she was about to get some company, because for the first time in his life Cadell wanted to commit murder. It was an ugly feeling; he hated it even as it rose in him. But he didn't let go of it.

George had already hurt Dory in ways she'd never recover from. If he'd killed her... Well, he was going to join her. He wasn't fit to share the air with another living soul.

GEORGE CAME CHARGING ON, sure the cop would swerve. But he didn't. There was no place to go except to drive around him. It was mowed flat on either side of the road, dry grasses waving. At the last second, he wrenched the wheel, expecting to bypass the oncoming vehicle.

Except those evenly mowed grasses concealed a ditch.

He jolted to a stop so hard his face hit the steering wheel. Searing pain erupted in his chest, but he ignored it. He pushed the door of the truck open and slid out, scrambling up the ditch and heading for the distant trees. He'd always been a fast runner. He could outrun some cop who lived on doughnuts and coffee.

"Police dog," shouted a male voice. "Stop or he'll bite you."

He kept running, ignoring the command, then he heard a word that made no sense.

"Foos!"

He didn't dare look back. He fixed his gaze on those trees and kept pumping his legs and arms, ignoring the pain in his chest.

CADELL WATCHED DASHER take off after the guy. Off lead, as fast as he could run. Cadell paused to look into the red truck. No Dory.

He stared toward the dog chasing the man and knew he had to go after them. The guy might shoot the dog. His partner. Some things a cop couldn't do.

But he called the news in as he began to run and was assured cops were converging at his place, with a chopper standing by if needed. They'd find Dory. He had to finish his job.

The sirens blared behind him. Then, to his great pleasure, other K-9s on the hunt fell into line behind Dasher. That meant not far behind them came their handlers.

George didn't stand a chance.

BACK AT THE RANCH, however, perplexity had set in. Several deputies stood around the ostrich pen, and they might as well have scratched their heads.

"I'm fine," Dory said, now sitting upright, legs tucked

"They didn't hurt me. But they're scared because that guy kept poking them with an electric prod. Just back away. Cadell will know what to do when he gets here."

"It might be a while, ma'am," answered one. "He was last seen running with his K-9 after the guy who abandoned the red truck."

For the first time since early morning, Dory felt like smiling. "He is, is he? I hope Dasher shreds my brother. What about my dog, Flash? He got shocked, too."

"The one that was found in town?"

"Probably."

At that the deputy smiled. "He's fine. The vet's going to look him over, but other than refusing to leave your house, he's okay."

Dory breathed a huge sigh of relief, then felt a warmth in her heart. For Flash. For Cadell. Imagine the dog not wanting to leave her house. "Couldn't coax him away?"

"Not from what I heard. He snapped at anyone who tried."

"He's had a tough morning."

"Seems like he's not the only one," the deputy answered.

No, she thought, letting her head fall back against the ground. No, indeed. All she knew was Cadell had better come back here safe and sound, or she was going to do something she might regret for the rest of her life.

GEORGE DIDN'T GET far into the woods. Dasher bit him on the forearm and hung on, even after George collapsed. Cadell caught up to find his dog holding George's arm like a stuffed toy, which he wouldn't release until Cadell told him to. Cadell pulled his service pistol, took a bead on George and told Dasher to release him. Not that George had much fight left in him. He was having trouble breathing, panting hard.

So instead of the pleasure of putting him in handcuffs, Cadell had to settle for allowing medevac to take him to the hospital. "Cuff him to the gurney," he told the medics. They promised, accepting a set of flex cuffs from him.

Then he and Dasher headed the rest of the way up his private road and found an almost fantastical scene. Under other circumstances he might have laughed.

But there was only one thing he wanted to know. He trotted up to the pen. "Dory? Are you okay?"

She smiled up at him from where she sat inside the ostrich pen. "I'm fine, but my new friends are going to need to see the doc. I don't know how many times George shocked them."

Then, to his utter amazement, one of those ornery birds craned its neck downward and nuzzled Dory gently.

Well, at least one of them had good taste.

"So," she asked, "do you think you can get me out of here?"

HE GOT HER out of the pen with surprisingly little trouble. The birds settled down in their hiding positions, which made him worry. Usually they seemed to take great delight in regarding him balefully from above. He hoped George hadn't hurt them beyond repair.

Though Dory claimed she was quite all right, the paramedics insisted on examining her for shock. When she seemed okay, they warned Cadell to keep an eye on her.

"It could hit at any time," Jess McGregor said. "If it does, bring her in to the clinic or the ER." Then he limped on his artificial leg around to the front of the truck.

Dory didn't want to leave until Mike Windwalker arrived to check the ostriches. Cadell didn't argue with her, although the thing he most wanted to do was get her home and check her out from head to foot. He couldn't believe she had come through this unscathed.

But for the moment all she wanted to talk about was the ostriches, how they'd avoided hurting her even when George was torturing them. She took clear delight in the fact that Dasher had locked onto George's arm and that her brother had been taken cuffed to the hospital. "I hope he has more than a bite," she said.

Cadell almost smiled. "I'm sure he has more. He crashed

his truck in the ditch, and when I got to him he was having trouble breathing. I'm betting broken ribs."

"Good. I hear those hurt."

"Like hell," he agreed.

He watched her with appreciation and amazement. The woman he'd first met had seemed pinched, locked inside herself, stalked by fear. Gradually she'd been emerging from her inner prison, at least with him, but right now she seemed to have busted the doors wide-open. The closest she'd ever come to this much happy animation had been in bed with him. Now she was showering the world with it.

He hoped, for her sake, it lasted. It could begin a whole new chapter in her life.

As he drove her home finally, she grew a bit quieter. He could sense her eagerness to see Flash. Mike Windwalker had said he had a bit of singed fur but no burns. She was still on edge about it, though, which he could understand.

But he was growing increasingly edgy himself. This morning, as he'd raced heedlessly over dangerous roads at unsafe speeds, he'd realized he wanted Dory Lake in his life from now on.

All the flags he'd planted after Brenda—warning flags telling him to avoid long-term relationships with women—had become meaningless. Just like that. Unfortunately, you could waste years trying to avoid getting kicked in the gut until you awoke one morning and found yourself utterly vulnerable.

So he was about to get gut punched again. Because now that George would be going to prison for a good long time again, she could pick up the threads of her old life, and he couldn't imagine why in the world she might want to stay here.

If she was emerging from her private hermitage, surely she'd want to test her wings, taste the world she'd been avoiding. Hell, she hadn't even really dated, from what he could tell. Wouldn't she want to do some sampling? Look for a life in a city with more action? Dang, she'd been in prison as long as her brother had.

And she'd only come here because she thought she could hide and she knew Betty. She'd be crazy not to look for something better.

The signs were all around anyway. She'd set up her office, but she was still using a rickety dining table in her kitchen. She hadn't prettied up even a single corner of the place by hanging a picture. Leaving almost no mark that she had been there.

So, she was planning to move on quickly. Nothing was permanent, not even the high-speed internet she'd had installed, and that was a cord that could be severed with a phone call.

Of course, he had only himself to blame. The flags had been there from the beginning. He should have known better than to break his own rule. Women couldn't be trusted to stay. Brenda had proved that.

When they got to her house, Flash was still on the porch waiting. Someone had put a bowl of water out for him, but he was concerned about only one thing.

When Dory climbed out of the SUV, Flash dashed toward her, forgot all his training and jumped up on her, knocking her to the patchy front lawn.

Cadell listened to her giggle as Flash licked her face, and he smiled faintly, poised to leave. She didn't need him anymore.

But then she freed herself from Flash's attentions and jumped to her feet. "Come on in," she said to Cadell. "I don't know about you, but I could really use some coffee."

He hesitated. "I was just about to go."

She froze. "Why?"

"You must have stuff you want to do."

"Stuff?" She tilted her head. "Okay, then. You're on my list of stuff. Come inside."

He took his usual place at the rickety kitchen table while she fed Flash, then started the coffee.

Then she faced him. "So tell me something, Deputy Marcus. Was I just a job to you?"

He felt almost sickened by the question. "What?" He didn't want to believe she'd just said that.

"All the nights you spent here. Was that just protection, like Flash? You said you were a protector. Was that all I was? A job?"

Her words punched him. "No," he said hoarsely.

"Then why are you in such a hurry to leave?"

His self-control was usually pretty good, but after the stressors of that day, it had frayed. The words burst from him, almost angrily. "Because you're getting ready to leave now that George is no longer a threat."

She frowned. "Did I say that? I don't remember ever saying that."

"Well, why the hell would you want to stay here?"

Her face changed, and he thought he detected a flicker of the fear that had once been there so often. When she spoke, her voice was small. "You?"

Astonishment gripped him. Before he could respond, she'd turned her back to him, reaching for mugs.

"I realize," she said, "that you don't want another woman in your life. I get it. Brenda must have been the witch of all witches. Anyway, maybe you're done with me. Maybe I was just a job to you. Regardless, I'm not leaving. I don't want to leave. I want joint custody."

Now he was confused. "Joint custody of what?"

"Itsy and Bitsy."

That did it. Circuitous as she was being, he got it. Being willfully dense would serve nothing. He shoved the chair back so hard it tipped over.

She whirled, startled by the sound, and he was amazed to see tears rolling down her cheeks.

"Those ostriches," he said firmly, "don't come without *me*."

She wiped the tears away with her sleeve, but her smile still hadn't appeared. "You'd better mean that."

"I never meant anything more in my life. We're a package, me and those birds. Take it or leave it."

The smile began to peek out. "I'll take it," she said quietly.

He grabbed her then, forgetting finesse, drawing her into a hug so tight she squeaked. "You take it, you can't leave it."

"I couldn't possibly leave those birds," she said shakily.

He closed his eyes, pressed his lips to her hair and muttered, "So I have to keep them?"

"If you want me."

"I guess I'm stuck with them. Because I love you."

She threw her arms around his neck, and he felt his uniform shirt dampen with her warm tears. "I love you, too, Cadell. I want you, the dogs, the ostriches...I want it all."

"Babies?"

Her head tipped back. "Babies," she agreed firmly. "But you get joint custody."

Finally he laughed. It was the most joyous sound that had escaped him in a long time. "I'll help with it all."

She pressed her lips to his, giving him a salty kiss. "Forever."

"Forever," he repeated. "Forever."

* * * * *

If you loved this suspenseful story by
New York Times *bestselling author Rachel Lee,*
don't miss out on previous books in the
CONARD COUNTY: THE NEXT GENERATION
series:

UNDERCOVER IN CONARD COUNTY
CONARD COUNTY MARINE
CONARD COUNTY SPY
A SECRET IN CONARD COUNTY

Available now from Mills & Boon Romantic Suspense!

Join Britain's BIGGEST Romance Book Club

- **EXCLUSIVE offers** every month
- **FREE delivery direct** to your door
- **NEVER MISS a title**
- **EARN Bonus Book points**

50% OFF your first parcel

Call Customer Services
0844 844 1358*
or visit
millsandboon.co.uk/subscriptions